Tamil: The Best Stories of Our Times, edited by Perundevi, brings together twenty-two outstanding short stories published over the past three decades by some of the finest contemporary writers of Tamil fiction. Traversing Tamil Nadu and the Tamil diaspora, these stories capture a society's encounter with the modern world, as its people grapple with what is irreducibly human in themselves and others. Along the way, they unravel the subtle intricacies of life, illuminating various transitions, identities and interiorities. Absurd, agonizing, humorous and poignant, this landmark volume offers an exhilarating glimpse into Tamil literature today.

OTHER BOOKS IN THE SERIES

Telugu

Urdu

TAMIL

THE BEST STORIES OF OUR TIMES

EDITED BY
PERUNDEVI

HARPER**PERENNIAL**
An Imprint of HarperCollins *Publishers*

First published in India by Harper Perennial 2025
An imprint of HarperCollins *Publishers*
4th Floor, Tower A, Building No. 10, DLF Cyber City,
DLF Phase II, Gurugram, Haryana – 122002
www.harpercollins.co.in

2 4 6 8 10 9 7 5 3 1

Introduction copyright © Perundevi 2025
English translations copyright © Respective translators 2025
Copyright of individual stories vests in their respective writers

P-ISBN: 978-93-6569-580-9
E-ISBN: 978-93-6569-854-1

This is a work of fiction and all characters and incidents described in this book are the product of the authors' imagination. Any resemblance to actual persons, living or dead, is entirely coincidental.

Each individual writer asserts the moral right
to be identified as the author of their work.

All rights reserved. No part of this publication may be reproduced, stored in a retrieval system, or transmitted, in any form or by any means, electronic, mechanical, photocopying, recording or otherwise, without the prior permission of the publishers.

Typeset in 11/15.2 Adobe Caslon Pro at
HarperCollins *Publishers* India

Printed and bound at
Thomson Press (India) Ltd.

This book is produced from independently certified FSC® paper
to ensure responsible forest management.

CONTENTS

Introduction	ix
HARMONIUM *Ashokamitran* Trans. N. Kalyan Raman	1
THE KING'S WAY *Kanmani Gunasekaran* Trans. N. Kalyan Raman	6
THE SAGA OF BUTCHERY *Keeranur Jakirraja* Trans. N. Kalyan Raman	20
THE BREAKING OF A STORY *Sundara Ramaswamy* Trans. Janani Kannan	40
THE FLIGHT *Vannanilavan* Trans. Janani Kannan	50
CHEENALATCHUMI'S QUEUE *Latha* Trans. Janani Kannan	54
THE RULES OF THE GAME *J.P. Sanakya* Trans. N. Kalyan Raman	69

THE KNOWN, THE UNKNOWN *Sa. Kandasamy* Trans. Yashasvi Arunkumar	94
CYCLE *Charu Nivedita* Trans. Nandini Krishnan	106
FOOTBALL AND HER *Sureshkumara Indrajith* Trans. Yashasvi Arunkumar	111
SCREENING *Aravindan* Trans. Yashasvi Arunkumar	118
THE HORSEWOMAN *Ambai* Trans. G.J.V. Prasad	128
CATCH A CHUNKY GOAT *Appadurai Muttulingam* Trans. Suchitra Ramachandran	134
SOUNDARAVALLI'S MOUSTACHE *S. Ramakrishnan* Trans. Yashasvi Arunkumar	144
BLACK BEADS AND TELEVISION *Salma* Trans. N. Kalyan Raman	154
THE GODDESS WAS WATCHING *Nanjil Nadan* Trans. N. Kalyan Raman	161

THE TOOL OF HIS TRADE *Devibharathi* Trans. N. Kalyan Raman	171
MIRAGE *Tamilnathy* Trans. Yashasvi Arunkumar	181
HEARTBREAK *Imayam* Trans. Janani Kannan	196
THE BLOUSE *Perumal Murugan* Trans. N. Kalyan Raman	215
UPRISING *Shobasakthi* Trans. Janani Kannan	224
SACRIFICIAL STONE *Jeyamohan* Trans. Suchitra Ramachandran	245
Acknowledgements	267
About the Writers	271
About the Editor	279
About the Translators	280

INTRODUCTION

TAMIL SHORT STORIES were first introduced to me by my mother in the late 1970s, when I was a teenager. At the time, our family lived in Cuddalore, a coastal town in Tamil Nadu. Initially, I read selections from the collected works of Kalki and Jayakanthan, and later, moved on to stories published in weeklies like *Ananda Vikatan*. Even as I was enjoying this new pastime, my mother assigned me a task: every Sunday morning, in the front courtyard of the large rented house where four lower-middle-class families, including ours, lived as tenants, I had to read the stories aloud. My audience consisted of four or five women, aged between thirty and seventy, who listened attentively as they sorted greens, ground flour, folded clothes and made bead dolls. If I made any mistakes or faltered while reading, my mother would chastise me, 'Someone should put vasambu [calamus] in your mouth. What's the use of going to school if you can't read Tamil properly?'

Back then, I had not heard of Ashokamitran, and Sundara Ramaswamy was an unfamiliar name to me. Even Pudumaippithan was still in the future. I would have to wait another ten years, till I came to the metropolitan city of Chennai to take up my first job, before I could begin my tryst with modernist Tamil literature. In Chennai of the late 1980s, I came across Ashokamitran's short-story collection, *Kalamum Aindhu Kuzhanthaikalum* (Time and Five Children) while searching for a novel by Jayakanthan on a shelf in the Kasturi Srinivasan library near my working women's hostel in Triplicane. The eponymous story in the collection featured a young man with a large canvas duffle bag slung over one shoulder, hence unable to lower his arm, 'like a bird with a single wing', running hurriedly to catch a train, possibly to make up for lost time, at that particular moment and in his life. That image felt close to my heart because I had to travel without exception every weekend from Chennai, where I worked, to Cuddalore, which was my home, to see my mother, who was falling ill frequently during that period. She would die two years later. The image haunted me for several months afterwards. I had never encountered such a powerful depiction or the solemn tone of the narrative in any of the stories I had read earlier. A new world of Tamil short stories had suddenly opened up for me – a world that, as I would soon learn, was the prerogative of 'independent' literary magazines (or 'little magazines'), funded and published by small groups of literary enthusiasts for a very limited readership.

It is worth noting here that not only Ashokamitran, but several other authors in this collection – for example, writers like Charu Nivedita, Perumal Murugan and Nanjil Nadan – have contributed to popular magazines like *Ananda Vikatan*, *India Today* (Tamil) and *Kalki*, besides independent literary magazines. In this introduction, my references to the literary world or literary tradition are intended solely to signify rigorous literary writing. In fact, from the beginning of the nineties, with the advent of magazines like *Subamangala*, edited by the renowned playwright Komal Swaminathan, which were identified as 'middle magazines', the conventional dichotomy between independent literary magazines and popular magazines became even more untenable and problematic. Since I consider that literary writing, by its very nature, stands on its own regardless of where it is published – and that the magazines which carried such works merely served as oysters displaying these treasures – I have edited this collection with a focus solely on the pearls.

Without elaborating on the history of how the literary short story in Tamil took root, flowered and thrived on the fertile soil of literary magazines, beginning with *Manikodi* in the early 1930s, let me recall the remarks of Pudumaippithan, the father of modernist Tamil literature, on its birth and status, situating it within the wider context of art. A contributor to *Manikodi* himself, Pudumaippithan notes that the Tamil short story achieved 'literary status' during the 1930s and asserts further: 'Only that which imbues life with meaning is art. The short story has shown how many of life's sutchumangal can be made intelligible in and through language. Reliance on old templates, where "Lord Siva visits briefly and grants a boon; the chaste woman's misfortune emerges and resolves" has disappeared, and stories that once shimmered with moonlit landscapes, love and heroes have now begun to look directly at life, at the truth.'[1] The word 'sutchumangal' cannot be translated to my satisfaction. While any translation is inevitably reductive, it refers to facets, phenomena and dimensions of life so subtle that they often escape perception through the senses, logic or reason. For the purposes of this introduction, I will refer to them as 'the subtler aspects of life'. In the same vein, Pudumaippithan also envisions the short story as a window onto life.[2] Building on his ideas, I hold that the strength of modernist Tamil short stories lies in their capacity to stage a direct engagement with life and truth, both shaped and inflected by the forces of modernity,

---

1 Pudumaippithan, 'Sirukathai', *Pudumaippithan Katturaikal* (Chennai: Star Publications, 1954), p. 29.
2 Ibid.

through narrative fiction. Of course, the meanings of life and truth vary with time and place, and across generations; they are neither constant nor singular. Still, through all these transformations and plural meanings, these concerns remain pivotal to modernist fiction in Tamil. A common thread that unites the stories in this anthology is their unflinching confrontation with life and truth, set against the shifting realities of the world outside of them. The authors have strung together various subtler aspects of life skilfully onto this thread, which now resembles a katambam – an assortment of fragrant flowers and leaves – as we call it in Tamil.

The subtler aspects of life that some stories reveal are often strange, eluding our comprehension or common sense. Consider Latha's short story 'Cheenalatchumi's Queue', for instance. What drives Cheenalatchumi, an elderly woman troubled by constant knee pain, to go out of her way to stand in serpentine queues only for the sake of company and conversation? Why does the Anglo-Indian woman in Sureshkumara Indrajith's 'Football and Her' propose marriage to a football player, who doesn't even speak her language and is already married – all out of her love for the sport? What compels Kattur Kokku Sami, an ascetic who is reputed to perform miracles, to invoke the name of a senior police officer and secure his release from police custody in Sa. Kandasamy's 'The Known, the Unknown'? Does the male refugee in Appadurai Muttulingam's 'Catch a Chunky Goat', locked up in a Canadian prison on charges of child abuse, declare his innocence or admit his guilt in his letter to the immigration officer? These short stories prompt us to recall, or at least acknowledge the possibility of, other similar moments that life might occasionally bring to us – vague, uncertain, and lacking tangible resolutions.

At the same time, some other stories seem to delineate straightforward truths of life that we can immediately recognize and agree with. In Devibharathi's 'The Tool of His Trade', when the tailor Thangarasu is pushed to sell the only tool of his trade and begins sharing his sorrowful tale with everyone he encounters, it portends a bleak future that is easily accessible to the reader. In Salma's 'Black Beads and Television', when Zakiramma chooses the tangible, sensual pleasure of watching television over wearing a symbolic chain of golden beads as thali around her neck, her decision does not appear outlandish to us; instead, it feels relatable. Similarly, when the female protagonist of Imayam's 'Heartbreak' cries, 'Perhaps this is how life is. Whether the problem is with the uterus or the sperm, it is always the woman who has to suffer', the reader may readily nod in agreement: 'Yes, it is.'

Comprising twenty-two short stories written in the 1990s and beyond, this collection exemplifies current Tamil literary practice while attesting to its uncompromising engagement with the world around us, particularly over the last three decades. Whatever undercurrents of life these stories seek to draw from, all of them bear the imprint of the contemporary world. In elucidating the term 'contemporary' used here, I would like to draw upon Brian A. Hatcher's reflections on the term in the Indian context, that 'contemporary' can only be meaningfully understood within a broader framework of certain 'developments' that characterize the modern era, such as 'colonialism, nationalism, anticolonial resistance movements, transnational migration, the global networking of diaspora communities, and the impact of new technologies – from steamships and telegraphs to television and the internet'.[3] While Hatcher's remark pertains to 'modern' Hinduism, its broad scope remains relevant to literary analysis. Moreover, as P.P. Raveendran reminds us, what we understand by 'modern' also encompasses a fluid array of concepts such as '"everyday", "worldliness", "sociality", "secularism", "bilingualism", "polyphony", "democracy"', "resistance", "nationalism", and so on' – not as static

---

3 Brian A. Hatcher (ed.), 'Introduction', *Hinduism in the Modern World* (New York: Routledge, 2016), p. 11.

ones, but with distinct 'resonances' within the Indian context.[4] The stories in this collection, since they are informed by developments of the modern era, also grapple with these resonances.

The birth of the magazine *Manikodi*, the pioneering avant-garde platform for modernist short stories, was driven by the currents of a modern nation in the making. *Manikodi*, as A.R. Venkatachalapathy points out, was 'self-conscious about its literary quality', and 'it was also received in the same manner'.[5] This very self-conscious quality attests to the magazine's distinct status and identity as a locus of modern writing. Furthermore, as Venkatachalapathy reminds us, its emergence was primarily enabled by the nationalist fervour ignited by the Civil Disobedience Movement against British rule, and the magazine's founders and many of its contributors were Indian nationalists closely associated with the Indian National Congress. It is no surprise that, as an author shaped by the independent literary magazine tradition, which has its roots in *Manikodi*, Ashokamitran reflects on the making of the modern democratic nation, particularly the stakes and participation of common people within it, in the story 'Harmonium'. The story features a Saibaba devotee and his wife, perhaps hailing from a nearby village, who sing bhajans accompanied by a harmonium on the streets of a sprawling metropolis to earn a living. As the narrative briefly references the harmonium's origins as a harmonica, an instrument once played by beggars in European cities, it is also punctuated by mentions of the aversion to this instrument expressed by prominent modernists such as Jawaharlal Nehru, Rabindranath Tagore and Subramania Bharati. The couple continues to perform in front of high-rise apartment buildings inhabited by

---

4 P.P. Raveendran, *Under the Bhasha Gaze: Modernity and Indian Literature* (Oxford: Oxford University Press, 2023), p. 3.
5 A.R. Venkatachalapathy, 'Manikodi', *Sahapedia*, 4 September 2017. https://www.sahapedia.org/manikodi, accessed on 8 October 2024.

middle-class or affluent residents, even though the latter may not hear them at all. Is it out of hope, or the lack of any other option? Ashokamitran poignantly captures the fractured image of the nation, reflecting on the misery of the lower classes alongside the indifference of the privileged through his characteristically astute and minimalist narrative style.

In Vannanilavan's 'The Flight', again we encounter a lower-middle-class man from a village moving into a bigger town to work in a three-storeyed textile shop to repay a loan. Subjected to constant surveillance by supervisors throughout the day, for him the distinction between a prison and a workplace disappears. As in 'Harmonium', the narrative revolves around the themes of hope and the lack of options for common people. The fractured nation also looms large in Nanjil Nadan's 'The Goddess Was Watching', along the persistent faultlines of the caste order and religious loyalties. Yet, hunger emerges as a grim force, binding some in these divided groups in a morbid unity.

'The King's Way' by Kanmani Gunasekaran similarly focuses on the condition of a class of artists, namely the therukkoothu (ritual theatre, associated with the Draupadi cult of the vernacular Mahabharata tradition) actors in the modern nation. This short story, close to my heart because of its resonance with my academic research, eloquently articulates the marginalization of traditional folk artists, not only in terms of inadequate compensation but also through the loss of dignity, attention, and respect for their profession in contemporary times. The title itself carries a note of irony – those who play the role of kings on stage at night must beg during the day for a seat on a town bus, often in vain – contributing to an insightful artistic engagement with their plight in modern Indian fiction.

The gender inscriptions and inequity in public and private spaces, and the resultant sexual and other kinds of violence that women endure, are the underlying currents in the short stories of J.P. Sanakya, S. Ramakrishnan and Imayam. S. Ramakrishnan's 'Soundaravalli's

Moustache' eloquently portrays a typical classroom in a school as an institutional space that regulates bodies along gender norms and punishes those who fall outside these norms through shame and exclusion. Imayam's 'Heartbreak' leads the reader into the nuclear, heterosexual family scene today, revealing how female pregnancy still determines the social status of even highly educated and employed couples, while the inability to have children subjects the woman to profound familial trauma.

'The Rules of the Game' by Sanakya alludes to the unspoken rules by which the normative family institution operates. Pregnancy functions as a central motif in this narrative. The 'game' is rigged against the female protagonist, Kanniyammal – a survivor of gang rape in a public space – who becomes pregnant, and is subsequently ostracized by her husband and his family. However, unlike the common stereotype of victimhood often seen in popular as well as literary works of fiction that deal with rape and ostracism, she quickly finds strength and forges her own path. bell hooks, in one of her works, reminds us that while 'unnecessary' and 'unchosen' suffering may leave a mark on our lives, '[W]hat we allow the mark ... to become is in our own hands'.[6] While Kanniyammal embodies this wisdom, Ambai's 'Horsewoman' also illustrates it. In this story, the protagonist, driven by youthful infatuation, faces familial violence and abandonment as a consequence of her decisions. Nevertheless, she manages to carve out her own livelihood with the help of a couple of horses. What if she must part ways with those horses at some point? Will she not know how to open a door, even when its handles are seemingly out of reach?

In his signature irreverent style, Charu Nivedita's short story, 'Cycle', critiques the hypocrisy surrounding female chastity and

---

6 bell hooks, *All About Love: New Visions* (New York: Harper Perennial, 2001), p. 209.

marital fidelity, the two pillars that support the institution of heteronormative family in the Indian social milieu. The affected parties – the deceived wife and the deceived husband – maintain a facade of normalcy in their marriages, adhering to societal expectations. As gossip spreads through the neighbourhood, the situation escalates, leading to a disproportionate exercise of police power. The narrative not only prompts reflection on the blurred boundaries between individual/private and societal/public, but also poignantly critiques the omnipresent power vested in the modern state machinery and its regulatory interventions in matters of the heart and relationships. In a similar fashion, Aravindan's 'Screening' dismantles the veneer of a 'perfect family' led by a man who is perceived to be an ideal father and husband due to his sense of propriety, dutifulness and self-discipline. Known for speaking politely and within limits always, an inadvertent remark shatters his image, exposing the brittleness of an intimate space like a family, and the lack of understanding that might count for a quality too lenient in the context of infractions of codes of morality.

Our contemporary world, where the dynamics of globalization and neoliberalism have shaped patterns of travel and migration, is marked by a paradox. On the one hand, global travel – facilitated by factors such as technological advancements, mobility of capital, transnational markets, and treaties between nations and economic interdependence – has become more accessible, enabling the movement of people across borders for work, education and leisure. On the other hand, this ease of movement contrasts sharply with the experiences of marginalized groups like refugees, who are often forced to migrate due to political conflict, persecution or poverty – issues that are themselves tied to the complexities of the global milieu.

The stories by Muttulingam, Tamilnathy, and Shobasakthi vividly depict the struggles of Sri Lankan Tamil immigrants in the diasporic spaces of Canada and France. Muttulingam's 'Catch a Chunky Goat' interweaves the formidable challenges that a Tamil immigrant faces within the immediate family circle and the perplexing legal system of the host country. In Shobasakthi's 'Uprising', the immigrant-protagonist devises a successful strategy of resistance to authority during security screenings at his workplace, a moment that also echoes the humiliation he endured during the political conflict in his homeland. Intricately tied to the history of ethnic conflict, civil war and Tamil resistance in Sri Lanka, the narrative at once undermines this 'success' by contrasting it with his personal life, wherein he adheres to conventional ideas of virile masculinity only to be 'failed' by them eventually. Tamilnathy's 'Mirage' explores the life-struggles of a casino addict, who is also a young Tamil immigrant woman navigating assimilation into the culture of the host country. As the narrative lays out the 'racial pain' faced by her, it appears to raise the question: Is assimilation in the host country as random and elusive as success in front of a slot machine?

Latha's 'Cheenalatchumi's Queue' is a captivating reflection on Tamil identity and its construction within the melting pot of immigrant communities in cosmopolitan Singapore. A standout feature of this story is its clever and innovative subversion of the typical search for the Tamil identity or nostalgic longing for it, which are common concerns in much postcolonial Tamil fiction emerging from outside the Tamil diaspora. The female protagonist, adopted by a Tamil family as a child, rejects the label of 'Chinese' (as implied in the name 'Cheena [Chinese] Latchumi' used by others in social settings) and insists on being called simply 'Latchumi'. Through her persistent efforts to assert her identity as a 'Tamil woman', the narrative poses a provocative question that we rarely come across in contemporary Tamil fiction: What are the criteria for an 'authentic' Tamil woman/person, and who has the authority to determine them?

The trope of identity is central to the narrative of 'The Saga of Butchery' by Keeranur Jakirraja as well. Ruefully reflecting on it in the context of history and local customs, it starts with a touch of humour, but gradually veers into dark comedy. The protagonist, planning to sacrifice a camel instead of a goat on Bakrid, hears an anonymous voice – probably his conscience as the narrative seems to suggest – remarking, 'Anything associated with you should bear the stamp of Arabia and reek of the Gulf, right? Only then would people accept you as a Muslim.' When the severed camel's head starts speaking in the same unidentifiable voice, we wonder who is being really sacrificed. The narrative opens up rich possibilities of interpretation regarding who speaks, who listens, and whether the conversation will ever end. Its lack of closure adds more vibrancy to its tapestry of inquiry.

Jeyamohan's 'The Sacrificial Stone' is one of the few intensely evocative stories in the Tamil literary realm. It constructs a nuanced narrative of the life of a poor Brahmin priest and his family, highlighting the politics of temple administration and, in a related way, the complexities of the caste order – topics largely overlooked in Tamil fiction. More significantly, the narrative illustrates how, when institutional justice fails the oppressed and vulnerable, a mysterious punishment can sometimes befall the wrongdoers. Here, the curse, a mythological and puranic motif, becomes a weapon that delivers the justice that the modern judicial apparatus fails to provide. We are gently reminded that betrayal, wrongdoing, regret, and the seeking and granting of forgiveness are universal human experiences that persist across time. Akin to Jeyamohan's story, the narrative of Perumal Murugan's 'The Blouse' also goes beyond the discourse of modern rationality. The doctor-son of the elderly protagonist despises her and inwardly curses her as an 'uncivilized savage' for not covering her breasts with a piece of blouse fabric. The family's attempts to 'civilize' her during his wedding preliminaries culminate in a strange occurrence: a sharp corner of the blouse plunges deep into her heart and emerges 'from her armpit in the form of a cyst as big as a newborn's head'. She would never be able to wear a blouse again. The cyst is at once a symbol and a physical manifestation of her resistance to being tamed against her will. It is as if the vulnerable woman is given a mysterious tool – albeit a bizarre one, this cyst – in her fight to assert her agency, although we are unsure about the course her future might take.

While mysterious elements beyond instrumental rationality are central to the narratives of these two stories, the fantastic takes centre stage in Sundara Ramaswamy's 'The Breaking of a Story'. Not only is this story a marked departure from the others in the collection, it is also a rarity within Sundara Ramaswamy's oeuvre as well, given that the author is known for his measured and modernist prose style, grounded in realism. It opens with an inexplicable event that defies everyday logic, capturing the bewildered reactions of onlookers. Eager to cover the breaking story, the media rushes to capture sensational images of the 'phenomenon' and provide continuous updates. This narrative addresses the contemporary trend of the media's constant barrage of information and its relentless drive to fill every moment with content. It challenges us to consider whether we are at all capable of witnessing a miracle, if and when we encounter it, without the external mediation of images, soundbites, or stories from the print or visual media.

As a reader, I have immersed myself in the creative works of the writers in this collection for over thirty years. As a writer within the Tamil milieu, I feel fortunate to have journeyed alongside many of them – through their texts and, at times, through personal conversations. I do, however, recognize the absence of a few other significant short-story writers in this anthology, but that owes largely to the limitations imposed by the logistics of publication. Ultimately, my selection was guided by two key criteria: the ability to convey the barely perceptible intricacies of life through writing and the effectiveness with which these narratives encounter today's world.

Given that Tamil as a language and culture is prominent outside Tamil Nadu as well, this collection includes a few renowned Tamil writers from countries other than India – Latha from Singapore, Shobasakthi from France, and Muttulingam and Tamilnathy from Canada. During the process of making this collection, conversations with translators such as N. Kalyan Raman, Janani Kannan, Nandini Krishnan, Yashasvi Arunkumar and Suchitra Ramachandran have been invaluable. I would also like to acknowledge G.J.V. Prasad for his contribution through the translation incorporated in this collection. My conversations with Kalyan Raman over the last several years have helped in familiarizing myself with the Indian literary milieu concerning translation. I owe a special gratitude to Rahul Soni, who has supported this project solidly from the very beginning, and to Kannan Sundaram, who introduced me to him. My sincere thanks go to Rinita Banerjee, whose attentive eyes steered this book to its current shape.

Ashokamitran once remarked, 'Creative literature reflects the changes in outlook, culture, tradition, and moral precepts of its time', adding that 'a good story should be worthy of being compared to any great story, written in any part of the world.'[7] Early Tamil writers were first exposed to the short-story genre through English and translations of Western and Bengali literature, as Dilip Kumar notes in his foreword to an extensive collection of Tamil short stories, translated by him and Subashree Krishnaswamy.[8] Much like their predecessors,

---

7 Ashokamitran, *Padaippukkalai* (Nagercoil: Kalachuvadu Publications, [1987] 2021).
8 Dilip Kumar, ed., *The Tamil Story: Through the Times, Through the Tides*, trans., Dilip Kumar and Subashree Krishnaswamy (New Delhi:

writers represented in this collection are familiar with pan-Indian literature, and have also engaged with global literatures, including Russian, European, Asian, Latin American and Anglo-American texts, primarily through translations, reflecting the evolving cultural and literary sensibilities of their time.

This global influence was deeply ingrained in the independent literary magazines that nurtured many of these writers. Authors such as Ashokamitran, Sundara Ramaswamy, Jeyamohan, Charu Nivedita and S. Ramakrishnan have penned lucid essays on pioneers of modern literature, including Chekhov, Márquez, Hemingway, Bukowski and Robbe-Grillet, revealing expansive literary horizons. A discerning reader may recognize how the styles and cadences in these stories share a kinship with literatures across India and the globe, even as they remain grounded in their own cultural milieu. In the collection, which resembles a katambam, such kinship is an asset. As long as it remains fragrant, who would not want to enjoy its medley of scents? Now it lies in the hands of readers.

Perundevi

Tranquebar Press, 2016), p. xvii.

HARMONIUM

Ashokamitran

TRANSLATED BY N. KALYAN RAMAN

A SONG WAS PLAYING in the street. Ramachandran ran and stood at the entrance of his apartment block. A man wearing a yellow veshti had kept a large portrait of Shirdi Saibaba on something that resembled a cycle-rickshaw and done it up like a mobile shrine. A baby slung on her back, a woman who could have been his wife was walking with the fellow in the yellow veshti. A loudspeaker in the vehicle was broadcasting a bhajan – devotional song – about Saibaba.

Ramachandran gave a rupee to the man in the yellow veshti. 'You have a tape recorder; so, why the harmonium?' he asked in Telugu.

'We play recorded songs only when we are pushing the vehicle. We stop and sing at street corners.'

'Can you sing a little now?'

'We have many more streets to pass through.'

'I'll give you five rupees.'

He sang a new bhajan. Now and then, the woman with the baby joined him. The bhajan was very moving, and they sang it fervently with their eyes closed. It would not be wrong to say that the harmonium played through his fingers. He seemed to press merely four to five bars, but the full shape of the melody came to life. On a couple of occasions, the harmonium sounded like a background instrument.

Ramachandran gave him ten rupees. Without being asked, the man in the yellow veshti sang one more bhajan. No one could appeal to Saibaba like him.

After singing the second bhajan, he moved on. At once, the tape recorder started playing. It sounded quite jarring, as though it were atoning for his singing.

Who had schooled this young man in music? Who had taught him to play the harmonium? Only a few days ago, when a little boy turned up with a decorated bull, Ramachandran asked him, 'Listen, don't you go to school? Are your parents alive?' The boy collected a rupee and said, 'Yes, they are.'

'What does your father do?'

'He also goes around with a boom-boom bull.'

Ramachandran felt sad and surprised at the same time. Even though the bull was short and stout, it did not appear to be starving. This little boy's father has trusted him with a bull. It is certain that the boy and his parents are not residents of the city. He must have come from a village somewhere on the outskirts. He could not have travelled with the bull in a bus or suburban train. The boy must have walked many miles to reach this locality. Had there been small, independent houses here, someone might have given him money, but there is no chance of that happening in high-rise buildings. It seems as if apartment blocks are expressly designed to eliminate all charity and giving to the poor. These days, a lot of robberies are committed in these apartments; murders too, now and then. Only after the stench begins to spread do some people make the effort to break down the door. An unsightly corpse will be hanging inside.

Apartment dwellers have another problem too. If food is left over, they cannot give it to anyone. These days, we rarely see people walking the street every night, crying, 'Amma … give me some food.' How can a lone watchman eat leftover kuzhambu and rice from so many apartments? Therefore, food cooked with groceries and vegetables bought at great expense has to be thrown out as garbage; we have to pack it carefully in plastic bags and deposit them in the garbage bin. We may feel uneasy on the first day. But in the course of time, we become inured to such feelings. It would be nice to give this boom-boom boy some food, but everything would have been dumped in the garbage bin by now.

As for the Saibaba devotee who lugged a harmonium around, his father must have taught him to play the harmonium along with this way of earning a living. If he were asked, 'Why didn't you educate your son? You have made a nomad out of him,' he would simply say, 'Saibaba will take care of everything.' Should we call this devotion or superstition? A family had given that son a bride as well. No Saibaba devotee worried about the future. Why should this young man worry?

Ramachandran climbed the stairs and reached his apartment. The boy with the boom-boom bull and the Saibaba devotee practised the same trade. They harboured no special enmity against the people who chased them away; felt no special gratitude towards those who gave them alms either. By now, that Saibaba devotee would have forgotten that he had received ten rupees. There was something he did not know: Ramachandran had asked him to sing not out of devotion to Saibaba, but to listen to the young man play the harmonium, for the music he produced out of the box.

There was a time when not all north Indian and Telugu singers considered it beneath them to use the harmonium. A harmonium provided the sole background music for stage dramas. It might have been the graveyard scene in Raja Harishchandra. But a harmonium player would be sitting on one side of the stage, visible to everyone, pumping the bellows with his feet. In fact, many harmonium players were stars of the stage. As the lead actor burnished his singing with a series of ornamentations, as if to compete with him, the harmonium players would play further variations. Was there a single Saigal song without the harmonium? There were songs that featured the piano and the harmonium at the same time. Songs by Pankaj Mullick, Juthika Roy, K.C. Dey … They said this K.C. Dey was blind. Was he born blind, or did he lose his eyesight in an accident? Whatever it might be, his most famous song was '*Baba, mann ki aankhein khol*'. ('Lord, open the eyes of my heart.') Jawaharlal Nehru wouldn't have heard this song; Rabindranath would have. The harmonium had a place in Rabindra Sangeet. But Rabindranath didn't like the harmonium.

Jawaharlal had communicated in writing that he disliked the harmonium. But the harmonium has been a life-giving instrument for so many indigent artists, mendicants and beggars! Jawaharlal would not know this. He did not know many things. He is known as a man of letters. However, even though he wrote hundreds of pages, he could not invoke a single literary quotation in a striking manner. His daughter was better than him in many ways. After all, she studied in Shantiniketan, didn't she? She knew that R.K. Narayan and his whole family considered Nehru a detestable individual. Yet, she bought all of Narayan's books, invited him to her residence for tea and got him to autograph all the books. Narayan had also been a member of Rajya Sabha, nominated by the President. He never used his position to make money, or abused it in other ways. But this man, who never wrote a letter of reference even for close associates, also didn't like the harmonium.

While travelling by train through Andhra Pradesh, Ramachandran had heard harmonium-singers countless number of times. Carrying the instrument, they would leap from one train compartment to another even when the train was moving at full speed. Risking their lives in order to beg! They sang only Telugu songs. How movingly they sang! How wonderfully they played the harmonium! Now the railway police have driven away singers and blind beggars from our trains.

But they couldn't do anything about the aravanis – transgenders. The aravanis embarrassed even policemen. Those who were afraid of getting beaten with lathis would run away or hide. But it was never easy for the police to handle the bold ones among them.

Harmonium. Harmonium. It had evolved from the harmonica. An instrument that has been in use for a few centuries. The harmonica, too, is a beggar's instrument. In European cities, people would beg while playing the harmonica in street corners. The harmonica can sound as if a whole band is playing. The harmonium is like that too. Carnatic vocal music is always taught with a harmonium. *Sa ri ga ma pa tha ni sa. Sa ni tha pa ma ga ri sa.*

The harmonium has had its enemies in every generation. What was the matter with Bharathiyar? His songs could be included among the finest of all his creations. But he did not like the harmonium. He wrote a whole essay elaborating on his dislike for the instrument.

There were no Saibaba devotees in Bharathiyar's time. Otherwise, he would not have hated the harmonium.

During Rabindranath's lifetime, Saibaba's power and glory had gained wide renown. Rabindranath might have disliked Saibaba, but he was a man who carried with him both Ramakrishna Paramahamsa and Keshub Chandra Sen at the same time. 'Throw away your prayer beads! God dwells in the man who breaks stones and the man who is ploughing the field!' Perfectly fine ... but the same god is also present in the harmonium player who sings Saibaba bhajans. Why, he is present in the harmonium itself.

THE KING'S WAY

Kanmani Gunasekaran

TRANSLATED BY N. KALYAN RAMAN

Kanniyakoil was the last stop on the bus route from Pondicherry to Cuddalore. None of the buses approaching Kanniyakoil slowed down to stop and pick up passengers. Daunted by the waiting crowd that came surging forward, they whizzed past. Even if, as an exception, a bus halted to allow passengers to get down, it would only stop at a distance from the bus stop. Before the sprinting crowd got anywhere near it, the bus would have started again.

Vathiyar Vadakkiruppu Kasiraja's vision was blurred from standing under the scorching sun for a long time and staring all the while at the black tar road. There was a terrible pain in his right arm from being held up repeatedly; it felt as though the arm was about to break off. Not a single fellow stopped his bus. Even if, by some miracle, someone did, he would say, 'Can't take your luggage on board, get lost,' and take off.

Vathiyar, the 'master' of a troupe of therukkoothu performers, looked behind him. His heart trembled at the sight. Costume bundle, tin trunk filled with jewellery, mattalam blocks, harmonium box – everything was lying under the naked sun. Inside the jewellery trunk were dresses and ornaments for Dharumar, Bhimar, Kannan, Duryodhanan, Panchali, Alli and other divine characters. They had moved the trunk under the shade of a neem tree, but whenever a bus stopped unexpectedly, they had to carry it back. If the bus refused to take them on board, they had to lug it back to the shade again. Exhausted from carrying the trunk back and forth, they dumped it under the hot sun.

Bored of standing next to Vathiyar for hours and holding up their arms to flag down a vehicle, his men retreated to the shade and squatted on their haunches, eyes inflamed and yawning continuously. They lounged there, sleep-deprived, drowsily watching the road. 'Kattiyakkaran' Nellikuppam Rasu spread a towel on the ground and curled up on it. After performing all kinds of roles through the night, whenever the audience began to doze off, Rasu kept them entertained with jokes, stories and songs; he worked harder than anyone else in the troupe.

Vathiyar's expression had turned grim. Sweat streamed down his face, streaking the make-up which had not been removed properly. He wiped it with a towel and draped the towel over his shoulder while continuing to stand there, his gaze fixed northwards. In twenty years of performing koothu with a troupe, he had never failed to keep his word or fulfil an engagement after accepting it – by formally receiving paakku – scented arecanut powder – from the host. Was he going to slip up today? The prospect filled him with dread. He kept glancing behind him repeatedly at the men lounging in the shade.

Even as he allowed them to rest after a long, exhausting night, Vathiyar could not afford to be complacent. There were wine shops here and there. Kanniyakoil was just across the border from Pondicherry, where booze was cheap. He was afraid that they might mess up yet again.

He had warned them yesterday as soon as they got down in Kanniyakoil.

As though his remarks were intended specifically for Kattukudalur Vadivelu, the actor who played the role of Sooran, Vathiyar turned in his direction and said, 'Just because liquor is cheap around here, don't get tanked and botch up on the stage. There is a performance tomorrow night in Palakollai. We must reach there on time. Buses going there are not frequent. Don't any of you dare to get drunk, pass out and wreck our engagement.'

Even then, Vadivelu was fidgeting as though he could barely contain the urge. It was true that only after downing a few could he spin around in step with the beat, raising a swirl of dust, and captivate the audience, but this was Pondicherry booze. For the price of a quarter bottle anywhere else, you could buy three here.

Everyone was annoyed with Vathiyar. 'Why is he so strict? Doesn't he know that no matter how much they drink, our fellows can sing in the right key and dance without missing a beat? Then, why does he come after us at every turn?'

The days when Vathiyar had such confidence were long gone, especially after the ignominy suffered at their performance in Chinnakalapattu last year. It was a koothu that his troupe had been performing every year, but it was Koravankuppam Sadagopan's troupe that was going to do it this year. That the gig had changed hands this time was both disappointing and humiliating for Vathiyar. All because of that Elavathadi Gopal fellow! Vathiyar had kicked him out of the troupe that very night.

Chinnakalapattu was a fishing village in Pondicherry. Vathiyar had told them that he would go home from the village where they had performed the previous night and come directly to Chinnakalapattu. When there was a slight delay in his arrival, those present had started the performance. They had designed the play in such a way that even if Vathiyar arrived a bit late and then put on costume and make-up for his role, the timing of his entry would be just right. Vathiyar always played Karnan. Elavathadi Gopal usually played the lead role of Duryodhanan. Encouraged by Vathiyar's absence, he had crossed his limits and swilled a large quantity of cheap booze. As if that was not enough, the villagers who knew him from his performance every year had cooked him a feast of mutton and fish. He had gorged on it like a starving beast let loose in a field of maize. Somehow he had managed to put on his costume and make-up, sing the curtain-raiser as well as one more song to herald his arrival, and circle the stage, ankle-bells jingling, a couple of times in step with the beat. That did it. Abruptly, he started running past the assembly. Watching this from a distance as he walked towards the assembly, Vathiyar started to shake all over. As he hurried behind the assembly, he came upon the sight of Duryodhanan Maharaja lying there in the dark, retching, and in no condition to resume the koothu. The stink was gut-wrenching. A dog rushed in and scavenged for bits of meat and fish strewn on the ground. Vathiyar stood in the middle of the assembly and apologized to everyone; then he got someone else to dress up and perform Duryodhanan's role.

All said, koothu is a divine art. It is a people's assembly where the learned are gathered along with ordinary folk. An assembly in quest of truth and enlightenment. This koothu, performed in a public space, is the same one that Lord Nataraja performed in the temple in Thillai. It is as retribution for insulting such a sacred assembly that the engagement has been snatched away from them, Vathiyar thought.

The strict instructions that Vathiyar had issued immediately upon his arrival were effective only through the nighttime. In the morning, after removing his make-up, Vadivelu rushed to the wine shop. Since his not messing up on the stage the previous night must have required supreme effort, Vathiyar pretended not to notice and did not intervene. He knew that a man couldn't sustain himself in this profession without drinking and that alcohol worked wonders for the sleep deprivation and fatigue that were endemic to koothu performers. But mostly it was the low prices that had seduced and felled Vadivelu. Even the man who set out to fetch Vadivelu failed to return; and the man who went in search of the man who had gone looking for Vadivelu did not come back either. By the time they could get everyone together and reach the bus stop, it was very late. Otherwise, they would have left a long time ago.

Vathiyar held up his arm at a van that was speeding past. As soon as it came to a halt, Pulavankuppam Panneer collected everyone who was resting in the shade and ran to the van along with them.

Looking at the jewellery trunk and the mattalam blocks, the van driver asked, 'Which town?'

'Cuddalore.'

'Will cost you a hundred.'

'How could that be? Atrocious!' Vathiyar said, sounding shocked.

'Ten people, plus your bundles and boxes – enough to fill a van and more. And you're shocked when I say hundred rupees.'

'We reach Cuddalore right after we cross the river. And for that…' Vathiyar dragged his words out.

'Then you buy salted peanuts for a rupee and come walking while you munch on them.' The van driver left.

Vathiyar looked mortified. His people, who had come running to the van as a group, returned to lounge in the shade. Vathiyar turned to look. Vadivelu was standing nearby.

Anger flared up in him. 'All because of you, useless wretch! But for you, we would have reached Palakollai by now.'

'I am Arjunan, the brave warrior who has earned glory and fame in the world. I have learnt many an art, and studied the Vedas and the scriptures. I hold a mighty bow in my hands. I am a man of character who goes by the name of Palgunan.' The vitality that had animated Vathiyar's leaps and jumps as Arjunan last night was entirely missing from his body. After standing patiently for hours till his legs throbbed in pain, he wondered whether he should finally go and sit in the shade. Just then, a private bus arrived. Vathiyar held up his hand without much hope. The bus stopped. Everyone picked up their baggage and ran to the bus.

From inside the bus, the conductor, holding a tin whistle between his lips, said, 'Yov, don't dump your sacks in the midst of this crowd.'

'These are not sacks, 'nga. Jewellery trunk and costumes for performing koothu,' Vathiyar said in a near-pleading tone.

'Yov, I don't have much time. Put them on top of the bus,' the conductor said. Vathiyar was dismayed.

'These are for our koothu, 'nga. They are like God's property. Allow me to take them inside; it will earn you merit.'

'Yov, put them on top or let me go. It will cost you forty rupees in all,' the conductor said in a tone of demanding a yes-or-no answer.

'Wait, wait. We will load everything on top.' Kattiyakkaran Rasu climbed to the top of the bus, and as Vadivelu kept passing the items from below, he arranged them neatly and tied them to the luggage holder with rope.

Everyone knew that at the Palakollai performance that night, Kattiyakkaran Rasu would narrate the whole sorry episode in front of the audience – how they had stood waiting for a bus in Kanniyakoil, holding up their arms, and how they loaded their luggage – mocking the troupe to make the crowd laugh. It was only by turning the humiliation they suffered in the world into a joke before the audience that they could console themselves.

They had boarded the bus carrying only the two big mattalam blocks and harmonium box with them. While they stood like bats hanging from the ceiling, the conductor came by. 'Forty rupees,' he said.

'Be lenient about the luggage, Aiya. It's nothing but props for our roles. Acting is our livelihood, Aiya. We must perform to survive. If we don't, we'll be in trouble.'

'This is why we should never carry people like you. You'll say yes to the fare when you come on board, and once you're inside you'll say something else. Give me forty rupees if you have it, or else…' Without another word, Vathiyar gave him forty rupees.

By the time the conductor took the money and issued the tickets, they had reached Cuddalore. Someone standing in front of him asked, 'Which company is this?'

'Vadakkiruppu Kasiraja Company,' Vathiyar cited his own name.

'In which village is the koothu?'

'In Palakollai, near Sendanadu. After Panruti.'

When the bus did a semi-circle at the bus terminus and slowed to a halt, a couple of blue-shirted men came running towards it. Vathiyar felt weary and despondent.

'Now we must wrangle with them. They'll grab our money like highway-robbers. Bastards!'

A blue-shirt tried to climb the ladder to the top of the bus before it came to a stop. Vathiyar jumped down and blocked him. 'They're only props for our koothu, 'pa. There's no luggage.'

'Let me see what you have there anyway…' He tried to climb up again. The other blue-shirt said, 'Go ahead, 'pa. Another bus might come in anytime now,' and hurried him.

'No, 'pa. They're only items for performing koothu. We'll unload it ourselves.' As soon as Vathiyar said this, the one who was about to make his way to the top of the bus said in a rage, 'If you unload it, what are we standing here for – plucking pubic hair?'

Meanwhile, the rest of the troupe had got down from the bus. The costume bundle and jewellery box were lying above. The blue-shirt stood with one foot on the ladder. Vathiyar repeated patiently, 'Don't mistake me. We are ten people here. If we need help, you can always unload it for us.'

'Yov, I don't want to abuse you. It doesn't matter how many people you have in your troupe. In this bus stand, only we have the right to unload. I have brought down your luggage so many times before. You speak as though you are new around here,' the fellow by the ladder said angrily.

Vadivelu lost his temper. His face, from which the red make-up had not been erased completely, grew even more red. 'Dei, watch your mouth. We have enough people. We'll take care of it. Abuse us, huh? Try it, man, if you dare.'

The man with his foot on the ladder stepped close to him instantly. 'Dei, who are you calling "dei"? Street-dancing clown. Dei, Thevarasu, Kuppa, come over here!'

Vathiyar became slightly fearful. Still, he was not fazed. 'Call whoever you want. Don't assume that only you have people here.'

One of the blue-shirted fellows who had turned up in response to the call looked at Vathiyar and those standing beside him, and at the goods lying above. Then he said, 'What's the matter, Vathiyar? Why don't you give us some change for tea and move on instead of kicking up a row?'

'Not like that, 'pa. We have enough men. If we didn't, then we would ask you.'

'How are we to survive, then, Vathiyar? When you perform koothu, you will net a hundred rupees per day. What about us? All right, climb on top, da. You don't know how to talk to these people. Vathiyar, move out of our way.' Two men brought down the goods.

'Give us twenty rupees, Vathiyar.'

Vathiyar was startled. 'Why, this is atrocious. That's why I said earlier … while we have so many people.'

'All right, Vathiyarey. Take five rupees off and give us the rest.' After rummaging through his pockets, Vathiyar gave the fellow six rupees and said, 'This is all I have.'

The one who had tried to climb to the top of the bus first asked, raising his voice, 'What the hell is this, six rupees?'

'Leave it, da,' the one who had come later appeased him.

The troupe picked up the luggage and went over to where the bus going to Panruti was parked. One of them tried to slip away. Vathiyar was annoyed.

'Elei, where do you think you are going? We must reach Panruti in time to get a bus to Palakollai.'

'Wait, Vathiyarey. I have a stomach ache. The idli we ate at the stall this morning must have had too much baking soda. The pain is tearing into my stomach,' he said, rubbing his lower abdomen.

'Only when there is work to do, you'll want to take a shit.' Vathiyar had spoken in exasperation, but when he thought about the condition of koothu performers, he could feel only pity. They leapt and roared all night as kings endowed with all kinds of powers, accompanied by a retinue of ministers and sidekicks; but once the day dawned, when they squatted in a corner of the pyol at the roadside stall eating piping hot idlis, their stomachs would be on fire. That, too, idlis made from sour batter with an excess of baking soda. Their stomachs would heave, turn, churn and settle before the pain started. Staying awake through the night and being fast asleep during daylight hours, not eating properly and not emptying the bowels regularly – they endured so many hardships.

Because it was a town bus that had no luggage holder on top, they escaped the usual hassle. Boldly they carried their luggage on board and took their seats. Vathiyar sat in a corner, the jewellery trunk and the costume bundle next to him. After stowing the mattalam blocks and harmonium box in the space below their seats, the players fell asleep immediately. Both were exhausted from having carried their instruments all this while.

Many more passengers boarded the bus once it started moving. 'Ticket, ticket…' the conductor demanded from Kattiyakkaran Rasu, who told him, 'The man at the back will buy,' pointing to Vathiyar.

'Ten tickets to Panruti and two for luggage,' Vathiyar said.

'What luggage?'

'Koothu items, jewellery trunk and costume bundle – that's all.'

'That will be fifty rupees.'

'What! Fifty rupees?'

'Yov, ten tickets to Panruti will be thirty rupees. Then, two luggage items. You pass through so many towns and villages. Yet, you talk without a clue about what's going on in the world.'

'So, what's the charge for the luggage – twenty rupees?'

It seemed the conductor couldn't bear the aggravation. 'What a hassle it is with you guys! I should never have let you into the bus.'

'All right. Give us the tickets.' After collecting fifty rupees and putting the notes into his bag, the conductor tore off a sheaf of tickets, gave them to Vathiyar and moved on. Vathiyar was so sleepy that his eyes were glazing over. He had not had a wink of sleep so far. He must reach Palakollai somehow and sleep for some time; only then would the fatigue leave him.

When the bus shook from a severe bump on the road, Vathiyar opened his eyes. He was shocked. A man was sitting on the jewellery trunk.

Feeling distraught, he said, 'Listen, 'pa. That jewellery trunk is sacred like God. Get up.' He woke the sleeping man.

The fellow appeared to be slightly drunk. 'It's not as if it's filled with gold and diamonds. Just four or five blocks of coral wood, and you keep shouting about your jewellery. And they are inside a tin trunk. And you're frightened like it has got dented or something.'

'It may be coral wood, but it feeds ten families. You are sitting on the deity that keeps us fed.'

'All right. Calm down, already.'

Sighing, Vathiyar closed his eyes again. 'You there! You haven't yet bought a ticket!' Hearing the noise, Vathiyar woke up again. He got up, did a head count of his troupe, and shut his eyes again.

The bus stopped at Pattambakkam and resumed its journey. 'Yov, therukkoothu! Check whether everyone from your troupe is here. Count them again.'

'It's fine, 'pa,' Vathiyar said, dismayed at being unable to snatch some sleep.

While counting them again, the conductor noticed that something was lying near the mattalam player's feet. Abandoning the count, he patted the sleeping man awake and asked him, 'What is that, 'ya?'

'Harmonium box, 'nga.'

Bending low, he asked, 'And that one?'

'Blocks for the mattalam, 'nga.'

'Who will buy tickets for all these? Fish out ten rupees for both.'

'Both are counted as part of the jewellery trunk, 'pa,' Vathiyar said from behind.

'Then you should have tied them both to the trunk and brought them,' the conductor said sarcastically.

'Not like that, Aiya. We have never bought tickets for them separately.'

'If you hide them under the seat like this, I'm sure you can travel without buying tickets.'

'No, Aiya. We've never been asked to buy tickets for them on any bus.'

'In this bus, you have to. That too, with me in the bus, you absolutely must.'

'Look, we are ten of us travelling with just two mattalam blocks and a harmonium box.'

'Even if a hundred more are travelling with those items, you still can't escape buying tickets for them.'

'What are you saying? They are sacred objects for a therukkoothu show. Mattalam blocks and a harmonium box. Both are very special for our God. And you're making such a terrible fuss…' Vathiyar rambled on.

'I don't want any talk about gods and spirits here. Take out the cash.'

'Not like that, 'nga. You see…'

The conductor took a few steps forward and blew his whistle. It was loud enough to clog everyone's ears. The bus came to a halt with a sudden jolt. Ignoring the pain from bumping his head against the vertical rod in front of him, Vathiyar took out the money and gave it to him. 'Here, take it.'

The vehicle was crossing Keezhkavarapattu. Vathiyar had faced such problems many times before, but this day had brought nothing but quarrels and harsh words right from the start; he felt sad and humiliated.

Of course, he could be generous and hand over fifty or hundred rupees to the conductor, and move on without a word of argument. But he couldn't afford to these days. Transport expenses ate up half of what he earned. He had to pay eighty or hundred rupees as salary to each member of his troupe. Then there were the costs of the make-up items: oil, senthuram (foundation) and face powder. If any of the costume props – sticks, shoulder blocks and wig – broke after being dumped on top of a bus, he had to spend on replacements. After meeting all these expenses, he had to scrape some money together and make an advance payment to each actor for the next year.

Somehow, by the grace of God, ten families can survive with enough food in their bellies – sighing, Vathiyar thought to himself.

It started to grow dark. Vathiyar was sitting in Panruti, feeling forlorn. Again, he turned to the man next to him and asked, 'Aiya, this bus that goes via Sendanadu to Palakollai…'

'It left just a few minutes ago.'

Vathiyar became agitated. 'When will it be back?'

'After returning from Palakollai, it will go to the depot and come here only at half past ten.'

If they started at half past ten, it would be half past eleven by the time they reached Palakollai. After refreshments, putting on their costumes and make-up, they would be ready to begin the show at one in the night. Vathiyar could barely stand on his feet. He could never justify this delay to the people of the village. His name would be mud. If they had reached Panruti just a little earlier, they could have caught that bus. In fact, the villagers had asked them to come by that bus.

Everything happened because of this idiot Vadivelu! He glared at Vadivelu standing before him. Vadivelu cast his head down.

After asking around, Rasu came back with some information. 'It seems there is a bus going via Sendanadu to Ulundurpet. Beyond Sendanadu, there is a place called Nari Odaipalam. Palakollai is only two miles from there. If we take that bus, get down at that spot and pass a message through some bicycle heading that way, asking the people there to send a vehicle, we can reach Palakollai in time for the koothu.'

Vathiyar experienced an instant surge of energy. He asked eagerly, 'At what time?'

'Seven-thirty. A private bus service called Neelavati.'

He made a mental calculation. At all events, they could start the show by eleven at the latest. Vathiyar asked his men to keep the luggage in a corner; then he undid his turban, and after loosening his hair and tying it back into a bun, wound his turban tightly around his head again.

As time went by, a large crowd had gathered at the bus stand. After making them wait for a long time, the Neelavati bus came at eight. A section of the crowd got up immediately and rushed towards the bus. Even before the passengers could get down, they pushed and jostled through every gap and cranny, and filled all the vacant spaces.

Vathiyar asked his men to bring the jewellery trunk and other items of their luggage and ran towards the bus. Rasu, carrying the jewellery trunk, followed behind. The conductor, who was standing inside facing the entrance, shouted, 'Yov, who is that with a trunk? We won't take any sack or trunk on board. Stand back.'

Pushing and shoving, they boarded the bus through the rush of the crowd. Except Rasu, who stood outside holding the trunk in his hands, barely able to bear its weight. Standing behind him, Vathiyar pleaded with the conductor, 'Not like that, 'nga. These are therukkoothu props, 'nga. We have a performance in Palakollai. If we miss this bus, there is no other bus tonight.'

Rasu, who was now carrying the jewellery trunk on his head, approached the steps. The conductor leaned forward and pushed hard at the trunk. 'Yov, I can't have it on board in this crowd. Move back,' he said.

'No, 'nga. We'll pay whatever you want for the luggage. If we miss this bus, we won't get another. Please do us a good turn.' Even as Vathiyar was imploring the conductor, Rasu made his way through the crowd and brought the trunk down, gently lowering it on the steps.

'Yov, you don't seem to understand if you are told once. Take it away.' Standing above the steps, the conductor kicked the jewellery trunk and pushed it out. Before Rasu could catch hold of it, it slid down from one step to another with a series of thuds. Each thud descended like a thunderclap in Vathiyar's heart. Before it could fall to the ground, he rushed along with Rasu to hold it and gather it in his arms. Then he broke down and wept.

'The God we touch with our hands and worship, he pushes with his feet, 'pa. He is kicking our God with his feet, 'pa. He is kicking and shoving the God who feeds us with his feet, 'pa.'

Vathiyar sobbed and wailed. Everyone stood around, feeling distraught. Turning the corner, the Neelavati bus was on its way.

THE SAGA OF BUTCHERY

Keeranur Jakirraja

TRANSLATED BY N. KALYAN RAMAN

ON BAKRID, ONE found enormous quantities of meat cooking on the stoves of all the households in the town. In this respect, there were none of the usual distinctions between the rich and the commoner. Meat meant meat of a slaughtered goat; to put it nicely, sacred meat of the holy day of sacrifice – meat harvested from butchering goats and cattle, then sectioned into parcels, and sent to relatives, friends and indigent folk. Even as the meat was cooking on the stove in the kitchen, packet after packet of meat would keep arriving in a steady stream. It was indeed a sight of surpassing beauty. But it was impossible for any household to consume all of it.

On that day, more than half the butcher shops would be shut with a sign on the door: 'Shop closed'. But once the shops were closed, the shopkeepers didn't go home and lounge in comfort. Based on prior contracts, they went to the houses where sacrifice was being offered and remained occupied the whole day, performing tasks like slaughtering goats and cattle as well as skinning and curing the meat. Sometimes these tasks went on for even two or three days.

Look! Over there! Bakrid is coming to town.

Because of the upcoming Bakrid festival, 'Vatti' Hussain – so nicknamed after the exorbitant interest he charged as a moneylender – had become a celebrity in the town. Reason? This time, he was not going to sacrifice goats or cattle. Then...? Like Ebrahim Nabi, who had dared to sacrifice his son Ismail back in the day, was Husain going to sacrifice his son? Nope. To generate publicity for himself in the town around Bakrid this year, he was all set to import a large animal from a north Indian state. A large animal meant ... not an elephant, a bear, a lion, a tiger and their kind. The rules of the faith offered no scope for sacrificing any of those species.

Vatti Hussain was bored of slaughtering goats and cattle. 'We've been sacrificing the same animals for ages. It's time we thought a little differently in a modern civilized world.' Just when he was honing his thought process, the local textile store delivered at his home some new varieties of lungis meant exclusively for his use. An attendant from the textile store had brought two dozen lungis packed in a large bundle and left it on his desk. It was the desk on which Hussain did his accounts.

At one time, lungis for Vatti Hussain meant only handloom lungis; that is, he wore only handloom varieties. But these days, only power-loom lungis were very popular; they looked dapper as well. The store procured them especially for him from a Senguntha Mudaliar in Ranipet. The brand was 'Caravan'. The name printed in Tamil on the label of the bundle was: 'The Ship of the Desert'.

After waking up that morning, Vatti Hussain drank a large bowl of mutton soup before brushing his teeth; then he went to the toilet, stayed there for half an hour and finished his ablutions. Emerging from the toilet in an agitated state, he ordered his wife to get his breakfast ready and went to his desk. When he opened the bundle from the textile store, he found on the label of each lungi a camel, with an enormous hump and a long neck, standing tall. Just as Archimedes had cried 'Eureka! Eureka!' in excitement, Hussain bellowed in Kongu

Tamil, 'I've found it! I've found it!' On hearing this, Hussain's good wife, Ummusalma, his children and grandchildren, close friends and relatives, employees and people from families in the neighbourhood gathered around him. Seeing the crowd that had collected, Hussain did not really shrink from embarrassment. Had he been shy and awkward, how could he, an illiterate who couldn't read four sentences together, have boarded a train without a ticket, travelled to some remote province in the north, started hundreds of pawnshops and earned in crores? How could he have given job opportunities, like a veritable government, to five hundred or a thousand callow young men? How could the man have got so many to leave their dusty native villages, and towns like Palani, Dharapuram and Udumalaipettai that were still villages in the twenty-first century, venture beyond their boundaries and board the Kurla Express from Erode Junction? How could he have got them to wander all the roads and avenues of Bombay city, and got their tongues, which would not defer to any language other than their mother tongue Tamil, to roll over fluently while speaking multiple languages like Hindi, Marathi, Urdu, Bihari, Gujarati, Assamese, Telugu and Kannada? How could he have got them to go to Juhu beach every Sunday to gawk at the bodies of Anglo-Indian girls and fuck them in their minds?

As soon as Vatti Hussain decided that the sacrificial animal this year would be a camel, not goats or cattle, his good wife Ummusalma's face turned sombre and minuscule as a speck. Since her husband was running – with great dedication and care and completely against the tenets of their faith – an extensive moneylending operation, Ummusalma strongly believed that, as a couple, they were both going to suffer endlessly in a cruel hell in their afterlives. Now she often dreamt of herds of camels advancing towards her and taking turns to stomp on her mouth, and woke up screaming in the middle of the night. She imagined that her bed was covered with desert sand that bore the imprint of camel hooves. She had told her husband many times about such dreams, but he would always dismiss her with a smirk. When a furious Ummusalma asked him to tell her what the joke was, he said, 'We have more money than we could wish for. We can perform three Haj journeys each, gather all our sins in a sack, and drop it into our local river. Now, shut up and go to sleep.'

'There is no water flowing in our local river, Rawuthar Aiya. It's a sprawling tract of sand,' she retorted.

'If we can't dump it in the river, we'll drop it in the ocean. Sleep, woman!' Hussain said.

'Where is the ocean in our town?' Realizing that Ummusalma was merely trying to provoke him, Hussain lay there without uttering another word.

Ummusalma had another problem with camels. She could not stand camel meat. She was allergic to its foul smell. On the day of Bakrid three years ago, a lidded metal pail filled with camel meat had arrived from a relative in Dindigul. In those days, she was not at all allergic to camels. But it was on that very day that her allergy had set in. When some neighbours who had come visiting after their Haj pilgrimage regaled her unwisely about the glories of camels, camel milk and camel meat, Ummusalma started drinking tea with camel milk in all her dreams. Camel milk was like spurge milk, thicker than all other kinds of milk, like cow milk, buffalo milk, goat milk, packet milk, coconut milk and cottonseed milk. Even its taste bore a scent reminiscent of the Gulf, not in reality but only in her dreams.

The moment she eagerly opened the lidded pail from Dindigul, she felt like throwing up with a loud 'eww'. Raw, uncooked camel meat with its famous stink was introduced to her on that day. After she realized that the smell was far worse than the rancid odour from a dead bandicoot, she spent the whole day in the bathroom, vomiting and passing loose stools more than fifty times, and became so completely dehydrated that she got herself injected with glucose in a hospital and returned home.

Vatti Hussain, who entered the house with opulent dreams of camel korma, camel dry roast, camel meatballs and camel soup, was taken aback on seeing Ummusalma's condition. All the aforesaid fantasies about camel dishes were ruined in a second. The man had gone out of his way to contact the famous chef Zachariah and made special plans for camel biriyani. It was a major disappointment for him that on this sacred day, this grand festival day, Ummusalma was laid up in bed. It was at this moment, when he was grieving, heartbroken and drowning in anxiety with a hand on his head, that the anonymous voice began to converse with him:

'This is why, Saheb, you must marry three or four times just for convenience. If one wife dies, you would have another; if she is gone too, you would still have another left. Do you think our ancestors guided us for nothing? If you don't obey the word of elders, you end up having to struggle like this. Suffer! Only then you'll learn. You don't lack for money, do you? The property you've amassed by robbing people from the north and charging exorbitant interest is there for you to enjoy. And you are not past ninety, are you? Just sixty-two. Here, just the day before yesterday, before your very eyes, didn't seventy-seven-year-old Jainulabuddin marry fourteen-year-old Barkat Nissa secretly at sunrise, the time for Fajr prayer? Ask him. He is reported to have said, "When ninety-year-olds get married, why should I worry? I am still a young man." If anyone asked you, you would say, "Jainulabuddin has nothing to worry about. He consumes the golden elixir, which keeps him young." He consumes only the golden elixir, whereas you can afford to swallow even gold nuggets. Well, whatever. How long are you going to stick with Ummusalma, who pukes at the faintest whiff of camel meat? But no, don't use that as an excuse to give her talaq. At this juncture, it will spoil your image. Why does a moneylender need a good image, you might say. Interest will yield more interest. Show me another business where this happens. Be that as it may. In the upcoming municipality elections, you stand a good chance of being elected chairman. Forget about party-sharty. You were born to stand as an independent and win without contest. Your symbol – what else? It must be your beloved camel! Anything associated with you should bear the stamp of Arabia and reek of the Gulf, right? Only then would people accept you as a Muslim. It is true, of course, that your ancestors were peasants farming in the remote interiors of the Kongu region. If anyone looks closely at your face, it would be obvious.

'Did you enter India as a descendant of Prophet Muhammad after a forty-day journey by ship from Arabia? Were you a Rawuthu who trained horses and let them gallop in the battlefield? A Moghul or a Mongol? Nothing of that sort. Your roots have penetrated deep into this soil. It is only to keep you from knowing it that you are given incomprehensible Arab names, made to shave your head smooth and bald, forced to wear a Turkish cap with silk tassels hanging from it. You can grow only a beard; you are not permitted, like a traditional Tamil, to keep a moustache. Why all these restrictions? What for? To make you forget your original identity … What is the meaning of "Hussain", dear? You don't know? Hahahahaha.'

Though the electric fan was spinning at high speed, Vatti Hussain sweated profusely. He wiped his face clean with the towel on his shoulder. He felt as if a road roller was trudging inside his head. As he kept perspiring, he wiped himself with the towel again and again. What happened just now? Who was speaking to him all this while? When he thought about it, he was perplexed. Was it his conscience that had spoken to him? How could it know so many things? Wasn't it the conscience of a fool who lacked even basic education? How could it speak in such a logical manner? It was indeed surprising that Hussain could even sense a kind of mockery in those words, as if they meant to instruct him on what was right. Hussain felt uneasy, though, when the voice taunted him about not being a real Muslim. It made him feel disgraced and hang his head in shame. It was a voice that spoke to him ... but was it distinct from his own voice? Whom could he consult to gain clarity on this? They would call him a lunatic. How disgraceful it would be if the great Vatti Hussain were to lose his sanity. Would anyone in the town respect him? Would his employees, who fulfilled his every command, respect him? Forget them, would Ummusalma herself respect him? Would he be able to contest the municipality elections? Even if he did, was he likely to get votes? What an ordeal it was. But he was determined to deal with it.

Hussain stood up suddenly and entered his secret chamber. What was this secret chamber? It was a room no one else could enter. Even his good wife Ummusalma was not allowed in there. The fate of people who had borrowed money from hundreds of shops belonging to Hussain was decided there. It was filled to overflowing with innumerable documents. Wherever one looked, there were bonds, poor people's fingerprints, traces of tears and wails. Like the villain in a black-and-white Tamil film, he entered the room with a gloomy expression, opened the cupboard, and touched and caressed his revolver. The anonymous voice was a sign that he was surrounded by enemies. He paced up and down the room for some time. Vatti Hussain had enemies across all the north Indian states. The name of a Madrasi like him was on the hit list of Maoists. He was fortunate to have survived sudden ambushes on several occasions. All this happened ten years ago. Now he was a prominent man in this town. But, but ... that voice?

Vatti Hussain was indeed quite perplexed. Had Ummusalma been in normal good health, she would have found out who it was. She had a natural ability to identify different types of voices. The only drawback, though, was that she would exaggerate everything tenfold. But three or four out of those ten yarns would be flawless. She could easily identify the voice that had spoken a short while ago. Hussain came out of the secret chamber and cast a quick glance around the room where Ummusalma was sleeping. She lay like a painting whose colours had faded. She had aged a bit. Disease had that effect on her. Sighing, Hussain turned his eyes away from her.

Sometime back, Vatti Hussain used to receive a mysterious call night after night just before he went to bed. As soon as Hussain lifted the handset to his ear, the voice would begin:

'Don't charge usurious rates, Hussain. You'll be ruined.'

'Hello. Who … who … are you?'

'Dei, Hussein. This is your conscience speaking. Charging interest is tantamount to committing homicide. You are a murderer.'

'What is conscience and all that rubbish! Tell me who you are, moron.'

'You brag about owning a hundred pawn shops. One hell for each shop. One hundred hells for one hundred shops.'

'Fool. Charging interest on loans is my trade. I have a right to pursue my trade.'

'Interest money is proscribed as evil. A terrible hell awaits you in the afterlife.'

'Who are you to tell me what is forbidden and what is allowed – God?'

'God's messenger.'

'Are you a prophet? If you were born to one father, tell me your name, you cretin.'

'I am not the Prophet. I follow in his footsteps.'

In this way, their conversation would continue well past midnight. Hussain wouldn't concede anything easily. The mysterious voice at the other end of the line wouldn't relent either. At some stage, Hussain would lose patience and spew a stream of abuse. All the abuses that were current in several Indian languages would roll fluently off his tongue. Swearing was routine with people involved in the moneylending business. Ummusalma would close her ears and move to the next room. Hussain filed a complaint at the local police station about the mysterious telephone calls. He invited officials from the telephone department to his home for dinner and requested them to help identify the culprit. Nothing happened, though.

Very soon, Hussain's suspicion began to fall on anyone who dispensed advice. Its worst victims were the Pesh Imams at the local mosques. Poor men. How were they to blame? What else could they do apart from offering advice during their sermons on Fridays? Any Pesh Imam who proclaimed that usury was a sin was dismissed and sent packing by the mosque administration. Needless to say, it was done under pressure from Vatti Hussain.

One of Hussain's numerous detractors in the town with a flair for statistics pointed out that thirty-seven Pesh Imams had been victimized in this manner. It was only later that Vatti Hussain began to follow a new strategy. He would invite any newly appointed Pesh Imam to his house and instruct him as if in a classroom: 'You can preach whatever you like, but don't open your mouth about interest.' It was by obeying this dictum scrupulously that the most recent Pesh Imam had lasted in office during the past month. It was rumoured that those who sought boons during prayers also prayed that the Imam's tenure in this mosque must continue. Chances of it being a false rumour were low.

The mysterious telephone calls continued to plague Hussain. That day, Hussain was in the toilet. Ummusalma had picked up the phone. She also received some advice. 'Whoever interacts with people in the moneylending business will also be condemned to a terrible hell. Islam prohibits charging interest as well as paying interest…' The same voice. The same tone. Ummusalma had held the receiver to her ear for no more than a minute before she put it down. A smile appeared on her face for a fleeting moment and disappeared. The voice that had evaded Hussain's detection all these days was instantly obvious to her. It was also an opportunity for her to realize what an idiot her husband was. Someone who couldn't identify the voice of his own son must be a complete idiot, right? The son spoke in an altered voice, but that was immaterial. He wasn't such an accomplished mimicry artiste either. As per the wisdom of the police in Tamil films, even an expert criminal would leave some clue behind at the crime scene. In the same way, someone who spoke in a completely altered voice would slip into his real voice at some point. It would be caught by those who knew him. That was how Ummusalma had recognized Salim's voice. She had recognized it as the voice of Salim who had been staying in Bombay against his own wishes for the last four years to manage the pawnshops established by his father. He had stoically borne innumerable abuses from his father in this regard. Ummusalma was immensely pleased by her son's principle, resolve and the tactic he had employed against his father. Whenever his phone call came, the redoubtable Vatti Hussain was shaken to the core.

When the phone rang the next day, Hussain, who was ready with a few more expletives he had coined, picked up the receiver. 'Hold on for a bit. Let me take the call this time,' Ummusalma came forward on purpose and answered the phone. Hussain was disappointed at not being able to spew the abuses that lurked in his throat. 'Hello,' Ummusalma said, smiling. Hussain was surprised. This time someone sang from the other end, with a lot of effort, in Nagore Hanifa's voice.

> Profit from moneylending
> is a flame that singes the poor
> Are dinars a substitute for justice?
> How can we disobey Prophet Nabi's teachings?
> How can we lose heart?

'Dei ... Salimu ... that's enough, da ... don't exaggerate so much.'
'Amma! You've caught on, then?'
'He is here...'

That did it. The connection was terminated from the other end. Hussain shot a bemused look at Ummusalma. That look of dread had not left his eyes.

'Who was that, woman?'

'Salim.'

'Salim?'

'Yes, yes ... do you remember that boy from Tiruppur, who was a collection agent in our Mulund shop in Bombay, the one who wrangled for a pay raise and ran away from the job?'

'That rabid dog? I'll fix him.'

'Don't gnash your teeth like Nambiar, the villain in MGR's films. Have some patience.'

'If you had given the phone to me, I would have made mincemeat of him. After all, a dog who did our bidding for his livelihood...'

'Oh, yes. As if you didn't pick up the phone and speak to him. Just shut up and go to bed.'

'What!'

'I asked you to cover yourself with a sheet and go to sleep. Can't you see the dew falling? It's become such a hassle with you every night.'

'My heart won't calm down.'

'Rub your chest with a lot of Nilgiri oil.'

'How dare a lowly servant get cheeky with me...'

'There won't be any phone calls from now on. Be quiet and go to bed.'

'If there are...'

'I'm telling you there won't be, right?'

Ummusalma had lied astutely to her husband and protected her son. The light was switched off. The phone matter came to a full stop that day. This was an old story. It was over and done with. But this voice that spoke today as though it was advising him anonymously – whose voice was it? Vatti Hussain was worried that Ummusalma was no longer fit and healthy enough to bring this new episode to a swift conclusion.

From the beginning, Hussain was always bewildered by the anonymous voice. As he kept brooding about it, even the few straggly hairs left on his head fell off. It was clear to him now that it was not the voice of his conscience. In a way, this brought him relief. Then he recalled several voices with which he was familiar and imagined them talking to him.

Over the telephone, the feeble voices that pleaded with him for a reprieve in the deadline for payment of interest, the ingratiating voices that asked for donations, the voice of the head priest who pestered him constantly to buy lights and a fan for the mosque, voices of employees who asked for credit during salary payment, the voice of Salim who complained, 'Why are you involving me in a profession I detest, father?', the voice of Ummusalma who rebuked him whenever he said anything tactless ... voices, voices, voices. A thousand and eight voices, of different types – garbled, clear, raspy, tender ... oh, my ... so many voices ... but none of them matched that anonymous voice.

There was nothing wrong in feeling frustrated that on this Bakrid day of all days Ummusalma had fallen ill and taken to bed, unable to cook and serve the camel meat that had arrived at their doorstep. This was a practical matter; so, why fret so much over it? What kind of voice was it? What did it speak about? Did he understand any of it? Hussain understood one thing very clearly. The voice importuned him to marry again while Ummusalma was still alive, and it did so in a mocking tone. It reminded him that legally there was scope for keeping four wives. It argued that age was no bar, pointing to the Jainulabuddin affair. It spoke about municipality elections ... he understood everything. But what it mentioned next was beyond his grasp. It used new words, words that he had never heard of, like 'roots' and 'ancestors'. Would Ummusalma be familiar with the meaning of these words, perhaps? She is more educated than me, thought Vatti Hussain.

When Ummusalma was studying in the eighth standard in Keeranur High School, both families had negotiated and fixed her marriage with Hussain. 'You are asking us to conduct the nikah even before she can write her final exams,' her father complained. In response, Hussain's father said, 'Exams! What about exams? Is she going to study and become a district collector?' He conducted the marriage with pomp and show. Being tall and well built, thirteen-year-old Ummusalma looked like a twenty-year-old woman at the time.

If he were to confuse the past with the present, even the strongest man would feel dejected. Diabetes and hypertension were Hussain's chief ailments. Using this voice, some invisible, clandestine forces were toying with Hussain. Sweaty and tired, Hussain sat immobile on the floor for a long time. Once he collected himself, he was unable to rise to his feet and walk; so, with his knees on the floor, he moved to the next room and saw the bedridden Ummusalma. Had anyone witnessed that scene, they would have taunted him: 'Did you look at where Hussain with his millions finally ended up? He couldn't even move his limbs.' Hussain was consoled that all this had happened within four walls, without anyone knowing about it.

Ummu was in deep slumber because of all the medicines she had taken. Her face was impassive like a rock, without betraying the slightest flicker. She has become a chronically ill patient so early in life, Hussain thought. Even so, he crawled up to her and asked her openly, like a child, 'Ummu, what is the meaning of "roots" and "ancestors"?' He asked her again and again. But what's the point of finding out the meaning of such words, he thought; instead, if he could learn a couple of fresh expletives, it would be a pleasure to use them on the slaves who did his bidding. With that, he forgot all about that anonymous voice and those two words whose meaning he could not discover.

The camel arrived in Hussain's house two days before Bakrid. It was a camel of good pedigree from Rajasthan. They said it had been brought from Bengaluru. The camel was tethered at the entrance of Hussain's mansion, amid a thick stand of trees. The townspeople were amused by the camel's hump, long legs and tall appearance. It chewed on the foliage of trees that were more than twelve feet high. Hussain's house was surrounded by the faces of the townsfolk. Most of them would have seen a camel only in movies. Since the camel was stationed there, Hussain's house became something like a zoo for both children and adults. This, too, was a source of pride for Vatti Hussain.

Bakrid arrived. The morning hours were particularly busy. In the houses of wealthy men, goats were slaughtered and laid on the streets. The stink of blood was everywhere. Vultures wheeled overhead, spying on the proceedings. It was prescribed in the Holy Book that blood must gush forth. It was also indicated in the same Holy Book that the meat of the animals they sacrificed never reached God.

Even though many goats and cattle were being slaughtered, people were fed up with watching those scenes repeatedly. Even when it was not Bakrid, animals were slaughtered daily in the butchers' shops, weren't they? Could anything give as much pleasure as watching 'live' a huge animal like a camel being sacrificed? People from Skanda TV, a local TV channel in Palani, laid siege to Hussain's house along with their camera. A news flash that this event was going to be broadcast live as a special programme with the title, 'How to slaughter a camel' was being scrolled on the TV screen in every house.

Hussain arrived at the entrance bright and early that morning and sat on the sofa that was exclusively for his use. A surge of pride was often evident in his body language. The men from the abattoir had arrived with their knives and other implements. They offered water to the thirsty camel. Patiently, it had its fill of an enormous quantity of water. After a lot of effort, the men from the abattoir managed to tie the camel's feet together. They realized that the effort had nearly taken the life out of them. However, thinking of the money they stood to earn, they calmed down. 'Give us a tall stool,' the lead butcher told Hussain.

The fun began. 'Why do you need a stool, da?' Hussain asked.

'To hack the neck, Muthalali,' the servant answered.

'To slit my neck, is it?' Hussain snapped in irritation from his seat.

'No, 'nga. To hack the camel's neck, sir…'

Hussain stood up and lunged forward with his arm raised as if to strike the lead butcher. He was taken aback. 'Wretched fellow. Idiot. Why would anyone hack a camel when it's standing? You must make it lie down, da,' Hussain hit the roof.

'Oh, no. We didn't know that, Muthalali,' the butcher said.

'How would you know a graveyard if you've never died? Dei, dei, didn't I ask you right in the beginning whether you knew how to slaughter a camel? You nodded your head like the bull from a Perumal temple, and now you stand there blinking. Otherwise, I would have brought some men from Dindigul instead, wouldn't I?'

Hussain's angry tirade had goaded the lead butcher. 'Dei, Majidu … Ilyasu … you hold the front legs, da. Khader, hold the hind legs,' he ordered.

'And what are you going to do?' Hussain had only the lead butcher in his sights.

'I will do the hacking, Muthalali…' he replied politely.

'You've come here only to slit my throat, da,' Hussain said and struck himself on the head in exasperation.

A large crowd had gathered in the front yard of Vatti Hussain's house, which resembled the venue of a public meeting. Shrieks and wails, a melange of voices. The place was in an uproar, with a giant wheel, carousel, ice cart, balloon vendor and snacks cart in operation. No matter which amusement they were engaged in, everyone had their eye on the camel. The people from Skanda TV had switched on their camera. Every now and then, the camera panned and zoomed in on Vatti Hussain's face. Wise to their move, Hussain sported a faint smile on his otherwise grumpy face.

Completely at a loss, the butchers lay prone at the camel's feet. Seeing them, Hussain's blood pressure shot up. 'Why are you prostrating yourself before the animal, as though you are pleading for forgiveness? Get up, da. Stand the camel next to the wall and pull its legs off the ground. It looks like you will turn even me into a butcher,' Hussain cursed himself. Some people felt pity for him. 'Serves him right,' some of his detractors thought, and felt happy. Following Hussain's instructions, the butchers led the camel close to the wall. It didn't strain and struggle like goats and cattle normally did. Like an innocent, it moved pliantly in whichever direction they pulled it. After leaning it against the wall, the butchers tried to pull the camel's legs off the ground. 'In our greed for the money, we got ourselves trapped in this awful situation.' Regret was writ large on the butchers' faces.

Hussain observed the large crowd outside. He pointed in one direction and shouted, 'Dei … those two young fellows over there … step inside, da.' As if they were only waiting for this call, four youths rushed in immediately. Addressing the men who stood before him with folded arms like servants, Hussain said, 'Here, take this money. Go and help them, da.'

'Yes, boss.' Their reply was redolent of the fragrance of Arunthathiyar Street.

As they approached the camel, the butchers winced. 'Muthalali, these are scavenger-boys,' the lead butcher expressed his displeasure in public.

'That's why I called them to help you, da.' Hussain was candid about the situation.

The butchers did not agree. It showed on their faces. The hold-up was a disappointment to the crowd; since the sun too was scorching hot, they squirmed in discomfort.

By now, the butchers had moved away from the camel and gathered separately to talk among themselves. Vatti Hussain found it insulting. 'How arrogant are these dogs who work for a daily wage.' He was seething with anger. 'What military secrets are you discussing, you morons?' he yelled at them. One of the butchers came towards Hussain.

'Muthalali, our leader is feeling bad that there seems to be no difference between those who slaughter pigs and us, who slaughter goats.'

'I called them only to assist you, da.'

'Even if it's only assistance, their hands will touch the object of holy sacrifice, no?'

For Vatti Hussain, this felt like a slap on the face. If the butchers walked away in a huff, the sacrifice ritual would come to a halt. At this stage, to find men locally or get them from Palani or Dindigul would require enormous effort. Naturally, his voice was subdued now. 'Look, this camel has come to our town by a truck all the way from Bengaluru. Who knows how many hands had touched it while loading and unloading. Is it practical to worry about such things?'

'All that happened before the day of the sacrifice. Once an animal is positioned for sacrifice, only the faithful can lay hands on it, master; infidels are forbidden to touch it.' Though he was one of the butchers, his words sounded firm and strict.

There was no history of Vatti Hussain ever submitting to the whims of daily-wage labourers. In the interests of getting the job done, he tried to be somewhat amenable. Once the butchers stood firm, Hussain's ego was aroused. 'So, what is it that you want now?' There was a slight tremor in his commanding voice. The sidekick who had come and spoken to him went away. Now the lead butcher stood before him. The earlier humility had disappeared, which was evident from his body language. 'There are so many men standing around here. If you wanted to call a few people for assistance, you could have summoned some fine peasants. But for some reason, as though you had decided it in advance, you call a few chakkiliyans.' Vatti Hussain could not give a reply to the lead butcher. He stayed quiet. 'I am leaving, master. The other men will stay back and complete the job...' the lead butcher said and walked away. Hussain stared vacantly at his receding figure.

No one knew what mysterious chemistry came to their aid, but once the lead butcher had left, the butchers and the Arunthathiyars got together and pulled the camel's legs, pushing it down. As if a whole mountain was sliding down, the camel fell on the ground. With that, the Arunthathiyars withdrew from the scene, which is to say, the butchers had given them leave.

Shoving a hand in an inside pocket, Hussain fished out three or four hundred-rupee notes and thrust them into the hands of the young men. 'We'll take your leave, master,' they said and set off at once. 'Appada, the problem is over,' Hussain breathed a sigh of relief. Just then, the three butchers screamed in unison, 'Master, the camel is weeping!'

'What do you mean ... the camel is weeping?' Hussain rushed to the camel and looked. It was true. Tears were pouring out of its eyes. The sight was indeed moving in some way. But Vatti Hussain in his sixty years of life on earth must have seen so many in tears, must have been the cause of tears for so many ... So, how could this dodgy move of a dumb creature like this camel succeed with him? 'Hmm ... hmm ... get on with the job. Don't delay it because it is weeping,' Hussain ordered.

The knives were sharpened noisily on stones and leather straps. People roared in anticipation. The cameramen kept zooming in, by turns, on the camel and Hussain. 'Dei, slit its throat after saying Bismillah. That's the halal way. That's why I called you people,' Hussain shouted. As instructed by Hussain, one of the butchers chanted 'Bismillah, Hir Rehmanir Rahim' and brought the knife near the camel's neck. At that moment, they heard a peculiar voice. 'Stop. Don't kill me…' the camel began to speak. Stunned upon hearing this plea, the butchers drew back.

Vatti Hussain was astonished. He, too, had listened to the camel's words with close attention. Now the butchers and Hussain exchanged glances. The roaring crowd fell silent. Everyone was amazed. But to Hussain alone, it sounded like a voice he had heard somewhere. The butcher with a knife in his hand said, 'Master, the camel is speaking.' Still, he brought the knife again near the vein in the camel's neck. 'Don't hurt me. Please let me go. Don't kill me,' the camel spoke again. Seeing and hearing the camel move its lips distinctly, the butchers were taken aback. It was the anonymous voice that Hussain had heard earlier. There was no doubt about it. The same enunciation. The same accent. The butchers dropped their knives and stood up. Their faces were frozen in shock and disbelief.

'We'll make a move, master,' they said, and started walking out one by one. Hussain remained calm for some time. Then, suddenly, he got up with a loud cry. 'Dei, dei, all this is Shaitan's work, da. It's Shaitan's mischief to prevent us from offering sacrifice, isn't it? Tell me, da.' His clamour travelled in all four directions. The butchers were walking away, totally unperturbed. Hussain addressed them in dismay. 'I'll pay twice the money we had agreed on, da. Slaughter the camel and offer sacrifice, da.' Hussain knew that the weapon of last resort was always money and that it had no substitute. Hussain's mantra of 'double payment' made short work of the butchers' resolve. They stopped in their tracks. Then they looked back. They walked again to the spot where the sacrifice was to be made.

One of the butchers, baring all his teeth in an ingratiating smile, asked Hussain for confirmation. 'How much will you pay, master?' Hussain replied with gusto, 'Whatever we had agreed on, I'll pay double that amount, da.' The knives that lay on the ground returned to the butchers' hands. Even when its throat was being slit, the camel kept saying all kinds of things: 'Muhammad, the son of Abdullah who was born in the Qureishiya clan, came to this earth as the messenger of God…' The blood gushed out. Instantly, the eyes turned red.

Vatti Hussain's face was glowing. Even after it was skinned and the offal removed, the camel's lips kept speaking with clear enunciation about all kinds of things. The people who stood around the camel watched in amazement.

Though Vatti Hussain had sat down to eat and was mixing the rice with his fingers, he did not have the courage to touch, leave alone eat, the camel meat on his plate. If even the cooked meat was still writhing and talking, who would have the heart to eat it?

THE BREAKING OF A STORY

Sundara Ramaswamy

TRANSLATED BY JANANI KANNAN

The phenomenon occurred at Sage Junction at four in the afternoon. At 3.58 p.m., to be precise. In a flash rose a colossal pedestal splitting the earth wide open. Revealed atop the pedestal was a real, live damsel. A tantalizing beauty.

The first to sight the beauty, an elderly man – seemingly well-educated – narrated to a bunch of buzzing reporters, who began to collect around him, the dread that had seized him when he first witnessed the mysterious creature, his uncontrollably slurred scream as he had darted away, and how, while doing so, he had involuntarily checked his watch. Though blurry-eyed from the shock of noticing the figure, he simply could not stop gawking at her. Was what he'd witnessed real, or a figment of his imagination, he asked himself repeatedly. The quivering of his voice, as if on the verge of tears, was pitiable. With his left index finger stiffened from pointing at the figure frequently, he remained with his melancholic gaze shuttling between the reporters' faces. His right hand was pressed firmly against his pounding chest.

The crowd multiplied by the second. The news spread through the metro, like the winds fueling an inferno. Everyone began to run frenetically towards Sage Junction. The hurtling vehicles sparked a vivid imagery of accidents captured in photographs. Reporters and photographers on motorcycles and in cars arrived in droves like the high tides. Just how they had sniffed out the news so quickly was a mystery.

'Sir, please stop staring at the lady and answer our questions,' the reporters implored the old man. While thrilled to have identified the first person to witness the sensational beauty, a concern that he may get distracted and draw himself away from their inquiries seized their minds.

Stiff as a bamboo shoot, showing not a trace of fatigue, the old man derived a mild high from talking more and more about the mystical figure; unbeknownst to him, the golden leaves of imagination and the fragrance of embellishments seeped into his descriptions. He swelled with pride upon realizing the richness in his narration. A stammerer, the old man began to speak with excessive shyness, a habit so long established that it had become one with his breath. For someone whose struggle with speech stirred discomfort in listeners within just a few seconds of him speaking, he found himself in a tempo of brisk delivery. Jubilant, he began to speak with resolute confidence.

What's this? Why are these reporters and photographers herding this way? Why are those who have come to sight the mysterious figure to their hearts' fill and to take scores of photos of her surrounding me instead? Do they really need someone to describe what they are seeing? Are they going to print my photo and cover what I say in all the newspapers tomorrow?

The old man could hardly believe what was happening around him.

With the characteristic craftiness known of their profession, the reporters stroked the old man's imagination, barely a bud, into a wholly blossoming flower with their nuanced questions. For wasn't it a win for them if, through his accounts, they could shape much of the story as they wanted to create? For the second or the third time, the young man with glasses from that popular daily – unclear why his fellow reporters called him 'Eagle' – inquired in English, 'Sir, when you first witnessed it, was the lady's bosom unconcealed?' All of a sudden, the elderly gentleman remembered his old talent of speaking in English, of holding his listeners enthralled by it. He cleared his throat and responded, in English, 'I doubt that the damsel's ample breasts have ever been concealed even by a bare thread.' The reporters' joy knew no bounds upon this response. The man's response in English further served as veritable proof of his credibility.

What transpired was this: that their city, a large one, being the capital city at that, projected a modern identity of its people the world over – everyone agreed. Not a denizen needed reminding of where the statue of the venerated individual who laid the foundation for their very existence, commandeering in its presence, was sited. Even less be told about how people referred to this location where he – an icon of their civilization and the overseer of their actions – sat prominently. After all, is not the image of his grand posture, seated facing north, deeply imprinted in their minds? That was where the phenomenon had occurred; directly behind him, to the south, at 4 p.m. Rather, at 3.58 p.m. sharp.

The ravishing beauty appeared to be a princess descended from a European royal lineage. The old man expounded to the reporters, 'I have seen beauties akin to this queen of beauties only in the bulky art books in libraries.

'Her neck is long and tight-fleshed, her shoulders broad and full as a man's. Those eyes exude a languorous pleasure, binding one in a spell. The way her eyelids lower over her pupils, like the flutter of a bird's wings, simply arrests the heart. The tips of her teeth catch the light of the evening sun and scatters its golden gleam.

'Everyone believes that she is fully naked. Inside that ornate pedestal with a vast circumference, she stands hidden from the waist down. Evidently, her modesty affords her only that much freedom.

'Her breasts, God almighty! Creation, seeing itself at its zenith, laughs exuberantly in triumph. Their eminence. Their ampleness. It is her rose-hued skin alone that, gliding down from her neck, holds them taut. The nipples, bright purple, like globe amaranth flowers, point upwards, fervently longing for the touch of fingertips.'

The crowd that germinated at Sage Junction within mere seconds of the idol arising was growing by the second. With no more space left for it to grow dense widthwise, the crowd only grew longer and rapidly so. When the people collecting at the back of the crowd were unable to lay their sights on the beautiful form, they jostled their way forward. Does letting another advance not imply one's own retreat? Small waves of movement arose out of the din that ensued. When sewer covers began to yield from the weight of the crowd, feet began to take over the steps of storefronts. And as the steps became fully covered with feet, plinths began filling with bobbing heads.

The police force began descending at Sage Junction. Black vans with metal mesh arrived in a line. The vehicles pulled over at the very back, behind the tail end of the crowd. As they arrived, the police presumed they were being judicious in parking there. Within a short span of time, the crowd thickened well beyond them, engulfing them entirely, seemingly rendering them insignificant. So completely were they consumed by the crowd that, even if an emergency were to occur, they would have been unable to move. Even opening their doors was impossible. Yet, the policemen, though trapped in their vans, relayed continuous, if slightly overwhelmed, updates to their stations and their superiors through the radio equipment. The few that escaped being trapped in their vehicles got crushed and humiliated as they ploughed their way through the crowd asking the store owners one by one to fold up their stores immediately. They warned them that they would not be able to protect them if the crowd went rogue and pillaged the stores.

It seemed that the entire metro was emptying into the crowd. Students, pickpockets, teachers, film industry folks, cheats, politicians, thugs, godmen, merchants, turncoats, writers, prostitutes, painters, industrialists, those working in all forms of media … was there any kind missing? Government employees were the ones who, even after work hours ended, still had a lot of work to tend to. They, too, put off their burden for the next day, tying their mountain-high piles tight with red tapes, and began to rush out. Empty streets drowned in darkness. There was no need to open ticket counters at the cinema theatres.

For a growing number of onlookers, the longer they gawked, the more they were convinced that this was a mere illusion. They suspected that what had occurred was a natural chemical reaction, which after combining a formless spirit, sound, cloud, fragrances, breeze and water, had solidified into that magical form. When the suspicion turned into a mental itch that could no longer be contained within, it began spilling out in small whispers. As words began percolating through the crowd, those who did not agree with them responded loudly. Can a lifeless form blink, they retorted. Indeed, a fair question. The beautiful form, even if only sporadically, did blink its eyes. Not just that, a keener look would also spot the faint smile blossoming on the figure. Countering arguments erupted, followed by angry outbursts rippling through the crowd. Like a threat made in broad daylight, news began to spread that those ripples could turn into squabbles any minute.

However, no one could explain that constant expression of astonishment that lingered on the enchantress's face. Among the crowd that had gathered was also a world-renowned psychologist. Commencing with the disclaimer that what he deduced was solely his presumptions, he went on to provide an explanation to the students surrounding him: 'This beauty may have never seen a sea of people like this in her life. She may find it perplexing that every pair of eyes in this mass is unblinkingly staring at her bare breasts. Why every face is brimming with thoughts of pleasure could be a question of great import rising in her mind, one possibly growing into a weighty concern. With all this on her mind, she may be mistakenly concluding that all these people are seeing breasts for the first time in their lives. No one can pinpoint the exact thoughts running through that lass's head.' And with that, the professor concluded his speech.

Excitement was aplenty at the offices of the newspapers, magazines and other periodicals. With each passing second, panic was on the rise. Phones were continuously engaged. With the phones causing them trouble by not providing the connectivity they needed, impatient employees found a reason to violently slam the handsets. What could the poor telephones do now that every phone number in that large city demanded to be connected all at once? Time, too, embraces the flight of the sun. Within a mere half hour, or forty minutes at most, the stories must reach the editors' desks. The editors had to read them all and either approve or redline them. If the editors deemed any story inadequate in juiciness, it may have to be rewritten entirely.

Never had a day like this dawned for the editors. Their minds raced. A historically unprecedented phenomenon has chosen our city to bestow the honour of manifesting at. Our people are so privileged to witness this with their own eyes. Blessed are we that this news will get published in newspapers globally. In leveraging this fortune maximally lies an editor's skill and creativity. Opportunity is at the doorstep.

There isn't much to breasts themselves. But the form and the bareness of those! It is their unique positioning that is making everyone hot-blooded. That is the motif for the story, all the reporters concurred unanimously. However, there were differences of opinion on the perspective that whenever nakedness featured in a story, imagery assumed prominence over words. As important as photos are in luring interest to a story, it is only words that have the ability captivate the reader, a few reporters contended passionately at a bar that they frequented. To their question on why pornographic books rife with gaps to be filled by the imagination sold better than those with images of uncensored nudity, featuring every imaginable sexual posture, no one had an answer.

The editors were all too familiar with these theories in publishing. Why else would they show such frenzied urgency in setting their eyes on the photographs of that day? Burdened by the sheer volume of work, they remained tied to their desks. Did they too not pine with the desire to savour the luscious beauty of the maiden, the reporters shared a titter amongst themselves.

When news that a huge riot had broken out at that location and that bullets may be fired any minute to pacify the crowd reached them, the reporters from all the newspapers took to their motorcycles and scurried back to the spot where the phenomenon had been sighted.

In the minds of onlookers, who had been continually gazing at the magical figure, a deep affection started developing subconsciously, drop by drop. Our sister may be holding a different point of view than ours on the subject of wearing clothes. But of all the places in the world, this queen has come seeking us. Shouldn't we respect that? What else can that smile that has made her face its abode from the instant she emerged from the earth mean other than to say, I love you? Many an onlooker, importantly youngsters, shared a few thoughts that were in line with their mores and asked her a few questions. It should hardly be surprising that there were a few in this massive crowd who were well-versed in any language she spoke, if she spoke one. However, wasn't the crowd justified in regarding the damsel's lack of response to any of their questions, her face bereft of any emotion, as a slight to their affection? Impatient, the crowd began asking questions utterly lacking in sensitivity. Using words that could hardly be repeated, much less printed, they tossed obscenities at her to mock her, hurting her tender heart, delicate as a sapling. That a photo contest was announced amongst those skilled at spinning obscene language to create even lewder obscenities, could only be construed as unfortunate.

When an assistant editor in Eagle's office asked a reporter for the kind of questions that the crowd had raised, he handed a stack of sheets to him. The assistant editor recognized that although the questions were meant to be emphatic, they would cause the paper they got printed on to rot, and in turn, took the stack to the editor. These are dangerous. They must be used tactfully, the editor thought. It suddenly occurred to him that the photos had still not made their way to his desk. He demanded them.

Eagle told the assistant editor about an itch nagging his mind. He had an unquiet suspicion that the police might have intervened. 'Why?' asked the assistant editor. 'The story from Sage Junction hasn't featured in the night bulletin on TV yet,' Eagle said, his face tightening. 'Could you not make some inquiries?' the assistant editor asked, his intonation betraying allegation. 'I am saying this only because I received the news, sir,' Eagle replied. 'They haven't broadcast it yet? Why, what is the reason?' the assistant editor asked loudly, more to himself, as he walked to the editor's room to update him.

Eagle made his way to the room where photographs were developed. All along his way, he greeted colleagues with the usual courtesies. The entire office was abuzz on why the Sage Junction incident had still not been broadcast on television. When they pointed out that throngs were gathered waiting in front of stores that sell televisions, Eagle said impatiently, 'Why? Didn't they all witness everything in person?' 'Yes, sir, but you get to see many angles at the same time on TV, don't you?' one of his colleagues replied. 'Don't ever underestimate people as fools, sir,' he advised. A reporter who shared a closer bond with Eagle whispered into his ear, 'Sir, the TV people deliberately started the rumour about police involvement. I do not believe it.' He continued, 'Do you know, sir, our photographers too have gone back to the junction.' To the question on Eagle's face, the friend replied, 'They say it is a technical problem. I'm not sure what it is about.'

A meeting of the editorial team was underway inside the editor's office. They decided, after much deliberation, that they would print the story on the front page, replete with photographs, in a big way, regardless of any constraints from the police. The emergency meeting had lent them an opportunity to recall and refresh their memories of the principles newspaper chief editors should adhere to. How could they surrender their basic rights as newspapers? Isn't providing news promptly without hiding anything a social responsibility of the newspapers?

When Eagle reached the room where photographs were developed, there was no one around. The lab doors had been left ajar. Everyone had rushed out in the office car. Eagle raced back to the editor and informed him. The editor quietly looked out through his glass window and asked, 'Will they be able to reach Sage Junction in this pouring rain?' Eagle did not say anything.

Only after Eagle came out of the room and looked at the street did he realize the fierceness of the rain. If it persisted for four or five hours, they would have to resort to boats to traverse even the main roads. Eagle didn't know what to do. His mind was restless. He headed upstairs, to the fifth floor, and peered out at the street through a window. All pedestrian traffic on the street had come to a complete stop. His team could have got stuck, unable to drive in the rain. The cars that were pulled over were standing in a line, soaking and shrivelling in the rain. Eagle tried to reach one of his staff-photographer friends through his mobile phone. His call did not go through. He tried calling his friends who worked in other media. None of his calls went through. Suddenly, darkness seized the window. The power went out. Eagle sat down heavily on a step. He felt the need to collect himself.

After a while, his mobile phone chimed. The photographer told him that he could see many of the other big metro-news magazine photographers on their way. 'Why?' Eagle asked. 'We are beginning to believe that they too encountered the same technical issues that we did, sir,' came the response. 'What is our issue?' Eagle wanted to know. 'Please let us not get into that now, sir. The problem is going to be resolved in a minute, we are very close to Sage Junction,' assured the response. 'In that case…' Eagle tried to continue, but the call dropped. A suspicion crept into his mind as he wondered if the call hadn't dropped but was disconnected.

Eagle descended the stairs letting his hand slide over the handrail and his feet drag over the treads. As he neared the first floor, he could hear the editor yelling. He had the propensity to yell without ever knowing when to stop, even when he was beyond the point of exhaustion. Just then, a call came through on Eagle's mobile phone. The voice was trembling. 'Sir, sir!' the voice shouted. 'Yes, tell me!' Eagle urged. 'The figure at Sage Junction has disappeared! There is nothing left here,' the photographer relayed hysterically. 'Disappeared? When, how?' Eagle shouted. 'Sir, no one is here. Only a deranged man is sitting here in this rain, sobbing.' The connection drew in a lot of static before finally dropping off.

Fortunately, the generator started working. Eagle went back to the photography room. As he entered, he looked all around. On a long table lay strewn a whole bunch of photos. He picked up a photo. It was clear. But in that photo, the maiden's breasts were missing. He scuffled through all the photos, checking them one by one. In none of the photos did the lady have breasts. Utterly distraught, Eagle hurried towards the editor's room.

THE FLIGHT

Vannanilavan

TRANSLATED BY JANANI KANNAN

'VE! WHAT ARE you doing there, scratching your head instead of doing your work?' The mean taskmaster Ebenezer's harsh tone jolted Devapichai and he snapped back to reality, like a person aroused from slumber. It was only then that he noticed the customer standing across from him, waiting to purchase some fabric. 'Sir, what do you want? Four cubit or eight...?' he asked mechanically.

Sesuvadiyaan, who manned the towels section next to him, murmured to him in a low voice, 'I tried to warn you a couple of times that the manager was staring right at you ... but you paid no heed.'

'... I was preoccupied with some thoughts ... Ayya, what did you ask for? ... Eight cubits of Gundanj veshti? What price range did you want that in...'

Ebenezer stood at the second counter and continued to watch Devapichai with a scowl on his face. Even though the air conditioner was running, Devapichai felt like he was oozing sweat. Right when he was in the middle of displaying the veshti the customer wanted to see, Ebenezer walked over to him and began to reproach him straightaway. 'Ve ... do your work properly and pay attention to the customers.

Or else, I will inform the owner and have you sent to the godown to tack stickers. There is no AC there … or anything else … You will die there, in that sweltering heat. Do you want to go to the godown?' he demanded brusquely, oblivious to the customer's presence. The customer gaped back and forth between the two of them. 'No, Ayya … I will do my work,' mumbled Devapichai, cowering down.

Ayya! Why does he have to address Ebenezer who was barely as old as his son as 'ayya'? Devapichai wanted to grab the measuring stick and whack him on his head with it. The air conditioner continued to run with a soft whirring sound. A large family stood gathered together in the children's readymade garments section on the northern end. A girl in that group looked exactly like his youngest daughter Annabhagya Mary.

Six years had flown by since he started working at the three-storeyed Santhosh Textiles. The only reason he had started working there was to repay a small debt he had accrued from the wedding expenses of Annabhagya and Gnanam, his two daughters. Even though Gnanam's husband had said to him, 'Mama, you don't need to go to work. This is hardly an amount to worry about. I will take care of it,' Devapichai's conscience couldn't allow that. Whatever said and done, he was his eldest son-in-law. How could he have him repay his debt?

The ground floor at Santhosh Textiles was entirely dedicated to saris. The next two floors had clothing for men. The topmost floor was for bedsheets, carpets, rugs and curtains. On the terrace was a shed erected for the forty employees to reside in. Each one of them lived, bathed, ate and slept there. The owner Chelladurai never hired anyone locally – he cherry-picked people from villages that were at least forty or fifty miles away to work for him. Every employee allegedly got a different day off from work every week. But none had anyone to visit nor anything to do in that town. Neither could they go home for just that one day. Consequently, all they could do, and did, was to spread their mats and lie around under that rusty, old canopy. Sometimes, when they were summoned to help out in the godown, even that one day of respite was lost. Working here was no different from being in a prison. To that end, the owner had 'supervisors', or three taskmasters, just like Ebenezer, to keep pushing the employees around constantly and to snitch about everyone's activities to the owner. Nothing the employees did, including eat, ever escaped their watch.

If an employee was Christian, he would get five days of leave from work for Christmas. For Muslims, it was during Ramadan, and for Hindus, the five days were around Deepavali. That was the only time they could make a trip home. Once, a man named Shanmugam from Nanguneri went home for Deepavali and did not come back at all. To make things worse, he had taken an advance of three thousand rupees on his salary. Two of the owner's men were sent over to find him and bring him back.

The labour officer never set foot into the building.

A week had passed since Devapichai had decided that he could not be in this jail any longer. But he still didn't know how to make the flight. The owner's men were posted everywhere. Even a visit to the church or temple was accompanied by one of the taskmasters the whole time. He just had to escape from here. Even if they tried to bring him back after that, his two sons-in-law together would protect Devapichai from them. Finding a way out occupied all of Devapichai at all times, including when that slave-driver Ebenezer had pounced on him and torn him apart.

They sent his salary – if he could call that pittance so! – directly to the family. After they deducted money for everything, including food, seven hundred rupees was all that was sent to his wife Rosappoo. Separately, though, every month he received an allowance of twenty-five rupees to spend on toiletries. He had managed to scrape together about four hundred rupees from that. Enough to get him home.

The only time the taskmasters were not with them was during lunch. Typically, four persons were allowed at a time to eat lunch. If he could somehow get to the third floor at that time, he thought, he could exit through the stairs at the back of the store which opened directly to the adjacent street. Those stairs only served to move large bales of clothing whenever they were delivered. Occasionally, the door to those stairs was inadvertently left unlocked.

That afternoon, Devapichai deliberately ate his lunch rather unhurriedly. Thangapandi and Manikandan said, 'Annachi, you take your time to eat, we will leave now,' and left him there by himself. Thavasimuthu, the server, had also gone into the kitchen to retrieve something. This is the moment, Devapichai decided, rinsed his hands quickly and set out. He snuck over to the third floor and checked the stair door. To his surprise, the door had been left open. He immediately slipped through the door and rushed down the stairs as fast as he could, walking and running at the same time. He reached all the way to the door that opened on to the adjacent street, only to find Sannaasi, the taskmaster from the sari section, standing there, smoking. 'Annachi ... what brings you here?' he asked Devapichai when he saw him. Devapichai squirmed slightly as he drew out his response: 'Nothing really ... the phlegm congestion is bothering me ... want to buy some medicine...'

'Why do you need to go out just for this? That manager, he has all the medicines you need...' the taskmaster said.

'Oh yes ... I completely forgot about that,' Devapichai replied, and retraced his steps back into the shop.

CHEENALATCHUMI'S QUEUE

Latha

TRANSLATED BY JANANI KANNAN

'WILL YOU BE going to the temple?' Dhanam asked Cheenalatchumi as she arrived. On any other day, she would have responded to her. But in addition to being in a celebratory mood from being able to vote for the first time in a general election, Cheenalatchumi's focus was entirely on the queue. She looked around frequently, turning her head this way and that. People standing ahead of her had moved forward. She strode to keep pace; she did not like that the queue was moving so fast.

Turning around, she noticed Kamala, her neighbour from upstairs, walk away slowly, from standing behind her to the end of the line, her eyes on the mobile phone the entire time. Cheenalatchumi had a few things to discuss with Kamala. 'Must be an important call, she must not have seen me,' she thought to herself. She stood on her toes, craned her head and scanned the people in front of her.

Everyone in the queue lived in nearby blocks. Cheenalatchumi had known many of them for a long time. Everyone was looking downwards, buried in their mobile phones. She coughed a little as if to clear her throat. A few people looked up, gave her a smile, and plunged right back into their phones.

CHEENALATCHUMI'S QUEUE

Every day, Cheenalatchumi scoured the Tamil, English and Malay newspapers to find out where and what she could stand in a queue for. If she had extra money at her disposal, she bought the dailies from the Seven-Eleven store located across the building. If she did not have enough money, she read the newspapers at the community centre nearby. Her next-door neighbour informed her promptly of any news on long queues in the Chinese newspapers.

Her mornings always dawned with excitement. Ever since she heard the news on the radio that voting was going to take place across all the constituencies this year, Cheenalatchumi had been keenly researching about voting queues. She had stayed up entire nights wondering what the queues for the elections would be like and who she might run into.

Did Kamala get off the phone, she wondered turning and tilting her neck to check. She was still on her phone. When she turned, the Chinese man standing behind her gave her a friendly smile. She said to him, 'This is my 611th time standing in a queue this year.'

'Really? It's only the beginning of September. You have already stood in so many?'

'Standing in a queue is like meditating.'

'Is this some new discovery?'

'Indeed. It is my discovery,' she said. The Chinese man smiled awkwardly.

It must have been about ten years ago now. Both her sons were away on National Service. Her daughter used to spend all her time immersed in her studies at the university. Her husband was always at the coffee, or 'kopi', shop with his friends. Cheenalatchumi, who went to the temple every day not knowing what else to do at home, stood in a queue for over two hours to eat at the temple one Purattaasi Saturday.

That day, she fell in love with standing in queues. Since then, she was always found bustling about, driven by a heightened sense of urgency. She woke up early every day to get through her chores quickly.

'Where are you off to in such a hurry?' Kannusamy, her husband, asked her one day. From that day onwards, if Kannusamy was at home when she was about to head out, she would share her plans for the day with him. 'Don't forget that I don't have an income,' he'd say.

Cheenalatchumi pulled out a small blue-coloured 555-brand notebook from her handbag. She used it to keep track of how many queues she had stood in – whether it was to buy the 4D lottery ticket, watch a football game, purchase a movie ticket, withdraw money from the bank or anything else – and for how long. She jotted down standing in a queue that morning to sate her hunger at the vegetarian Chinese restaurant next to her building complex and added a note next to it: *He was his usual low-minded self.*

It was more for the long queues than for the plateful of mee, which cost just a dollar and a half, that she went only to his shop every day. Since she could chat with the other people standing in the line, it didn't matter to her that the shopkeeper never spoke to her. That day, she was angered because he spoke to the person in front of her in English but asked her what she wanted in Hokkien. Because she had lived close to a Chinese settlement in her childhood, she could speak both Hokkien and Cantonese fluently. But if anyone who knew English or Malay spoke to her in Chinese, it made her angry. Writing that note full of rebuke quelled her anger; then she added '*425th food line*' with a star next to it.

Cheenalatchumi could stand in queues for any length of time for food. She would wait for hours on end at Japanese and Korean food places. She also stood in queues for hours in temples. On Fridays during the month of Aadi at the Vadapathira Kaliamman Temple, Saturdays at the Perumal Temple in the month of Purattaasi, or the temple on Tank Road during the Tamil month of Karthikai – she had a roster just for this. She also went to the Abdul Gafoor Mosque to receive the porridge served during fast. For Cheenalatchumi, all gods were the same. Any tasty food was worthy of the divine. To stand in queues with family and friends for long hours, sharing a laugh or a story, and eating that food was akin to worship.

But, to take a token and sit for several hours at a hospital caused her extreme anxiety. Nor did she like to wait for anyone anywhere – she felt paralysed if she had to wait in one spot. She would irritate that person who kept her waiting by calling them incessantly.

Standing in a queue in motion was the only meaningful form of waiting for Cheenalatchumi. She preferred winding queues over straight ones. It was her discovery that a queue that meandered did not hurt one's feet; nor did one feel the passage of time while in it.

She envisioned each queue as appearing like a dark line from the sky above, where every individual was equal. Whenever it occurred to her how every dot in the line had a meaning, she felt pride in being part of one.

She checked her watch and made a note of the time of her arrival at the voting queue in her little book. She looked back and forth again to check who all were in the line. That was when she noticed Gunavathi standing two spots ahead of her. Before she could move her eyes away from her, Gunavathi noticed Cheenalatchumi looking at her. She stretched her lips slightly to form a thin smile. 'Jealous woman,' Cheenalatchumi murmured under her breath and turned her face away. Although it had been a year, Cheenalatchumi was still upset.

Last year, when Gunavathi's uncle-in-law had passed away, it didn't bother Cheenalatchumi that she wasn't invited to the eighth day of offering for the dead. She took part in it anyway, telling herself, 'This is hardly an auspicious occasion to be invited to.' As soon as she entered their house, Gunavathi's mother-in-law said, 'Here's Latchumi! She will give you the right directions. Few people know our Tamil rites and rituals like Latchumi these days.' From making kopi, arranging for vessels, to making sure everything was available for preparing the meals, Cheenalatchumi took on a lot of the tasks.

'Aunty, for the eighth day, should the offering be served in odd numbers?' Gunavathi asked. Then, as she was sautéing some meat she added, 'Do you eat beef?'

'How can you ask that? Isn't cow a god we worship? How can we eat that?'

'What about pig? Isn't it because they consume pig fat that the Chinese have such healthy skin and hair? Even at this age, your skin is glowing…'

Before Gunavathi could complete the sentence, Cheenalatchumi left the onions that she had picked up to peel on the table and walked away. This was the first time since that day that she was seeing Gunavathi in person. 'That is why her only son is going after a Chinese girl. She deserves it!' Cheenalatchumi said to herself. As she tried to calm herself down, she was flooded with more memories.

When she was studying in a Tamil-medium school, her classmates used to keep feeling her skin. 'How come you are so fair?' Zeenat would say and sit next to her dotingly. Immediately, Rathna and Bhagya would chase Zeenat away saying, 'Don't get enticed by her fair skin, she is a pig-eater! That, too, the dirty kind that strolls around the settlement.' Whenever she heard the term 'white pig', Cheenalatchumi would burst into tears. Why that made her cry still puzzled her; after all, she used to delight in being called a white pig affectionately at home by her parents and husband. As she recalled how much she cried hiding on the stairways or in the bathrooms, she felt sorry for herself.

After her fifth-grade exams, the teacher had conducted a contest of riddles.

'Aaso's pig had 17 piglets. His wife delivered their tenth child. How many piglets will our "white pig" have?' Rathna had poked fun at her. She still felt humiliated thinking about how the entire class had roared in laughter. '11! 15! 20!' they had shouted in response.

Cheenalatchumi stopped going to school after that day. Her mother didn't see a point in her continuing school either, and made her stay at home to learn cooking. Her mother did not express her affection in the same way that her father did. However, wherever she went, she took only her along and introduced her proudly, 'This is my daughter.' Any task that demanded a sense of responsibility was assigned only to her. Once when, during a visit home by her older brother's friend, he handed her a bag of fruits, her younger sister Rani had asked her, 'Are you showing off you fair skin to lure men?' It was only when her mother had added, 'Don't you know that you should go to your room whenever men come home?' that it occurred to Cheenalatchumi for the first time that her real mother would never have said something like that.

After extensive inquiries and only after she had three children of her own had she been able to trace down her biological sister. When Cheenalatchumi visited her house for a get-together a day before the big Chinese holiday, she served herself veggies over rice and started eating with her hand. 'Why are you eating like an Indian?' her elder sister had asked. Later, when they were in the middle of a conversation, her sister had remarked, 'Have you applied oil to your hair? That is why you smell,' and sat a little further from her. Even though she never saw her sister after that, she could not erase that incident from her mind.

As she recalled Kannusamy's often repeated quote, 'Only if you experience hardship in life can you truly enjoy the happiness in it; if everything is sweet, you will feel glutted,' she realized that she was getting very close to the voting spot. She immediately pulled out her mobile phone and walked back to the end of the line while looking at the phone.

When Cheenalatchumi had arrived at the voting tent at 7.30 that morning, there was no crowd. So she had gone to the market close by to eat something. Any queue had to be long for her to be in it.

It had been more than a month since she'd seen her grandson. When she was trying to decide what gift to buy him, he had said to her, 'Aatha, get me a Hello Kitty.' Her daughter had said, 'Amma, you would need to get in the queue very early for that. Don't bother with all that.' But Cheenalatchumi had immediately begun to wonder what kind of queue it would be. She then found out where she could get the gift and stood in line the very first day to buy the toy and take it to her grandson. Waiting in lines for hours to achieve something gave Cheenalatchumi unbounded happiness. She considered it the sole purpose of her life.

Cheenalatchumi had noted down standing in line to pay her final respects to the Old Man – prime minister LMY – as an achievement in her notebook. She reminisced occasionally about the many hours she spent standing – three times in all – in a queue that extended from the City Hall all the way to the Parliament, bearing the pain in her knees, pangs of hunger, nature's calls, and everything else.

Kannusamy had tried to dissuade her citing all sorts of reasons. 'It will be crowded, your knee pain will worsen, you won't have access to a bathroom if you need to go…' But Cheenalatchumi did not heed anything he said. She went all three days. She wanted to pay her respects to the Old Man only because that would allow her to stand in a queue.

She didn't go with Kannusamy; because no matter how long the queue, he would find a way to cut into it and finish the task quickly. When the first iPhone was launched, he had somehow found some person to stand in the queue for him and bought the phone in ten minutes. Cheenalatchumi had felt utterly cheated. Not only was she robbed of the opportunity to stand in a queue, for hours, ahead of the entire city to buy the phone, but because her belief that, of all places in the world, it was only in Singapore that people properly followed the decorum of queuing, had proven false, she was also left deeply worried. Yet, she never gave up standing in queues or stopped talking about the greatness of Singapore.

Every day of hers started in some queue.

Long queues becoming news items with photographs on television and in newspapers was one of the reasons she liked being in them. If a part of her, even if somewhere distant, was identified in one such feature, that was enough to make her jubilant for an entire week. She would have something new to talk about.

Cheenalatchumi's decision-making process to pick an occasion to stand in a queue was quite interesting. She often observed with amusement the eagerness that rose in her.

She was following the news about the Old Man's death and the last rites like any other. She had been saddened by how long he had suffered being in the hospital with so many tubes connected to him and found peace in his passing. Whenever anyone was too incapacitated to speak, it troubled her. 'How can anyone live without the ability to talk?' she would bemoan. She was especially affected by older people who couldn't talk or didn't have anyone to talk to. She had told her children strictly that they should not take her to a hospital should anything happen to her. It was only when the media began to carry news that throes of people were waiting for hours to pay their respects to the Old Man and the queues were snaking through the entire city that she became enthusiastic.

As Kannusamy was a long-term member of the party, Cheenalatchumi was concerned that he may get to go directly to the body without having to wait in a queue. 'When has Singapore ever seen the whole city stand in a queue? When will it ever witness that again? Convention dictates that respects be paid by duly standing in line. I will wait in line and see him,' she declared and left. 'Try complaining when your feet hurt at night and see what happens,' Kannusamy said with a scowl, but she turned a deaf ear to his words.

Following that, for a person longing for any opportunity to be in a similar queue, the general elections brought a sense of relief.

She woke up before dawn, showered, and wore a green sari with a red border that her daughter had bought her for Deepavali. The traces of turmeric on her face, the patches of white talcum powder over her neck, and the vermilion dot in the middle of her forehead further brightened Cheenalatchumi's yellow skin tone. If anyone so much as looked in her direction as if to enquire where she was headed, she said, 'My mother always says dress up well so that the people around look at you with respect.' Even if she was going to the shop at the lower level of her building, she combed her hair and applied some talcum powder before heading out.

Like her mother, she only dressed in saris. Her children still kept pushing her to wear nighties at home, and salwar kameezes, trousers and tops when stepping out. But, regardless of what anyone said, it was always saris for her. If anyone pressed on, she would say, 'We are Tamils. It is upon us to preserve the Tamil culture,' and quieten them.

'This Chinese girl, doesn't she embody the goddess of wealth?' her maternal relatives had once stated, when they visited them from their hometown for the first time. And that had triggered a major altercation. Even as a child, if someone asked her whether she was Chinese, she promptly replied with a grimace, 'Don't talk to me about being yellow, black, or any colour. Don't you see the vermilion dot on my forehead?' She did not acknowledge the name Cheenalatchumi, which stood for 'Chinese Lakshmi'.

When she was little, she had liked the name Latchumi. But as she grew up, because there were so many Latchumis around them, she tried to change her name several times. Each time she tried, she ran into some hurdle or another; so she decided to keep it. From then on, she wore her name with pride. 'My mother always said to me,

"You have come into my life like Goddess Latchumi,'" she'd say, or, 'Whether it is my family or the family I am married into, I am their lucky charm. I am the Latchumi of my house.' If anyone had a baby girl, she advised them, 'Name her "Latchumi", the whole family will prosper!'

It is true that her mother used to coddle her by saying that during her childhood. She also told her that they had thrown away into the garbage bin the milk tins and money they had found next to her as she lay outside on a napkin. Every time Cheenalatchumi heard the words 'You are our Latchumi', tears flowed uncontrollably from her eyes.

After she counted the money in her wallet and looked up, she noticed some people engaged in conversation. The queue was moving slowly. Maran, who was standing behind her, mentioned that he was going to cast a vote for the first time even though he was thirty-four years old. Cheenalatchumi began to narrate how she hadn't had the opportunity to vote until that day:

'My father, my paternal and maternal uncles, all worked at the port and were members of the ruling political party. Election to them was like a festival. The whole house would be full of beer bottles. They took off from work and did election-related work all day. In those days, our constituency had contests too. But because their party was always certain to win, the contest was more among the members of the party, around who planned the better celebration. That was how they measured their wins and losses. My father's competition was the party office manager, Quake. He would want to buy a large garland of orchids, my father would tell us. But my father would have already ordered garlands of roses and jasmines a week earlier. What they primarily competed about was whose garland was the longest and whose was worn first. If my father won, he would celebrate for a whole week by drinking Lalang water. If he lost, he would drink too much Lalang water out of anger and pick fights. My father did not provide for the family. Any savings came from my mother and me doing odd jobs here and there. Still, it was during that time when we all really celebrated. We got meals with chicken and new clothes. Everyone showered, dressed up, and went out as a family to cast their votes first thing in the morning. I, too, would go along for the fun of it. They would buy us ice and boiled peanuts.

'Ever since I was little, I have loved elections. But I have never voted. This is my only regret marrying Kannusamy mama. People who lived next door said, "That man is no match for you. He is twelve years older than you. He would look like your father." But see, no one else showed up asking for my hand. From the time I can remember, my mother kept on telling me, "You will be the wife of Kannusamy," and that always stayed in my head. There has never been an election held in the localities we've lived in. That is my only regret. Only after fifty years of independence are elections being held in all constituencies now.'

She looked at Maran's face to see if he would ask her any questions. But he simply nodded and didn't ask any. He was well aware that if he engaged her even a little, Cheenalatchumi, in her enthusiasm, would begin listing all the times that she had waited in a queue until then. But that did not deter Cheenalatchumi from carrying on. She could make friends very easily.

That was how she had become friends with Le Hong, her neighbour from downstairs, for over a month now, just so that she could read his newspaper. If anyone else who lived in that building block saw Le Hong by the lift, they would choose to take the stairs no matter how many flights they would have to climb. Even if no one said a word, he would start talking about a lot of things. If they tried to leave, he would grab them by their hands and stop them. He spoke a mix of Chinese and Malay; it didn't matter to him that the listener didn't understand him. He bought the newspaper every day. Cheenalatchumi would spend a few hours talking to him daily just so she could borrow his newspaper and cut out snippets of news items to stick in her collection. Doing that helped imprint the news deep in her mind. She felt a sense of grandeur in effortlessly recalling information and dropping them during conversations.

'Because voting booths have been set up conveniently in so many places, there isn't much of a crowd here. Looks like people have gone to the ones closest to where they live,' she said to no one in particular.

'Apparently, many people with PR status have moved into this area now. That's why there aren't many voters. More than half the people in this country now are immigrants,' Ameena from the opposite block, who was standing in front of her, reacted, turning her head halfway.

It was with Ameena that Cheenalatchumi had waited to pay her respects to the Old Man on the first day. If the wait was long and especially if the queue was outdoors, it was fun going with Ameena and her family. They always packed water and food. Ameena's son and grandson brought their guitars with them. They sang old numbers by Ramli, Elvis and The Beatles while playing their guitars. They sang Mohammed Rafi and Kishore Kumar songs too. 'Those are songs for oldies. We should sing songs from our time,' Cheenalatchumi would say and dive into Illaiyaraaja songs. Whenever she said the words, 'We grew up on Illaiyaraaja's music,' her voice grew softer. With the same tenderness, she would launch into the song, '*Naane naana*' in her nasal voice. Within a short while, everyone would begin to find something else to do. Undeterred, she would continue to sing, believing that they were still listening to her.

When Cheenalatchumi reached the queue that day, it was extremely long. The people there estimated that it would take eight hours. Ameena, who was ahead in the line, turned around to find Cheenalatchumi standing tall and majestically. A smile flashed across Cheenalatchumi's face and faded. She instantly straightened the bag hanging from her shoulder, changed her facial expression and looked at Ameena's husband. 'You didn't bring your guitar,' she said sorrowfully.

'No one told me what kind of songs the Old Man likes; I don't know if he even likes music! Why bother the poor man with music that he may not care for,' Ameena's son responded. Cheenalatchumi became quiet. The line had started at the City Hall MRT station. People were walking in groups instead of in a queue. Ameena's family moved quietly and fast. Cheenalatchumi strolled along observing everything around and fell behind. It was strange to walk quietly. She tried starting a conversation with Ameena a few times. Ameena ended them with a word or two. Later, she resorted to humming a sad song to herself: *'Thenpaandi seemaiyile…'* A profound sorrow engulfed her. Tears welled in her eyes.

When they crossed City Hall and began walking on the lawns, a group of middle-aged people cut the line ahead of them. Cheenalatchumi stepped aside to allow them room and Ameena became annoyed.

'If there is a line, there will always be people who will break it or have others hold a spot for them. Don't we also sometimes hail a cab in front of people who are already waiting for one, pretending not to see them?' Cheenalatchumi attempted to pacify Ameena. But she would not accept her explanation. She turned away sharply to show her disapproval and stood with a frown on her face.

'My mother has told me about standing in queues during the Japanese rule and later for food and water. I have also stood in them when I was little. The man who eliminated the need to stand in such queues has now made us all stand in one greater than any of those,' Cheenalatchumi said, hoping to assuage Ameena's anger. Instead, it fanned it and made it worse.

'That's right, we are the ones to wait in line for everything, unlike some others,' Ameena announced. The group that had cut in the line exchanged glances. Looking at those well-dressed people, Cheenalatchumi assumed that they held high positions and felt troubled that she couldn't help them out.

When she suspected that Ameena was angry even now because of the long queue at the voting booth, Cheenalatchumi lost interest in talking to her. 'Her anger is quite like this queue. At first glance, it may appear long, but in the end, it will add up to nothing,' she said softly to Maran. She turned her attention to Ameena's grandson Rashid, who was standing in front of Ameena, and asked him, 'Are you going to vote for the Opposition party?'

Rashid and Cheenalatchumi's son's son were great friends. They were voting for the first time ever. She had seen her grandson's posts on Facebook attending gatherings by the Opposition party and had 'liked' them. She assumed that he and his friends were all in support of that party.

When his turn to cast his vote arrived, Rashid stepped forward and went in. It was Cheenalatchumi's turn the very next minute. The people standing there checked her identity card and the voter card that she held in her hand readily and let her in. The disappointment over how quickly the line had moved overshadowed the joy she had felt about voting; she marked her choice and dropped the ballot in the box.

When she came out, Cheenalatchumi spotted Devan's mother, who lived in her block, standing in the queue with her friends. They were all dressed up. 'Where are you off to?' she asked them from where she was.

'To the parliament,' Devan's mother replied. Her friends' laughter reached her ears. Cheenalatchumi laughed along too. 'No matter the reason, isn't laughing always good?' she mused.

'Isn't that why you made your son study political science?' Cheenalatchumi remarked. As far as she was concerned, she wouldn't let go of the slightest opportunity to chat.

'Is that so?' asked one friend, to which Devan's mother replied, 'Just ignore her,' and took her phone out from her bag to answer an incoming call.

'You can only stand in this queue once. You cannot come back and stand here again. Just saying,' Cheenalatchumi commented, without really meaning to say anything specific.

'Why, were you going to vote twice?' the person standing next to Devan's mother asked, mockingly.

As Cheenalatchumi pondered over whether she could have stood in the queue twice, whether in fact they would have let her cast the same ballot twice, she realized that she had ambled her way to the market. She straightened her head and looked up at the shops. Only the chicken and rice shop and the soup shop had long queues. She counted the heads to see which one was longer. The chicken and rice shop had 27 heads waiting; there were 29 at the soup shop. She began to make her way towards the latter when a Chinese woman hurried past her and joined the queue in front of her. 'These old ladies, they always do this,' Cheenalatchumi muttered, irked. Then she went on to start a conversation with that very lady. 'It would be nice if they provided water to those who stood in queues to cast their votes … mm … What do you think?'

THE RULES OF THE GAME

J.P. Sanakya

TRANSLATED BY N. KALYAN RAMAN

1

DEPLETED IN SUMMER, the lake looked like a sinuous snake lying along the edge of a broad avenue. Astrologer Kaliyan had stretched out on the far bank of the shrivelled lake. Since the sun had risen high that morning, his old bicycle, which was parked next to him, had cast its shadow to waver upon the undulating sand. The astrologer's sling bag was hanging from the bicycle. Its handles, discoloured by thick layers of grime, glistened in the sun. The bicycle and the sling bag knew the astrologer far better than the villagers did. His whole person – grey hair, shrunken chest, two-yard veshti, long shoulder cloth and dirty sacred thread – lay sprawled on the sand.

'Since when did Kaliyan, who has never known the smell of liquor, start drinking?' Men on their way to take a shit on the lakebed gossiped among themselves as they walked past.

News of the astrologer's dishevelled state was spreading slowly through the wind that swirled about in the village. Many tried to rouse him, but he was simply unable to get up. After energetic goading by some villagers, he sat up, opened his eyes and looked around blankly; being in no condition to keep his eyelids open for very long, he shut his eyes again and curled up to sleep. Everybody felt a kind of pity for him. Now that he has started drinking, how can we trust his astrology any more, they said. It was Kaliyan's fortune-telling and frank speech that had bound him to the villagers. Wherever they stopped him to ask for predictions – on the street, under a tree, or in the fields – explosive laughter and planetary positions would stream forth from him. His teeth were stained brown from a habit of chewing betel leaves. He had made predictions against their will even for those who ridiculed astrology, and they had foundered, unable to dismiss his forecasts. 'Aiya, I learnt this from my grandfather, Veera Siva Shanmugam. I didn't just pick up this bundle to earn a living. Your father would know about my grandfather. He was a mystic, a sage for the whole village,' he would say with a hearty laugh.

For more than twenty years, his ancient bicycle had roamed around in the villages of the region. The trails it had traversed were many. Bereft of bell and brake, the cycle would obey no one but Kaliyan. The red letters painted on the rear wheel guard as on a bicycle for hire – 'Kaliyan Josiyar' – would shiver and writhe as if running a high fever. Once he sat on it, he was not known to have travelled fast ever. It was like a royal procession while he amused himself gazing aimlessly on both sides. As he pedalled slowly, swaying from side to side, the bicycle would chat with him through a steady series of squeaks. Emitting a moan when he got on and a fond rumble when he got down, the bicycle was an amiable companion to him. It would shudder when he slapped the seat with his right hand just before getting on to it. Kaliyan was emotionally attached to that bicycle.

'No king can lay a hand on my bicycle,' he would say.

More than the men, the women of the village were attached to him. As the go-to man for many important tasks and occasions, including naming a child, school admission, attainment of puberty, selection of dates for auspicious functions, the annual ceremony for dead ancestors, funeral rites, and fixing dates for young men's sports matches, his face was imprinted in many a villager's heart. Even so, when it came to the fee for examining horoscopes or marking dates, he was satisfied with whatever people gave him. He would make obeisance with folded hands and receive the money. He was remarkably adept at handling those who got drunk at death ceremonies and insisted on ritual propriety, disarming them with jovial banter. In certain villages, Kaliyan had become an integral part of all family functions and death ceremonies. Even if he had quarrelled at a house the previous day, he would make certain that he dropped by the next day and chatted amiably with the family. On the astrologer who had become a feature of their village, the residents bestowed affection and privileges without any reserve. Of his four children, the three boys had left their father's vocation and moved to other towns. Kanniyammal, his youngest child, had left her husband's place to come and live with him.

2

Kaliyan had set out from Aasiriyar's house after having made predictions for his four sons and reckoned the likely period of his death as per calculations based on his first-born's horoscope. The sun was scorching hot. Just as Kaliyan reached the front door, Aasiriyar said, 'Do you know Kala's son in Sathamangalam, Josiyarey?'

Kaliyan turned to him and said, 'Sadasivam is a distant relative. The boy is a tailor.'

'Yes, that's the boy … He has opened a shop in town now. They asked me if I knew of a good prospect for a bride.' The astrologer knitted his brow, reflected for a brief while, and said, 'Hmm.'

'He is a fine boy. If it's all right with Kaliyan, shall we seek an alliance with his family for Kanniyammal?' As Aasiriyar spoke,

Kaliyan seemed startled. Even as Aasiriyar continued, 'Your girl is also getting older. They are fine folks,' Kaliyan put the cycle on the stand and rushed back into the house. 'Between you and me, Kanniyammal will be thirty after Thai begins,' he said with diffidence. He seemed excited suddenly. 'I've seen the boy too. A fine boy. He speaks with respect whenever we run into each other,' Kaliyan said. 'In any case, ask them to bring the horoscope. We'll see if they match,' he said, looking at Aasiriyar's face.

'Why bother with horoscopes? If the hearts are aligned, the families will come together…' Kaliyan objected immediately. 'Being a learned man, you shouldn't say such things. Nothing happens without the influence of planets. If we go by your thinking, I should have got her married off in the second year after she attained puberty. We received plenty of horoscopes. Nothing matched. Sometimes I feel dejected and wonder why she was born at all.'

'Look here, Josiyarey! This palm here, why can't it be like this elbow? Why should there be lines on it?'

'Show me your hand.' Kaliyan reached out and held Aasiriyar's hand. Then, kneading and turning it, he scrutinized it intently.

'Do you know how to read palms, Kaliya?'

'I know a little, Vathiyarey … but not as well as I can read horoscopes,' he said and asked in a whisper, 'Is your wife at home?'

'No.'

'Before you married her, you must have kept another woman in the position of a wife,' Kaliyan said. 'It would be no surprise if you had married her formally.' Stunned for a moment, Aasiriyar withdrew his hand casually.

'Please don't take it amiss. I did blurt out something. Whether I was right or wrong is between you and your conscience. You don't have to tell me.'

Aasiriyar's opinion of Kaliyan changed abruptly. He felt awkward even to show his face to Kaliyan. As if he understood Aasiriyar's predicament, Kaliyan said, 'I'll be going, Vathiyarey,' and took his leave. As he was about to step out, he said, 'Ask them to bring the horoscope. If it matches with hers, we will fix the alliance.' He turned the bicycle and gave the seat a hard slap. 'Ahn,' Aasiriyar responded from inside.

Swaying from side to side, Kaliyan pedalled his bicycle in the scorching heat. His shadow accompanied him on the red dirt, also pedalling the bicycle.

3

Kanniyammal stood under the scorching sun and toiled all day; her face was always dark as a shadow. The villagers used to say that she was 'half woman, half man'. In a way, they were right to think of her as half woman. Now that she was past the seasons of youth, she resembled a half-woman. They said it was because of her age. Since they had been searching for a groom for her from the time she attained puberty, it would have been no cause for surprise even if they had called her a hag.

Kanniyammal was dark and beautiful. Men tended to stare at her chest before they looked at her face. At one time she used to find it awkward, then she got used to it. It's natural for men to ogle, she told herself. During her faceless existence spent working in fields and orchards in the company of elderly women, someone had taught her this facile phrase. Past noon, when the harshness of the sun began to subside, Kanniyammal started gathering twigs for the woodstove at home.

Kanniyammal had no aptitude for studies. If anyone asked her, 'What is four and three?' she would answer, 'Seven.' If she was asked again about 'three and four', she would say, 'I don't know this sum.' Her brothers got an education and progressed in life. This girl occupied her mother's place in the kitchen. Motherhood dripped from her face, words and fingers. She was inseparable from the soot-smeared kitchen. 'If you know cooking and how to work in the fields, someone will definitely marry you,' she would say with an innocent laugh. For her, the time of youthful dreams was over. All her girlfriends had children by now – a toddler crawling on the floor and a baby on the hip. She would hug their children with enormous affection. 'If you like them so much, why don't you tell your father?' her friends would tease her. 'Give me one of yours, why don't you?' she would retort.

'I don't know if it's the planets or just plain misfortune,' she would say about her life. The strand of dissatisfaction was slithering secretly inside her. To her, all the modern things of the world were but fables. Her only true realities were the deccan hemp, a type of spinach with a sour taste, and idli-dosai. She had no interest in new information either. She wouldn't listen if she were told. Sometimes she turned into an old woman herself and listened avidly to family stories narrated by old women late into the night. In fact, most of her friends were old. 'They got married, delivered children, raised them to adulthood and married them off, managed the household and had grandchildren … There's nothing they don't know,' she would say.

'Had she been married, she would have had two to three children by now,' the old woman walking beside her with a firm step said. Today Kanniyammal came upon twigs that were mostly thick and long. In the plantain grove, she tore off a strip of bark from a tree, wrapped the twigs in it and knotted the bundle. Then, half-kneeling, she lifted the bundle to her knees and then to her head, and stood upright. After balancing and adjusting the bundle on her head, she bent her knees and picked up the food pail with one hand and started walking. Until she had walked home from the riverbank, she would not touch the bundle, not even casually. It was beneath her dignity.

In the evening, the streets were lively with the bustle of people. Her house was situated behind two houses near a channel with flowing water, with an abundant growth of screw-pine thickets on both banks. She was walking down the street past rows of houses. Men's eyes shot a glance at her breasts as she passed. In the beginning, she had experienced a mix of excitement and revulsion at this. Now she was able to judge a man as soon as she set eyes on him. 'These men only make me want to laugh. Not one woman's husband is faithful,' she would say.

Propped up against the side wall of her house, touching the thatched roof, stood Kaliyan's bicycle. It was a sign that Kaliyan was at home. Easing the firewood bundle off her head and dropping it heavily on the ground, she scratched her scalp briskly through her hair. The hair on the crown of her head turned scruffy and rose in clumps. 'Who is it?' Kaliyan called. 'Aangh,' she replied.

Later that week on Friday, the astrologer's house was filled with people as well as the smell of toddy. As usual, Kanniyammal was sitting with a few women in the kitchen. Meanwhile, Aasiriyar came by and took Kaliyan with him. Kanniyammal was shocked when she heard that her father was drunk, but when she looked at everyone there, she recovered her composure. She thought that all of them must have got together and bought some liquor and forced Kaliyan to drink it. When a woman teased her, she retorted, 'Menfolk get drunk. My father is a man too.'

Not only Kanniyammal, but all the others too liked the groom. 'Befitting the name Maniyan, our boy is truly a gem. Yes, he is our gold, sovereign and diamond!' a man said as he yawned with the back of his hand over his mouth. Maniyan sat stiffly in a black chair as though he were chained to it. Unlike Kanniyammal and the other women who stole glances at the groom, Maniyan kept sitting there without a similar opportunity coming his way. He did look like a tailor. The knuckles on the fingers of his right hand were callused from constantly wielding a tailor's scissors. The men kept themselves busy, going inside the house, hanging out at the doorway, and gathering in the alley to chat among themselves.

A woman said, 'Hope the horoscopes match at least this time.' The groom's family had brought an astrologer with them. His chunky spectacles sat precariously on his flat nose. Behind his glasses, his eyes appeared small or big, depending on their movements. Sometimes he seemed to have no eyes at all. He was drunk too. 'Where is the bride's mama?' said the new astrologer. Kanniyammal's maternal uncle, who was standing next to him, responded, 'Don't I look like an uncle to you?' He was drunk as well. 'How would he know unless he is told?' Sadasivam interjected. 'Yes, of course,' the uncle nodded his head like a serf.

To the question, 'Where is Kaliyan?', some people replied, 'Aasiriyar has gone somewhere with him.' 'What is he doing there when the ceremony is going on here?' a man protested with an air of responsibility. 'An important matter, it seems.' 'What kind of important matter?' 'Who knows?' 'Of course.' They babbled again. From his vantage on the chair, Maniyan trained his eyes inside but could not spot the bride in the dark. When the collective laughter of the women came floating outside, he felt nervous, presuming that it must be about him. 'It's getting late, 'pa,' Sadasivam said. 'Late for what?' someone wanted to know. 'For what, you ask? For a crab to sting your wife,' Sadasivam replied. The crowd burst into waves of laughter.

When Aasiriyar entered the alley with Kaliyan in tow, Kaliyan's face appeared as though he had swallowed a turd. 'Hmm, the bride's father is here.' Guests who were scattered all over gathered in the front hall. Kaliyan was intensely preoccupied with something. He showed no signs of being drunk. Making his way through the crowd, he stood in the dark and stared at Kanniyammal. His heart started pounding. His intoxicated state had erased any inhibition he might have had about Kanniyammal being a grown woman now. When he drew closer, Kanniyammal stood up. Kaliyan started crying. At first, Kanniyammal and the other women were shocked; then they fell quiet, thinking that he was shedding tears of joy over sending his child away to a new life. His tears flowed down his cheeks in two strands. Kanniyammal stood perplexed, not knowing what to do. 'Why are you crying like this?' an old woman chastised Kaliyan. He looked up at her. Face contorted and lips trembling in a surge of emotion, he held down his tears. As he inhaled deeply to lessen the intensity of his grief, his rib cage swelled in his chest and then subsided. 'Go on. Go and do what needs to get done,' the old woman said. One thing was clear to Kanniyammal: her marriage was fixed. Then, as if he had regained his composure, Kaliyan stepped aside, cleared his nose, and wiped his face with a towel.

'Because my daughter is thirty and still unmarried, they are talking ill of me, 'ma,' Kaliyan said. As he kept staring at her, Kaliyan was yet again overcome by the urge to weep. Kanniyammal's eyes welled up. 'Why are *you* crying, di? Sit down. Don't people get their daughters married off? Why cry about it?' the old woman shouted. She tugged hard at Kanniyammal, making her sit on the floor. Kaliyan went out.

The astrologer with the chunky glasses had already drawn the charts and jotted down the planetary positions. Kaliyan came in and took his seat amidst the gathering. Pointing to the astrologer's notebook, Kaliyan asked to have a look at it. With a secretive expression on his face, the astrologer looked at Aasiriyar and Sadasivam by turns. 'Hmm,' Aasiriyar said. Scrutinizing the horoscope chart, Kaliyan winced. 'What sort of calculation is this!' he exclaimed. Parting the heads of guests who were seated on the floor, Aasiriyar made his way through the crowd and sat next to Kaliyan. The others shifted to make room for him. Aasiriyar took the notebook and glanced through it. He handed it forthwith to the astrologer. 'Vathiyarey,' Kaliyan said. 'Keep quiet,' Aasiriyar rebuked him. The new astrologer muttered his calculations like a devotional verse. Some people were watching him. Then he concluded, 'Everything is just perfect,' and glanced at the crowd. Kaliyan sat motionless.

'Fix the date for the marriage on the upcoming muhurtam day,' Sadasivam said. The astrologer turned the pages of the almanac back and forth. 'If we skip the coming Friday, the Friday that follows next is auspicious,' he said.

'Kaliya, shall we agree on that date?' Aasiriyar said. Kaliyan looked blankly at Aasiriyar. 'Yes, note it down,' Aasiriyar said.

'The groom owns a tailoring shop in town. It's best that we negotiate right now what the bride's family is prepared to give him as dowry,' a relative of the groom said.

Sadasivam retorted right back, 'They'll give bollocks. Don't we know this idiot?' Then he turned to Maniyan and asked, 'Look, Maniya. What do they need to give you for you to marry the girl?'

'Don't want anything, Aiya,' Maniyan replied.

'Did you hear that, Maari? You, too, Amma?' Sadasivam said, addressing Maniyan's mother.

'All you men are doing this together. How can I say anything?' she said.

'Am I going to push your son into a well, then?'

'Oh, for goodness's sake. Why are you upset? Sit down,' Maniyan's mother said.

'You won't get a girl like her in this whole district even if you searched with a fine sieve.'

'Why should I talk to you? I will speak directly to my nephew,' Sadasivam said, playing the entitled kin. 'Elei, you want to get married to this girl, don't you?'

'I am fine with it, Aiya,' Maniyan said.

'Listen carefully, everyone. The groom has opened his mouth and said that he will marry Kanniyammal.'

'What's next, then?'

'I still haven't seen the girl,' Maniyan said. The crowd laughed. 'Oh, god.' Sadasivam laughed too. Aasiriyar called out to the people inside the house.

Kanniyammal entered the hall accompanied by an old woman and stood close to the wall. The new astrologer was busy writing the scroll for the marriage.

'Have a good look at her, dear nephew. The old woman who is at the back is married already. The one in front is the bride,' Sadasivam said. The crowd laughed again.

4

After Maniyan married Kanniyammal, her dreams had begun to roam freely along with her. Just as Maniyan found Kanniyammal adorable, she, too, loved Maniyan. Kanniyammal believed that her marriage had been delayed for so long only so that she could meet and marry Maniyan. Maniyan brought her sweets and flowers every day. Every day, she spoke to him regretfully about her father's loneliness. He would listen without saying much. Kanniyammal's complexion, which was dark back in her village, had not only begun to turn fairer, but she had also put on weight and become radiant with happiness. Maniyan's mother brimmed with pride when she heard the villagers say that it was only after an auspicious period began for Maniyan that he got himself a good wife.

Kaliyan went to look up Kanniyammal nearly once a week. There were only five villages between her native village and her marital home. Making frequent visits to look up Kanniyammal was awkward for Kaliyan. However, when Maniyan's father told him that he liked Kaliyan's visits and that he should come by regularly, it made them all happy. Moreover, the various types of kuzhambu prepared hitherto in Maniyan's family began to taste different after Kanniyammal's arrival, which pleased everyone. Her mother-in-law, too, went around singing praises of Kanniyammal all over the village. She marvelled at how, in spite of garnishing the dishes with very little oil, Kanniyammal's cooking was phenomenally tasty. She also gave some of that kuzhambu to her elderly woman friends and established the veracity of her claim.

A year later, the issue that had been troubling not only Kanniyammal but also the rest of the family reared its head. Because she was still childless, Kanniyammal and Maniyan expected every month that her period would be delayed, only to be disappointed. Yet, both clung to the hope that they would have a child soon.

Whenever Kaliyan paid a visit to Kanniyammal, what bothered him at present was her horoscope. He had begun to have serious doubts about whether the horoscope he had been scrutinizing until then was genuinely hers. He believed that there was no chance of an error in the time of her birth as recorded. He began to suspect his own astrology practice of so many years. Since, in recent days, the idea caused him extreme torment, he talked about his distress to Aasiriyar whenever they met. Not only did Aasiriyar chastise Kaliyan but he also advised him to be happy that a marriage that should have happened in the natural course was conducted at least now. Since Kaliyan had fulfilled his duty, no one could find fault with him. He sent Kaliyan away with these words of consolation. But like a slab of granite dropped in water, the idea endured in Kaliyan's mind without fading away.

Her mother-in-law believed beyond a shadow of doubt that the reason why Kanniyammal had not been blessed with a child yet was because of some transgression against God. She claimed to have taken three different vows to propitiate three deities: Ayyanar Sami, Ayyappan Sami and Mariyamman. She told Kanniyammal that, except a visit to the Ayyappan temple, she should fulfil the other two vows. She had a plan to send Maniyan to the Ayyappan temple. She ground some medicinal herbs into a potion and gave it to Kanniyammal to drink. She bought red plantains and asked Kanniyammal to give them to Maniyan, telling her strictly not to reveal to him that they were given by his mother.

Every month, the family began to wait secretly for Kanniyammal to conceive. Complying with her mother-in-law's wish, Kanniyammal participated in the maiden puja of Ayyappan's devotees that year. Draped in wet clothes after bathing, she knelt in front of the devotees, and received morsels of food as alms from devotees who had taken their vows and consumed them.

On full moon day in the month of chithirai, she laid some food on the bare ground in the Mariyamman temple and, with her hands tied behind her back, bent forward and ate the food lying on the ground. At the time, her mother-in-law shed tears of fervent hope. Kanniyammal cried too. Though she loved children herself, she yearned wistfully for a child to be born to her at least for the sake of her husband and in-laws.

Right from the beginning, Kanniyammal had been insisting to Maniyan that they should go to the movies together as a couple. She had seen a few movies now and then, in brief segments when they were screened on television sets in the street during weddings in the village. Afraid of being groped by men in the teeming crowd, she would come back home early. She never went to anyone's house to watch television shows. The few houses she visited regularly did not have a television set. Besides, none of this was important to her. All the married women in her village went to the movies with their husbands; she felt like going too. It held a certain glamour for her, that was all.

Maniyan, too, promised her that he would take her some day. Since the shop was new, and he had to earn a good name, attract customers and retain them, he was keeping it open even on holidays; this was the excuse he gave her. Still, she kept pestering him fondly all the time.

5

On Sunday that week Maniyan set out along with Kanniyammal to see a film. Kanniyammal was overjoyed.

Maniyan's mother sent them off with an admonition to be careful and come back safe. Kanniyammal's pale yellow sari was a-bloom with green plants and red flowers. Merging in some fashion with those colours, her figure sparkled. Maniyan wore a shirt and trousers that he had had stitched for himself. They started walking down the red clay street lined with tamarind trees on either side. Yesterday, Maniyan had returned home by afternoon. Because he had to take her to the cinema the next day, he wanted to make sure that she got ready in time. Even though she had pestered him constantly about an outing to the movies, she might say at the last minute that she had a lot of work to do. Besides, he had guessed that he would have to ask his mother in advance for permission.

When they reached the bus stop, it wore a deserted look. When she wondered aloud why there was no sign of other people, he told her that he was wondering about it himself. Once they crossed the abandoned channel, the cinema theatre was only a short distance away. The woman from Ayipettai who sold tapioca for a living was walking back quietly with her basket full of tapioca. Maniyan asked her what was going on. 'Haven't you heard!' she exclaimed in surprise and told them in detail. She said that they had arrested the leader of that caste-community and therefore, no bus was running since the previous night. A lot has happened in one night, and we had no clue about it, Maniyan said ruefully. Kanniyammal's face had wilted in a second. She wanted to know whether no bus would be plying henceforth too. The woman said that she had to go up to the abandoned channel and she had walked all the way from Ayipettai. Kanniyammal felt that all her dressing up and joy of anticipation had gone to waste. Maniyan could not bear to look at her face. He was startled that she appeared so woebegone, like a little child. He told her that they could walk to the cinema, but he wasn't sure whether the show would be on. She wondered how they could run the show amid all the commotion. After remaining silent for some time, they turned around and trudged back home. Wanting to divert Kanniyammal's mind, Maniyan tried to talk to her about sundry topics. She responded with a tired smile. Her pace, too, had slackened. Then both husband and wife walked in silence, with only the patter of two pairs of chappals in the background. Maniyan tried to talk about other things she liked but even they failed to win her attention. Finally, he said, 'Why would a grown up feel so dejected because they couldn't go to a movie?'

'I am not dejected,' she said. 'I feel out of sorts. I want to lie down and go to sleep.' She had pined for so many years for a husband, a child, and going to a movie together as a couple. The child didn't materialize either. Of late, she treated, and talked about, small and big obstacles as though they were the same.

They tired themselves out telling everyone in their street why they had to come back. Since even ordinary news from the world reached their remote village in the boondocks only after considerable delay, they were amazed by his news. Karikalan said that he had heard the news on the radio in the petty shop. He added that they were likely to release the community leader by noon that day.

Once she entered the house, Kanniyammal spread a mat and curled up to sleep without even washing her feet. Maniyan sat down next to her and stretched his legs. He had the impression that she was crying. He looked down at her. She was indeed crying. It pained him. He hugged her tight and consoled her. She told him through her tears that nothing she wished for came true, that she was a luckless wretch. Offering her more words of consolation, he kissed her many times. Like a child quaking in fear, she buried her face deep in his chest and hugged him tight. He had not expected at all that she would get so worked up over such a trifling matter.

6

Maniyan went out that afternoon, and upon his return, told Kanniyammal the news he had heard on the radio: that buses would run after six that evening. Though she was not tired, she hesitated. Maniyan tried to cheer her up. She thought to herself that her husband was taking a lot of trouble over her, and if she refused, he might feel bad.

That evening, he rushed down the red clay road, dragging her along with him. She felt like giggling. With an air of urgency and quick strides, he was walking down a deserted street like a man pushing his way through a crowd. She walked and ran, keeping pace with him. 'Are we running so hard merely for a film?' she said to herself and laughed. Seeing some people waiting at the bus stop brought them some relief. Both of them were sweating profusely. Whenever she looked at him and he glanced at her, they struggled to suppress the laughter that bubbled secretly between them. One or two buses, heavily crowded, went by. 'That bus is so densely packed, it might explode,' someone said. They pushed and jostled their way aboard the next bus that arrived.

Just before they reached the abandoned channel, the conductor stopped the bus and started issuing tickets. She whispered to him, 'The show would have started.' He bent close to her ear and said, 'Around here, they start the show only at seven.' It was difficult to breathe amid the congestion. The conductor kept banging on the tin roof with his palm and shouting at the passengers to buy tickets. 'Tell me, why is this called the abandoned channel?' Maniyan asked. Mindful that others should not overhear their conversation, Kanniyammal said in a low whisper, 'Hmm ... because it has run dry?' Both laughed together.

When they got down at the bus stop in the town with the cinema hall, darkness had begun to fall. As they walked past the taxi stand, where Ambassador cars were parked in a row, the gang of drivers standing there passed comments. A driver whistled and called out, 'Hello!' Presuming that he was calling out to them, the couple exchanged glances and walked on without looking back. As the cinema hall drew closer, Kanniyammal's joy at the prospect of watching a film kept mounting. When they started walking fast after crossing the market area, she reached out and caught hold of Maniyan's hand. Maniyan adjusted the pace of his stride to match hers. When they entered a lane and reached the compound of the cinema hall, they were shocked to see that the doors were closed. They were told that the show had started at six. A pang of disappointment gave way to a strange eruption of laughter. Maniyan looked at her and laughed. Seeing him, she laughed too. Both came out and, as if their secret had leaked out, shook with laughter.

'What a farce,' she said.

'On a rare day unlike no other, a woman went to the festival. But the festival day, too, turned out to be an ordinary day. It's like that story,' she said. 'What can we do?' Before she could end the sentence with 'except go home' she started laughing, turning those final words into laughter instead. 'No one in the whole world would have run so desperately for a movie.' 'They would have,' Maniyan said. 'Yes, of course. They are us,' she said. They broke into laughter again. As though the idea came to him just then, Maniyan said, 'Shall we go and eat something in a hotel?'

'It will cost a lot of money,' she objected.

'No, it won't. After all, we didn't go to the movie. We can spend that money on food and go home happy,' he said. Kanniyammal nodded. They went to a Muslim eatery and had parottas. Then they ordered a biryani and shared it between them. She said she liked the taste. She was tasting biryani for the first time since she had it with her brothers as a child.

When they came out of the eatery after the meal, she said, 'Why does our plan for watching a movie fall through every time?'

'What an odd question,' Maniyan said. They arrived at the bus stop. Maniyan counted the money in hand. 'We haven't spent that much,' he said. Kanniyammal laughed. 'Shall we catch the second show?' he asked eagerly.

'What an idea! Athai will scold us,' she protested.

'I'll tell her.'

'Ah, of course you will tell her, but once you leave for the shop, I am the one who has to face the music,' she said.

'No, she won't scold you,' he said.

She clammed up. They watched the buses coming into the front yard of the market and turning to go back, and the people running to scramble aboard. 'All right, let's go,' she said. He grinned at her. They started walking once again towards the cinema hall. 'After the show, there's a bus that leaves at one o'clock. We can go back on it,' he said. Nodding, she walked on.

'Before marriage, I used to return home in that bus after watching the second show,' he said.

She was troubled by constant thoughts of her mother-in-law. Both kept walking in silence.

'What if she says, "As a man, he might say a thousand things. What happened to your good sense, woman?"?'

Maniyan smiled at her. A small crowd of people were waiting for the second show. The couple stood along with them.

7

When they came out after watching the film, the street lay abandoned like an orphan. They walked down a street where rows of closed shops stretched into the distance. In front of the downed shutters of a few shops, a few men and dogs lay asleep. Walking at a brisk pace, they arrived at the bus stop. Most people from nearby villages had come on their bicycles. Sounds of cycle bells went past them.

A film song was playing in a tea stall. Apart from a couple of small shops, light in the garbage-filled street was confined to a small circle around each lamp post. Maniyan enquired about the bus at the tea stall. 'It's been two weeks since the bus was cancelled,' the stall owner said. A flicker of anxiety was visible on Kanniyammal's face. Maniyan said in an apologetic tone, 'Let's walk.' She nodded and started walking immediately.

'Are you even fit to be housewife, your mother is going to ask me,' she said. 'I'll take care of that,' he reassured her. Though Kanniyammal had liked the film, the joy of watching a film had ebbed out of her. They started walking fast in the darkness.

'Why did they cancel the bus?' she said.

'Not enough passengers, perhaps. Even earlier, the crowd would vanish once the bus crossed our village; the driver and conductor would be the only ones left on board,' he said. After crossing the buildings, they started walking on a long tar road that stretched between uncropped fields on either side.

'We've roamed around so much since morning. We set out for the movie, then went home, set out again, got on the bus after a lot of pushing and shoving, came to the theatre, then wanted to head home but went to a hotel instead, came back to the theatre, watched the movie ... Appa ... I am wiped out ... I wouldn't get this tired even if I worked all day in an orchard or a field,' she said. Maniyan, too, was exhausted by now.

'These people stay awake and drive the bus. Do they get extra money?' she asked. Maniyan hadn't thought about it until then. Meanwhile, she asked the next question. 'These people who drive buses on festival days like Pongal and Deepavali, don't they feel bad about not being able to celebrate with their families?' 'Yes, they would.'

Though her questions gave him a few moments of perplexity, Maniyan realized that there was no one to whom she could address such questions apart from him. Then they kept walking in silence.

Listening in that silent darkness to the actual sound level of their chappals, they walked on.

Past the roadside Ayyanar temple, dense clusters of black babul trees had started on both sides of the road. 'If Athai asks me, I'll tell her that you are the one to blame for everything,' she said. 'Suit yourself,' he replied. As they were going up the bridge across the abandoned channel, they saw a man, smoking a cigarette, coming down in the opposite direction. As they went up the incline, he asked them, 'Which village are you going to?' Maniyan told him the name of their village while he kept walking. At the end of the side walls of the bridge, four men climbed up the downward slope. As a sign that something untoward was going to happen, Maniyan felt his body tremble. As if she sensed it too, Kanniyammal grabbed Maniyan's hand. The men who came up the slope from the other end tried to walk past them casually; then they caught hold of Maniyan. They clasped Kanniyammal's mouth and lifted her up with ease. She fought with all her strength to break free. Someone grabbed hold of her legs, which were kicking wildly, and held them together. Maniyan groaned and screamed. They covered his head with a blanket and kicked him. The pain spread across his entire body and sank in. Babbling and disoriented, he lurched forward and back, dragged by them in every direction. Carrying Kanniyammal, they ran along the gravel road on the left that led to the Nachiyar Amman temple. They lifted Maniyan and carried him to the downward slope on the other side. Kicking his legs, Maniyan struggled to break free. Holding his head in a firm grip, someone shoved a piece of cloth into his mouth. The sound of a switchblade being released was heard clearly. A nameless fear spiralled up inside him and choked Maniyan's throat. A man was stationed near the Nachiyar temple, too, beside the dilapidated old bridge. They bundled Kanniyammal into the Ambassador car that was parked there. When two men arrived at the downward slope, the pair who were guarding Maniyan handed over the knife to them and went away. The new arrivals kept chain-smoking. With his hands and feet bound by rope, Maniyan lay curled up on his side. When he rumbled and turned over, they warned him; standing a little away, they continued smoking. Maniyan overheard them whispering to each other that she had good tits. A short while later, as though they had received a sign, they left him there and started running. He could hear the sound of the Ambassador car's engine growling on the bridge.

8

Both had cleverly concealed the incident from people at home. Kanniyammal came down with a fever. But from the day after the incident, the mother-in-law kept screaming at them. That neither of them behaved like their normal selves made her suspicious. For all the grilling she did, she couldn't get a handle on what was going on. Initially, whenever he saw Kanniyammal, Maniyan would weep in secret. Laid up in bed with all colour drained from her face, Kanniyammal's grief became protracted on seeing her husband cry. At night, he hugged her tight and sobbed bitterly. She sought refuge in him like a child. Both of them were fearful, imagining that every night was fraught with danger. He took her to the free clinic nearby. Whenever they saw someone looking at them closely, they were reminded of that night. She covered her head whenever she went out of the house.

Kanniyammal, who resembled a chronic patient, started recuperating. When her period was delayed that month, she believed that God had rescued her from all kinds of evil. The news bestowed a new radiance on everyone in the family.

After she returned to normal health, Kanniyammal started doing the household chores. Maniyan watched her perform various tasks. She was pleasant and cordial in her interactions with people. This surprised and shocked Maniyan. He had expected that Kanniyammal would hang herself – that she would take her own life somehow. He indulged in extended fantasies like, after he had rendered all the services she needed during this difficult period, leading her to accept him as a good husband, she committed suicide and passed away, that he howled and wept from grief, and the villagers consoled him, and to compensate for his sorrow at losing his wife, his parents got him married to another girl, or that Kanniyammal remained a chronic patient and died eventually, and he contracted another marriage two years later.

After Kanniyammal started going for work in the fields, his fantasies died away entirely. She felt that Maniyan was gradually withdrawing from her. Then she consoled herself that it was her own imagination. At night, he unbuttoned her blouse and stared at her breasts in the light from a chimney lamp. No longer comfortable with such intimacy, she drew her sari over them. 'You are seeing my body like a stranger,' she said, turning over to lie face down, and cried inconsolably. During coitus, she felt that he was less equanimous now than he had been earlier. Many times, she noticed that his expression kept changing as he reached different levels of intensity. She began to be afraid. It was that fear which made her feel that he was moving away from her. Some days, after tossing and turning right next to her, without any forewarning he would abruptly start fucking her. She was troubled by a premonition that something bad was going to happen. After the third month passed, news of her pregnancy spread throughout the street.

Her mother-in-law started lamenting that a tortoise had entered her house, and her family would surely go to ruin from now on. 'So what if there were several men? Shouldn't a woman have run away?' she said. Kanniyammal became very angry with Maniyan. The house was in turmoil. Kanniyammal was bewildered. She didn't know what to do. Both had decided together to conceal their secret, but why had Maniyan spilled the beans first, without telling her? It confused her.

Not knowing exactly what he might have said about her, she believed that he had portrayed her in a very derogatory manner. For her part, her mother-in-law neither asked nor said anything about her own son. As if she had been treated unjustly, she lay sleepless at night at the doorway of their house with her elderly friends, exchanging conspiratorial whispers.

Gradually, everyone in the village came to know. Many imaginary versions of the incident began to circulate. Kanniyammal felt deeply ashamed even to step out into the street. Well, if she didn't step out, the villagers came to that house on their own, wanting to know what had happened. Except the family that was affected by the incident, most of them spoke in favour of Kanniyammal. The mother-in-law must have come to some decision in her mind. As though she was waiting to implement it, she sought advice from everyone who visited their house. She kept sniffling her nose as if she was the affected party.

Kanniyammal stopped talking to Maniyan. As arranged by her father-in-law, two young women kept her company, always, to make sure that Kanniyammal did not do anything untoward out of bitterness or frustration. He kept saying that she was no longer one person, but two. His general perspective on the incident had transcended the decisions made by his family. One day, as instructed by his mother, Maniyan took Kanniyammal to his father-in-law's house and left her there for what was to be her prime delivery. It was a big relief for Kanniyammal. She was happy that, in her house, she wouldn't have to encounter the faces and murmurs that sprouted behind her as she walked down the street to catch a bus.

9

On the third day after reaching home, Kanniyammal confessed everything to Kaliyan and broke down. Kaliyan felt a surge of pity for his daughter. Cursing the Almighty, he laid his hand on her shoulder and consoled her. Then he came to the front hall, hit himself repeatedly on the head and started sobbing like a small child. He went to Maniyan's house. 'Who was responsible for what happened?' Maniyan's father spoke in generalities. Kaliyan was not really pleased with what the mother-in-law said. She was very curt and rude. Kaliyan waited there because he wanted to meet Maniyan. Having returned from work, Maniyan saw Kaliyan's bicycle at the entrance of his house; he turned around immediately and parked himself in Karikalan's petty shop. Pointing out that Maniyan seemed to be delayed, the mother-in-law persuaded Kaliyan to leave. Kaliyan departed, pedalling his bicycle in the dark. He was crestfallen at not having been offered even a sombu of water to drink or something to eat in the house of his daughter's in-laws.

Weeks turned into months, but no one from the son-in-law's house came to visit Kanniyammal. Kaliyan was filled with dread. For Kanniyammal, not having to meet anyone from Maniyan's family was a relief. Kaliyan travelled back and forth on his bicycle between Maniyan's house and his own. He could not manage to meet Maniyan. Spending a little money, he went to the town where Maniyan ran his shop. He was able to meet Maniyan there. Maniyan fetched a stool for Kaliyan to sit on and bought him a cup of tea. His behaviour brought some degree of comfort to Kaliyan. But the problem of who should broach the matter first had surfaced awkwardly between them.

'At this time, when Kanniyammal is pregnant, she feels that it would do her good to see you often. She is a motherless child, as you are aware.'

Maniyan replied in a single word: 'Sure.'

Kaliyan brought his palms together as a mark of respect and took his leave.

They said the child looked like Kanniyammal. Everyone in her family was elated that it was a male child. As for speculations about the reason why Maniyan's family did not visit her, Kanniyammal put an end to them herself. She narrated boldly to anyone who asked her everything that had happened to them on that day. She had the courage to keep articulating what she felt in her heart was right. Kaliyan resigned himself to fate. He thought that he had done everything possible within his resources. None of the negotiations mediated by Aasiriyar and Sadasivam was effective. Even the minor confabulations held in the front pyol of his house failed to yield any outcome in Kaliyan's favour.

The mother-in-law stood firm in her stance. 'Why should my son look after a child sired by someone else?'

Sadasivam and Aasiriyar met Maniyan in his tailoring shop and spoke to him. When it appeared likely that he would consent to live with Kanniyammal, they suggested renting a house near Maniyan's shop and shifting the family there. They advised Kanniyammal too.

In the end, no one could dent Kanniyammal's resolve. 'It will be just me and my child for the rest of my life. I have no need of anyone's charity,' she told them.

None of the pleas advanced by Kaliyan on behalf of all parties found favour with Kanniyammal. As if she had turned her back on the whole world, Kanniyammal lay awake at night showering the child with care and affection. 'I have to admit you in a school,' she cooed to the child, 'and buy you a slate and notebooks. You will put on a shirt and trousers. You will study well like a good boy and grow up to be like our Appadorai Vathiyar.'

THE KNOWN, THE UNKNOWN

Sa. Kandasamy

TRANSLATED BY YASHASVI ARUNKUMAR

It felt like the car was flying at eighty kilometres per hour. It was an AC car, so the inside was cool. I leaned back comfortably. Light violin music played from the car's tape recorder. I like instrumental music better than vocals. As a child, I had wanted to learn the violin. But it was Appa who had stopped me. He was of the opinion that the arts posed a danger to succeeding in life. Chithappa, my father's younger brother, went to college to study law. But by his second year, he had fallen in love with the cinema. So he left his studies and started acting instead. He even acted in a couple of films. Then he married an actress. Once married, he fought with my father over splitting their inheritance. Appa gave him his share, and Chithappa never returned to our village again. Since then, Appa has feared the arts. And he spread that fear to everyone else in the family.

I tried to learn the violin after I joined the police force. I even went for violin classes for two months. I was happy. But then I was transferred to Thoothukudi. I brought the violin with me, along with the rest of my belongings. But it was bad timing – the riots started just after I moved. Three people were killed. More than sixty houses were set on fire. Eleven constables, four sub-inspectors, and one inspector were wounded and admitted to the hospital. As the Superintendent of Police, my workload increased. My violin simply stood collecting dust.

The car got off the bridge over Paalaaru. The bottle on the backseat rolled and fell. I bent down to pick it up.

'The road is smooth. We should be able to reach Manakkudi no later than five-thirty,' Vijayan observed.

I looked at my watch once before taking a gulp of water. It was warm water, with jeera. The warmth was soothing. All thanks to Vijayan.

Vijayan always brings water with him on journeys. He never drinks water from anywhere else. He fell sick with jaundice one time. The doctor told him it was because of contaminated water. He is the kind of person who strongly believes in doctors and science. He stopped drinking water from outside. As a police officer, I cannot really pay that much attention to these kinds of things. I handed the bottle to him after I was done.

The car slowed down abruptly. After making way for the lorry behind us, the car got off the highway and stopped under a tamarind tree on the side of the road. The driver got out of the car urgently. I suspected the car may need repair. I swiftly opened the door and stepped out. The driver had opened the hood and was peering inside. I turned back to look at the road. I could see that the oil had dripped all along the way.

'Driver, what is the issue?' Vijayan stepped out of the car as well.

'It is an oil leak, sir.'

'Is it the engine oil?'

'It is leaking from the oil sump, sir.'

'So the car won't run.'

'The mechanic has to come, sir.'

Vijayan turned to me. 'So we cannot reach Manakkudi by five like we thought.' I did not give him an answer. I stood, hands crossed, staring at the cars and lorries that zoomed past us on the highway.

'What is this, driver? You should have checked the vehicle's condition before travelling out of town. Instead, you stop in the middle of the road and announce there's an oil leak. How will we go now?' Vijayan was growing angrier by the second. The driver kept his head down, wiping away the oil stuck to his fingers. The driver was under Vijayan's employ. I felt like it would not be right for me to be around while the driver was being reprimanded. I turned around and started walking alongside the oil drips on the road.

This entire Manakkudi trip had been for my sake. My friend, auditor G.R. Dharmaraja, is in the real estate business. On the way to a plot in Kovur, he was in an accident in which his leg got fractured. He was now being treated by his younger brother, Giriraja, who is a bigshot doctor. I was planning to pay my friend a visit. I had happened to mention this in passing to Vijayan one day.

'Dr Giriraja is a very good friend of mine. Ever since he built his new hospital, he has been inviting me to come visit. But I never found the time. I can use this as an excuse to finally visit him,' he had offered.

I thought it was a good idea. So I agreed. Vijayan is the odd one out amongst all my friends. He does not reveal much of himself. He gets the job done quickly and vanishes without a trace immediately after. That is the reason I enjoy travelling with him.

Just as we were starting our journey, Vijayan had said, 'Giriraja is a good man. It is hard to find a man like him in these times. He won't know head or tail the moment he sees both of us. I am sure he will host a huge party for us. We will not be able to leave that very night, we will have to stay until the morning after.'

'I am not going to tell you anything about Dharmaraja,' I had replied. 'In four hours, you will find out for yourself. Nothing I say can fully describe him.'

'Really?' asked Vijayan.

Vijayan is the type of person who believes everything I say. Even the 'really?' was not an expression of doubt. It was his way of accepting my comment.

I took a short stroll and returned to the car. Vijayan was standing by its side, his arms crossed in front of him. His face bore a look of concern that our trip to meet Dharmaraja had run into such an obstacle. I am not the kind of person who gets upset over these things. I believe that whatever happens, happens. That is one of the reasons why Vijayan and I have been friends for the last seven years.

'The driver is an idiot. He's stranded us in the middle of the road now.'

'Right.'

'If he'd just told me in the morning, we could have taken Selvam's car. It's a new car, he bought it only last month.'

'The driver didn't know.'

'What did he not know? This is all just his complacency. As soon as we return, I am going to fire him.' As Vijayan spoke, the driver came back on a motorcycle with a mechanic.

The mechanic, wearing half-trousers, bent under the hood and checked the engine. The oil had collected into a little puddle. He turned to the driver and scrunched his lips. Vijayan could bear it no longer. He approached the mechanic.

'It is a crankcase leak, sir. The oil is empty. We have to remove the oil sump and fix it again with a gasket.'

When Vijayan stared at him, the mechanic continued: 'He is a good driver, sir. He stopped the car as soon as the oil started leaking. If the car had gone just a hundred feet more, the engine would have seized up.'

'Fine, when will the car be ready?'

'Around ten to ten-thirty in the morning, sir.'

Vijayan continued to stare him down.

'There are seven vehicles in the workshop, sir. On this highway – that side forty kilometres and this side thirty kilometres – we are the best, first-class mechanics. If any vehicle needs repairs, or if there's an accident, they come straight to our workshop. There may be a little delay, but our work is clean, sir.'

'We are on our way to meet someone urgently.'

'So what, sir? We have taxis. You can go and come back comfortably, sir. In that time, the vehicle will be pakka ready.'

Vijayan looked back at me.

'Leave the driver and go, sir. When you come back, the car will be ready,' the mechanic repeated.

Vijayan took out five hundred rupees from his purse and handed it to the driver.

I suddenly remembered Kattur Kokku Sami. Sami lived at the foot of the Kattur hill, on the banks of the Paavur lake. Kokku Sami was a mysterious man. It was very unusual for him to walk using both his legs. Keeping one leg folded, he would move around by hopping on the other leg. That's why they called him Kokku – 'crane' – Sami. Soon after, he became the Kattur Kokku Sami.

I have known Kokku Sami for only about nine months. I say 'known' very loosely. It was Dharmaraja who had first taken me to meet him. He had offered Kokku Sami two packets of beedis and one packet of biryani.

'Is it for me, sami?' Kokku Sami had asked.

'Yes, Sami,' said Dharmaraja.

Kokku Sami came hopping on one leg, happily took the biryani packet and hopped away towards a rock to eat it. I was astonished at the speed with which he ate. I kept looking back and forth between Kokku Sami and Dharmaraja. After he was done eating, Kokku Sami screeched twice like a crane, shook his arms up and down like they were wings, and started climbing up the hill. The way he climbed the hill, it really looked like he was flying. In just a short while, he had made it to the top.

'I don't know what happened, Sami has gone away,' commented Dharmaraja, holding my hands. Maybe he was upset that Sami had not spoken to me. 'This is how he is, sami. If he feels like it, he speaks to people, or sings songs. Otherwise, he simply stays silent. But I don't know why, today, he went back up the hill.'

'So what?' I reassured Dharmaraja. Yet, I felt a niggling sadness in my mind.

Six months later, I happened to pass by that route. So I went to see Sami by myself. I remembered Dharmaraja's words: 'No one knows where Sami came from. No one knows his name or anything about him. Even if someone goes to meet Sami, no one asks him his name, about his work, where he came from, about his relatives, anything.'

Sami spotted me from a distance. Pushing aside the wildflower creepers, he welcomed me, 'Come, sami.' There was no one around. It was only me and him. Monkeys were swinging from the branches overhead. Peacocks spread their wings in flight. I stood gazing around. Sami carefully opened the turkey biryani packet I had kept in front of him. Separating the rice, meat and egg from each other, he laughed. It was a kind of laugh I had never heard before. My entire body erupted in gooseflesh. I shook my head. Sami screeched like a crane two or three times. The peacocks and monkeys came closer to him. He grabbed handfuls of the rice and meat with both hands and scattered it in all directions. It felt as if the entire hilly landscape had been transformed.

'Vijaya, as soon as the taxi comes, let's go to Kattur and meet Kokku Sami before going to see Dharmaraja,' I proposed.

'Why do that? There is a bar inside the wine shop. Let us down two pegs instead and come back,' he responded. Vijayan is an atheist. He does not believe in gods, godmen, rituals, etc.

'Okay, then you stay. I will go and come back.'

'What do I do in the meantime?'

The taxi came to a stop near us.

'You stay in the bar. I will be back in half an hour.'

I got into the taxi. Sitting behind the driver, I turned to Vijayan and repeated. 'Stay in the bar. I'll be there soon.'

The driver was about to put the car in gear. I don't know what Vijayan had going on in his mind but he hurriedly got into the car. That made me happy. I lightly patted his back. He turned towards me and laughed.

The taxi stopped in front of the Mahua tree in the Kattur bat grove. A number of bats were hanging upside down from its branches. Huge, huge fruit bats. If there was ever a feast in my eldest uncle's house, they would serve bat meat. I tried my first bat meat without knowing what it was. I had tasted a slight difference. When I finished eating, I asked my aunt about it. She told me it was bat meat. I never ate bat meat after that.

Under the tree, next to the fence, there was a board: 'Bat hunting is prohibited in this area. Shooting and catching bats is a punishable offence. Offenders will be penalized with a fine of one thousand rupees and/or three months jail.' Vijayan made me wait for a minute while he read the board before following me. I pushed the vines aside before walking along the narrow trail. In the distance, I could see the wide lake and the hill.

'This is the first time I have been in these parts,' Vijayan confessed. He kept looking at the wild prickly pears, veldt grapes and bimbi plants that had grown along the way. The trail twisted and turned. From atop a short mango tree, two peacocks screeched and landed on the ground.

The sound of the peacocks echoed from the walls of the ruins of the Kattur Mandapam. As I walked on, I looked in every direction for any sight of Kokku Sami.

Kattur Kokku Sami was not someone who could sit in one place for long. He was always moving around. On some days, he would climb the mango tree and hang upside down like a bat from it. On some others, he would dive into the lake and stay there, submerged up to his neck. On yet some other days, he would hop around on one leg. There was no way of telling what he could be doing on any given day. I have seen more than twenty different Samis. Kokku Sami was the most unique one of them all.

'This godmen-craze is the curse of our society. There must be something lacking in our society if despite all our efforts to eradicate these evils, these Samis have persisted,' Vijayan kept murmuring as we walked.

'Just like we know some things,' I took one step forward, 'we don't know many others.'

The leaves rustled. I held Vijayan back with my left hand. A peacock pecking on the ground let out a terrible screech and flew to the beech tree.

'What?' asked Vijayan.

'A cobra! Must have been six, six and a half feet.'

'Oh, but I didn't see…?' There was a tinge of doubt and disbelief in his tone.

I walked ahead without responding. Sami stood leaning against a palm tree right next to the ruined Mandapam, his arms crossed. There was not much difference between the tree and him. His black hair hung in dreadlocks around him. Black body. A dirty towel was wrapped around his waist, up to his knees. I could not deduce if he was asleep or awake.

Stopping opposite him, I called out, 'Sami.'

He looked at me and laughed. Those white teeth looked terrifying. I shook my head and brought my hands together in reverence.

'Have you come, sami?' he asked. The magnetism in his voice seemed to sink right into my soul.

'What, Sami?' I was confused.

'There was some drama yesterday, sami.' He broke into a thunderous laughter. The sound of that laughter echoed through the entire forest. Peacocks took flight in terror. Monkeys started jumping from one tree to another in fear.

I turned to look behind me. Vijayan stood holding my shoulder tightly. It seemed like he too was frightened.

'Is that so, Sami?'

'It was all a big joke, sami.' Kokku Sami sat down. He gestured to us to sit down. I sat down opposite him, Vijayan to my left.

'It must have been around this time yesterday, sami. Two police samis came. They told me that Inspector Ayya was asking to see me.

'I asked them: "Me, sami?"

'As soon as they said, "Yes, Sami," I immediately went to the police station with them. The inspector was getting into his jeep just then.

'When he saw me, he threw me a glare. He got into the jeep and left after instructing the others, "Lock him up, I will come back and deal with him." They made me sit in one corner, sami. I sat there quietly, looking around.

'One sami came and saw me, and told the others, "Why, da, why have you made the Sami sit near this stench of urine? Seat him in the back over there." When I went there, I could hear the sound of beating. One lady ran out crying. I could not remain seated, sami. I got up and started pacing. Later, one sami came and told me that Inspector Ayya was calling for me. I went and stood in front of him. He did not even look at me. He kept talking to the others, pretending he hadn't seen me. I stood on one side by myself. After they left, he turned towards me. He wagged one finger at me, his left hand, and called me forward, "Come here."

'I stood in front of him and asked, "What, sami?"

'Inspector Ayya looked me up and down once before questioning, "So for how many years have you been walking around in this guise?"

'I told him, I don't know, sami. That's all. But he got really angry.

'He slapped me. "What do you mean by you don't know, huh? How dare you fool around with me!" It looked like his hand really hurt because of that slap. Shaking it a few times, he turned to me again. "What happened yesterday evening?"

'I replied, "Inspector Ayya only should tell me."

'He kicked my hip. "What, da, you think you are so great?" I stood still. He shook the leg with which he had kicked me a couple of times, sami. I continued watching him, standing wherever I was. The more I saw him, sami, the sorrier I felt for him.

'Inspector Ayya leaned against a wall. Twirling his moustache with his left hand, he spoke again. "I will tell you what happened, you tell me if I am right."

'What could I say? I continued to stare at him.

'"Yesterday, two thieves came to the Kattur Mandapam, dug a hole near it, buried all their stolen jewellery, and told you to keep watch. You kept guard over them. Later that night, they came back, took the jewellery and left. While leaving, they gave you a packet of biryani. And you gobbled it all up greedily, your mouth watering." After saying all this, he looked at me menacingly.

'"I ate the biryani," I said.'

Sami laughed, before continuing.

'I didn't know what else to say, sami. I remained there, continuing to stare at Inspector Ayya. He kept saying many things. I didn't say a word, I just stood listening, sami. Finally, as if he had remembered something, he asked me, "Who all do you know?"'

I kept looking at Vijayan's reactions.

'I told them your name, sami. Inspector Ayya was taken aback, he stuttered, asking me how I knew you. How can one answer that kind of question, sami? I simply nodded back. "I know him, that's all."'

I am the Superintendent of Police. But I had never told Sami that.

'He asked me again, "Who else do you know?" I told him I knew him, sami.

'He was terrified. He asked, "Me? What do you know about me?" I didn't give him an answer. If I know something, does that mean I should tell it to everyone, sami? I remained quiet and simply kept standing, sami.

'I don't know what occurred to Inspector Ayya after that, but he called two police samis, asked them to get me a biryani, and chased me away. I thought of you and came back.'

I didn't know what to say. So I handed him the packet of beedis. He took it and turned it this way and that. Happiness spread over his face. He pulled out one beedi and held it out to Vijayan. After hesitating for a moment, Vijayan accepted it. Sami gave me one as well. I accepted it and put it in my mouth. He lit it for me. I blew out the smoke. He lit another beedi for himself.

Vijayan continued looking at both of us in turns. I lit his beedi for him.

'Good friendship,' commented Sami.

Vijayan does not smoke beedis. He coughed a couple of times. His eyes started watering. Holding the beedi in his hand, he looked at Sami. Sami's eyes were shut as he puffed out the beedi smoke.

The wind was chilly as it blew over us. A peacock spread its wings and screeched. As the sky darkened, it looked like it would soon start to rain.

Vijayan pressed his palms to the ground and lifted himself up.

I turned to the Sami and bowed to him, hands clasped.

Kattur Kokku Sami bid us farewell. 'Come again, sami.'

I never leave before he gives me leave to go. But the Sami has never made me wait even a minute longer than I would want. Maybe he had lots more to take care of than I did. He would always quickly dismiss anyone who came to see him.

THE KNOWN, THE UNKNOWN

I turned around. Vijayan took a step forward. I joined him on the narrow trail once again, pushing away the wild physic nut bushes on the way, thinking about the Sami's mysterious ways.

Fifteen days ago, Inspector Ravindradas had come to my office. He had received a suspension. According to a complaint filed by the Human Rights Commission, he had been temporarily removed from his posting. After reading that order, I had given it back to him without a word.

'Kattur Kokku Sami spoke a lot about you, sir,' he had said.

I had looked up at him.

'One of our constables brought the Sami to our station one day. It was me who got him a biryani and sent him back respectfully, sir.'

'Oh really?'

'He is a big Sami, sir, he performs many miracles. But no one really knew about his powers.'

I walked ahead wondering what happened to Ravindradas after our meeting that day. We came by a tiny brook. Vijayan jumped across the stream. A water snake was swimming speedily against the current. Seeing that, Vijayan held his hand out in front. 'There's a snake, be careful, sami.'

'Okay, sami.' I took his hand and crossed over to the other side of the stream.

The snake vanished from sight.

CYCLE

Charu Nivedita

TRANSLATED BY NANDINI KRISHNAN

T HE SIGHT OF the crowd before my house sent my heart straight into my mouth. It was only when I drew closer that I realized they had gathered before the house across from mine.

Rupavati's husband was raging away.

'I'll hit you', 'I'll stab you', 'I'll punch you', 'I'll kill you', 'I'll tear you to pieces…' and several other threats and words that are not suitable for publication barraged from his angry mouth.

His opponent was the wife of Shanmugham from the next street. Some ten to fifteen others were engaged in holding the two back from a violent fight. One got the impression they were ready to fly at each other's throats and wrestle right there on the road. If their restrainers let go, they might just roll about on the dust. Or, they might lose all enthusiasm for the fight and go about their own respective businesses. One can never tell with such things.

Screaming at the other had taken a toll on the voice box of each. Rupavati's husband now shouted in a high-pitched woman's voice, and Shanmugham's wife in a man's baritone. Either because the restrainers were too tired to hold on any longer, or because the fight had lost its panache, a sense of ennui hit everyone at some point. The audience began to lose its strength, bit by bit.

If I were to say Rupavati's beauty lived up to her name, I'd be lying. That said, she wasn't exactly ugly. She was a little taller than the average woman. She had piercing eyes and a charming laugh. We don't know which of these assets had infatuated Shanmugham, but he was entirely besotted with Rupavati, to the extent that he threw aside the running of his shop.

Rupavati had two sons. The elder was in Class 8, and the younger in Class 5. Her husband worked as a driver in a government department. He was often out of town, on what he claimed were inspection tours with officers. Even if he was in town, the 'side business' he ran, as a real estate broker, ensured that he was rarely home before ten o'clock at night. He had a motorcycle to get around.

However, it appeared his wife preferred a bicycle. And if that cycle belonged to Shanmugham, its appeal was heightened.

Soon after the roar of the motorcycle signalled her husband's departure from the house, the bell of the cycle would herald Shanmugham's arrival at Rupavati's door. He would sound the bell before he got off the cycle, one leg on the ground and the other on a pedal. The moment the bell rang, no matter where she was, Rupavati would run outside, blushing and giggling. (She would actually run. If one saw her then, one wouldn't guess she was the mother of a pre-teen boy. She would run and skip with the abandon of a schoolgirl.) Sometimes, Shanmugham would simply chat for a couple of minutes, without bothering to get off his cycle, and be on his way. At others, he would lean the cycle against the wall of the house and go inside.

I've observed all this from my window, where I stand to shave. On the occasion curiosity led me to peep outside, my wife would say, 'Why are you so interested in other people's lives?' and close the window. When she did this, I was forced to switch on the light so I could shave without nicking myself.

'Why can't those lovebirds divorce their spouses and marry each other?' I once asked my wife.

'Where do you think we are, America? Keep quiet now. What will people think if they hear you talk like this?' she said.

She had a point. I remember reading a report in a foreign newspaper. A judge made his quotidian entry into the court premises and was startled by the number of couples he saw lined up. He then figured he knew what the matter was and said kindly, 'Ladies and gentlemen, you seem to have got the addresses mixed up – this is not the marriage registrar's office, this is the court.' The couples chorused, 'Sorry, milord, but we know this is the court. We are all here to get our divorces.'

Once the fight was done with and the street had quietened down, I ascertained that my wife was in a good mood and put myself to some trouble to sound disinterested as I asked her what the morning's duel had been about.

'I know your head will burst unless I tell you,' my wife said. 'Rupavati's husband found them out. Hence the drama.'

It struck me that the husband was always the last to learn of such things.

From that day forward, the clash between the cuckold and the cuckquean became a daily affair.

'Keep your wife in check,' Shanmugham's wife said.

'If your husband steps foot in here, I'll eviscerate him,' Rupavati's husband said.

No one bothered to separate them now.

Their argument was bookended by Shanmugham's wife gathering fistfuls of dust from the road and throwing them at Rupavati's house, cursing. She contrived to do all this with her one-year-old infant on her hip.

Even as the spouses fought, I never failed to spot Shanmugham's cycle in the house opposite.

'Nowadays, the cycle is there through the day,' my wife offered up, even before I could ask.

Things were going on as usual when, one fine day, the police arrived and took Shanmugham away. Apparently, Shanmugham told them it was Rupavati who kept badgering him to visit and had written him reams of letters to that effect. He even came back home to get them and produced them as evidence at the police station, I heard. Literally heard, for Shanmugham's wife would wail about it all as she stood before Rupavati's house and hurled mud at it, every day.

The police then came for Rupavati. Her husband accompanied her to the station.

When the couple returned, I happened to be passing their house. (My wife would object to my claim that this was a coincidence. My telling her it was a Sunday and I didn't have much to do but wander the street wouldn't cut much ice with her.)

Rupavati's husband beamed at me. His smile appeared victorious. He seemed to be aching to tell me something. I grinned back at him. As if I'd just given him the green light, he poured it all out.

'Saar, do you know what she told them at the police station? "I have no idea who that lout is. He comes to our house all the time and harasses me," she said,' Rupavati's husband told me, pointing at his wife with great pride.

'Then, what about the letters your wife wrote him?' I was tempted to ask, but having mulled it over for an instant and concluded that it wouldn't have been the most nuanced response to what he had said, I went instead with, 'Oh, is that so? Well, then.' I gave him a grand nod, and then went homewards.

Word on the street was that the police had warned Shanmugham that they would skin him alive if he so much as showed his face at Rupavati's door.

However, we realized just how serious things were when the cycle continued to make its daily appearance at Rupavati's home. Although it was none of my business, the sight of the infant at Shanmugham's wife's hip gnawed at my insides.

Then, the police came for Shanmugham again. Rupavati's husband had greased the right palms, we heard.

By evening, the street was rife with the rumour that Shanmugham had been stripped naked at the police station and beaten to within an inch of his life. Could this be true? Several of the neighbours claimed to have seen it for themselves. Some bravehearts made their way to the police station to ascertain the facts.

I mustered the courage to join them.

The rumour turned out to be the truth. Shanmugham lay all in a heap, his skin shining with bruises and torn to reveal flesh in several places. He was buck naked, thrown like garbage outside the police station. Some of his neighbours wound a cloth around his waist and took him home in a rickshaw.

The next day, as I returned from office, I saw a crowd gathered outside Shanmugham's door. I rushed to see what the fuss was about.

Shanmugham was hanging from the crossbeam. Several of our neighbours were engaged in the effort of cutting his large body down from the beam.

The cycle lay abandoned on the road outside his home.

FOOTBALL AND HER

Sureshkumara Indrajith

TRANSLATED BY YASHASVI ARUNKUMAR

He was fair-skinned, with a clean-shaven head and catlike eyes. 'Name?' I asked. He did not speak. His wife, who was standing near the bed, answered instead. 'His name is Pidrik.' She wore a cheap cotton sari. A dirty thali hung on her neck. She had glowing black skin and a sturdy body.

He corrected her, 'Frederick Johnson,' with perfect English pronunciation. I realized he was Anglo-Indian. Next to his pillow, an English novel lay face down, open on the page he had been reading.

It was as if the woman had noticed me observing their dissimilarity. 'My husband,' she let me know. 'How is he doing?' I asked. 'His thoughts are no longer on the drink. But it's not like he can leave the hospital to get some, no? I don't know what he'll do once he comes back home. I hope he'll behave,' she replied. 'Have they taken good care of him?' I enquired. She laughed and said, 'Very good.' Her body gleamed as if anointed in oil. When she laughed, her charms increased.

I moved on to the next bed. My friend Dr Devasagayam had been inviting me for a long time to visit the De-Addiction Centre run by him. So there I was. I called the attendant and asked for more information about the couple.

'He's some mix with Anglo-Indian, sir. His wife's name is Madathi. Do you see the combination! His father was a Thevar, used to work as a surveyor. His mother was Anglo-Indian. Somehow, sparks flew between the two of them. Apparently all his relatives have moved away to Australia. He works as a watchman in a school. His missus had come as a construction worker when the school built an additional building. Sparks flew here also.' He chuckled.

'You must have noted down his father's name in the register, right? Can you check and tell me what it is?' I said.

He went off, checked the register and returned to say, 'His father's name was Easwaran alias Davidson.'

I had had a hunch when the attendant told me about the man's family history, but it was now confirmed. 'I know his father. He used to work for me. I have seen his mother as well,' I told him.

Many years ago, I used to work a government job. On one particular day, I had taken the jeep out for some personal errands before arriving at the office. I had been sweating. After requesting for some tea to be sent to my room, I took out the packet of peanuts I kept in my table drawer. I crushed the peanuts inside the packet, took them near the window, and blew on them. The outer skin of the peanuts came off and fell on either side of the window. Gathering the now bare peanuts, I put them back inside the packet and stashed the packet inside the drawer. Keeping the drawer half open, I started munching on the peanuts.

Just then, one of the office assistants entered the room and informed me that a 'shirt-woman' had come to see me. Why would such a woman want to see me, I wondered. I told the assistant to let her in. An Anglo-Indian woman clad in a gown came inside. There was a boy with her. She wore lipstick: a fair woman of average beauty.

She had a black mole on her left cheek. Below her knees, her hairless legs showed white. She wore high heels.

'I am Easwaran's wife, he works under you,' she told me in English. I did not understand what she wanted.

'Which Easwaran are you talking about? Isn't he a Thevar?'

'Yes, he changed his name to Davidson and married me. Here is the ring he gave me.' She showed me the ring on her finger.

I realized what had happened. It appeared that Easwaran was keeping this woman on the side. I asked her what the matter was.

'He does not come home these days. He hasn't given us any money either. You are the only one who can talk to him and set him right,' she said.

'I will try talking to him and help you as much as I can. How did you come to marry him?' I asked.

'That man is a football player,' she started in English. 'Don't you know?' Her face brightened with just these words. I told her I did not.

Her narration shifted into elegant English.

'Have you not seen the way he dribbles the ball with his handsome legs? He used to dance with it! His game was so beautiful. He'd wear those football shorts, and when he kicked the ball, his calves would jiggle. No one could steal the ball from him. I cannot describe the grace with which his legs and the ball would move in tandem. The ball seemed to seduce his ankles. And then, when it did part from him, it would escape the goalie's advances, reach the goal and mock everyone else. What a player!'

I was astonished at her openness. I was just a stranger, someone she did not know. But I got the impression that this was how she could speak about his game, and that if she had the chance, she would say even more.

What luck that Easwaran has! The boy has managed to bewitch this woman with a football, I thought.

After speaking a while about more general matters, she took her leave. When she was leaving, I stared at her white legs. Her son turned to look at me, waved, and followed his mother out. Cat-eyes, reddish-brown hair, Easwaran's son.

That day, Easwaran did not come to work. He only came the following day. I called him to my room and asked him to sit down. It seemed the others in the office had already informed him of the woman's visit. He sat squirming, as if embarrassed. I asked about her.

'Ten years ago, I used to go to Railway Colony to play football on the grounds. Back then, football matches used to happen every day. It's rare to see a match there these days – if it happens, it happens. I've been a football player since I was young. It's only now that I can't play like I used to. Back in those days, she would come every day with her friends to watch. We'd drink water from her house. After the game was over, they'd serve us tea. Ginger tea. It used to be so tasty. One day, when I was alone, she praised my playing and offered me her hand. After that, we started meeting regularly. We used to go to the Regal Talkies to watch films. Things progressed from there. I married her.'

'Does your first wife know about this?' I asked.

'She does. If I don't go home even for a day, she scrunches her face and tortures me.'

'Of course she would. Which woman would willingly give up her husband? But shouldn't you be taking care of this girl too?'

'You know my situation. My income's gone down. That's why I'm trying to move to another office.'

'Give her at least something. Aren't they also dependent on you?'

'She works in a school. She will make some money one way or another. But the one in my house stays at home. Where will she go for money? … Okay, okay, I'll adjust somehow and send some money. I've put in a request for the GPF. You have to sign the form.'

'Where is it?'

'It's right here.' He found the file and handed it to me. I signed it and gave it back to him.

Within a few months, he shifted to another office with better pay. When he bid his farewells, I spoke to him again. 'Please take care of both your families.' A few months later, on the day before Christmas, he came over to invite me home for lunch. I went.

The house was decorated with colourful serial lights for Christmas. A picture of Yesu hung in the front room. The house was clean and tasteful. Photos of Easwaran and his wife in their wedding attire hung on the walls. Her father was ill and stayed in one room in the house. He went back to his room after greeting me. They showed me around the house. I was quite surprised by it all. In the bedroom, two footballs lay on the bed. I could not stop thinking about them.

Before lunch, she poured wine into two fancy wineglasses and offered them to Easwaran and me. Then she took a glass, poured herself some wine and spoke to us while twirling the glass in her hand.

They had prepared biryani. They did not seem to have plain rice or curd. I did not ask for it either. They did have raita for the biryani. While we ate, I wanted to hear her talk more about his football skills. She spoke casually in English. Her fluency and pronunciation were attractive.

'I did not have the chance to watch him play back in those days,' I told her in English.

'Yes. His game had a beauty of its own. Everyone except him would vanish from my sight. He would dribble the ball while his calves would contract. Yesu Himself must have blessed him to play football. He usually wore blue-coloured drawers – the colour of the clouds. After all, he played football in the skies. How many goals he's shot! The entire stadium would blush when he walked in. Have you ever seen flowers blush? Fear would grip the hearts of those who were supposed to play against him. It was like their feet were tied. The football would nip teasingly at his ankles. He would walk on the ball. Stand on it. He would boost the ball up with his feet and send it flying to the goal using his head. The ball looked pleased when it stayed at his heels. And it would move at the slightest touch of his foot! You wouldn't even notice he'd touched it. When you kick a ball, it moves a particular distance depending on the force of the kick. But when he kicked it, I would see the ball go farther than I thought possible. It was a mystery how it happened. It was all Yesu's grace.' She kept talking while drinking her wine and twirling the glass between her fingers. I did not know if Easwaran understood everything she said. He didn't know English very well. All his attention was devoted to relishing the meat on the bone from the biryani.

I asked after their son. She told me that he was at the neighbour's house, that he spent all his time there, and that it was the house of her periyamma. Just as I was about to leave, the boy returned home with a friend. He had on a coat, suit and tie. He seemed like a lively child. He turned to me and held out a hand, speaking in English, 'Hi, uncle, glad to meet you.' I shook his hand.

A few months after that dinner, I was transferred to another town. I no longer had any contact with Easwaran, he was not even in my thoughts. It has now been two years since my retirement. One day, I happened to come across someone from the survey department. I enquired about Easwaran. He told me that Easwaran passed away a few years back.

After urging the attendant to take good care of this Frederick Johnson, I went back to the boy himself, Easwaran's son. He was now reading an English novel. Madathi stood up from her stool the moment she noticed me.

I spoke to him directly. 'Your father used to work with me. I just found out. I came to your house many years ago, on Christmas eve, when your father had invited me over for lunch. You were only a small boy then. Where is your mother now?'

'Appa abandoned our family long ago. Amma died even before my father did. He did not even come for her funeral.' He took out a framed photograph from under his pillow and held it out to me. 'This was my mother.'

In the photograph, his mother stood hugging a football.

SCREENING

Aravindan

TRANSLATED BY YASHASVI ARUNKUMAR

When Padmanabhan woke up, he looked all around him dazed. He couldn't make out where he was. He could hear the sound of a moving vehicle. A few familiar faces became noticeable. Padmanabhan rubbed his eyes. He looked out the window. It was bright outside. He realized the vehicle was moving fast. It was a train, and he had boarded it the previous night. His head cleared. When he tried to sit up, the berth above hit his head. He hunched down and carefully stepped down from his berth. A number of his relatives were packed into the opposite and adjacent berths. Keerthivasan, Geetha, Vembu, Krishnaveni, Krishnan…

Padmanabhan rubbed his eyes once more. He smiled in their general direction. One or two of them smiled back at him lightly. He was fully awake now, the events of the past few days coming back to him: *We are returning from Ganesan's wedding in Tirunelveli. Vatsala was not feeling well; Radhika had a college exam. So Krithika and I went to the wedding by ourselves. Our relatives came along with us. The train is now approaching Chennai…* 'Where is Krithika?' Padmanabhan turned to Keerthivasan for a response. Keerthi responded slowly,

'She is standing near the door.' Nobody else was talking. He was surprised to see the usually chatty group sitting in silence.

The train approached Tambaram. Padmanabhan went to the toilet. He brushed his teeth. Why is Krithika not near the entrance, he asked himself. Maybe she is standing at the entrance on the other side of the bogie. When he returned to his seat, he took out their luggage and arranged the bags neatly. Everyone else too sorted their own luggage; and then checked again for any misplaced belongings. No one said a word. Padmanabhan was astonished. But it was not his practice to question people on their silences. He remained silent too. He quietly wondered why Krithika had not returned to her seat yet.

No one said anything even after alighting at Egmore railway station. Each of them hailed their autos and taxis and left without a word. Padmanabhan was confused when Krithika continued to remain silent. He asked her, 'What happened? It was a wedding we went to, wasn't it? Why is everyone acting as if it was a funeral instead?' Krithika did not respond. She did not even look at him. She carried her own bag and walked straight ahead. Padmanabhan, now more confused than before, followed her. He had never seen Krithika in such a state before. He wondered if their family had had a fight while he had been asleep. Had Vembu or Krishnan said something offensive? Or maybe Krithika fought with Geetha? Padmanabhan could not make sense of anything.

When he got inside the auto, he phoned his sister's husband, Keerthivasan. He did not answer. He tried calling Krishnan and Vembu; they did not answer either. He tried asking Krithika in a slightly angry tone. She did not offer him any response.

When they reached home, his mind became occupied with leaving for work. He left as usual.

Padmanabhan was someone who observed a sense of discipline in everything he did. In all his social circles, be it family, friends or office colleagues, his image was equal parts duty, patience, honesty and dignity. Systematically organized daily tasks; actions full of patience, propriety and dignity; even-toned speech; helpful character; one could list Padmanabhan's virtues on and on. He would wake up every day around six. Even on days of extreme cold or rain, his habit would not change. Sundays and holidays too were not exempt. Vatsala had tried telling him many times to sleep in a little bit longer but he would laugh each time. 'But I just can't stay asleep any longer, what am I to do?' Even when he was up early, he would never disturb others' sleep. He would creep out, catlike, and shut the door to the bedroom before completing his morning ablutions and making himself a cup of coffee. After a fifteen-minute walking routine, he would return to read the newspaper. He had read only *The Hindu* from a young age. After shaving, he would then read the news on his phone. Then there would be a few phone calls. He would open his computer next and look at his emails before reading international newspapers online. Once that was done, he would turn on the TV and watch the news. Mostly BBC or NDTV. Then he would go to the kitchen and help around. Or he would go to the shop to buy whatever was needed that day: coconuts, maybe some chillies, sometimes bread. Then he would leave for his office.

Even in selecting his clothes for the office, he followed a strict system. Each day of the week was organized into a specific clothing style and colour. Depending on the colour of his trousers, the shoes and belt would be changed. On Fridays, he wore dark-coloured shirts. Saturdays were for T-shirts, and they were always collared. The colour of the pen in his shirt pocket would depend on the colour of the shirt. In the evenings and on holidays, he could be found watching cricket or tennis or Discovery Channel or National Geographic.

Vatsala could not believe her ears. She would not have believed it if she had heard it from anyone else except Krithika. In all these years, such a word had never come out of Padhu's mouth. Vatsala knew better than anyone that it was impossible for him to use such a word. Even in their moments of intimacy, his speech never turned crude. When they had just been married, before having children, Vatsala herself had crossed many limits of propriety. But Padmanabhan had never once spoken out of bounds. Even in the dizzying heights of their cosying up, his language had remained polite. When she saw pleasure overtake him, Vatsala would expect him to say something. But Padmanabhan maintained his boundaries strictly.

When talking about intimate matters, his language would remain discreet. He would avoid speaking directly about sex or sexual attraction. When the family would go out for a movie, and the girls would be giggling between themselves about love and romance, he would pretend to not notice. Krithika would say something just to get a raise out of her father. But he would never fall for her trap. He would just say 'Naughty girls,' give a small smile, and move on.

When she started narrating the events from the train to her mother, Krithika could not control her tears. Vatsala was confused and concerned; she shook her daughter, cajoled her to tell her what had happened. 'I don't know how to tell you, Amma,' Krithika spoke hesitantly before it all came out. Vatsala struggled to make sense of it all. She screamed at her daughter, 'What are you blabbering on about? Have you gone mad?' Krithika leaned on her mother's shoulder and cried, 'I promise this is what happened, Amma, how could I lie about something like this?'

Krithika could not forget that moment. As soon as it happened, everyone's gazes had turned towards her. Krithika had teared up and bowed her head in shame. She had left abruptly and locked herself inside the toilet. She felt flustered. She did not know how she could step back outside and face everyone. She held her handkerchief to her mouth and sobbed into it, muffling her tears. Disgust and helplessness consumed her. After a long time, with a lot of effort, she calmed herself down, washed her face and stepped out. Geetha and Krishnan stood right next to the toilet, worrying. Avoiding their gaze, Krithika opened the entrance to the bogie and looked outside.

Krithika was struggling to breathe as she finished narrating her story. Vatsala was frozen. She still could not believe it. But since it was Krithika herself who was narrating it, she couldn't not believe it either. It was common for Padmanabhan to talk in his sleep. On those rare days when he would wake up slightly later, he would blab about something or the other. 'Is the coffee ready?', 'Who won the toss?', 'Have you paid the EB bill?', 'Bring me my purse…', 'Where is the toothpaste?' The three of them would laugh at him. They would not wake him up just so he would speak some more nonsense and they could tease him later. He would often say the same thing in different tones. If he said, 'Bring me my purse', he would say the same thing forcefully, slowly, urgently, with some light distress, and in many other ways, and then he would jerk his eyes open. He would blink like a man who had gone to bed in his house and woken up deep in the forest the next day. After that, he would get out of bed and begin his daily tasks. There would be no trace of his blabbering from before. His customary manners would return to him naturally. He would be drinking his coffee when Radhika would bring up what he had said and tease him. That is when he would find out about it himself. Embarrassed, he would just smile and return to reading his newspaper.

Vatsala thought about his words and where they had been uttered. She turned speechless. Her heart felt empty, her eyes teary. She felt sick from her stomach.

As far as Vatsala knew, Padmanabhan had never really admired any woman. He had never been seduced by their glamour or beauty. She had never seen him pay more than a second's attention to the glamorous pictures in newspapers. Vatsala had seen him change the channel when item songs would play on TV. That was his habit, not only when there were children around, but even when he was watching by himself. Once, Vatsala had purposely pointed to an actress and asked, 'Isn't she sexy?' But Padmanabhan had only responded with, 'Sexiness is based on one's perception. I can only think that she looks fit.' Vatsala had replied, 'What do you know? She has so many fans only because of her figure.' Padmanabhan would not offer any further comment. Some days, he would spend hours on the computer watching films. Vatsala had peeped in out of doubt a few times without him noticing. Not even once had there been a porn film playing, or even a sex scene.

Even though Vatsala herself did not watch such films, she was still worldly enough to know things. It is not like she did not understand what the men in her office would discuss secretively amongst themselves. She had also heard her female colleagues talk casually about pornographic films. Even though she herself had seen a few such films in her youth, it had all stopped after marriage. That Padmanabhan was such a saint had in some ways restricted Vatsala as well. She had been astonished when the married women in the office spoke freely about such matters and when she learned they also watched these films with their husbands at home. She could not even fathom talking about it with Padhu. That a man like that would behave in this way! That he would say such a thing! The mere thought of it made her retch. Even more pressingly, the question 'Him?' kept repeating in her mind.

None of their family who were on the train that day had called Krithika or Vatsala. There were no messages either. Usually, there would be at least one call every day from someone or the other. Just from the way Radhika looked at Vatsala and Krithika after returning from college, they could tell she knew. The news was starting to spread. Radhika only asked, 'Did it really happen, Krithi?' Krithika nodded. Radhika sat down, stumped. The three of them did not say a word to each other.

When he returned home that night, Padmanabhan remembered the weird events from the morning. He noted how silent the house was, it reminded him of how everyone had been silent on the train too. Even Krithika had not spoken to him. When he tried to say anything, he only got one-word responses. It used to be that even before he could ask her what was for dinner, Vatsala would tell him, 'I made chapati and channa masala tonight', 'I have made lemon sevai', 'Today it's dosai and chutney'. But this time, Vatsala only nodded slightly, gestured him towards the food, and left him alone. When he served himself the food and sat down at the dining table, Radhika and Krithika stood up and left for their bedrooms. It was clear that the three of them were hiding something. But he couldn't fathom what it was they would not share with him. No matter how hard he tried, he could not figure it out.

He tried asking Vatsala privately. That did not lead to anything. She refused to look him in the eye, just said 'Nothing' and moved away. Padmanabhan was not the type to probe or cause a commotion around situations. He worried if Radhika was in crisis. He tried calling Keerthivasan, Vembu, Krishnan and Geetha once again. Only Geetha answered. Her voice did not sound all right. 'I am outside. I'll talk to you later, Chithappa,' she said and cut the call. Padmanabhan was stunned.

He could see that something big had happened. Something serious enough for everyone to collectively avoid him. But he did not know what it was. Did someone say something horrible about him? But what was there to say? Even after much thought, he could not think of a single negative thing someone could say about him. He could not think of anyone who might hold a grudge against him. His mind drew a blank. Love, money, work – he had not gone against anyone for anything. He had never been caught in any troublesome situation. Whether it was anger or desire, he had long learnt to lock it away inside himself. After so many years of such discipline, what kind of disgrace was this?

The more he pondered, the more Padmanabhan felt as if his head would explode. He thought of writing a letter explaining his situation and disappearing. But where could he go? It felt as if it would be better to be gone forever. As more time passed, the thought grew stronger. He decided to try one last time. Whatever happened must have happened on the train. Out of everyone there, Keerthivasan was the eldest and most responsible. Padmanabhan would try reaching out to him one more time, and if he did not get a response, he would have no choice but to take the next step.

He took his mobile phone and typed patiently. In clear and concise English, he wrote:

Dear Keerthi, I can see that I have done something wrong. But I don't know what it is. This is killing me on the inside. If I knew what happened, I could make amends. But I am being punished without even knowing my crime. It would be easier for me to die instead. I am not saying this lightly, I hope you understand. If I don't hear from you in two days, you will no longer see me alive. That is a promise.

After sending off that message, Padmanabhan felt his mind calm down. Keerthi called him within the next ten minutes. He asked to meet alone. They met that very evening.

'I think you should see a psychiatrist,' said Keerthivasan, right at the outset.

'First tell me what happened, Keerthi,' Padmanabhan replied. 'Tell me what it is. And then admit me to a mental hospital or sentence me to death, I will accept whatever you say.'

'I don't know where to start, this is new for me as well.' Keerthivasan was hesitant.

'You have to tell me one way or another,' said Padmanabhan. Keerthivasan took a deep breath and started speaking.

It was dawn by the time the train had reached Chengalpattu. Everyone was waking up by then. They finished their morning ablutions one by one and returned to their seats. Padmanabhan, who was on the middle berth, was still fast asleep. Nobody had the heart to wake him up. Some people were waiting for him since his berth needed to be put away for them to sit comfortably below. Seeing them struggle to find a place to sit, Krithika asked them if she should wake her father up. But they refused. It was rare for an early riser like Padmanabhan to sleep in. 'He must be tired, we should let him sleep.'

Everyone spoke in low tones so as to not wake him up. As usual, conversation moved around a mixture of cinema, cricket and politics. Krishnan said, 'If Kohli had not hit that shot, India would have won yesterday's match.' Krithika argued, 'If that one shot was the reason we lost, why even have other players in the team?' Krishnan did not back down. 'Don't talk like an idiot. Everyone can't play well in the same match. Whoever is in the best form in one match has to win it for the rest of the team.' Krithika was irked by then. '*You* are the idiot. None of the other batsmen even reached a double-digit score, and you are blaming the player who hit 55 runs. And when questioned, you find dumb excuses like form, what nonsense!'

In that moment, Muthukrishnan cut in the conversation to show them something important on his phone. 'Look at her, da, she's back to acting after marriage,' Vembu told Muthukrishnan. Keerthivasan laughed and said sarcastically, 'Yes, yes, that is very important news indeed.' Vembu turned towards him. 'Isn't it true, 'pa, that you don't step away from your seat even for a second when you watch her films?' Seeing Krithika laugh at that, Keerthivasan felt embarrassed. 'That's just because she is a good actor.' Vembu did not let go: 'So you are glad she is making a comeback.' Keerthivasan cautiously stopped himself from saying anything further and just smiled in response.

Just then, there was a noise from Padmanabhan. Everyone turned towards him wondering if he was awake now. He was still asleep, but he spoke. Everyone paid close attention to what he was saying. He named a leading contemporary actress who was famous for her beauty. They were surprised that he had even said her name out loud. But what he said next replaced their surprise with cold horror. He said it again and again. The last two times, he said it in a very distinct tone and with emphasis. His hands were moving frantically. After uttering that actress's name, he had clearly said, 'Pussy, her pussy…'

THE HORSEWOMAN

Ambai

TRANSLATED BY G.J.V. PRASAD

She realized that she didn't know very much about horses only when Tulsi told her this.

'If you shampoo your hair with a horse's urine, your hair will stop falling. It will grow lustrous and jet black.'

Tulsi was the garbage collector in her building. She belonged to Uttar Pradesh. When you answered the doorbell around seven in the morning, she would be standing there with a smile, a long blue plastic drum in her hand for the garbage. Sometimes, she would sit on the steps saying, 'Auntyji, give me some ice-cold water.' Even that morning, it was after drinking cold water that she said, 'Why Auntyji, why does your hair fall like this? Your braid is like a rat's tail now.'

Tulsi was always blunt in her speech. She didn't have the time to speak with respect, circumlocution or with preambles. Analogies and proverbs studded her speech brilliantly. Once, when Tulsi had said how her husband came home drunk and beat her up, and she had asked how Tulsi could bear living with him, she had replied with great precision. '*Gale pada dhol bajana hi padega*' (one has to play the drum that has fallen to one's lot). When demonetization was announced, she said '*Kothewala roye, chapparwala soye*' (The bungalow dwellers will weep, the hut dwellers will sleep).

It was with the same directness that she asked about the hair fall.

'I fell ill, didn't I? It's been like this since then.' Listening to this explanation, she spoke about horse urine as remedy.

When she was a young girl in Bengaluru, there used to be a lot of horse carriages. They were called jutka. During the mango season, her mother and she would go to the fruit wholesale market and take a jutka on the way back. Mother would give a mango along with the fare to the driver. She has seen horses feeding from the bags tied to their mouths. When walking with caution around the vehicles some horse would pass a waterfall of urine. Another would drop dung generously.

This is how she knew horse urine. Also, when grandfather would come back from some wedding, all the womenfolk and children would surround him and ask, 'How was the rasam?' The quality of the rasam was a sure indicator of the quality of the wedding. Grandfather would clear his throat. Everyone would wait eagerly for the words from his mouth. 'You want to know about rasam?' He would begin. Then, he would pronounce, 'Rasam was like horse urine!'

No one knew who in that family had ever drunk horse urine to determine its taste and quality, but everyone would laugh heartily and clap their hands as soon as grandfather made his pronouncement.

And now Tulsi says that horse urine can stop hair falling. She had heard of cow urine, cow dung. This was the first time that she had heard of horse urine. She was slightly tempted by the vision of jet black and shining hair. She had already tried every oil from the Ayurveda shop. Oil bottles and smells multiplied in the house but the hair did not stop falling. She had to wash the floor of the bathroom carefully to prevent people from slipping and falling on any spilt oil. She herself nearly slipped and fell twice.

She couldn't tell Madan about the horse urine. Already the smell of Ayurveda oil had got him down. He declared he would rather that she had an expensive hair transplant than buy these oils. She thought of the horse that would take children for a ride in the colourful open carriage along Juhu beach. On the Versova beach there were many with horses who would offer rides to children. That was stopped when a child had an accident.

When she was trying to think where else she would have access to a horse, she remembered the horsewoman. She was known by the name Ghodewali (horsewoman) in that area. The twists and turns and drama in her life far exceeded those dreamt up by those who wrote sensational stories in tabloids. They met one evening when she had brought her horse along to the beach. She immediately poured out her entire story.

Her father worked in the Indian Army. He was stationed in Ooty. She had studied there. Which was why she knew Tamil though a North Indian girl. She knew how to ride a horse. She fell in love with the horse-riding instructor. Divine love. She eloped with him. (As she narrated the story, the references to him turned disrespectful. Finally, she referred to him only as sala and bastard.) He showed his true colours only after they arrived in Mumbai. He tried to exploit her to make money. She knocked him unconscious with the lid of the pressure cooker and ran. But where to? If she returned home, her father would kill her. She didn't have a mother. She boarded an electric train, a Mumbai Local. She boarded a train heading to Virar planning to commit suicide by jumping into the Vasai creek. Got caught. Was placed in a Women's Shelter. She escaped from there but was caught again. With the help of an Inspector, she came out of the Shelter and joined a tourist agency, stayed in a Working Women's Hostel and accepted the Inspector's love and, because he was a Muslim, converted religion and married him as his third wife and got beaten up badly by his first two wives. She was pregnant, and as soon as a son was born, he pronounced Talaq thrice and took away the son. It was then that the horse entered her life. She heard that a racehorse was being sold because it had an incurable cold. She bought it for just two hundred rupees. She knew home remedies for horses. She brought the horse home from the stables. Since her building was a cooperative society like most apartment blocks in Mumbai, the Secretary said he would take legal action against her. When she argued that when residents can keep dogs and cats why not a horse, it became a big fight. She then tied the horse outside on the sidewalk. Mumbai Corporation objected to it. In the meanwhile, since it was on the road, a horse that belonged to another horse owner mated with it and it was clear that her mare was going to foal. One night, she called a vet who lived nearby, and the mare gave birth. Now, she had two mares. It was only after horses were banned on the beaches that a new idea dawned on her. That she could rent out her horses for baraats. In North Indian weddings, the bridegroom would arrive on a horse accompanied by his family and relatives. She immediately printed a banner and tied it to a pole. 'Horses available for hire at discounted rates for Baraat. Contact Reshma.' She had given a phone number. Because she knew what kind of calls she would get if she printed a phone number with a woman's name, she had given the number of the petty shop opposite. The owner was aged and was willing to help her.

When she wondered what a long story it was in just twenty-five years of age, she replied that she had, in fact, left out some portions of the whole story.

She had Reshma's number. She called.

'Hi, Mami,' said Reshma.

All women from Tamil Nadu were Mami to her. The Tamil 'mami' instead of 'aunty'.

'Reshma, I haven't been to the beach often recently. Do you still have your horse?'

'Yes, Mami. Whose marriage?'

'Not for a marriage.'

She didn't know how to say it. She hesitated a bit.

'Reshma, I need some horse urine.'

'What?'

'Horse urine.'

'I don't think the connection is alright, Mami. I heard something like horse urine.'

'Horse urine is what I said.'

'Mami, why Mami?'

I told her why. She said, 'Mami, I am getting Rani (the name of the horse. The young one was called Rajkumari.) ready for a baraat today. The baraat will go by your street. Just see. As soon as she comes back, she will pass urine. Would a milk can of urine be enough?'

'Reshma, sorry. Only the urine that she passes in the morning…'

'Aiyo, that's difficult Mami. Let me do one thing. The boy who looks after her sleeps nearby in the petty shop. I will tell him. He will be accompanying the baraat. You give your milk can to him. I will instruct him.'

As soon as she heard the sound of the band and the baraat, she stood near the gate to her block, can in hand. Other than the band, the usual sound of fireworks wasn't there. That was because Reshma would give clear instructions when sending the horse along with the boy. This horse had been a race horse for many years. If she heard the noise of a cracker, she may think it is the gun shot to start a race.

Even though his face was veiled by strands of flowers, it was clear the bridegroom was a youth. When the procession was passing her gate, she gestured to the boy to come. Before he could, a young man lit the fuse of a huge series of crackers. As the first cracker burst, Rani sprang forward on all her four legs and began to gallop. 'Bachao, help', shouted the bridegroom holding on tightly to the reins. The young people dancing in front of the horse which had been walking slowly till then screamed and scampered out of the way. Rani was running with the bridegroom to the village of Versova. The family and relatives of the groom were giving a dressing down to the youth who had burst the crackers.

Someone managed to call Reshma on the mobile and she came rushing on another horse. One could see from the gate how she raced towards Rani and called out to her and stopped her by the reins. The groom jumped off the horse and came running back towards the crowd. Reshma brought back the now calm Rani but the groom refused to mount her. He was in a funk. His legs were trembling still. They gave him water and soda to drink, calmed him down and then took him along to the wedding.

Reshma left with Rani. The next day, following complaints, she had to leave her place. It was said that she had sold her horses.

The hair that did not grow a shining jet black with a rinse of horse urine had to be cropped close to the scalp.

CATCH A CHUNKY GOAT

Appadurai Muttulingam

TRANSLATED BY SUCHITRA RAMACHANDRAN

With the blessings of Lord Ganapati, Om

The Immigration Officer
200 St. Catherine Street, Ottawa, ON
K2P 2K9.

(I humbly request the translator of this letter, translating from Sri Lankan Tamil into English, to kindly preserve the order of the conversations in it, to represent my ideas correctly, and to explain our cultural nuances clearly in their translation.)

Respected Sir,
Myself, Shanmugalingam Ganesaratnam, arrived at the Toronto airport on the evening of 90.03.18. As instructed, I gave my application for asylum to the officer who was there. My wife's sister Vijayalakshmi and her husband Balachandran came to the airport to meet me. This was the first time that I was meeting Vijaya. Her face resembles my wife's, so I had no difficulty recognizing her.

They took me home and made me stay with them. It was a small house, but they gave me a room all to myself. All my life, I had never had a room of my own. So my respect for my brother-in-law increased.

Both my brother-in-law and Vijaya took good care of me. Everything was new to me. The postman came right up to the house to deliver the post. At all times, everywhere, hot water gushed out of the tap on the left, and cold water out of the tap on the right.

They taught me how to get a transfer ticket on the buses, how to use the telephone cards. On the fourth day following my arrival, I got a job at a restaurant. I did the dishes and got paid in cash.

In the beginning, I was happy with my new life. I could now rent new films on VHS from time to time. I could eat things that I had never heard of back home. They advised me to invest part of my salary in a chit fund. I paid them a monthly rent for the room and put $250 towards the chit fund. From the money that was left, I was able to send some home.

My brother-in-law had two jobs. It would be eleven in the night before he got back home. Vijaya left early in the morning for her job at the daycare centre, wearing pants and a coat, a handbag on her arm. She worked only half a day. My first shift got over at three in the afternoon. I would come home and rest for a while. Then I would help them with the chores around the house. Getting things from the market was usually my responsibility.

At night, after my brother-in-law came back from work, we had dinner together. Vijaya was a good cook. The taste of her shrimp kuzhambu is particularly memorable. Actually, that was the last time I had shrimp. It was the day the police came for me. Since then, it has been two years of endless torture in this jail.

The food I get here is very different from what I am used to. Two eggs, five times a week. So that's ten eggs. Fish four times, chicken drumsticks three times, and salad – their name for uncooked greens – four times a week. I have high blood pressure. I have diabetes. I am sick, I am depressed, and I am utterly miserable.

I did not come to Canada as a tourist. As I have said repeatedly in my application and during the investigation, I emigrated so that I could flee the war in my home country. I came leaving behind my wife and my children, my angels. I hoped that I could finally shore my family's fortunes.

That was the only reason I travelled for three months to get here. I did not arrive here by plane directly. First a boat, then a train, then in a lorry transporting jackfruit – they kept rolling down on me all night long, I had to keep awake to push them away – then in a container ship, and finally a plane. I travelled for eighty-nine days in all, and it took Columbus only seventy-one to reach America. I had nothing on me except for my bag of dreams.

My little ones are far away, at home. I am here, suffering. They will forget me. I do not know if they even remember my face any more. When I left home, my oldest was seven, the second was five, the girl – a doll, a goddess, my little idol – she was four. The baby was only six months old.

My oldest is very smart. He does well in school. But even then, he didn't know that he could run straight out when we tried to make him drink castor oil. He would instead be running around me in circles. The second one, he always stood close, facing me, when I bathed at the well. He liked getting drenched in the same bucket of water I'd pour over myself. My daughter wore dresses edged with white lace, she would toddle over to me. The children fought to sleep close to me, to touch me, when I stretched out on the mat at night. I don't know when I will see my little gods again.

In our country, the full moon always glows gold. When I saw the blue moon here, I immediately knew that something evil was coming my way. The man in the next cell died last night, God knows why. I owe him an egg. I do not know his name. But he did not agree to go with death in peace. Even in death he kept staring at the world, his glazed eyes wide open.

He was from an African country; I cannot pronounce its name. There, he told me, they have one name for a red cow and another name for a black cow. The shoe on the right foot has one name and the shoe on the left foot has another, he said. Perhaps they have two different words for owing a man one egg and owing another two.

I have some comforts here. I was not used to these comforts earlier, so I had a hard time in the beginning. For instance, I trained myself to not lose my keys. All the doors in Canada are self-locking. They are dangerous. They take up a lot of your memory. Here, the guards with caps on their heads and long batons on their sides open the iron doors for us with an almighty clang; they even lock them behind us. We do not need to do a thing. It is not our responsibility to fret over whether the doors would lock by themselves. Just walk in, walk out, arms swinging – that's all we need to do.

I was very cautious at my brother-in-law's place. The doors locked on their own there. You had to keep your hands on the keys at all times. We went to work and came back home at the stipulated hours every day, always clutching on to our keys.

Sir, this was when my life started taking an unfortunate turn. I slowly realized that they cared about nothing but money. The family was slightly dysfunctional too. I was somewhat uneasy with the way Vijaya would speak to me. I had decided to move out as soon as my application for asylum was approved. I was waiting for the right time to detach myself from this family – but amicably, you understand! – they had really done a lot for me. But it seems like God did not want that.

The trouble began when we started watching TV late in the night. Vijaya's speech and mannerisms grew somewhat odd then. When she spoke to me, her gestures were unusually dainty. Her fingers and the rest of it reminded me of my wife. One day, I got back from work very tired and went to bed early. That day, Vijaya had served me dinner. There was a fried red egg on my plate.

But when the husband came in, he got only vegetables. From my bed, I could hear them fight.

Another important thing. They had a daughter. Their only daughter. Her name was Padmalochani. At first, they called her Padma. But it was not stylish enough for them. So it became Lochani. Then, that got shortened further to 'Lo'. She was a stout child, quite plump. Vijaya scolded her all the time. 'Leave your uncle alone, he is tired,' she would say; or 'Go study', or 'Go get that book from the neighbour downstairs'.

Although she was young, she was very shrewd. She was not good with school, though. She had a crafty mind. Never one to do anything in a straightforward manner. Always full of mischief and tricks and deceit. She had very sharp ears. She could guess who was coming just from the footfall on the stairs. 'This is the uncle who lives upstairs, he is going home', 'That is the aunty from downstairs, she is coming here to borrow the video,' she'd announce, and she was always correct. When we watched Tamil films at home, she could always tell precisely when the romantic scenes were going to show up: 'Ah, so they are going to hug and break into a song now!'

She had the habit of staying back in the living room after everyone had gone to bed. She said she wanted to finish her homework. But when all by herself, she played adult content on the TV. She would mute the soundtrack and watch the perverse visuals silently. She got used to such things over time; one could even say that she started liking them.

She had ten times more brains than any adult. One day, her mother left the house saying that she was going to the video store. This child went to the phone and hit the redial button. 'She is lying,' she promptly announced. 'She has gone to the aunty who runs the chit to look at some saris.' You couldn't bullshit this kid.

The doors in that house were capable of banging themselves shut and locked on a whim – all, except the bathroom door. One day, I happened to open the bathroom door by mistake and found Vijaya in the shower. I started panicking. But she stood there, as if nothing had happened, with a smile on her face. She did not even try to grab the towel hanging from the rail next to her to cover herself up. Uh … okay, I thought. I left immediately.

This fat kid had witnessed the whole thing. 'Uncle saw mother naked,' she boomed. It must have taken a great big bribe to keep her mouth shut. In any case, when my brother-in-law returned that evening, the kid did not open its trap.

That was an innocent mistake. In a couple more days' time, though, there was another incident that was not so innocent. That day, I swore to myself – never again. I cannot vouch for how successful I was in keeping to my resolution. The reason being, within a few days of this incident, I was caught by the police.

At night, Vijaya had the habit of lounging around, crossing her legs at the knees, taking slow sips of her strong black tea with a dash of 2 per cent milk in it. My wife used to do the same thing. It was a pleasant hour. Vijaya never missed an opportunity to laugh. She let peals of laughter ring out even at the silliest of jokes.

On one such day, when it was particularly difficult for me to keep myself in check, Vijaya went into her room to change. I think she knew that the door was a crack open. She slipped one leg into her tight jeans, and then the other. The fabric rose up rapidly and came to a halt under her broad bottom. With a fine jiggle of her rump, she pulled it up. Those thighs, they filled the jeans perfectly, hardly a wrinkle to be seen. I cannot describe how hot and bothered I got that day. How long had it been since I had touched a woman! And then, a scent that I knew all too well rose in the air. It made my body burn.

Sir, that was when this happened. You might find it hard to believe. Unless God himself come down to bear witness, who would believe me. This pudgy kid, she never let me rest. Even if I kept the door closed, she would open it, she would come in. And then she would turn on the fan, fiddle with the radio, open the windows, close them, move my things around. Always messing around.

You could not find a bed like mine in any store in Canada. It was a small bed, quite cramped, especially made to order by the carpenter. The kid climbed on top of it and jumped around. She made me lose sleep in every way possible. It was the same story on that day. She came in dragging a rag doll by the leg and screeched at me, 'Let's play something!'

'Don't bother me now. I'll tell your mother,' I said, trying to get rid of her.

'Amma isn't home. She has gone to talk to the aunty downstairs,' she said. Then she started a game of 'Catch the chunky goat!' (This is a game we play in our homeland. The translator must explain.)

'I will catch the chunky goat!' I whooped as I chased her. 'I will brand you with the fire,' she chanted as she ran. The two of us were shrieking and running round and round the bed. I did not realize when, in the heat of the game, the cloth around my waist had come undone. I told you, the kid had sharp ears. I don't know how she missed it that day.

Suddenly my door opened with an almighty crash. It was my brother-in-law. He strode in with his hair trussed up, his shirt buttons undone. All I could see were his hairy black arms and sturdy fingers. A blow from him landed right on my neck. I was thrown into the air and hit my head on the wall; I lay on the floor in a heap, bleeding. The kid was making gurgling sobs. 'I did nothing. It was all Uncle's doing,' she said repeatedly.

I do not know when he dialled 911. When I looked up, there was the police. The child's knickers were on the bed. That was the first thing they picked up. They did not so much as ask how I got the wounds on my head. I had to wait until the blood had dripped and dried on my shirt before someone came to bind it up. There was not even a dog to care for me in this country. I do not know what they wrote to my wife to poison her mind. I stopped receiving the letters she used to write me – letters on fine, translucent paper, the kind used to wrap jewellery in, where you can see the ink seeping through on to the other side.

I have no reprieve from this hell. One cannot account for that child's cunning. Her body was well-developed, so was her mind. She planned this. She framed me. I will never see the $6,500 they took from me for the chit fund. They sent me to jail, but they go on living comfortably. I have not breathed a word about any of the depravities I witnessed when living under that roof. The family will be entirely ruined if I did.

My cellmate is gay. He is always depressed. He just sits there all the time, staring at an old letter folded into eights, tearing at the creases. There is a rumour that he is involved with Daniel in Cell 27. There is just one problem: Whenever I want to take a piss, he follows me. I have never seen him sleep. He stays awake for a long time, his legs dangling over the side of the bunk above me, repeatedly crossing himself. If I wake up in the middle of the night, sometimes I see his feet dangling down the side, like long stockings washed and hung up to dry.

As night approaches, the shadows emerge. A left-handed cockroach lives with us. We get alarmed if he's missing for even a day. We look for him all day long. The slender ash-coloured beech is always the first to shed its leaves. The other trees follow suit. But the maple leaf on the flag hoisted at the entrance of the prison? That never falls.

They have separated me from the angels in my life. I sit here all day long thinking of them in my long jumpsuit, dyed in the colours of the robes Buddhist monks wear back home. The names of the first five prisoners who were placed in this jail, 160 years ago, are engraved here. At least a thousand people must have slept on the bed where I lie now. Some may have gone to sleep, never to wake up. Perhaps, some day, my name too will be engraved here. 'There once lived here a prisoner from a foreign land – a prisoner, who never made collect calls, who never received any letters, who was never allowed to have any visitors – and this was his name.' I don't know.

'*On July 1, 1867, the confederation of provinces led to the creation of the new Dominion of Canada. Today, Canada has 10 provinces and 2 territories. The first Prime Minister of Canada was John A. Macdonald. I swear that I will be faithful and bear true allegiance to Her Majesty Queen Elizabeth II, Queen of Canada, Her heirs and successors, and that I will faithfully observe the laws of Canada and fulfil my duties as a Canadian citizen.*'

Honourable sir, I learned the phrases above by heart in the hope that, some day, I will obtain Canadian citizenship. Now, I kindly beg you to discount my review appeal and send me back home. You can put me in a container ship again, if you like – I will go back home the same way I got here.

I learned that my wife had given birth for the fifth time now. That is impossible in my absence. It is an atrocious lie.

Ten thousand miles from here, there is a village where the iluppai trees shed their sweet white flowers all night long; where the folks pare their wicks and go to bed at seven in the night to save lamp-oil; where, on a clear night, on a mat that curls up at a moment's notice, lies my wife, with two children each on either side – how fairly she shares herself between the four of them! – staring up into the helicopterless sky, at the red planet glowing next to Venus. To that beautiful land, I must, I must return. I will haul bricks to make a living if I have to. Once again, I swear. I had absolutely no idea that the chunky, well-developed girl would only be ten years old.

I give you my word. I will forget all that I learned by heart in the hopes of becoming a citizen of your country, I swear. Please, just send me home.

Yours truly,

Your humble servant,

Shanmugalingam Ganesaratnam

Cell 37
Kingston Penitentiary
555 King Street W.

SOUNDARAVALLI'S MOUSTACHE

S. Ramakrishnan

TRANSLATED BY YASHASVI ARUNKUMAR

When one of the boys in seventh standard stood up and announced that Soundaravalli had a moustache, she was seething. And when the science master heard the boy's words, he made her stand up in front of the entire class. The girls near her giggled coyly with their mouths closed. Soundaravalli bowed her head and sat back down. When the science master continued loudly, 'Ey, Indrani! You check and tell us if she has a moustache or not, 'pa,' the entire class burst into laughter.

Indrani had been sitting on the same bench as Soundaravalli. She grabbed Soundaravalli's head and tried to raise it, as if she had spent her whole life wishing for such a moment. Soundaravalli kept her head bent forward and tightened her hold on the bench, refusing to budge an inch. But Indrani wouldn't give in – she ducked under the table to catch a glimpse of Soundaravalli's face. Soundaravalli started grinding her teeth together. She wanted to slap the shit out of Indrani.

'Sir, she's gnashing her teeth and refusing to lift her head. May I ask a couple of girls to help me lift her head?' The science master seemed to get more excited at what Indrani said. 'I don't care what you do, the truth has to come out.'

As soon as he said that, Shankari, who sat behind Soundaravalli, took hold of her braid and gave it a pull. Even when the back of her head hurt, Soundaravalli did not raise her head. Marikkani who sat on her left started tickling her sides. Even as she wiggled her body, Soundaravalli's face remained hidden.

Only Nirmala, who sat in front of her, seemed considerate. 'Ey, leave it, di,' she said, 'Soundaravalli does not have a moustache and all.' But no one took her seriously. Aavudaiyappan, the class leader, jumped up eagerly. 'Shall I pull her head up to see, sir?' The teacher held him back, saying, 'What, da, does this look like a jallikattu match? Each of you wants to have a go. Wait, da, we will see what happens.' The students began whispering among themselves.

Reaching under the table, Indrani managed to grab hold of Soundaravalli's chin in her hands. Even when Soundaravalli pinched her hands using her nails, Indrani did not let go. Holding Soundaravalli's chin, she started hefting her head up. Soundaravalli reared just as Sornam pulled her braid from behind, and her face was brought into the light. Soundaravalli hastily brought her hands up to her face, not knowing how to hide herself from the exposure. But Indrani did not let go even then. She pried Soundaravalli's hands apart and presented her face to the class.

The entire class stared at Soundaravalli's face. The science teacher came near her and took a closer look. Then, with a loud laugh, he announced, 'Yes, da. Soundaravalli has a moustache.' The boys started banging on the benches, laughing. Soundaravalli bit her lips, unable to bear the disgrace. Tears brimmed in her eyes.

The teacher asked her, 'Have you seen your face in a mirror at least once in your life?' She could not respond. She felt as if someone had gripped her throat tightly.

'Do you bathe every day?' he continued. She nodded. When asked where she went to bathe, she spoke up hesitantly, her arms folded, 'In the stone kidangu, sir.' As soon as she said that, a boy piped up, 'That's a lie, sir. No girl goes to bathe in the stone kidangu. It is two men deep.'

'Ha, I know that just from the state of her face … You don't need any other proof.' That said, the teacher turned towards her. 'When did you last take a bath this year?' Soundaravalli felt enraged. She stood without giving him any answer. The master struck his cane against her skirt.

'Grow that moustache nice and long, just like those chandiyars … Only then will you have that same swagger. None of the boys in the class have grown a moustache yet. But see, da, this *girl* already has one.'

Even the girls in the class started laughing loudly after that. Like a good girl, Indrani spoke up: 'Sir, I take a bath every day using turmeric. I will never have a moustache.' The science master gave her his stamp of approval: 'That is what is seemly for a girl child.' After that, the taunts were relentless until class ended.

When the school bell rang for lunch, the science master exited the classroom. The minute his head vanished from sight, Soundaravalli pounced on Indrani. She pushed her out of the bench, seated herself squarely on top of her, and started hitting her. Indrani did not let go either. She caught hold of Soundaravalli's hair and pulled at it. Both of them rolled on the floor.

Indrani reached out to grab the drawstrings of Soundaravalli's skirt to unfasten them. Soundaravalli caught hold of her hand and bit hard. When her hand started to bleed, Indrani raised a loud cry and started sobbing. Soundaravalli ran out of the school, without even taking her bag with her.

Two boys went to the teachers' staffroom and narrated Soundaravalli's biting incident to them. When Naarambu sir came inside the classroom with his cane, Indrani showed him the bite marks on her hand. He consoled Indrani, 'Let her come tomorrow, we will take care of this,' and instructed her to apply crushed kuppaimeni leaves to the wound. But Soundaravalli did not return even when classes started after lunch. Only Nirmala and C. Murugeswari felt bad for her. Not one of the male students refrained from making fun of her.

Even though she had exited the school premises, the taunts and insults seemed to stick to Soundaravalli's body like ants. She wanted to throw herself into some dilapidated well and die. She continued walking alone, kicking and crushing the thumbai plants she found on the side of the path.

When she reached the boulder near the Kaatu Muniyamman temple, there was not a single human in sight. Only a neem tree, and above, a few white clouds and the wide sky. In front of the temple, four to five rusty bells hung between two stone pillars. Sitting down on the sun-heated boulder, she felt like looking at her own face just once.

Narrowing her gaze, she tried focussing on the tip of her nose. But there was no way to find out if there was a moustache or not. These damned eyes, they can see things like the moon so far away. But they can't see a moustache right above the lips! She was angry at her eyes. Tilting her head this way and that way, she tried her best to see if there was a moustache. But she could see nothing at all. The mirror in their house had lost its silvering over the years. The reflection was blurry, as if it were cast on still water. Soundaravalli had been using that mirror only to place her pottu on her forehead every day. She was convinced that unless she checked for herself whether she had a moustache or not, that very day, she would not feel better.

She sat on that rock until evening set. It was the time when the well-diggers would return to their homes. If she did not leave now, those in her house would start looking for her. As a heavenly breeze tousled her hair, she started towards her house slowly.

She did not know what to say if her family questioned her. If she told Amma, she would hit her. None of her older brothers cared about her much. And night would fall by the time Ayya even came home. Not knowing what to do, she decided to meet C. Murugeswari once before going back home and started walking towards her house.

C. Murugeswari was sitting on the verandah and assembling matchboxes. Every day, after returning from school, she would prepare at least four bundles. Just like her, more than half the girls in their school had made a routine out of sitting under the streetlight and assembling matchboxes. Soundaravalli was very good at sticking the bottoms of those boxes. She could finish them very quickly.

Pushing aside the scattered matchboxes on the verandah to a corner, Soundaravalli sat down. C. Murugeswari continued sticking her matchboxes while informing Soundaravalli that Aavudaiyappan had handed over her bag to the headmaster's office and that Naarambu sir would nicely cane her when she came back to school the next day.

'Let them be. Ninnies, all of them! All of this was the doing of that monkey Indrani. I would have bitten her lifeline out, but she escaped. Does she think I don't know all the shit she's up to?' Soundaravalli started ranting.

C. Murugeswari responded thoughtfully, 'Kodhandaraman, Chinnamuthu, and Vavvaalu – these three boys are the ones behind everything. They keep digging up stuff about you.'

Soundaravalli wondered if she could ask Murugeswari directly. She hesitated. 'Is it true, what they say ... Has a moustache really sprouted on my face?'

C. Murugeswari shifted closer to Soundaravalli to take a look, so close it seemed as though she were blowing away dust from her eyes. 'Abba, how many hairs have grown,' she said without smiling. When Soundaravalli cautiously asked if they had a mirror in the house, Murugeswari directed her to the mirror fixed on a window inside the house.

Jumping down from the verandah, Soundaravalli rushed inside. The mirror in Murugeswari's house had lost its silvering too. She drew the mirror extremely close to her face to see. It was just like those boys had said: light hair had indeed begun to grow above her lip.

Cursing whatever was making those bristles grow, she gingerly stroked them with her fingertips. They were like a cat's whiskers. She kept the mirror at a distance to check if it looked ugly. In the image, she could see how her collarbones popped, how her eyes looked sunken in her swollen face.

Indrani's reflection would never appear like that. Her cheeks were nicely filled in. Her hair curled near her ears and swayed in the air. Every day, she applied mai to darken her eyebrows. Her father worked in the Panchayat Board. In their house, they had a big dabba of powder as well.

Soundaravalli only had one dabba of bindi paste in her house. Not even a dabba of mai for her to line her eyes with. Besides, her mother would not have bought it even if she asked her to. 'Why does a schoolgoing brat need to apply mai to her eyes, ears, everything? Whatever beauty you already have is enough. In another two years, we are going to marry you off to some well-digger. This much beauty is good enough for that.'

The more she stared at the mirror, the more the sight of the moustache repulsed Soundaravalli. She tried tugging at one of the bristles, as if she were going to pluck them out one by one. But her fingers couldn't catch hold of any of them. They had just started growing, and looked like lines drawn with a black pencil.

She felt like crying. Fixing the mirror back on the window, she covered her mouth and started to weep. The pain of not knowing how to get rid of this moustache burnt her from the inside. Wiping her eyes, she went back and sat down next to Murugeswari. With a sad voice, she asked, 'Now what do I do, di?'

Murugeswari did not know what to do either. 'Just try grinding and applying lots of turmeric. It should vanish in four to five days,' she offered. Soundaravalli made up her mind to not go to school for the next couple of days and started walking back home.

Her eyes wandered to the face of every woman on the street. She could see that one or two women also had moustaches. She wondered if they too had been humiliated like her.

When she reached home, Amma was frying up dried chillies in the kitchen. There was smoke everywhere. As soon as she popped her head in the door, Amma threw the ladle at her. 'Why did you bite that Indrani, di? Are you a dog? Or are you so starved of meat that you wanted to get a taste of it from her?' she shouted. Soundaravalli scowled back, 'I didn't bite her without reason.'

Amma used the ends of her sari to hold and remove the pan from the heat. 'Her Amma and Ayya stopped me on the way and took me to task. If I had caught hold of you then … I would have pulled you apart nerve by nerve. Where in the hell have you been all this while?' Soundaravalli did not want to tell Amma about the incidents at school. Gathering her usual matchbox-sticking supplies, she went and sat down at the end of the street. But she could not focus on her job. The pain in her chest kept increasing.

She waited for Amma to finish cooking and come out to the front of the house, before stealthily making her way into the kitchen in search of the turmeric tuber. The tuber had shrunk in size because of constant use. She rushed to the makeshift fence on the back of the house, rubbed the tuber vigorously on a stone, and quickly smeared the paste above her lips. Her hands were covered in yellow.

As soon as she heard her mother returning to the house, Soundaravalli dropped her head and quietly went back outside. But Amma chose just that day of all days to join her in the task of sticking matchboxes. As soon as she sat down, she saw Soundaravalli's face.

'What is this guise, di?' Soundaravalli lied that she had some irritation on her skin. Her mother glared at her. 'So? Does that mean you have to smear turmeric like this all over your face?'

Even Amma's face had catlike whiskers like hers. But neither Ayya nor her brothers had said anything about that ever. She kept staring intently at her mother's face. Amma did not even notice. Soundaravalli could not control her pain any longer. Nervously, she told her mother about the moustache growing on her face. Amma pulled her closer and looked at her face. 'That will go away on its own. Is that why you applied this much turmeric to your face?' But her mother's words did not satisfy Soundaravalli.

She hardened her face before declaring, 'We should buy a new mirror for our house.' Amma frowned back at her: 'We will buy everything on the day we marry you off.' Soundaravalli's anger reached a peak. 'Should I walk around with a thick, ugly moustache on my face until then? What would you know about how the boys laugh at me in class?' Amma responded, 'What can I do about that, di? There's already so much on our plate to deal with. Is your moustache such a big problem now?'

Soundaravalli decided she would never confide in her mother again.

Her brother came out from the house in search of Amma. They started talking and walked away.

Soundaravalli had faced no problems until fifth standard. But as soon as she started sixth standard, the school had started doling out many restrictions: the skirt should be long enough so that no part of the legs was visible, girls should not wear men's shirts, and so on. Her body too had started undergoing many changes during that time. As if that wasn't enough to irritate her, her mother had started bringing up her imminent marriage for anything and everything.

That night, she assembled matchboxes until sleep pressed her eyes shut. The thought of having no one by her side was depressing.

She considered going to Indrani herself to ask her what to do to stop the moustache from growing. That night, she went to bed without eating.

Over the next three days, Soundaravalli rubbed the turmeric tuber and applied the paste on her face whenever she remembered or felt like it. But the hairs did not go away. Instead, the turmeric stained her face yellow, making her look jaundiced. The news soon reached her father's ears, and he blew up at and thrashed her mother. 'Doesn't know how to raise a girl child properly. If you let her roam around like a temple cow, of course she will grow a moustache. Why, she will even grow a beard!'

That night, Amma took someone's advice and ground some herbs along with the turmeric and applied it on her face. And yet, the hair did not give way. Without anyone's knowledge, Amma had even got some donkey urine and applied it on her face. Soundaravalli had not been able to bear the stench.

After that, Amma started lamenting to every woman she met on the street: 'Who will marry my daughter now? Why, why did this have to happen to her?' Soundaravalli did not return to school after that. After four or five days, she started going for construction work along with her mother. No one had the time to pay attention to anyone or to make fun of them at the construction site. Soundaravalli and her mother worked hard.

Every day, on her way to work, Soundaravalli would pass by the school. Even from a distance, she could hear the sound of students studying inside. Keeping her head lowered, she would walk away.

Now and then, she would wonder if she could go and get at least her bag and books back from school. But she never went inside, too embarrassed to meet the students who used to study with her.

After many days had passed, Amma brought home a face cream from a medical shop in the city. Resigned, as if she did not care for it any more, Soundaravalli refused to take the cream. 'This is enough to marry a well-digger, ma.'

'Why did you have to be born in our house, di? What have I been able to do for anyone?' Amma started hitting her own head, trembling and crying. Soundaravalli, too, felt like crying. Each held on to the other and sobbed. They knew it was not just for Soundaravalli's moustache.

BLACK BEADS AND TELEVISION

Salma

TRANSLATED BY N. KALYAN RAMAN

THE COLOUR TV set that Shaukat Ali had brought home from Dubai was enough to make the whole village gape in open-mouthed wonder. Since there was no easy way to mount an antenna on top of his tile-roofed house, installing the TV set had turned into a big problem for Shaukat. When he thought of going to Habib's house, which was two doors away, and asking whether he could fix the antenna on their terrace, Mahmuda dissuaded him. 'Aiyo, even if that man agrees, his wife Farida won't. The whole village is already envious of our television set,' she informed him.

This was true enough. It was midnight when Shaukat Ali had entered the village. If he arrived during the day, the whole street would gawk at the number of bags and boxes being unloaded, attracting the evil eye – Mahmuda had forewarned him in a letter. 'To avoid making everyone jealous, take a flight that will bring you home at night,' she had insisted during an urgent telephone call too. Just as she had feared, as soon as his car entered the village and stopped in front of their house, Shaukat realized that the lights had come on in two or three of their neighbouring houses and many pairs of eyes were staring at him.

When Hazrat from the opposite house, who was among those who called on him after the morning prayer, remarked, 'It seems you've brought home the devil too,' it was no great surprise for Shaukat. He knew that Hazrat could only regard a TV set as the devil. He nodded without a word and smiled. When Syedamma from the neighbouring house told Mahmuda, 'Elei, it seems a whole lot of boxes were unloaded last night,' and laughed derisively, Mahmuda sensed her envy.

'A man who left his wife and child behind for four years, didn't even know if they were dead or alive, worked day and night in the scorching heat without proper food or water, has finally come home, and the wretched people in this village are so full of jealousy. May they lose everything they own!' While Mahmuda vented her anger at them by cursing without restraint, Shaukat Ali sat in silence on the pyol flanking the doorway of his house, not knowing where and how he might install the antenna.

'Instead of building a house with the money he's earned, he has lugged home a TV...' Amma's constant grumbling since that morning did not fail to reach his ears. 'It's not as if I haven't earned money. It was an old television set lying in my room. If I bring it home, does she have to grumble so much?' Shaukat muttered to himself. Proud of the distinction of being the first in the village to own a TV, he got up quickly and went out in the direction of the local bazaar. If he met Habib at his house and made his request, his wife might have a chance to intervene. So he decided to meet his neighbour in the market.

'What's the matter? You seem lost in thought.' Shaukat Ali looked up and was startled to see Habib standing before him. 'Ada, may you live a hundred years. I was coming to see you.' Shaukat held his neighbour's hand and greeted him.

'Is everything all right? Tell me,' Habib said.

'Nothing's the matter, really,' Shaukat said. 'I've brought a TV set. Only when the antenna is fixed high above the ground will the picture be clear. The antenna consists of just three rods. Can I fix it on your terrace and run a cable to the set?'

'I see.' Habib pondered this for a while. 'No problem. You can fix it there. I am not going to stand there with an antenna on my head, am I?' Habib said with a laugh, before he dropped his voice and inquired, 'Are you sure that no thunderclap will hit the antenna, mapillai?' From his tone, Shaukat could sense Habib's anxiety that he had perhaps consented in haste and his wife was going to scold him for it.

'Why would you even ask, machaan?' Shaukat said, worried that such irrational fears might induce Habib to withdraw his offer. 'You are a smart man, Habib, and yet you have such doubts. There are so many houses in the world with an antenna on the roof, and here you are, asking me whether it's safe.'

Once he had been pronounced a smart man, Habib decided he could not turn down Shaukat's request. 'Oh ... it's all right, then. You can fix it on my house,' he said with an impassive expression on his face.

However, worry about giving his consent without checking at home and how he was going to appease his wife was evident on Habib's face despite his calm demeanour. This caused some degree of discomfort, but Shaukat Ali got the job done without bothering much about his neighbour's predicament.

From Habib's terrace, Shaukat brought the cable down through the alley between the houses. He inserted it through a window in the flat-ceilinged extension of his tile-roofed house and placed the TV set at one end of the long veranda. The set received a solitary channel, in Hindi. Even then, if the wind was strong sometimes, there would be no signal, and only a jumble of dots would appear on the screen. If they were watching a programme at the time, they saw human figures for five minutes and only dots over the next five.

On top of everything else, the language, too, was unfamiliar. Shaukat was fed up. Did I bring this TV all the way here and go through all this trouble and humiliation only for this, he asked himself. He decided not to go anywhere near the TV set. Yet, his heart was brimming with pride.

Though he felt this way, it was quite a different proposition for his wife. From six-thirty onwards in the evening, women and children from all the houses on the street began to invade their house. Regardless of whether they understood the programmes or not, whether the picture was clear or not, the crowd did not get any smaller. Mahmuda, who in the initial days had proudly welcomed her relatives, served them tea and played hostess, started wondering why her husband had brought this wretched TV. When *Chitrahar* got over after eight and the crowd dispersed, she would grumble to her heart's content as she swept up the sand brought into the house by the visitors' feet. As far as she was concerned, the television had become a burden that outweighed their pride over it. Shaukat felt pity when he saw Mahmuda doing these chores. Zakiramma from the neighbouring street was the only one who stayed back to help Mahmuda with cleaning the house.

Even if on occasion Mahmuda handed her ten or twenty rupees in cash, Zakiramma wouldn't accept it. 'No need,' she'd say. 'Don't I watch your TV for free? Then why should you pay me?' In the lone cinema theatre in their village, they changed the film every week. Zakiramma would always be the first person at the opening show. She was fifty-eight and crazy about cinema.

Extremely annoyed at her ways, her husband Sultan would vent his anger out loud. 'Look at her, thambi. Does it look proper when a woman of good family, a Muslim woman, loiters around? If there is an MGR film playing, she watches it every day. She is burning up all the money I earn carrying loads in the market,' he would protest.

'Yes. What about it? I'll go when I want to. I love MGR movies like my own life,' Zakiramma would reply.

'You whore ... Gruel is all you eat, and you want rosewater to rinse your mouth, do you?' Sultan would yell at her. Mahmuda and Shaukat Ali had to listen to their quarrels all the time. One day, Mahmuda said to her husband, 'Look at this Zakiramma wiping our TV set, see how lovingly she does it. The way she keeps patting it, I hope it doesn't get damaged in the process.' At times, she would follow Zakiramma on her way home, pick up some dirt from any spot trodden by her feet, mix it with salt and seven dried chillies, and along with twigs from the roof of their house, wave the items in front of Shaukat and the TV positioned next to each other, in a ritual to ward off the evil eye.

'Right. This is all we need,' Shaukat would grumble to himself.

If Zakiramma had watched a film the previous night, she would, while cleaning the dirty dishes the next morning, offer an elaborate analysis of the film's plot. The listener would feel as if they had seen the film themselves. Barring one or two women, no other woman went to the theatre to see films. No matter what the film was, Zakiramma would sum up her experience of watching it in a single word: laddu. For her, all cinema was sweet and delectable. In her view, there was no such thing as a bad film.

One day, when Shaukat happened to remark, 'That film was just no good. I also saw it yesterday,' Zakiramma retorted, 'Why, bhai? Think about the amount of money they would have spent to make this film and how hard they must have worked on it. Is it fair that, after paying only thirty-five paise to watch it, we trash the film as garbage? That's why I will never say that a film is bad.' When Zakiramma said this while meticulously wiping the dust off the TV set, Shaukat Ali laughed, mostly to himself.

Mahmuda noticed that, of late, Zakiramma's eyes seemed to float in a dreamlike state. At times, she would call out the old woman, saying, 'What are you brooding about when you still have work to do?'

'It's nothing,' Zakiramma would say and resume her work.

Over the past fortnight, after Tamil programmes from Chennai Doordarshan began airing on their TV, Zakiramma rarely ever went home. She was unable to sleep a wink these days. 'Why should I go to the theatre to watch a film? Why can't I bring the film home, like in Mahmuda's house?' She began to dream.

'If television can be installed in a rich household, why can't it be put in mine too?' she mused. The constant brooding began to hamper her work.

Her activities were reduced to passing her days in deep reflection. All kinds of plans were being constantly worked over in her mind. Whenever her eyes, wrinkled from a lifetime of washing utensils, fell on the glossy smoothness of the TV set, she was transported with delight and pleasure. She began to develop an intense disdain for her life without a TV. More than the lack of good clothes to wear, jewellery, a house or children, it was the lack of a TV that was eating into her. It was more pleasant to think of the TV set as an essential rather than an unnecessary item in the household. It seemed as though she had completely forgotten that she was living with an old man called Sultan.

Since Zakiramma hadn't turned up for work till noon that day, Mahmuda went to her house looking for her. She could hear Sultan's screams even from outside their home.

Since she knew that such quarrels were nothing unusual between the couple, Mahmuda pushed the tin door open and entered the house. The screech of the door's hinges drew Sultan's attention, which fell on her.

'Come in, Amma. Will you look at what this woman has done?' In the corner where Sultan was pointing, Mahmuda found a large

TV set next to a cardboard carton. 'Why do we need this? This useless woman paid four thousand rupees and bought it.'

Mahmuda blinked, unable to understand. A television set for four thousand rupees? How had Zakiramma come by so much money? Mahmuda looked over at her in confusion. Zakiramma was seated majestically on a low wall abutting the kitchen. It seemed like she hadn't heard a word of Sultan's outburst.

Zakiramma was gazing exultantly at the TV in front of her. Mahmuda thought that she might be wondering about whom she could request for hosting the antenna.

'Do you know where the money came from? She sold her chain of gold beads. When I ask her, she says a string of plain black beads will do. To whom can I complain about this travesty?'

Ignoring Sultan's fury, Zakiramma said, 'Why does he insist on hanging around my neck only as a gold chain? What's wrong with plain black beads?'

Before her gratified desire, Sultan's wails came to nothing and melted away in the breeze, even as Mahmuda watched in wonder and amazement.

THE GODDESS WAS WATCHING

Nanjil Nadan

TRANSLATED BY N. KALYAN RAMAN

Sunday morning. It was not even eight yet. Subbiah had woken up, scooped some charred husk onto a strip of palm leaf hanging from the eaves, stepped into the thereykal river, cleaned his teeth, rinsed his mouth and washed his face. Squatting at the edge of the gravel road that branched off to the east towards thazhakkudi, the downstream quarter, he had defecated, then washed himself in the stream that flowed down from the Nachiyar pond. Afterwards, he walked to the culvert next to the bridge over the sluice gate and sat down. Shade from the banyan tree. The gurgling sound of the thereykal river flowing below. Opposite the banyan tree, Sudalaimadan, the village deity, stood facing east, resplendent after a fresh coat of manjanai, a paste made of turmeric, sandal and vermilion. Stuck on the front wall of Sudalaimadan's temple was a handbill exhorting people to vote for T.S. Ramasami Pillai, the Praja Socialist Party's candidate in the Kanyakumari Assembly Constituency in the 1962 general election.

The Sudalaimadan temple of yore had been upgraded now to Sri Sudalaimadaswami Devasthanam in a proper Sanskrit rendition. If a goat kid tried to shit like an elephant, wouldn't its arsehole split open? Even so, on the last Friday of every Tamil month, the family priest would anoint the idol with manjanai, light the lamp, make a votive offering of a bunch of peyan bananas along with betel leaves and areca nuts, pay obeisance with frankincense smoke, break a coconut and place the two halves in front of the idol, wave a flame of camphor in worship and then take everything home with him. Only the manjanai and garland of oleander would be left.

How could Subbiah get any work done if he sat gazing at Sudalaimadan? If he went home, his mother would hand him a palm-leaf basket and ask him to collect twigs for the stove. Upon his return, by way of something to eat, he would receive leftover rice soaked overnight in water. Because it was Sunday, it might be gruel made of broken rice, or green gram, or black gram. In that case, it would be a feast.

Yesuvadiyan – the name stood for Servant of Jesus – was heading down the Tirupatisaaram Road from the south with a brass pail, clutching its handle with his right hand. He was Subbiah's classmate in the eighth standard. Like Subbiah, Yesuvadiyan, too, was always seen in torn and patched second-hand shorts bought in the weekly market fair. As Yesuvadiyan drew closer, Subbiah said, 'Where are you rushing off to in the morning, da?'

'They are distributing powder milk in the church. My mother got some in a vessel and came back. I also went there and collected milk in this pail. I am going to thazhakkudi to deliver it to my sister's house,' Yesuvadiyan said as he walked on in a hurry.

It occurred to Subbiah that he, too, could go home, pick up a vessel and set off to collect some milk. If he carried a pail and they filled it to the brim, everyone in his family would get a tumbler each.

He walked fast and reached home. His mother was collecting dung in the barn. Now she had to carry it to the manure vat. Without making a sound, he searched for and found the brass pail normally used to carry gruel to the fields for Appa. The pail was missing its lid. He could not find it in the kitchen. 'Let it be,' he said to himself, and came out of the house with the lidless pail that was coated on the inside with lead.

Kolusammai Aunty must be garnishing a dish of flat rice at home, he imagined. He started walking on the Tirupatisaaram Road. To secure the shorts that kept slipping from his waist, he had fastened it with a length of knotted cord. Though the name of the village was common to both hamlets, a quarter mile separated Vadakkur in the north from Therkur in the south. Vadakkur comprised a landlords' quarter, four or five houses of pandarams (priests), a maravars' quarter, and a house each for the achari (carpenter) and the vaidyar (medicine-man). Therkur, inhabited by 'untouchables', was called colony.

The bathing ghat by the river was the southern boundary of Vadakkur. As sentinel and to offer shade as well, there stood a banyan tree that was seventy or eighty years old. At the foot of the banyan tree, facing north, sat Isakkiyamman, a local deity. Goddesses like Mutharamman, Muppudathiyamman and others were mostly north-facing deities. As he walked south towards Therkur, the river was flowing on the left. Matching its vigorous flow, Subbiah walked briskly alongside, carrying the pail in one hand and swinging the other.

A couple of men were perched on the protective wall of the bathing ghat with their backs to the river and to the women who came to bathe in the river and wash clothes. The banyan tree shielded their backs and heads from the rays of the morning sun. Seated on the wall facing west, with his back to the river and to Arunan, the sun god, 'Kaduvai' Pothi, a foul-mouthed old man, bent down to massage his kneecaps. He had rubbed some oil on them perhaps. His kneecaps were as shiny as black grams coated with oil. Directly opposite the wall was Amman Koyil Street, which went up to Saatthan temple before turning into South Street. On the right-hand corner, at the beginning of Amman Koyil Street, was an eatery called Bhagavati Vilasam, which sold sukku coffee prepared from dry ginger. Breakfast was idli and rasavadai on all three hundred and sixty-five days in a year. The eatery could seat four to five customers.

Subbiah walked fast, anxious to reach the church before they ran out of milk. As he approached the colony, he saw a tempo on the right side of the road, parked in front of the east-facing church. He could see a knot of men, women and children gathered around the back of the tempo.

He was used to calling it 'church'. He did not know whether it was a Catholic, Protestant or Pentecostal church. He had heard a phrase called 'Salvation Army'. Those who were called pastors wore full-sleeved white shirts and white trousers. Only the shoulder strap of the shirt was maroon in colour. A golden cross was pinned to it.

Even after he had grown up, Subbiah had no clear idea of the divisions and sects in Christianity. Later, he became friends with a Catholic priest who took an interest in his welfare and prayed for the well-being of his family. One day, he had asked the priest directly, 'Father, how many sects are there in the Catholic church?' The priest had replied in jest, 'Christ himself wouldn't know that!'

Around the back of the tempo, which held large open containers filled with powder milk, a small crowd had queued up. Women who had received the milk paused briefly to laugh and chat with those who were still waiting. Standing inside the tempo next to the containers, two men were scooping the milk in large mugs and pouring it into the vessels brought by the women. With veshtis folded back up to the knees and towels wrapped around their heads like turbans, both seemed energetic and diligent. Milk had spilled and splashed on their bodies and on the floor of the tempo, and its odour pervaded the air.

Subbiah knew the man who was standing below, trying to regulate the people who had come to collect milk. Dark and wiry, with a flat stomach, the well-built man was called 'Nondi' Solomon, because one of his legs was a bit short, and that gave him a slight limp. The sun's heat had begun to sting. The sloshing milk containers on the tempo and the waning crowd gave Subbiah the hope that he, too, would get milk. Nallayi Akka, who was standing slightly apart, smiled at him. She was Nondi Solomon's mother. She knew Subbiah. Everyone called her Nallayi Kizhavi, old woman.

'So, you actually went there and got milk?' In his mind he could hear Amma asking in a disapproving tone. Still, she would of course keep the milk vessel on the burning stove right away. After boiling the milk, they could have ginger coffee with it, which was a rare treat. Or, if there was some Kottayam sugar or palm jaggery lying in a pot, she could grate it and add it to the milk; then she could cool the milk by airing it, and, depending on the quantity, pour half or three-quarters of a cup each into eleven tumblers. Or she could get a little buttermilk for setting curd from Kolusammai Aunty and make curd from the milk; the next day, she could prepare sour white pumpkin gravy or mixed vegetable curry. If there was cucumber at home, she could even put together a curd-based relish like pachadi.

He moved forward tentatively and went closer to the tempo. The unease in his mind was evident in his posture. A man who was standing in the tempo and throwing his weight around turned to look at Subbiah. Recognizing the boy, he started shouting:

'Why does a boy from the landlords' quarter come and stand here? If something is available for free, it seems they will go and queue up anywhere. But once they put a stake in the ground to announce their temple festival, will they allow us to enter their hamlet?'

There was a mix of irritation and contempt in his voice. The other man, who looked up after hearing him shout, said in a sharp tone, 'Look at him, turning up here without any shame, carrying a pail. Get away from here. Scram northwards!'

The folks standing around the tempo tittered. Perinbam, a girl in Subbiah's class, stared fixedly at his face. He was overcome by feelings he could not express. Mustn't cry, he told himself. He felt that there was no point in waiting any more.

It was a phase in his life when derision, mockery and humiliation had begun to wound his heart. He was not old enough yet to have learnt that, after being hurt again and again in this manner, his heart would grow hard and callused.

Watching the goings-on, Nondi Solomon scolded the two bullies inside the tempo. He raised his voice in anger:

'Just shut your trap and do your work, elei! Does Christ have a caste, you punks sired by a cadaver? Have mercy on this poor boy. He is a good student. He is forced by poverty to come here carrying a pail. Don't abuse him and tear him to shreds, you stupid oafs! Bring that pail here, boy...'

Almost snatching the pail from Subbiah he gave it to the young man in the tempo and said, 'Fill it, lei ... let his poor family drink it up. There are five or six children there...'

He got Subbiah's pail filled to the brim and gave it to him. Subbiah lifted his eyes to the older man's face in gratitude and took the pail from him. With his head downcast, he turned and set out northwards. Subbiah felt demeaned and hurt. He walked gingerly, taking care not to let the lidless pail shake and spill milk on the ground. As he walked back to Vadakkur, the river was flowing on his right. Right and left depended on the direction of his walk. Koonangaani Patta, an old man from his hamlet, was grazing a couple of water buffalos down on the riverbank. Subbiah wondered whether he should keep the pail on the ground, get into the river, pluck a leaf from the shrubs of Indian kale that had burgeoned along the water's edge and cover the pail with it before walking further. But if he kept the pail down, a black crow might come and sit on the rim and topple it, or it might, after having eaten all kinds of prey, dip its whole beak into the pail and drink the milk.

'Chhee.' His mind reeled in revulsion. He kept walking northwards, careful not to swing the pail and spill the milk. At the border of the hamlet, seven or eight men were sitting on the culvert next to the bathing ghat on the riverbank. Kaduvai Pothi was dragging hard on a suruttu, a variety of country cigar. Rolling up the veshti and shoving it under the crotch, wearing the head wrap as a garland around the neck, chewing on betel leaves, areca nuts and strips of tobacco, stuffing snuff up the nostrils, exchanging playful banter and laughter – the gang on the culvert seemed lively and relaxed.

That morning, they must have had their fill of leftover rice soaked overnight in water, or baked rice dumplings, or garnished flat rice, or rice upma, or adai or dosai, or boiled and garnished pulses or millets, or fermented rice water.

Their existence had atrophied these days because they had no work to do in the fields. It was the time of the year when the paddy crop had sprouted and grown, weeding was over, manure had been topped up, and the dark green stalks were swaying in the breeze.

Mature samba crop is a sight to behold, they said. These men would have returned after watering the fields early in the morning. The soil was so fertile that, as a Sangam poet described it, 'a peasant's heart would shrink from touching it with the sharp point of his ploughshare'. Spreading the water with one's feet was quite enough. Gathering dung, milking cows, cutting grass, bathing the cattle and calves and tethering them – all these tasks would have been completed by now.

'What's sown is plucked,' they say in Malayalam. In Tamil, we say, 'You reap what you sow.' From now on, they would have to wait to pluck that flowering. Words like 'reap' and 'pluck' were used to mean harvest. For now, they could only go home for the afternoon meal.

Many dice games, board games and card games would be in progress on the pyols of the temple under the shade of the banyan tree. A man might pass that way after stealing green papaya fruit from some farmer's tree, a marker of desperate poverty.

'Ei! What's the matter? Do you want to give your wife an abortion? Or your sister-in-law perhaps?' the gang would jeer as they watched him pass by.

'Shut the fuck up,' he would retort. 'I've plucked some fruit to make curry.'

'Oh! I get it now. Look at this cadaver's plight, having to make curry out of unripe papaya.'

'Sounds fair, I must say. You guard all the proceeds from selling paddy like a ghoul and let it rot. What's it to you if I steal papaya or greens from some poor chap's grove?'

They would enjoy themselves with a hearty laugh for some time.

Walking along the riverbank, Subbiah didn't feel the heat of the sun. Fields and orchards lay on the other side. Mynahs were chirping endlessly. Egrets, storks and herons were busily hunting worms. Half in the river and half on the road, there was a lush growth of mast wood on the riverbank. Bunches of white flowers like pearls. Thickets of arka, chaff flower, castor, senna, firebrand teak, chaste tree, prickly poppy, Indian mulberry, twisted spurge, square spurge and jungle geranium had burgeoned along with wild grass. Near the riverbank, amid the gurgle of flowing water stood thickets of reed, bulrush and Indian kale.

As he drew closer to the stone wall of the bathing ghat, some men sitting on it turned to look at Subbiah. One of them was Kuttalingam, who transported loads in his cart for the landlord in West Street. Seeing the pail in Subbiah's hand, he asked, 'Where are you coming from?'

Stepping aside, Subbiah walked on without saying a word.

'You won't answer when I'm asking you?' Kuttalingam got up, walked over to Subbiah and glanced at the pail.

'Well. A fitting honour, I see. So, you went to the church and got the powder milk they doled out? How ridiculous!' he berated Subbiah and tried to snatch the pail.

Filled to the brim, the milk sloshed a little, a few handfuls spilling on the road.

'Let go, anney. I have to go home,' Subbiah said in a polite, submissive and pitiful tone.

Grabbing the pail from Subbiah, Kuttalingam took the milk and showed it to the men sitting on the culvert. Middle-aged Pandurangam Pillai put his left hand inside the pail. Scooping some milk out, he examined it and said, 'The milk is thick, dey! You can add an equal amount of water.'

'Those chaps are already insolent and strutting around. Look at you, going there, swallowing their insults to get this milk. You've brought us shame,' Paradesiya Pillai said. His son, Sankara Coutralam was in the same class as Subbiah.

'Anney, anney! Give it back, anney. Let me go,' Subbiah begged and pleaded.

Another man said harshly, 'Do you have to batten your meat by drinking their milk? Beggar!' He was furious.

Holding the pail in his hand, Kuttalingam continued to rebuke Subbiah, 'From now on, don't ever get up to such nonsense. Do you hear me?' Then, taking a couple of steps forward, with one hand supporting the bottom of the pail, he tilted it and poured the milk into the river.

'Elei! Elei! Poor boy, lei! What have you done!' Kaduvai Pothi grew agitated. The rest enjoyed a hearty laugh. Kuttalingam held out the empty pail, from which milk was still dripping, to a tearful Subbiah.

Snatching the pail in a flash, Subbiah climbed down the steps to the river and stood in knee-deep water. He dunked the pail in the water and rinsed it clean. Catfish and carp rolled over and moved away. He washed his tear-stained face with water from the river and wiped it. When he returned home, his mother would ask him, 'Where did you go with that pail?'

As he stood gazing at the river, the sun was directly in line with his forehead. He turned back to climb the steps. To the right of the bathing ghat, for a few feet along the riverbank, sissoo spinach had grown in abundance. He went over and, standing near the edge, started pulling out handfuls of the greens and filling the pail. North-facing Isakkiyamman of the banyan tree had watched him all along!

THE TOOL OF HIS TRADE

Devibharathi

TRANSLATED BY N. KALYAN RAMAN

THANGARASU TAILOR SOLD off his old sewing machine. There was no other way out for him.

Was it a machine at all when he sold it?

To have kept it for so long was no mean achievement. He had endured all its torments only because he wanted to hold on to this last remnant of the dowry from his wife's parents. It wasn't his lawfully wedded wife, after all, that he had to put up with it forever.

Thangarasu had always got a special kick out of comparing the machine with his wife Soundhiram. His love for the machine was not a whit less than the affection he showered on her.

In the past, he had quarrelled with his wife and packed her off to her parents' house. He had even thought about getting rid of her, once and for all. But Thangarasu Tailor could never contemplate parting with, leave alone getting rid of, his machine.

As a child is to the mother and a field ox to the farmer, so the sewing machine was to Thangarasu Tailor.

When he sat at the machine and started sewing, his whole demeanour was transformed. By nature, Thangarasu was a rough sort. But as soon as he sat at his machine, that roughness disappeared somewhere; instead, he was overcome by shyness and exultation, as if touching a new bride. When he got four or five orders together for new dresses, he even did a special puja for the machine.

As soon as he opened his shop in the morning, he polished the machine to shine like a mirror; nothing less would please him. He oiled it frequently. On Fridays, after adorning it with a string of flowers, he waved a camphor flame in front of the sewing machine and lit incense sticks. He was very particular about not allowing anyone apart from himself to come anywhere near it.

He would often scold the machine as though it was animate and had feelings; or whack it hard with a pair of scissors. During moments of great stress, he was even ready to give up his profession. Yet, his love for the machine had never wavered.

But all this was in the past, ten or fifteen years ago.

The day he brought Soundhiram as a new bride to Loganathapuram was the happiest ever in Thangarasu Tailor's life. The entire population of that locality was amazed and delighted at Soundhiram's arrival. The houses of Loganathapuram, draped with tattered jute curtains in the doorway, and its streets engulfed by the stench from overflowing gutters and rotting garbage, welcomed her with boundless love. To have such a beauteous girl come to live in Loganathapuram was an honour that far exceeded what those streets and houses deserved. Not all girls in Loganathapuram were unsightly, though.

Keshavan Nair's wife, Unni Mary, had teeth that were somewhat uneven, but her eyes were beautiful, like a mullet's. Though Vasantha Ruby, Thomas mechanic's eldest daughter, sported a largish nose, which other girl could match her long, thick, jet-black hair? Subramaniam Gounder's wife Sampooranam was dark, yes, but women with a voluptuous figure like hers were rare. The beauty of Parimala's eyebrows, Elizabeth Teacher's rows of pearly white teeth, Usha Rani's rosy feet and calves coated with soft, downy hair – you could look at them for as many hours as you wanted without feeling tired.

Though all this was true, everyone readily agreed that Soundhiram possessed, in her single person, all the aforesaid markers of physical beauty.

However, apart from Soundhiram, there was another reason for Thangarasu Tailor's delight and pride. The arrival at his doorstep by a horse cart of a brand-new sewing machine, as part of the dowry from his father-in-law, had made him doubly happy.

To everyone who dropped by to look at his new bride, he showed off his machine and sought their opinion. While prostrating at the feet of elders for their blessings, he boasted, 'See the machine I've got? Doesn't it look just like Karna Maharaja's chariot?'

For him, it was a matter of deep regret that he couldn't bring the machine along when he took his wife to the tent theatre, bazaar, or on visits to relatives' houses.

On the third day following its arrival, Thangarasu rented a shop beside the big portia tree in Loganathapuram and set up his new machine. He named his shop 'Soundhiram Tailors' and started plying his trade. Soundhiram performed drishti, a simple ritual to ward off evil eyes, for both the machine and Thangarasu.

The shop did very well during the initial months. Thangarasu lived happily, looking after his wife with as much love and care as he lavished on the machine. But there is such a thing called time, isn't there? Does it ever stand still?

Take an example: our country, which is a free nation now, was still a slave to the white man when Thangarasu was born. Thangarasu was not a tailor then either, nor was tailoring his career of choice at the time. As a child, when his father yelled at him, 'Go to school, da!', he went. Later one day, his father said, 'You've had enough schooling. Go apprentice yourself in a tailoring shop,' and placed him with Sayabu Tailor. Obeying his father's command, Thangarasu started training to work as a tailor.

At first he stitched buttonholes by hand; later, he sewed buttons.

Initially, he hadn't liked his vocation at all. Sayabu, who suffered from chronic bronchitis, had adopted cuffing Thangarasu frequently on the head and pinching him sharply on the thighs as duties appropriate for a master.

The little boy Thangarasu, fearful of his guru's aforesaid proclivities, kept sewing buttons with his head bowed, never looking up. 'When you're free, go over to the machine and practise tailoring,' his father urged him. But whenever he went near the machine, Sayabu hit him with a pair of tailoring scissors.

Poor Thangarasu.

He believed firmly that he was never going to learn tailoring from that Sayabu, that he would keep stitching buttonholes and sewing buttons through his entire lifetime, that as long as he possessed a head and had flesh on his thighs, this Sayabu would cuff him on the head and pinch him on the thighs.

Countless summers, winters, and seasons of rain and wind arrived in turn, year after year. Even the games children played – gilli, top, kabaddi, marbles – changed frequently. These changes came about without any particular effort from anyone. However, no matter how much he tried, Thangarasu could not to go beyond stitching buttonholes, sewing buttons and suffering corporal punishment at the hands of Sayabu.

'Whatever happens, I won't go to Sayabu Tailor's any more,' he declared one day, and tried staying at home. But on that day, instead of Sayabu Tailor, it was his father who scolded and thrashed him. He preferred getting this treatment from Sayabu Tailor; Sayabu at least bought him a cup of tea when it was nearing dusk.

So, resolved that this was his ordained fate and it would never change, Thangarasu continued to perform his daily chores.

However, contrary to what Thangarasu himself had imagined, he did learn tailoring well; once he attained the status of an independent tailor, he married Soundhiram, received a spanking new sewing machine as dowry and set up a tailoring shop in Loganathapuram. How life had changed for him!

That the country, which was a colony under the white man when Thangarasu was born, became independent later has already been mentioned. But Thangarasu was not aware of that change for a long time. No one could blame him for that lapse.

When the country gained freedom at midnight, Thangarasu was fast asleep. He was a little boy then. Since he did not know that the country was going to become independent later that night, he came home from the shop, ate his gruel and went to sleep. As soon as he fell asleep, Sayabu appeared in his dreams. Even in the dream, Sayabu was his usual self: he cuffed and pinched Thangarasu. At the very first cuff, Thangarasu's skull was broken and blood gushed out. The flesh on his thigh was yanked out until only the bone was left. Sayabu twisted Thangarasu's ears, and then the head itself disappeared. Sayabu had looked normal at first, seated at his sewing machine and coughing incessantly. The next moment he was sitting on top of a buffalo. His eyes were large as coconuts. His whole beard was bunched up into a big moustache on his face, and his measuring tape had morphed into his lasso of death. Sayabu came in hot pursuit of Thangarasu, roaring now instead of coughing relentlessly…

'Buttonhole, button, Lord of Death, his lasso, measuring tape, skull, thigh, blood, aiyo…' Poor Thangarasu woke up screaming. Alarmed and concerned that something had happened to their son, his father and mother calmed him down and made him go back to sleep. Amid all the commotion, Thangarasu did not learn about India becoming independent that night. Even now, he didn't know much about any of that. His life was confined to his home and his work. When he grew up and became eligible to vote, and somebody called him to vote, Thangarasu asked him, 'Vote-aa? What is that? Why should I vote?'

'We have to choose our own leaders, Thangarasu ... ours is a free country, don't you know?'

This was the sum of what Thangarasu knew about the nation's independence.

Even if many such changes took place without Thangarasu Tailor being aware of them, he had not really gained or lost a great deal in consequence. However, only when the number of families and residents in Loganathapuram increased and still newer tailoring shops sprouted here and there was Thangarasu able to understand that events in the outside world could also affect his life.

First, Bahadur Tailor's shop came up in Kattabomman Street.

Young Bahadur knew how to stitch clothes in the modern style. The man, too, looked handsome and stylish. He sat in his shop dressed in a different outfit every day, looking tip-top always. His manner suggested that he bore testimony to his own professional skill. Even the name he had chosen for his shop was very appealing. It was the name of a voluptuous actress who was then at the peak of her popularity. In ninety-nine per cent of her films, she danced with nothing on except her undergarments. As soon as Bahadur named his shop after an actress who hardly wore any clothes and hung up her portrait, the citizens of Loganathapuram started frequenting his shop, if only to pass the time.

Such ploys were beyond Thangarasu. First: no matter how hard he tried, Thangarasu could not turn into a young man like Bahadur Tailor. Second: he was no expert in stitching clothes in the modern style like Bahadur was. At his age, he couldn't really apprentice himself to a tailor, enduring cuffs on the head and verbal abuses just to learn the modern style, could he? Nor could he afford to employ such a tailor in his shop.

Feeding four people and sending his two children to school were onerous tasks in themselves. There were two reasons why Thangarasu Tailor sent his children to school. First, he did not want his children to grow up ignorant like him. Though he himself didn't know when the country had gained independence, at least his children should grow up knowing something about current events. Such was his wish. Second, he didn't want his children to become tailors like him, hard put to earn even their daily bread; he wanted them to study well and take up white-collar jobs.

Moreover, Thangarasu Tailor's machine was not as new as Bahadur Tailor's. It had become old, and several of its parts were worn out. Because of the loud clatter that rose from his machine whenever he sat down at it to work, citizens of Loganathapuram who lived next to his shop had begun to think of Thangarasu as their mortal enemy. Hanging up the picture of a screen vamp was the only thing he could do in that situation. As for the shop's name, he was of the firm opinion that no other name could be more appealing than 'Soundhiram'.

It slowly became clear to Thangarasu Tailor that he simply could not compete with Bahadur.

So what?

Would the planter fail to water the sapling? Would their Creator forget to feed them regularly? What was he going to achieve by scrambling to earn a lot of money? Four small stomachs in his family – how could they go empty? Come what may, we will live as we do now – Thangarasu began to console himself by indulging in such philosophical reflections.

However, the march of time did not spare him. Just as Bahadur had set up shop in Kattabomman Street, Peter and Raghavan settled down with their sewing machines in Anna and Ambedkar streets respectively. But neither their professional skill nor the appeal of their shops put any fresh dent in Thangarasu Tailor's fortunes. By then, his sewing machine had already become unfit for sewing. One or two cloth-pieces were brought to his shop once in a rare while. But Thangarasu had neither the threads for sewing those clothes nor oil for lubricating his machine. If he completed the job by borrowing some money from the customer himself, he was left with only a rupee or two for his labours.

Even that piffling amount had to be smuggled home to Soundhiram after proffering clever excuses and abject pleas to a phalanx of dunning creditors. Only then would she feed him gruel without showering him with abuses. Or else…

'You call yourself a man! Do you see other men carrying on like you? If a man with a family to look after won't even earn a tumbler of rice in a day, how can the woman run the household? Those two children – if they don't go to the workshop at their age and earn a couple of rupees, there will be no food. You said you will educate them, you couldn't even do that!'

Thangarasu's only answer to her was silence. Poor thing, what could she do? She was just like the machine she had brought with her as dowry. Like so many women, she, too, had stepped into her husband's home laden with many dreams about the future. But life brought her only grief and tears.

Even in the face of such penury, Thangarasu held on to his machine. Instead of sitting in his shop and waiting for the orders, he started going where the orders were. He fitted a wooden plank with caster wheels, placed his machine on it, and wheeled it all over the locality, mending old clothes.

Did it matter where he plied his trade? He did not steal, or cheat anyone by lying to them, did he? He tried to cope with life's challenges by earning his daily bread through honest toil.

However, since the protagonist of our story was neither a political leader nor a character in a movie, throwing and accepting challenges were matters he was not used to.

Could a man ever challenge his creditor?

Thangarasu Tailor was forced to sell his machine because he could no longer fend off his creditors. We don't have to go into the antecedents of how Thangarasu got himself into debt.

All that was quite normal.

We hear that there are innumerable crorepatis like the Tatas and the Birlas in our country. Even they are reported to be in debt to the tune of hundreds of crores. India is such a big country; even so, it owes thousands of crores to America.

Compared to our great nation, what was Thangarasu? Just an ordinary tailor. He, too, owed someone two hundred and fifty rupees. On that fateful day, when his creditor tracked down Thangarasu with his machine and held him captive with a towel around his neck, Thangarasu had no other option.

He sold his machine.

He had scolded that machine so often; kicked it a few times. He had even looked forward to the day when he would be rid of it. But the way he brooded and cried inwardly when it actually left him was a secret no one else came to know.

What would Thangarasu do now? It was something he himself didn't know.

After paying off his creditor, Thangarasu took whatever little money that remained and went to a liquor shop. It was a long time since the machine had earned him so much money. He came out of the liquor shop with bloodshot eyes and staggered all the way to Loganathapuram.

Bahadur's tailoring shop on Kattabomman Street was humming with activity. Thangarasu stood and stared at the shop. New machine. Bahadur Tailor, still a young man. Seeing him, Thangarasu Tailor was reminded of the times when he had sat at his machine as a young man. His eyes filled with tears.

Reeling on unsteady feet, he entered the shop. He grabbed the remaining notes from the pocket in his underwear and held them bunched up in his fist.

'Bahadur!'

He held the rupee notes directly in front of Bahadur's face, spreading them in display.

'Look, I've sold the machine. Do you know how long I've had that machine with me? I nurtured it like my own child. I sold it today. What kind of machine was it? Only fit for plucking pubic hair. With that machine, you couldn't even mend old clothes. To hell with it! Never mind, I'll get another one. A new machine, I'll show you! I'll buy a machine newer than yours! Do you think I am babbling after a few drinks? Yes, I've had a few. I drank for fifteen rupees, do you know that? What's the big deal? I'll drink even more. I'll drink for all the money in my pocket. What do I need money for? It means less than nothing to me. Do you feel like having a drink?'

Thangarasu quarrelled with Bahadur Tailor. The story of how he bought the machine, sold it, its grand features – he narrated everything over and over again, and then wept.

He would narrate the same story to many more people. He would tell it to Peter Tailor on Anna Street, Raghavan Tailor on Ambedkar Street, and to all other residents of Loganathapuram. He would narrate it every time he came across a human face.

He would talk about his machine to his wife Soundhiram and his children too; he would end up weeping. He would also quarrel with them.

My pen is not potent enough to describe all that he might do.

MIRAGE

Tamilnathy

TRANSLATED BY YASHASVI ARUNKUMAR

It WAS A red-coloured seven … It had eyes and lips. It came skiing through the snow and passed her by. It was thrilling to watch the contrast between the black–red figure and the spotless white snow. The seven vanished from sight for a while before coming back. Two other sevens also turned up from somewhere. The three of them rolled into one straight line. She raised her hands and shouted in joy.

For a little while she laid there, in a state of euphoria between dream and reality. The neat and orderly line of sevens held her captive. She was overwhelmed by a weariness towards herself and the excitement of gambling. 'Only god can save me,' she told herself.

It was rare for her to think of god. When entering the casino, she would pray for a win. When the realization of an imminent loss coursed through her veins, she would appeal to god to take her away from there before she lost everything. Aside from these instances, she did not really think of god very much. Anyway, she had Amma to pray for her instead. One of Amma's prayers was indeed to cure her daughter's prodigal ways.

'If you have money, please give...' Amma looked up at her daughter's request.

'Why...?'

Before answering that question, she hardened her face. She knew that by doing so, she could get the money after just one or two questions. Appa often remarked, 'Your mother is like the World Bank.' Amma's savings, preserved in multiple inner, outer and secret compartments, had rescued their family from debt many times.

She did feel remorse for swindling the fives and tens her mother saved and depositing them into the casino machine. It was a money-devouring monster. A monster with numbers, letters, flowers, pigs and mermaids hidden in its depths.

But she would console herself each time: 'If I win big, of course I will give it to my mother.' She had won. She'd never given.

'I am going with my girlfriends to Niagara...' she informed her mother.

'How many times will you see that place?'

She stood without speaking. She was Amma's only child. The mother was used to the daughter's silence.

Back then, she used to be unable to take her eyes off the Niagara, losing all sense of time. Captivated by a fantastical world made entirely of water. Her companions would all but vanish in the thick mist. The sublime nature of the waterfall scared her sometimes. The Niagara fell with a deafening roar, with unmatched prowess and purity, and with a beauty that seemed to invite one to jump to their deaths. But ever since her casino addiction had started haunting her, she had never gone back to it. One day, when she had returned to her hotel room, silently crying over her losses at the casino, she had noticed the Niagara pouring from the corner of her eye. Shaken, she had returned to her senses to see the white plummet of the Niagara through the window. A soundless cascade.

Amma took out a hundred dollars and gave it to her. She released the next arrow in her arsenal.

'I may be stuck in an unknown place with no money … What if I have to stay overnight…?'

Another fifty came out. She had also slyly slipped in that she wouldn't be back home that night.

The seven that came skiing on the snow reminded her of a penguin. The blaring sound of that machine, relentless like the siren of an ambulance, now started ringing inside her own head. She felt a heat wave pass through her. She touched her own cheeks, her body burned.

She met all the expectations of her community with ease: at home, at work, she read books, listened to music, went on evening walks, had a few friends … one boyfriend, and so on. Her boyfriend Sudhan had even teased her about it.

'You fool everyone with that innocent face of yours.'

He was the only one who knew about her weakness. As soon as the thought of the casino would cross her mind, she would forget everything and become a new woman altogether. She would fearfully observe how her own thoughts sprouted like a magic stalk, originating at her feet and rapidly progressing up her body, branches struggling to break out of her skull.

The multicoloured neon lights, the blinking digits – they were all things that excited her. And the number seven in particular – if she happened to catch it glowing somewhere, that was it! Even the sound of coins being poured into the coin counter made her go berserk. The clanking of coins afflicted her with a feeling of both happiness and sadness. She would gravitate towards the sound like iron to a magnet. Thoughts of her relationships, belongings, her duties, her 'good girl' reputation – everything would start to turn foggy like streets on a wintry night. She would try protesting the urge by reminding herself of all kinds of things. But the gambler in her, the one who didn't give a damn about anything, would become one of the mice running behind the pied piper. All preparations for the trip would begin in full swing.

Her mind started calculating. She had three hundred and twenty dollars in the bank. She could use up to two hundred on her credit card. If she added the hundred and fifty she had got from her mother, the amount would cross six hundred and fifty. After travel and hotel costs, she would have five hundred and fifty left. That was more than enough! Further, the voice inside her head kept assuring her that she was not going to lose this time. She recalled that winter night she had returned home with eighteen hundred dollars.

It was Sudhan who had first taught her how to operate the slot machine. In the days that followed, he had regretted it deeply.

'Truthfully speaking, even an idiot can play this. You have to place your hand on this circle and press once. The numbers and letters inside the machine will turn around before finally stopping in place. If you get a row of the same numbers or fruits or whatever, you win. If a spot moves even one place up or down, you lose. You can win a small amount, or a jackpot. That's all there is to it!'

He had revelled in the joy of teaching something new to his girlfriend. At first, she had called it a 'mindless game'. Then she had started nagging Sudhan to take her to play that very same mindless game. When he began lecturing her about responsibility, she started to go by herself without telling him. She was not a regular. Once in two or three months, a light would suddenly go off in her brain. That was all it would take! She would bolt out of her seat like there was a fire burning under her bum and set out for the casino.

She packed a few books and DVDs along with a day's worth of clothing into her travelling bag. She found herself thinking: If I win the jackpot this time, I will stay there for two days and rest. But just as the thought ended, reason prevailed on the impossibility of such an event. Damned woman, she scolded herself.

'Have something to eat before leaving,' Amma called out.

She was not in the mood to eat, but was moved to action at the thought that she could go directly to the casino if she ate at home.

Amma commented that her face had lost its radiance that day. She did wonder if her mother knew her secret. No … wasn't she such a model daughter? She laughed to herself. She felt guilty for fooling her mother. Briefly considered throwing away her plans, and staying home and reading instead. But the mermaid stood right at her doorstep, shiny scales and all, beckoning. A '7' horse neighed, shaking its shiny mane.

While waiting for her bus, she saw a family – Tamilians – in their car, chatting and laughing merrily. It was a Saturday; they were probably going to some restaurant. She imagined what they might say if they knew she was going to a casino. 'Ruined woman!' they would say. Most of them would probably look down on her, as if she were an abnormal creature. They would start a thousand rumours about her. 'That girl…'

A man in a jogging suit kept turning back and looking at her as he passed her by. She wondered if he could guess where she was headed. Maybe he, too, had a habit of going to the casino. After a while she realized she had been unintentionally staring into the eyes of everyone who went past her. How happy these people look, she mused. Her sense of self-pity increased. She tried to justify her actions using self-pity, reminding herself of the poverty of her childhood, how she had been a refugee, and all her struggles as an immigrant.

If only she could escape to the casino without anyone noticing … if only it weren't so far away and she could be there in a second … if only she had the money, she would have moved away close to the Niagara. She felt frustrated by her middle-class lifestyle, one that revolved only around one's job and family.

How beautiful and grand was the casino! With its entrance, constructed like an upturned bowl and lit up 24/7. The hotel building rose up behind the entrance, the English word 'CASINO' shining in bright red letters. One day, she had walked out of the building in tears after losing money. Those letters, with their shimmering, seductive aura, had reminded her of the women who walked on Queen Street with flashy bags and high heels. Many times, she had experienced the terror of walking into a wild animal's den when entering the casino. But the thrill of gambling had always triumphed.

Just beyond the main entrance, there was a round crystal showcase. Mini fountains rose and fell delightfully inside. People always hung around its edge, taking pictures. She would judge them: Ignorant fools, they do not know the pleasures of gambling.

It was roughly a two-hour journey. Along the way, barren trees announced the start of winter. The deep-blue river was calm. Tied to its shores, boats jostled slightly in the wind. The rusted boats, tied to one another, were reminiscent of sailboats from antiquity. She was sure they predated the century at least. She wondered why the slot machine did not use figures like boats and cars.

She did not know how to play poker. She had never tried to learn, neither did she wish to do so. She had seen those players, deep in thought, with scrunched-up faces, stroking the edges of their casino-issued poker chips. There would be Tamil faces amongst them as well. Mostly men. Very rarely women. Numerous men had shot her looks of righteous censure. 'A Tamil woman … you should be responsible and stay at home … What are you doing here?' She knew that rules like 'Tamil women should not drink' also extended to gambling. Earlier, she used to fear those looks and leave the place hurriedly. Later, she learned to casually throw a look back, as if to say, 'Well, what the fuck are *you* doing here?'

She decided to try the same slot machine again. She had relived that day many times in her head.

It had been a joyful day!

The slot machine was shaped like a telephone tower. At first, the screen had stopped counting at twenty. Then it went on to forty. Then sixty, eighty, hundred, thousand, ten thousand, and it kept going until it reached its peak.

Six thousand two hundred and thirty-five dollars!

Jackpot!

The horn that announced the 'Jackpot' started blaring. As if that wasn't enough, the light on top of the machine started swirling with a 'Win … Win…' too. She wanted to scream out of ecstasy. She had an uneasy feeling in her stomach. But with the composure of an experienced gambler, she smiled and sat quietly. People gathered around. Those playing on the other machines looked at her with jealousy. Yet, even as their faces darkened, they cloaked them in a polite smile and wished her well. She genuinely felt sorry for them. She could see herself in their eyes – the girl who had been on a losing streak just a moment ago. But the exhilaration of winning took over her senses quickly. She could still remember how her body had felt as weightless as a fleck of cotton or a feather. It was truly a miracle that she had won such a large amount from that machine, where one could only bet a maximum of twenty-five hundred dollars.

Sixty-two hundred-dollar bills, patiently counted one by one. The employee placed them on her outstretched palms. The remaining thirty-five dollars came separately. She gave the whole of it to him as a gift. She felt on top of the slot machine. When he left, thanking her profusely, she looked carefully to see if there was any surprise in his eyes. This was a secret game between her and the employees. She had seen how those at the desk completely changed their attitude when an unassuming Asian woman surprised them with hefty tips. Sometimes, she did it to make them happy. Other times, when they treated her dismissively because of the colour of her skin, she did it to momentarily unsettle them. Yes, indeed, she did this for the honour of all Asians.

She always kept a mental note of everyone she would share her money with if she won big. In her mind, that money was a fine she paid for the crime of gambling. The white women and the yellow-faced women who came to the casino did not seem to feel that kind of guilt, she mused.

She finally checked into the casino hotel and flung her travelling bag on to the bed. Then she touched up her make-up and made her way to the casino. As she waited for the pedestrian light to turn green, she considered returning to her room and reading something or watching something on her laptop instead. But those neat rows of cherries beckoned her. Pigs purred. She started walking faster. The wind felt extra chilly that day. Maybe it was because the waterfall was so close. The violent wind tousled her hair.

None of the slot machines that looked like telephone towers were free. She waited.

In the early days, she used to play an absurd game while waiting. She would stand outside and imagine the machine in her own head, one in which she could neither win nor lose. But she soon grew tired of the bluff and stopped. She became one of those women who could breathe only after they had finally sat in front of the slot machine. The process of waiting became bitter.

It didn't look like anyone was going to move away from those specific machines. She went in search of another machine.

Reassuring herself that she was not going to lose today, she sat down in front of a one-cent slot machine. These machines had been recently introduced in the casino. It took her only a little while to figure out it was a scam. There was no way to bet one cent on that machine. You had to bet a minimum of ninety cents to have a decent chance at winning. By the time she realized the scam, she had already lost a hundred and sixty dollars. The machine continued to buzz, as if to say, 'THERE … You are almost there … You are going to win!' It conjured up words and set them on her. She grew flustered, her agitation slowly spreading inside.

She went in search of yet another machine. She lost another twenty on the way. Since it was a Saturday, the casino was crowded. Aside from the gamblers, there was a crowd who had come just to pass time and watch others play. Men and women sat drinking in the bar, both in pairs and alone. She noticed that those who sat alone sat with their faces downcast. She reasoned that maybe they had lost. She also noticed a yellow woman sitting with tears streaking down her wide face. Must have been from either China or Korea.

Scantily dressed women laughed boisterously as they walked by, clinging to the arms of their male companions. She saw a few others drinking so much free coffee it seemed as if that was their one true calling. She felt an inexplicable rage.

In just a little while, all the humans around her vanished. She felt tired, as if she were walking alone on a never-ending road lined with machines. She crashed into other people. The magnificent ceiling seemed to collapse on her head. She felt out of breath.

She moved to an uncrowded area and sat down in front of a deserted machine. Coloured sevens swirled in its belly – one of them, a bright red seven. Black accents on the edges of the seven had transformed it into a sporting horse, just like the one in her dream. She remembered her mother telling her that dreams do not occur without a reason. Her mind started chanting, 'Oh god … Oh god…' Each time she pressed the switch, she waited anxiously. It will come now … it will come now…

It wasn't a mean-spirited machine. It gave. Then it took. It gave. Then it took. One time, she landed a line of black horses. She won a hundred dollars. When the wheels turned, her heart would palpitate. The figures would come tantalizingly close to a straight line, and then slip away. What a deceiving game! 'If not you, who else?' it seemed to goad her. One seven … another seven … the third seven would almost be on the verge of making it but slip away into hiding. The machine stole back the hundred dollars. She only had the satisfaction of having been allowed to play for a short while. She stood up to leave the machine that had decimated sixty dollars. Damned woman, she rebuked herself. She must have been loud. A white woman standing nearby threw her a strange look and moved away. She felt ashamed.

She opened her purse and counted the remaining cash. She had exactly ten twenty-dollar bills and a few coins. Two hundred dollars. She felt her head spinning. She thought of her mother, how she had commented that morning about her face losing its radiance. She felt guilty.

Even then, she believed that her luck could turn around any second. It had happened before. Everything would work out. That magical second ... everyone around her would transform into angels and fairies. She would take her winning money and walk out of the casino without looking back. She would then have time to properly admire the small fountains near the entrance. After that, she would return to her hotel room, heart brimming with joy. If she felt like it, she might even walk all the way to the falls. Night would coat the street like gold dust. She would perhaps order in a pizza, or maybe a kanreki. All she needed to do was one thing: find the right machine to play.

'You give your money to the machine. Then you fall at its feet and beg it to give you back the money it took. Do you think those who run casinos are out of their minds? If everyone could win a jackpot, the owners would have to close the establishment and go home. Every single person who comes to play believes they will win the jackpot. But the thing is ... we can't win all the time ... You can only win once in a while, that's the first rule of gambling.' She remembered Sudhan's words.

She was hungry. She took out her phone and checked the time. It was eleven-thirty at night. She had a missed call from her mother. She felt enraged, she didn't know why, and turned on the silent mode on her phone. The restaurant inside the casino would close in half an hour.

The entire place looked like it was covered in smoke. Since smoking was prohibited inside the casino premises, she realized it was not cigarette smoke. Maybe her vision had blurred because she had been squinting at one thing for a long time. She grew slightly dizzy.

Enough … she wanted to go back. The letters on top of the exit glowed a bright red. 'Go … go…,' said the angel. 'So, you're really going?' teased the mermaid. She walked towards the nearest exit. The restaurant was right next to it.

On the way, she saw seven or eight people gathered around one machine. She peeked at the scene. Jackpot.

Twenty-five hundred dollars!

That man – an old man – stood grinning with shaking hands. He looked like someone who had never won before. His face showed poverty … his clothes too. A woman was loudly narrating the story of someone who had won fifteen thousand dollars the previous week. To be honest, there was nothing to narrate. One press of a button … a straight line of figures … that was all!

One needed a million eyes to take in the figures that stood in a straight line announcing a jackpot. One time, a line of piggies had yielded her fifteen hundred dollars. The win had come with the last twenty dollars she had had with her, just as she had been about to miserably walk out. From then onwards, she had grown extra fond of pigs. Another time, a group of mermaids had fallen in a line. She stroked their scaly tails lovingly. Dust covered her hands. Red sevens covered in flames had won her five hundred dollars on many days.

She felt like trying one last time. Her stomach grumbled in hunger. Her head continued to spin. Things appeared out of place. She feared she would faint. The machine she selected next was ravenous, it gobbled up her money with unmatched determination. It did everything except give her a win. Even though she knew she was losing, she kept stuffing bills into the machine with a vengeance.

Her stomach had drawn in, her jeans were starting to slide off her hips. Even without looking in the mirror, she could sense the dark circles under her eyes. Shrivelled face, messy hair, she probably looked like a beggar, begging from those heartless machines. She wanted to cry. Her self-hatred increased. If not for rules of propriety, she would have screamed her lungs out and run out of there. But she could not behave howsoever she wanted. 'Shit,' she cursed under her breath every second. She was afraid that they would throw her out if she spoke or acted in a violent or disruptive manner.

There were rehabilitation centres specifically for those who wanted to get out of their gambling addiction. She had seen a number of people walking out of the casino, tired after weeping away their losses, all the world's sorrow pooling in their eyes. She had also seen many couples stepping inside the casino with their fingers interlaced, but walking out like sworn enemies after losing their money and fighting about it.

How many days had she taken herself to the casino, as swift as the wind, without even a glance back! How many times had she languished inside, as if she were in hell, chanting 'Oh god … oh god…' in her head! Those at the restaurant might remember the Asian woman who had walked in past midnight, looking like she was going to pass out. Just before she reached the point of no return, her self-inquiry began:

'Why am I like this?'

'Because I am alone,' she answered her own question.

She conjured up an image of herself in her mind and spat at it in disgust.

'No more … no more…' she started blabbering. She had pretty much lost everything. Meaningless words started floating around in her head. She had twenty dollars left at hand. It would suffice for dinner. She had the hundred-dollar security deposit paid to the hotel. They would return the deposit when she checked out. It was more than enough for the return journey. Her stomach troubled her, she couldn't make out if it was from hunger or fear.

Not knowing what to do, she sat down for a few minutes. She felt like sobbing. An idea struck her: to use the eighty dollars she had set aside in the monthly budget for paying the telephone and TV bills. She could give her luck one last chance. As soon as the thought crossed her mind, she started walking towards the ATM machine. She firmly believed that money would raise her from the grips of hell.

Everything will change in a second! Yes!

As she indiscriminately fed each twenty-dollar bill into the machine, foregoing all sense of shame, she loudly implored to god to somehow deliver her from her infernal misery. But her prayers were lost in the din of the casino.

Those eighty dollars also vanished. She thrust her credit card into the ATM, pleading for just twenty more dollars, but it gave up on her. She wondered if she could borrow money from someone, but who to ask at that hour? It was one-thirty in the night. The restaurant had closed. Her hunger adamantly reminded her of its presence.

'Have you ever thought of cheating on me…?' Sudhan had once asked her playfully.

She had replied, 'I don't know if you can call it cheating. But … if a man had offered me five hundred dollars to go with him on the days I have sat not knowing what to do after losing in the casino, I would have gone with him.'

Sudhan had not taken her seriously; he was used to her brazen and fatalistic ways.

She stayed sitting, her face drawn in sadness. She came to the shocking realization that she was moving towards the exact same position she had told Sudhan about. She observed with horror as thoughts of suicide rose to the surface from the depths of her mind. She shook her head and walked towards the restroom.

When she looked at herself in the mirror, she noticed her eyes had sunk in. Her self-loathing rose to a crescendo. She flung open the heavy doors of the casino and walked out. She bought herself a sandwich and a water bottle outside. The 24/7 convenience store offered the combo for eighteen dollars. She mentally calculated that the balance would suffice for breakfast.

When she came back to her room and threw herself on the bed, her mind would not stop murmuring, 'Never again…' She slapped herself hard. She took out her mobile phone. Amma had called her again. Sudhan had called her six times. She wanted to call him and cry, to ask him to take her away from this netherworld.

When his name showed up on the screen again, she took the call and placed the phone against her ear.

'How much did you lose?' he cut to the chase.

She remained silent.

'Will you never learn your lesson?'

He asked her again, 'How much?'

'Five hundred and forty.'

'Seventy thousand rupees.' He sounded severe.

She wept soundlessly. Hiccups rattled her body. He could not bear it.

'This is the last time. I won't come here again…'

'Tell me the truth, how much did you lose in the machine? I will give you the money … but you have to get out of there immediately…'

She swiftly sat up on the bed. A flash of happiness passed over her. She wanted to kneel down and thank god at that very moment. Sudhan's status rose up in her mind.

'There are no buses at this hour.'

'Okay ... then you should leave by the first bus in the morning...'
'Mhmm ... I will not come here again. If I do, you can leave me.'
'All right.' She could hear his light laughter on the other end.

⚡

She had slept well. As soon as she opened her eyes to the morning, memories of the previous day swarmed her mind. Her eyes misted in self-pity. The more she thought of Sudhan, the more love flooded her heart. She checked out of her room. Once she got back the hundred-dollar security deposit, she procured a copy of the timetable of buses to Toronto.

Once she exited the hotel, she took out the hundred dollars. She carefully counted out twenty-five dollars for the bus fare and kept it aside. She started walking towards the casino.

HEARTBREAK

Imayam

TRANSLATED BY JANANI KANNAN

Sangeetha unlocked the door and entered her house. She dropped her bag on the sofa and was just about to head to the bathroom when Ashok said, 'I am going to step out for some time, Sangeetha.' She stopped and asked him, 'When did you get back from work?'

'Just ten minutes ago,' Ashok said, in English. 'Urgent work,' he added, as he put on his shoes.

'Come evenings and you seem to have urgent work every day,' Sangeetha commented, sizing him up with a scorn on her face.

'Let's talk after I get back,' Ashok replied, as he looked for the keys to his motorcycle.

Sangeetha knew what he meant by 'urgent work'. She knew he would leave, then tipple beyond control and return late at night. Glaring at him, she asked, 'If you keep running away from home, will the problem resolve on its own? For how many years are you planning on running away like this?'

'What did you say?' Ashok turned to Sangeetha, abandoning his search for his bike keys. She offered no response; she had recognized that both the manner in which she had posed the question and the manner in which she stood would be deemed a little out of line by Ashok. She tried to make her way to the bathroom instead. Ashok stopped her and asked her again, teeming with anger, 'What did you say?'

What did I say? Why is he getting so angry? Sangeetha stood fuddled, unable to decipher what was going on.

'What did you say? Tell me!' he persisted. The sight of him sweating and shaking in anger frightened her.

Last week, as Ashok was getting ready to go out, she had asked him to buy some fruits on his way back. He said he would but forgot to get any. 'You are all talk and no action,' she had remarked, casually. But Ashok became furious. 'What do you mean by "no action"? Why did you say that?' He had badgered her for over two hours. Is he going to do something like that today too? I must get out of this situation, she thought. But before she could take a couple of steps towards the bathroom, he got in her way and barked at her, 'First, answer me. Why did you say that?' He then added, 'Am I trying to run away?'

'You said you had some place to go to. Come back and we can talk…' But even before Sangeetha could finish her sentence, he roared loudly, 'Am I trying to run away?'

Trying to avoid his question, she said, 'Move aside, please. Let me go to the bathroom.'

'That can wait. Answer me first.'

'Give me a second, I will be back,' she said and tried to go past him to the bathroom, but he shoved her and growled angrily, 'Give me an answer and then go.'

His imposing stance, the forcefulness with which he shoved her, the sternness in his voice, all made it clear to Sangeetha that he was not going to back away without causing trouble. When it occurred to her that the only way out of the situation was to be submissive, she replied in a subdued tone, 'It hasn't been a minute since I got back from work. It looked like you were literally waiting for me to get home just so you could leave. That's why I got angry, and I said that. I'm sorry!' But that wasn't enough for Ashok. 'What did you insinuate with those words?'

'I didn't insinuate anything—' Sangeetha replied, but he cut her off. 'I know what you were implying with those words,' he said, and punched the wall arrogantly. He stepped close to Sangeetha and asked in a pleading voice, 'Please tell me.'

'Let me go to the bathroom.'

'Tell me the truth and then go.'

'I will not say things like that again. Please, Ashok.'

'Whether you say things like that again or not is not important. What did you mean by those words? That is what I want to know now! That is important.' Ashok's voice grew more stubborn, his face, tenser.

'Let us talk later. You go on as you planned, please,' Sangeetha urged, annoyed that she let herself be trapped in such a situation.

'No, no!' he said, kicking the floor a few times. Then, suddenly seeming weary, he sat down on the sofa and said, 'This is my mistake.' He looked in Sangeetha's direction and said imploringly, 'If you tell me the truth, my anger will ease up a little. Just tell me what you meant, please.' Continuing in the same tone, he added: 'My body is my enemy, my body is the one that brings me shame.' And then, out of the blue, he began to slap himself while shouting, 'This is all my mistake, this is all my mistake!'

'Please don't, please don't,' cried Sangeetha, as she rushed to him and tried to hold both his hands.

Enraged as an animal, he hurled Sangeetha away. Sangeetha lost her balance and fell down a few feet away. She didn't know what to do. She crawled towards Ashok tearfully, hugged both his feet tightly, and said, 'I said all that without any intention to hurt you. I will never utter those words again. Please don't hit yourself. Hit me instead.'

Ashok shook his feet free in an instant, stood up and lit a cigarette. But something stirred within the man as he stood exhaling lengthy, languid puffs of smoke, for, all of a sudden, as though driven by madness, he pressed the lit end of the cigarette on his left arm. A calmness descended on his face with the burn. Seeing him light another cigarette and sear himself in a masochistic fashion, Sangeetha panicked, snatched the cigarette from Ashok's hands, and threw it away. 'Don't bother me,' he said, and went on to willingly inflict eight burns across both his arms. The eight spots seethed like marbles. He kept gazing intently at each of the spots by turns. Usually, he just broke things around him if he got angry. But seeing him hurt himself today terrified Sangeetha.

Looking at the boils on Ashok's arms, she said, tearfully, 'Instead of doing this to yourself, you could have just killed me.' Ashok pushed Sangeetha aside swiftly, removed the shoes off his feet and began to hit himself on his face with one. The agonized Sangeetha screamed and tried to wrench the shoe from his grasp. 'Leave me alone, leave me alone. I feel ashamed,' he said and shoved her. Even though Sangeetha lost her balance and fell down yet again, she got up and tried to take the shoe away from Ashok's hand. Overcome by rage at losing the shoe, he kicked the fish tank that sat beside the TV. The fish tank crashed to the floor and shattered into smithereens. In his frenzy, he stomped on each of the six fish that lay writhing on the floor and killed them. He then seized the television and smashed it to bits. He grabbed the photo frame with a photo from their wedding and crushed it into pieces.

Sangeetha did not once question any of his actions. Objects can be replaced. As long as he doesn't hit himself or burn himself with cigarettes. Ashok's mobile phone rang. He pulled it out and flung it to the floor. 'Why does the impotent need a mobile phone?' He then lit a cigarette as though his life depended on it and came over to the sofa to sit on it. After he smoked the entire cigarette, he approached

Sangeetha, who had sunk to the floor, and said, 'Get up.' When she remained seated, he held her by her hair and pulled her up.

Unable to bear the pain, Sangeetha stood up. He began to interrogate her like a policeman. 'Yesterday, when you were on the phone with your friend Asha, you said I have all the luxuries, but no life. That there's abundant food but nothing has salt, did you not? What did you mean by that?'

That moment completely rattled Sangeetha. How does he know what I spoke to Asha about at eight o'clock last night? How did my mundane conversation with her sound venomous to him? He makes capricious connections from conversations. Ashok is not going to calm down easily now. He will not stop torturing me with his questions. There is no way to mollify him. Keeping mum is the only solution even if it means getting in harm's way. Otherwise, he will grill me with more questions based on what I say. She looked at Ashok, trembling with fear.

'What did you mean when you said that to Asha?'

'...'

'Don't make a fool of me, Sangeetha. Give me an answer and this problem will get resolved now.'

Stay quiet, stay quiet, her mind cautioned her. But her mouth did not heed it.

'Why did you call me at lunch today and tell me that we should get a divorce and go our separate ways? What crime did I commit? Am I gallivanting around town engaging in illicit relationships? Do I chat with strangers? Am I talking on video calls? On the mobile all night? Posting TikTok videos? Posting selfies? Partying all the time? Don't I have a heart? Do you know that since your call this afternoon, I haven't eaten anything?' Sangeetha asked, and began to sob.

'Since you talk so much, tell me why you said those things to Asha. Just tell me that alone.'

Sangeetha looked at Ashok in disbelief. Is this the same Ashok who said when we were still courting each other, 'Being in love is like meditating; I forget myself. Without you, my life and my world are as good as destroyed. You are not just in my heart, you are my heart'? She was still immersed in her thoughts when Ashok said in a voice, soft as one would use to teach mathematics to a very young child, 'I still stand by what I said, Sangeetha. It is best that we part ways. I'm saying this for your good. I am absolutely certain about this.' Sangeetha was engulfed by an inexplicable surge of anger hearing him speak so decisively. She raised her voice as she asked him directly to his face:

'If you want to be in love with me, I should be too. If you want to get married, I should too. If you, for no apparent reason, decide that we should get a divorce, I have to submissively agree to that too, right? If I challenge you, you will say, falling in love and getting married is like committing suicide?'

'I am saying this for your own good. You just don't understand,' Ashok replied, rubbing his forehead.

'What is up with you today? Why are you so stressed out? Did you try a new clinic today? Did you see a new doctor? Why are you putting yourself through all this trouble and inflicting it on me too…?' Tears took over before she could even finish talking.

'Let's suppose I made all the mistakes. Why did you say nothing has life, nothing has salt? How can I be with someone who says things like this, you tell me!'

'I did not say it the way you think I did.'

'Then, in what way did you say all that?'

'…'

'How many people have you told about my low sperm count?'

'How is this a matter to share with others?'

'Did you not tell Asha?'

'I promise I did not.'

'I wonder how many more people you mentioned this to just like you did to Asha. Just thinking about it makes me want to kill myself. You would have told your family, your relatives, your friends, everyone, that I am a useless impotent.'

'I have not told anyone. Even my own family does not know about us going to the hospital, did you know that?'

'You know whether I am a man or not. Am I one only if I beget a child? The whole world says so. And you do too, do you not? How can I be with you knowing that you called me a blank shooter? Either you leave me, or I die,' Ashok said.

'You don't need to die, I will.'

'Good,' Ashok replied in a quieter voice and lit another cigarette.

For the first time in six years, Sangeetha questioned her decision to fall in love with and marry Ashok. After Sangeetha completed her BE, she got placed at TCS following a campus interview. Ashok was her senior there by three years as well as her team leader. Unlike other team leaders who cracked silly jokes, called often for idle chat or sent text messages, he only spoke to her about their project and only when needed. Because he had an image of being a 'terror', others didn't talk to him unnecessarily either. He had earned the reputation of being sincere in the firm. Sangeetha maintained a distance from him, far greater than other juniors. About a year and a half after she started working, he said to her candidly, 'I like you. Shall we get married? If you have other options, then don't bother with this. I don't care for falling in love, then going through a break-up and all that.'

'Let me think about this, sir,' is all she had said in return. Only then had she found out more about him – that he was of the same caste, both his parents were teachers, and he had only one younger sister, who had also completed her BE and was working at IBM. Ashok is well-educated, has a good job and looks quite smart too, she felt, and made sure there were no sticky details before she gave the number of her father's mobile phone to Ashok. Ashok started engaging in conversations directly with her father, mother, younger sister and other relatives. Four months later, they were married.

'Sangeetha is lucky to have found a husband like this,' her relatives and friends said. He was not the type that drifted about or spent money unnecessarily. He had a reputation of being a gentleman both at work and amongst relatives. All that held true until nine months ago. Everything turned upside down since then. Is Ashok a good person, or bad, she wondered looking at him. He was standing by the window, smoking. The same question arose in her mind again. She stopped mulling for an answer and instead, regretted going to the hospital. Why the hell did we ever go to the hospital!

Nine months ago, Ashok had brought up the subject himself. 'Everyone at home and even our friends are asking why we don't have a child yet. It is very embarrassing. Why don't we consult a doctor?' Many had asked Sangeetha the same question too. 'We have decided to postpone it for now,' was her standard response. She had also been wondering how to broach the subject with him; when he raised the topic on his own, it made it easier for her. However, because she didn't want to hurt his feelings, she said to him, 'What is the hurry?'

'We should not delay this any more. It is already too late,' he insisted and took her to the doctor.

The doctor said, 'I will prescribe medication for a month. Please have it. After that, if needed, we will follow up with some tests.' They both agreed. After the prescription ended, Ashok was the one to want a second consultation. 'Let's continue for another month,' she said. When two months passed without progress, the doctor prescribed some tests, first for Sangeetha. She underwent all her tests, anxious the whole time. While they were waiting for the results, the doctor, who returned after finishing his rounds, made a suggestion to Ashok. 'Since you are already here, why don't you take yours as well? That way you don't have to shuttle back and forth.' 'Why not, doctor? With pleasure,' he replied in English. Not stopping there, he went on to collect his 'specimen' for the test the doctor had prescribed.

All the test results returned normal for Sangeetha. The problem was with Ashok. 'Your sperm cell count is low. The ones you have are not the correct size, and they are not swimming fast enough towards the ovum. We can address this with medication. Take the medicines and come back after a week for another check-up. We will decide on the next steps then.'

Sangeetha was worried about Ashok's reaction to the results. But he didn't say anything. He simply purchased the medicines and followed the prescription diligently. When there was no change in the semen test a week later, the doctor said to him, 'Try to minimize laptop use. Keep your body cool. Make sure your testicles do not get too warm. Let's check if there are any issues in the tubes in the penis. There may be a blockage there, or in the sperm sac. Or the tubes may be twisted. We should get a scan done and check for that too. You need more of zinc, copper, selenium and folic acid. I will prescribe tablets for that. It is a simple matter. We will fix this, don't worry.'

He went through all the tests the doctor advised. He also took the tablets the doctor prescribed based on the results. But even after four months, the doctor told him there was no improvement. That was when he took to smoking and drinking.

If only the test results had come out to be favourable, Sangeetha reflected as she got up, picked up a broom and began to clean the hall. Ashok rushed over to her, seized the broom from her hand and said, 'Don't make a savage out of me. Give me a response to the question I asked and then do whatever you want.'

On many an occasion, Sangeetha had wanted to confront Ashok for telling his friends, 'Sangeetha has some problems. That's why we don't have kids yet.' She had instead pretended not to know about it. Though she was reminded of that now, she knew that if she brought it up, he would only yell at her, hit her, smoke and drink even more. So, she decided against it.

She did not open her mouth. As she stood dreading that even her breath may provoke a confrontation, he lifted her chin and said, 'Every time I have to get my semen tested, I'd rather die than be there the ten minutes I stand in the dark room. You stand outside. The nurse waits a little further away. When I hand her the bottle, she asks me, "Did you spill any?" Can you imagine how I feel then? You know how many times I have gone for the test. Do you even know how I feel each time I am in that dark room, when I take the bottle from the nurse, when I give the bottle back to her? Yet, what do you say? "Nothing has life. Nothing has salt. That I'm trying to escape." Right?'

In anger, Ashok couldn't find the right words. He was shaking, and his body was covered in sweat. Sangeetha stared at his face, not knowing what to say. She felt sorry for him.

In the past nine months of frequenting the hospital, she realized that Ashok was far better than most other men. Hearing hundreds of stories of men from the women she sat next to in the waiting area had shocked her. There were men who sent only their wives to the hospital, to have only them examined; they would rather die than undergo a semen test. Men who would assert categorically, 'There is no problem with me, all the problem is with you. You should go to the hospital', men who drank incessantly to hide their problems, those who diverted attention from themselves by accusing their wives of loose morals and abusing them, those who demanded a divorce, those who put up a show about how disrespectful the wife was to his parents just to cause trouble, those who framed the wife as a hustler, hit her and chased her away. That way, Ashok was a gentleman. He only drifted from doctor to doctor, lab to lab, without paying heed to the doctor's words or to Sangeetha's to not be in a rush and give it time to improve.

'If the problem is with the female, we try going with a test-tube baby or a surrogate pregnancy. Since the problem is with the male, it takes a little time. But it will settle down. Shots and medications that help with the production of semen, fixing the shape of the sperm, steering the sperm towards the ovum are available...' Ashok interrupted the doctor and compelled him to prescribe those medicines for him. He tried a shot called S.H. Next, he tried a shot called S.H.C. He also tried a medicine called Herbal Viagra. Any advice to not rush and to slow down fell flat on his ears. To increase semen production, he ate lettuce, pumpkin seeds and mackerel fish for two months. The only advice of the doctor's he heeded was: 'Please make sure you don't have kidney or thyroid issues. They can also cause problems. Don't eat fast food.'

Watching YouTube videos on childbirth became Ashok's obsession. How many lakhs of sperms are present in a drop of semen? What should the consistency of semen be – more dense or more liquid? What should the shape of the sperm be, of its tail? In what speed should the sperm travel to the ovum? What should the desired rate of sperm progression be? Ashok mastered all this. Two or three weeks ago, he asked her, 'Did you know? Just as how in school or college, many young lads compete with one another to fall in love with a beautiful girl, many lakhs of sperms vie amongst themselves to unite with just one ovum. Take me as your partner, they contend, they plead, you know? It is so cool to think about it. In a way, it is fascinating,' he said with a laugh. Back then, too, she had said to him, 'Let's drop this problem for now. We can try again in a year. Don't make a big issue of this, and let's not talk about this any more.' But Ashok had not listened to her.

Sangeetha said she would make tea and went into the kitchen. Afterwards, she held out a cup to Ashok. Instead of taking the tea and drinking it, he asked her, 'What do you think of me?' She stood perplexed, not knowing how to respond. The day before, noticing a new bottle of medication, she had said, 'Whatever you do, keep me informed. I won't take it the wrong way,' and he had gone on asking her the same question over and over again for more than three hours:

'What do you mean you won't take it the wrong way?' Scared that the same may occur again, she stood there trying to avoid looking at him. But equally concerned that he may ask if she 'didn't want to bother responding to a loser', she said, 'Would you like to lie down for some time?'

'Let's go our separate ways, Sangeetha. That will solve the problem. You can remarry, have children. If you stay with me, you will get nothing,' he replied. She said instantly, 'Don't talk rubbish.' Ashok harked back, 'Am I the one talking rubbish? Did you not say that there is no life or flavour in anything, or was that me?' and struck her hard on her face.

'Hit me more,' she said.

'Who would want to deal with an ass!' he hissed and walked out of the house at lightning speed, enraged like an animal. After staring at the door blankly for a short while, Sangeetha turned her gaze on the smashed fish tank, the television, the wedding photograph, and the water that had splattered all across the hall. She shut the door and lay down. Does everyone without a child get a divorce, she asked herself.

Did she do the right thing by falling in love with Ashok and marrying him? The question kept taunting her. Instead of typical domestic issues of incompatibilities with either the mother-in-law or the father-in-law, or financial stress either from not having enough money or not having a job, she had to contend with this unusual marital problem.

How did Ashok change so much? It was only after their visits to the hospital that his temperament began to undergo a change. From smoking a cigarette occasionally, he began to smoke two or three packs a day. From drinking a beer occasionally with friends, he began to drink liquor every day. From having intercourse two or three times a week, he insisted on doing it every night. It didn't matter if she said no, he didn't listen to her. Or if she said enough, he did not let go. He became violent. 'Why are you behaving this way? I am not reading anything into all this, don't worry,' she blurted one day. He held on to that and kept questioning her intent all night.

One day, when she asked him, 'Have you forgotten that the doctor said smoking and drinking only makes the problem worse?', he replied, 'So be it. All he is going to do is talk about me to another patient who has a similar issue, isn't it? What do the nurse who takes my sample, the lab technician who analyses it, the typist who types the result think of me? Just thinking about all that makes me want to kill myself. I just want to snip out my semen sac and be done with this.'

'We are not going to talk about this. Swear on me.'

'You won't get it, Sangeetha. Every time the doctor says, "I need the average, give a semen test every three days," the nurse hands me a bottle and says, "Go to the room," when you stand in front of the dark room, waiting, despite me asking you over and over again not to come with me, when I come out drenched in sweat and have to hand the bottle to the nurse whom I have to go looking for, do you know how I feel? When the doctor says, "We can get a semen donor," when I receive a copy of the results, when the doctor says, "Come back in a week," how do you think I feel? You have no clue. Because you are all right, isn't it?'

To that, Sangeetha responded, 'Do we have to go through so much anguish to have a baby? We do not need to go to any more hospitals. I do not want any children. Let's drop this right now.'

'You don't have problems, you can drop this. But can I? Are you saying this with the arrogance of not having any problems? Or with joy?' That question had felt like a slap on her face.

'What did I do wrong?' Sangeetha asked, instantly provoking Ashok. 'Everything is my fault. Falling in love with you, marrying you, and now shuttling between hospitals – all of it. Aren't you rubbing it in that the problem is with me and not you?'

More than any other time, he was angriest whenever he returned from the hospital. He would drive recklessly, would not pay heed to any of Sangeetha's repeated pleas to drive with caution. She rode with him plagued by a constant fear of an accident.

'Why are you taking this so seriously? Be normal. We aren't the only ones going through this. There are so many people like this out there,' Sangeetha said once. He stopped the motorbike immediately, pulled it to the side of the road and created a scene. 'If you had the problem, would you be preaching sermons like this?'

Sangeetha had to beg him before he turned his bike on again. 'Sorry that I said that. Let us go home and talk it out. Let's not stand by the road and do this. People are staring at us.'

It was impossible to predict what Ashok was going to say or do, or which words might trigger his anger. The last time they went to give the sample for semen analysis, she asked him if they could go to the temple on the way back. He glared at her and said, 'Who told you that going to the temple increases sperm production?' Two months earlier, his manager reprimanded him for not completing his projects properly and for taking too much time off from work, and stripped him off his team-leader role. He quit that job promptly and took up another in a less notable company for a much lower salary. When Sangeetha said to him, 'Why didn't you talk to me about it? You have made a big mistake. You could have been more patient,' his response thundered across the apartment: 'Mind your own business!'

No matter how much she contemplated the question about falling in love with and marrying Ashok, she was not able to come up with a response. 'He was gold until nine months ago. Now he feels like cheap brass.' The words slipped out of her lips unwittingly.

Since they got married, Sangeetha had quarrelled with Ashok only a handful of times. She had never raised her voice in anger or bickered with him for not buying her what she asked for. Ashok's sister Viji got married only a year and a half ago. She became pregnant within two months of the wedding. When Sangeetha asked him why his mother and sister informed only Ashok of the news and not her, he managed the situation with, 'Whether they tell me or tell you, isn't it the same?' She let it go even though she had been angry about it. It was only when they did not inform her of the valaikaapu ceremony that she became furious.

'They invited only you. You alone go to the ceremony,' Sangeetha said adamantly.

'Don't make a mountain out of a molehill,' Ashok said.

'How is this a small issue? They are deliberately shaming me. I'm not coming. This may be a small issue for you. You please carry on,' she replied.

'Come for my sake,' he insisted and forced her to attend the valaikaapu ceremony with him.

They called on all the women in attendance to smear the pregnant sister with sandalwood paste, adorn her with bangles and put vermilion on her. Till the very end, though, they did not call on Sangeetha.

Sangeetha waited for her turn. When the event was about to come to an end and they still hadn't called her, she said to Ashok, 'I have a headache, I am going home,' and left.

Ashok apologized to her a thousand times, but Sangeetha was not consoled. It was her first serious fight with Ashok.

'For the last couple of years, I have been attending fewer engagement ceremonies, weddings, valaikaapu ceremonies, and avoiding visiting newborns. Even if I do, I know what kind of reception I will get at those ceremonies. You know it too. In this case, women are worse than men. It is one thing for acquaintances or distant family to embarrass me or avoid me, but why would our close relatives treat me like this? Isn't your family educated? From now on, do not invite me to any of your family events,' she had said categorically.

When the baby was born, only Ashok was informed.

'They didn't feel the need to share the news with me. Then why should I go? You go, I will not stop you. Please don't ask me to accompany you.' She stood her ground for a few days.

'Come for my sake. Let others be on the wrong, you don't have to do that too. Please,' Ashok beseeched her.

She agreed on a cursory visit. After all, she wouldn't have a satisfactory response to give if they said 'Isn't informing your husband as good as informing you?'

'The baby is asleep, you can see the baby later,' they said, and left them seated in the waiting hall. No one invited them to see the baby for a very long time. It was only when the couple informed them that they had to leave that Ashok's mother said, 'One minute, see the baby before you leave.' She took the baby and placed her on Sangeetha's arms. A mere five minutes passed before Viji's mother-in-law said, 'The baby hasn't been fed in some time, she's going to cry any minute, she has to be fed.' Even though she knew exactly why Viji's mother-in-law had said what she had and what she meant by it, Sangeetha didn't delay a second in handing the baby over and stepped out. She cried all the way home.

'Why are you being so emotional about this small thing? Let it go, Sangeetha, please,' Ashok said, but none of his conciliatory words fell on her ears. That night, too, Sangeetha and Ashok had a huge fight. She had enumerated every family function from Ashok's relatives' side that she had attended and every single way she had felt humiliated.

'Don't we also want to have children? Are we refusing that on purpose? Why are people treating us like this? It is so humiliating,' she had said and wept through the night.

⸺ ⋮⋮⋮ ⸺

She heard the mobile phone ring. No matter who it was, she could call back later, she thought, and kept lying down. When the phone rang for the fourth time, she became wary. Maybe it was Ashok calling.

Three weeks ago, as usual, Ashok told her that he had 'some urgent work to attend to. I am going out' at six in the evening, but did not return by even ten at night. He didn't answer her calls either.

She was anxious and kept calling him persistently. When he didn't answer any of her calls, she called his friends to check on him. With every one of them replying that they did not know where he was, her anxiety turned to panic. She had rushed outside the apartment building and stood there looking for him. He arrived in an auto at eleven. He had a wound on his forehead, both his palms were bruised and his knees were bleeding. Utterly shaken by that sight, she exclaimed, 'Accident!'

'We'll discuss it at home,' he said, and didn't utter a word until they rode the lift and reached their apartment.

'Let's go to the hospital,' she said.

'It is only a minor accident, everything will be all right after a good night's sleep,' he replied and went to bed.

She undressed Ashok, who was inebriated to the point of being barely conscious. She cleaned all his wounds and applied ointment on them. Seeing Sangeetha cry, he snapped, 'Am I the only one in the world to meet with an accident?'

'What happened to the vehicle?'

'I've left it at the workshop.'

'What happened to the phone? I called you many, many times. You did not answer at all.'

'The phone fell down and got damaged. I have given it for repair.'

'Did someone knock you down from your vehicle?'

'Let me sleep,' he said pulling the blanket over himself, and fell asleep.

That night, Sangeetha didn't eat. Ashok never found out that she was up until two that morning crying, wondering about their relationship.

In the past, he used to apologize multiple times for the tiniest infractions. Nowadays, he brazenly commits big mistakes. Not only does he not apologize, but he scowls, yells and wants to hit me. During our courtship, he used to tell me that I was like the tender petal of the banana flower. Over the past last nine months, he has only been pushing me away.

When she saw his motorbike, which he brought back the next day, she said, 'This doesn't look like it was in an accident.' Ashok admitted to what had transpired. 'On my way home yesterday, I had to piss. I stopped the bike and got off to the side of the road. My leg slipped slightly. There was a pit there that I was too tipsy to notice. I fell in head on. The pit was ten feet deep. Couldn't be made out in the dark. I didn't know where my mobile phone fell, my wallet fell. A lot of effort went into just getting out of that pit. It was only in the morning that I went back and got my things.' The callousness with which Ashok narrated all this astonished her. 'Please order your drinks online and drink at home from now on. Don't go to the shop any more,' Sangeetha had begged him, but nothing changed.

What if he has fallen somewhere in a drunken state, like that day? Fear gripped her, and she swiftly got up and looked for her mobile phone. She noticed that the phone was ringing from inside her handbag next to the sofa. She pulled it out quickly and checked to see who was calling. It was her sister Subhashri; she answered it. 'Hello.'

'I called you so many times. Why didn't you pick up? Are you busy?'

'I fell asleep,' she replied, but her sister went on hastily, 'My son got admitted to pre-KG at Kendriya Vidyalaya. Called to share that news.'

'Congratulations. Have you informed Amma?' she asked.

'Not yet. What happened to you? Are you not feeling well?'

'How did you secure the admission?'

'I gave a minister four lakh.' She could hear Subhashri's laughter. A laughter that clarified that securing the admission was the accomplishment, not the payout.

'Four lakh?'

'Four lakh's hardly big money in 2022!'

'Okay, I am a little busy now. Will call you later.' Sangeetha hung up hurriedly. She wanted to sit down for a little while. She looked around at the hall. She was overcome with emotion as she regarded once more the shards of the fish tank, their wedding photograph, their TV, scattered everywhere and soaked in splattered water. 'Right now, I don't wish to buy a big house, or a car, or make more money. None of that. I simply wish to die, I want to kill myself. That's why I am smoking pack after pack of cigarettes, drinking bottles and bottles of brandy. I am causing my own death. And I'd like to speed it up,' she recalled Ashok telling her the day before. 'There is no cure for madness,' she muttered under her breath, walked over to the bedroom and lay down.

She heard the phone ring again. She picked it up, saw that it was her mother who was calling, and put it away without answering the call. She wondered if she should tell her mother. Every time she called her or met her, her mother would tell her, 'Despite marrying after you, our Subhashri has given birth to two children by now; you still have none. Why don't you go see a doctor?' 'Keep quiet. What is the rush?' is all Sangeetha would ever say. She never mentioned a word about visiting the doctor already or Ashok's problems to anyone, or the fracas that Ashok had been causing over the last nine months.

She heard the doorbell. She wondered if Ashok had returned as she opened the door. She saw somebody standing in front of the apartment across from hers and shut the door. As she walked back to the bedroom, she stepped on a shard of glass and her foot oozed blood. She pulled out the glass piece and wiped the blood. How will I ever forget this day, she thought. Wish I could say goodbye and disappear forever. 'One day that will happen,' she muttered grinding her teeth. 'Perhaps this is how life is. Whether the problem is with the uterus or the sperm, it is always the woman who has to suffer,' she said as she picked up a piece of glass from the fish tank that lay broken and hurled it on the floor, smashing it to bits. Then, she broke down in tears.

THE BLOUSE

Perumal Murugan

TRANSLATED BY N. KALYAN RAMAN

His MOTHER'S BREASTS had become a serious problem for him. He cursed her inwardly for being an uncivilized savage. Whenever he got up late and sat on the front pyol with a toothbrush in his hand, he found her walking up and down the front yard, gathering cattle fodder or carrying a dung basket on her head. A part of the free end of her sari, from the waist down to the back of the knees, was drawn up to the crown of her head, where it was wound into a circular pad for carrying loads. Her swaying breasts, drooping down her front like dried-up shells of palm fruit, grated on him.

He couldn't sit there for long. Meanwhile, she remained immersed in her work, oblivious to the existence of her wrinkled dugs. This troubled him even more and caused a feeling of extreme revulsion to surge within him. That he had once grasped those breasts and drunk milk from them for nourishment made him feel ashamed. The very thought that he had actually emerged from her womb made him feel deeply embarrassed. She should at least cover her breasts when she comes out of the house, he thought. He had tried to communicate this to her through a variety of antics, from averting his face to looking down whenever she stood before him. Nothing seemed to have any effect on her.

Just to avoid facing those breasts, he sneaked away to the fields or to the public well on the outskirts of the village. Still, as if she was giving chase to him, his mother followed him there on the pretext of performing some task or other. Feeding off the radiant light of love that gleamed on her face, her breasts heaved and swayed. As he fantasized about lopping them off with a sabre, he broke out in a sweat and blabbered incoherently. His innate sense of alarm urged him to run away from there. Even after he had taken refuge inside the thatch-roofed quarter on the terrace built exclusively for his use, the sight of those breasts glimpsed through the gaps in the fronds drove him to distraction. Once he closed his eyes and lay face down on the cot, the feeling subsided to an extent.

Whenever he heard his mother's voice in the house, he resolutely avoided coming down to eat. Swinging back and forth like strange little animals as she bent down to serve him, her breasts threatened to dash against his face. However careful he was to keep his head down while eating, he could not avoid them. He remained intent on washing his hands and fleeing up the stairs as quickly as possible.

During the last one month that he had spent at home after his studies, he never felt like venturing out of the house. He was scared that some villager he came across might ask him about his mother, about her breasts. He thought that people might mock his family about it and even laugh behind his back. No matter who he spoke to, a sense of foreboding, that observations on her breasts might come up anytime and lay siege to him, kept forcing him to flee that place immediately. As if trying to find a solution to this problem through medicine, which he had studied for so many years, he would keep plodding through the fat tomes till he was exhausted and eventually fall asleep. He felt shy to even step out of his room on the terrace. How could he without deciding how to react if he ran into his mother?

He wondered if he should broach the subject with his elder brother's wife. What would he say to her? Words that were about to roll off his tongue, doubled back, retreated, curled up, and died in his throat. He was hopeful that his sister-in-law would understand his problem, but he found it difficult even to begin talking about it. He faltered like a man who had stumbled into a foreign country. He tried to say at least a couple of words about it during mealtimes, but never managed to actually say them. Without raising his bowed head, he kept stirring the food with his fingers to buy some time, then got up and left.

His nights were spent seething in helpless rage. Why should I alone have a mother like this, he asked the house lizards on the wall. Busy in their hunt for insects, they paid him no heed. There was no flaw in his mother's good health, no fissure in her love for him. In spite of all that, those breasts she bared to the world ... He lay on his cot and stared at the ceiling as he wondered whether he should sever all ties with the village and run away somewhere. Was it really those breasts that had sustained him for so long, nourished his body, and crowned him with a prestigious degree? Why had his life turned out this way?

When the owner of a movie theatre in the city and father to a very beautiful girl came with a proposal to make the doctor his son-in-law, along with an excellent plan to cram critically ill patients into halls as big as warehouses and make the son-in-law in charge of the whole operation, the doctor's life became more complicated.

When his prospective in-laws sent word that they were planning to call on him, his family was overjoyed. They turned in the direction of his imminent good fortune and paid obeisance, but he showed no interest in such matters. He wanted to make sure no stranger ever set eyes on his mother.

When his sister-in-law enquired gently, wanting to wipe away the anxiety clouding his face, he gulped and stammered before blurting out finally, 'Amma's breasts...'

His sister-in-law was relieved that the matter was so trivial. At the same time, she was also thrilled that, for the first time in her life, she had been entrusted with a problem she could solve on her own. She, too, had had an eye on her mother-in-law's breasts. She went around the town singing praises of her young brother-in-law and his worry. Like him, everyone in his family was also more or less aware of the drawback and agreed with him that something had to be done.

His sister-in-law proposed a very simple solution and collected a sackful of concurrences and praise from everybody. 'We'll stitch a blouse and make Athai wear it before the bride's family comes here.'

They were relieved and happy that a major problem that had plagued them all their lives was eliminated in no time. From the fields, houses, and the snouts of goats, water buffaloes and bulls, arose a cry in unison: 'We'll get a blouse stitched for the old woman.'

No one was eager to find out his mother's preference in the matter. Everyone was infected by the conceit that they were about to weed out an obscene practice that had become entrenched in their midst since time immemorial. Whenever they spoke to her about the blouse, they wore a mischievous smile. They thought that she too must feel ecstatic like they did, lower her eyes and act bashful, or at least express such feelings in words. But she was struck dumb by their scheme.

As soon as she heard about the blouse proposal, she cringed, as if strange hands were wandering all over her body. With her tongue pulled back and teeth clamped together, she became wordless. Her face turned as hard as a field never touched by a ploughshare. No one paid any heed to the shadow of self-pity unfurling from her face. To be fair, however, they had only wanted her to be happy.

She caressed and gazed at her breasts, drooping down in a state of exhaustion from having suckled and nurtured all the children who roamed every part of the earth. Innocent of the family's plans and arrangements, her breasts swayed wearily, brushing lightly against her stomach. When she was in the prime of her youth, they had grown behind the free end of her checked cotton sari with the sheen of fresh coconut buds. After marriage, when her husband had touched them with his tongue, unbeknownst even to the darkness, and buried his face between them, her breasts lay intoxicated, sending currents of pleasure throughout her body. She mulled over the ooze of milk from her breasts that had dripped into the mouths of her children and on to her belly, and the importance the breasts had been accorded in those days. Her sari had only partially covered her breasts; it had been quite enough then. She couldn't recall anyone ever thinking or talking about covering them.

But her family was utterly pleased with their initiative, as if they were giving her something she had never received in the past or had lost since. It made no sense to her, though.

Her elder son's wife enthusiastically oversaw the wedding arrangements, as if the young brother-in-law's bride was coming from a foreign country. The matter of the blouse had also been assigned to her. She wanted her mother-in-law to wear one of her own old blouses so she could check her measurements. When the old woman screwed up her face as if the garment in her hand smelt of excrement, the daughter-in-law was incensed. Look at the woman's gall! I won't give up until I've made her wear a blouse, she vowed to herself. When her anger caused the garment in her hand to shake lightly and brush against her mother-in-law, there rose a screech like the shrill cry of a young mynah, cutting a line across the tasks being performed at that moment.

In that cry of hers, the old woman felt a pain she had not experienced even during any of her childbirths, and her veins stood out. Barring that lone cry, all her movements ceased. Harnessing all her willpower, she managed to suppress her pain. She sensed a sharp corner of the blouse plunging deep into her heart and emerging from her armpit in the form of a cyst as big as a newborn's head. She could not lift her arm fully even if she tried. Though her daughter-in-law turned pale and moved away, a terrible fear lodged itself in the young woman's heart, one that kept rolling inside her. What can this old woman do, after all, she told herself over and over again to gather the courage she needed so badly.

On the day they set out to buy fabric for the blouse, the house bustled with activity, as if in preparation for a grand function. No one had any hesitation or inhibition in talking about the day's mission. Why had I been so scared of such a trifling problem that everyone rallied around so readily, mused the doctor-son, and laughed at himself. In his dreams now there were no traces of dried-up dugs. He was no longer afraid to look directly at his mother. He imagined her wearing a blouse and was no longer fazed by the sight of those saggy breasts rearing up at him like cobra-hoods. His hours were spent in highly satisfying fantasies of marriage, of presiding as chief medical officer in a multi-storeyed building. He accompanied his sister-in-law to a textile shop in the city, whose welcome messages had reached them well in advance from twenty miles away.

After they left for the city at dawn along with ten or fifteen relatives, the old woman lay all by herself in the emptiness of the house, silently enduring the pain from the abscess in her armpit. Once it became certain that they would somehow make her wear a blouse, she puzzled over how she would walk about after that. It was doubtful whether she would be able to walk at all. She also wondered if she could continue looking after the buffaloes and their calves, the goats and their kids. Once her breasts were covered, would the animals recognize her? She imagined the blouse as a hacksaw that would cut off all the fingers of her daily activities. She also felt a thrill when she thought of how she might experience its touch on her breasts. Lost in thought and quite alone after the din of birds had died down, yet too distracted to do any work, she sat in a daze, leaning against the wall.

When they came back, their bodies baked in the afternoon sun, they saw her in the same terrible condition. The abscess had grown to cover the entire armpit. It was only now, when the abscess was big enough to peep out, that everyone became aware of it. Shocked, the doctor-son rushed inside, fetched his brand-new stethoscope from its case and examined her. Everyone was anxious. They were afraid the blouse might become useless now.

Touching his mother after a long time made him shake and tremble. He kept his eyes trained upwards to avoid looking at her breasts. Then, laughing at the gloomy faces that surrounded him, he said, 'This is an ordinary cyst. It would be easy to cut it out. Even if we don't, there won't be any problem. When she puts on a blouse, it will cover the cyst as well.'

The moment he mentioned the blouse, everyone was pleased. Not only did they wonder at the vastness of the textile shop, but they also babbled on about the countless varieties of blouse fabrics available there. Though their chatter fell on her ears, she observed that none of them was holding a blouse piece in their hands. They had bought not just one or two pieces but a dozen. These included half-a-dozen of the smooth nylon variety, shiny like snakeskin, to wear for occasions outside the home. The doctor-son boasted that the fabric was a fine product of that English-speaking country, which presently ruled the entire world. And for home-wear, there were half-dozen pieces in the domestic coarse cloth. At all times and in all places, her breasts had to stay covered. They had made all the necessary arrangements. Even the tailoring shop they had chosen for stitching the blouses was big and famous, and employed ten people just to take measurements. Many were envious of the old woman's luck in having a blouse stitched in such a grand shop.

After receiving information that the blouses were being readied, and the cyst had completely closed up her armpit, she stopped doing any of her usual chores. Nor could she lift her arm very high. What was the big problem if she couldn't work? Things were difficult in the household for a couple of days, that was all. It was decided that the entire flock of goats would be driven to the market fair and sold off, and the headcount of buffaloes brought down.

Without the bleating of the goats, she became restless and took to roaming the fields. Watching her goats being grazed by some stranger helped her pass the time; her soul was still contained in their cries. She sat amid some small boulders surrounded by palai and neem trees, staying close to the deities who stood guard over her at night, and fell asleep right there. The goatherd boys had to scour the area to find her and bring her back home.

News arrived that the fabric had been marked and cut. Even after a couple of trips to the city, the blouses were not ready. 'It is a big shop; naturally, there is a big crowd of customers. They will take their time, but the stitching will be perfect…' – such were the excuses offered. Meanwhile, the date for the visit by the bride's family was approaching fast. It was a major cause of concern for the doctor; he feared that the blouse might not be ready in time. He heard from someone that, since it was a big shop, the garments would be delivered on time if he got the right person to put in a word. So, he got busy trying to find someone.

After he had informed the tailoring shop that all the blouses were not needed at one go and that just one was enough, the doctor-son was told that they would be delivered as per schedule, that there was no need to worry. It struck him that he could have given the job to a small tailor and had a blouse ready by now. He asked around and found a way to work that plan as well. He contacted a tailor who could turn any piece of fabric into a blouse within an hour and received confirmation from the man himself. If the big tailoring shop failed to deliver, he was confident that he could give the job to this man and get the blouse in time for the in-laws' visit.

How could a big and famous shop fail to meet their commitment? They delivered the blouses on the eve of the in-laws' visit. Like the crowd that thronged around the man who auctioned shawls in the light of petromax lamps, the whole village turned up at the house in droves to gawk at the blouses and admire their beauty. 'Adengappa, see what a great run of luck she is having right now,' they raved. No one in the house slept a wink that night. Suggestions were also made about the chair in which she should sit after she had bathed and put on a blouse, and where the chair should be placed during the visit from the bride's family.

When they went to her the next morning, she was still sitting where they had left her the previous night, shorn of her memories, her eyes searching for something in the sky. The cyst in her armpit had grown and hung down to the elbow like another breast stuck to her side. She couldn't lift her arm at all. Like the sculpture of a woman sifting grain in a winnowing pan, it was arrested midway. No matter how hard they tried, the doctor-son and his sister-in-law could not raise her arm.

Engulfed again by revulsion towards those breasts, he felt nauseated. 'Chey!' he took his hands away. They swayed from the impact before coming to rest. He shook free of her breasts that were little more than wrinkles now and stormed out. His sister-in-law was left feeling helpless. She couldn't do very much on her own either. She heard the car of the bride's family in the distance and ran inside the house, dragging her mother-in-law with her.

After an exchange of mutual courtesies, the visitors were formally welcomed and the ball was set rolling between the two families. Beyond the heap of blouses lying scattered in the backroom, from a corner of the cattleshed with its slush of dung and stink of urine, penetrating the silence of the inner rooms and cutting through the happy laughter and words came the steady and feeble sound of moaning.

UPRISING

Shobasakthi

TRANSLATED BY JANANI KANNAN

1

AZHWAR THARUMALINGAM, WHO was born in Saravanai East and resides in Paris, will turn exactly forty-seven this Purattaasi. He works as a labourer of the lowest grade for a very famous scooter manufacturer in France. It has been thirteen years since he arrived in Paris. Until now, he has never set foot in an airplane.

Fifteen years ago, Tharumalingam got married to Asokamalar, who hailed from the Thangodai region of Karainagar. They were married at the Varatharaja Perumal Temple in Ponnalai. Even for those times, Tharumalingam was given a lavish wedding gift of five lakh rupees in cash, in addition to property and thirty sovereigns of gold jewellery. All this for a groom who was neither educated nor employed. But the man was an excellent farmer, a hard worker who managed a field of two thousand tobacco saplings all by himself. Above all else, he was a teetotaler and a non-smoker. A truly devout person too, he was the chief volunteer at the Ilandhaiyadi Pillayar temple. He spent his time either working in his field or in worship or service at the temple. He neither opposed nor supported any ideological movement, but his deep-rooted political belief was that they would never get a leader like Amirthalingam.

Although the property in Karainagar he had received as a wedding gift was under the control of the navy, his father-in-law had assured him that the navy would leave soon. Tharumalingam wasn't particularly worried about it either; rather, he was quite content in that it was one more to call his own.

Two years passed by, yet there was no sign of a child from the Tharumalingam-Asokamalar couple. Slowly, the town began to refer to him as 'malattu' Tharumalingam, mocking him for supposedly being sterile. While everyone in town taunted him, Tharumalingam's mother alone began to torment Asokamalar, calling her barren. The old lady spun spiteful tales that poked and prodded at the poor daughter-in-law all the time. During all those times, Asokamalar wept no end, but not once did she say or do anything hurtful to Tharumalingam. Tharumalingam quietly observed everything that was going on around him; his mind began to ferment in the deep despair and anger suppressed in him.

It was the issue of irrigation that caused the argument between Tharumalingam and Killian, the owner of the neighbouring farm, early one morning. While they were still in the middle of their altercation, Killian spat out derisively, 'All this for a sterile man's property that is after all going to go to who knows who!' Hearing those words that morning unleashed all the anger Tharumalingam had repressed until then – anger at the people of his town, anger at his own mother, anger at himself – which compounded into a massive rage that besieged his soul. He was engulfed by a momentary blinding darkness. Tears gushed from his eyes as he tried to bring himself back under control. He flung down the manvetti that he was holding in his strong hands, picked it up again but this time by the blade, and hurled it at Killian, aiming the short hoe's sturdy handle at his knees. 'Aiyo, machaan!' Killian screamed and sank to the ground grabbing his legs. Without turning around to look at him, Tharumalingam briskly returned to his farm and continued to work on redistributing the water.

At eight the same morning, Killian walked into Tharumalingam's farm along with two military soldiers. In those times, there was an abundance of soldiers in that region. With rifles on their backs, they roamed about on their cycles without a care. They took apart the doors and windows in abandoned houses, drank toddy and sang Baila songs loudly in the evenings and at nights, and trespassed into homes of young nubile women. What's more, they also took upon themselves the task of settling any dispute in town and meting out punishment at will.

The two soldiers Killian brought along with him were already very tipsy that early in the morning. In Saravanai, if six in the morning was when the toddy tappers brought down the toddy from the palm trees, the military men would squat under those trees, ready and waiting, by five itself. Some even climbed the palm trees in the middle of the night to drink surreptitiously from the earthen pots tied up there to collect the toddy. But to whom could the tappers possibly complain about the missing toddy? Especially when it was common knowledge that the very top leader of the soldiers for that region had amassed land by furtively registering several acres of arable land along the sea in the names of his relatives?

Even though Tharumalingam felt a bit jolted on seeing the soldiers, he wasn't quite that alarmed. It turned out that he was fairly acquainted with them both. The two of them – Uday and Fernando – were always seen together. They often stopped by Tharumalingam's coconut grove looking for coconut water. They would climb the trees by themselves, pluck the coconuts they wanted, and take leave of Tharumalingam with a salute. Tharumalingam dropped the manvetti from his hand and looked at Killian; a faint smile began replacing the shock on his face. Killian could not stand that smile on Tharumalingam's face.

'Machaan, you made a mistake laying your hands on me,' he threatened as he paced about with a hobble.

Then the taller soldier, Fernando, asked Tharumalingam, 'So, you support Thileepan, sir? Kili said so.'

That was when he realized what was going on.

It was an incident that even he had forgotten about. A small incident that happened in his tiny village when Thileepan, the leader of the Tamils, was leading a fast unto death in Nallur.

Tharumalingam was twenty then, and a lot more religious. At that time, too, he was neither in support of the Tamil organization nor against it. But that Thileepan fasted for twelve days, and more significantly, died within the premises of the Nallur Murugan temple, had aggrieved him deeply.

Tharumalingam was working in his farm that afternoon when the supporters of the organization drove by announcing the death of Thileepan through large speakers strapped to their vehicle. That by itself had not affected him as much. But right after the vehicle passed, from the direction of the school he had heard voices, wailing in sorrow, soaring in sadness. He had dropped whatever he was doing, leapt out of his farm and run towards the school.

On the street leading to the school was a picture of Thileepan with lamps lit in front of it. Teachers and students had gathered; they were crying bitterly. Pillaimuthu kizhavi, the grand old woman who was in the frontline of any funeral in the village, had been there too, bouncing nearly a foot off the ground as she thumped on her chest and wailed elegies. That scene had turned something inside Tharumalingam. The man had returned home but remained completely possessed by what he had witnessed. He did not eat a morsel that whole day even though his mother tried to make him; he had remained awake all night.

Early the next morning, he went to his coconut grove, dug out a whole young coconut sapling and dragged it all the way to the Puliyankoodal junction. His manvetti hung from his shoulder. An Indian peacekeeping army vehicle went past him. There was still time before the civil war would break out.

There hadn't been much foot traffic in the market. None of the shops had opened yet. Right in the middle of that market, where two streets intersected, he had hurriedly dug up a pit with his manvetti, planted the coconut sapling in it, and sat himself down facing northwards and cross-legged under that sapling. A short while later, a small crowd had gathered around him. He hadn't uttered a word to anyone. The news that Tharumalingam was acting crazy had somehow reached his mother. She had rushed over as soon as she could, tumbling through the streets and crying all the way. But Tharumalingam didn't say a word to his mother either. It was only later, when the supporters arrived, that he opened his mouth to speak.

'Now that Thileepan anna himself is no more, what do I have to live for?'

The eyes of the organization's local custodian had welled up. He bit his lips to fight back his tears yet managed to give out some orders. Within half an hour, a small tarp pandal was erected to shelter Tharumalingam and his coconut sapling. Sad songs oozed from the two speakers that were fixed to a telegraph pole nearby. A new mat and some pillows and blankets were provided to Tharumalingam for him to lie on. Someone brought an electric fan and placed it near his head. Four youngsters, including this storyteller, sat around Tharumalingam and continued to fast along with him. Tharumalingam's mother continued to weep.

By evening, Tharumalingam had withered a little as he had not consumed even a sip of water since the previous afternoon. Around eight that evening, he had lain down on his mat, curled up like a ball.

At nine, a vehicle with representatives of the organization arrived from Jaffna. They made their way to the pandal and informed him that the headquarters had decided to end all fasts. They had also brought along some fruit juice to end the fast. But Tharumalingam had refused to end it. His mouth gently kept murmuring the words, 'Thileepan anna is gone.' When they tried to force-feed him the juice, he spat it out on the face of the person who had tried to feed him. Finally, the followers of the organization had lifted him carefully together with the mat, put him in the vehicle and admitted him in a hospital in Jaffna. The next morning dawned with Tharumalingam waking up blinking cluelessly – he had not a hint about what had possessed him the previous two days! Besides, what remained for a long while after the incident was only the guilt that he had caused so much anxiety to his mother. For not even a month did anyone else remember his protest, as the very next month, protests far more momentous and deaths way mightier ensued.

Nevertheless, the incident did rear up in people's memories when Tharumalingam was discussed in matrimonial circles. 'Tharumalingam is a nice boy, with no bad habits, but now and then he gets caught up in a sort of delirium. At those times, he has no control over his actions,' they opined. Because no one who lived in his town would give him their daughter in marriage, he had to go to Karainagar to find himself a bride.

That morning, after so many years, this incident had resurfaced in Killian's memory, and he had shared it with the army men.

From a distance, the farmers from other neighbouring farms observed closely the happenings at Tharumalingam's. They remained watching as Tharumalingam stood in front of those men quietly with his head bent down. How could that mouth that religiously chanted holy hymns every morning and evening spell out a lie?

The soldier named Fernando went behind Tharumalingam, pulled both his arms backwards, twisted them, and held them tightly.

Tharumalingam's face turned skywards automatically. The other soldier, Uday, stood in front of him and spat on his face. When Tharumalingam tried to lower his face in reflex, pain shot through his shoulders. The saliva landed on his face, coursed down in a straight line, and dripped to the ground below. Uday then grabbed his AK-47, tossed it in the air and caught it upside down. With the same motion, he landed the butt of the rifle directly over Tharumalingam's testicles. Tharumalingam instantly lost consciousness. Fernando, who was holding his arms in a lock, put him on the ground and turned him over so he lay on his back.

When Tharumalingam opened his eyes, there was not a creature on his farm. His testicles were in excruciating pain. He sat up slowly and parted his saram to examine them. Both his testicles were heavy and swollen like large mangoes of the dark, Colombo variety. His penis had shrunk and was stuck to his body like a jamun fruit. A drop of blood glinted at its tip. He gently rose to his feet and walked home slowly, keeping his legs wide apart. Halfway over, he saw Asokamalar rushing towards him with tears in her eyes.

That night, he said to her as he sat leaning against a wall:

'No, this place is not right, this place is pushing me out. I am going to leave.'

'Where are you going to go?'

'No, Malar … this place is forcing me out. I should not remain here even for a moment.'

The next month, Tharumalingam was one of sixty people who boarded a fishing boat from Negombo to Italy. After two months of sailing, he reached Italy and eventually arrived in France via train.

His first words to Asokamalar's younger brother, who had come to receive him at the Gare de Lyon station in Paris, were:

'This is good, thambi, this place is all right … the setting feels right.'

2

To live in Paris without a visa was no joke! Tharumalingam shrunk to half his original size. Asokamalar's brother had fixed up a small storeroom that was behind their house for Tharumalingam to live in. Whether he had a job or not, the rent had to be paid promptly at the beginning of every month.

Tharumalingam was a determined and hard worker. Whatever work he found, whether it was in kitchens, farms or construction sites, at a printing press or in a Tamil store, he performed his tasks with utmost sincerity. He sent money to Asokamalar every month without fail. He wrote letters to her promising that he would get his visa soon and that he would bring her to France as soon as he got it. He also never forgot to send a contribution of twenty-five thousand rupees for the annual festival at the Ilandhaiyadi Pillayar temple every year. But it took him twelve years following his arrival in France, when he was forty-six years old, to get his visa.

As soon as he got his visa, he came straight to see this storyteller, his only friend in Paris, to share the news. Everything that was in his mind – his hardships, his trepidations, the pain from being separated from his wife, the craving for a child – he shared only with this storyteller, candidly and truthfully, with words dripping with sorrow and self-pity as he spilled them out.

It was under the guidance of this storyteller that Tharumalingam landed a job, through a private placement firm, as a labourer at the shop floor in a two-wheeler manufacturing plant located in one of the suburbs of Paris. It was a job that involved collecting nails and nuts, washing and drying them. He was actually quite happy doing that. He also learnt to speak a little French. Asokamalar arranged for food to be donated at the Selva Sannidhi temple in honour of him getting his visa. Tharumalingam also got busy with arranging for Asokamalar's visa to bring her to France. An astrologer from Andhra who was camped in Lachapelle had predicted with absolute certainty that Tharumalingam had a chance at progeny at the age of forty-seven. However, it was going to take two years for Asokamalar to join him in France legally. They were entangled in a complex web of paperwork and immigration laws.

'Let my coming over to France take its course, but, in the meantime, won't you come here to see me at least once?' a tearful Asokamalar often said over the phone. She would end every call with the words '*endra rasa*' – my love – and let out a sigh filled with sadness. Those words kept tormenting Tharumalingam.

Tharumalingam took two months off from work. But he was unequivocal in his decision to not set foot back on Sri Lankan soil, whatever be the reason. Every time he thought about Sri Lanka, his hands automatically reached for his underwear to reveal a sight that unfailingly reminded him of rotten, dark Colomban mangoes. Thinking about Sri Lanka, the mango-shaped island, only evoked in his mind an image of his testicles.

At that time, Asokamalar was staying in Colombo to take care of some work at the French Embassy. Tharumalingam directed her to meet him in Chennai, in India, and set off. This storyteller was the one who arranged for a rental place in Nungambakkam for Tharumalingam and Asokamalar to stay in for two months.

This was Tharumalingam's first time flying. He reached the Paris airport four full hours before his flight's departure time. He didn't carry much with him – this storyteller had told him that everything that was available in Paris was available in India for much less. He was only taking with him a few eatables for Asokamalar, a couple of sets of clothes to wear, seven or so bottles of eau de cologne, and a sweater to be given to his mother. He remained quite nervous the entire time he was in the airport. Half his life drained away from him while they checked his passport and his face over and over again. After managing to stumble through immigration services, he had barely sighed in relief when he came to know that he'd have to go through a security check. This was where they examined everything he carried with him.

They trashed all his eau-de-cologne bottles right in front of his eyes. Half of the eatables too ended up in the bin. Tharumalingam stood staring at the bin, nervous and clueless. Meanwhile, a few more items were tossed into the bin. They eventually reduced his load by half its weight. Then they made him remove his jacket, shoes and belt, and sent them through machines for inspection. Even though he understood what they said, at first, Tharumalingam felt as though there was something wrong only with him. He later noticed that the people in front of him were barefoot and semi-naked too and were holding on to their pants from sliding off their waists. He continued to hold on to his pants with his left hand as he collected his things that lay scattered on the examination table with his right hand. By the time he stuffed them back in his suitcase, he was sweating profusely and felt sightly delirious too.

When he eventually managed to pull himself together to move on, the next thing he was put through was body search. In front of him stood a circular machine. Next to the machine was a man, six and a half feet tall, standing stiff as starch, with a long black object in his hand. He waved that wand-like object in front of Tharumalingam's face and gestured him to come forward through the circular machine. Tharumalingam got reminded of 'Gemini Circus', a circus show he had been to at the Muniyappar temple as a little boy.

When he passed through the circular machine, it started beeping loudly. They made him walk through the machine again. The machine beeped again. They made him come through the machine for a third time. This time, the machine shrieked with a vengeance.

Tharumalingam was ordered to stay within a circle. He was then asked to stand with his legs apart and hands lifted up in the air, which made Tharumalingam perspire and tremble even more with nervousness. That must have surely made the officials suspicious, for they began to search him manually.

The six-and-a-half-feet-tall official with a firm face first patted down Tharumalingam's hands. He patted harder as he moved his hands over his chest and stomach. He patted all over his back and his buttocks and the area around it too, squeezing him as though he was kneading dough. Then, starting with his feet and moving upwards, he patted his legs. When his hands were patting and searching northwards of his thigh, Tharumalingam felt as though one of the officers' fingers stroked his testicles for a flash of a second. Tharumalingam shuddered. He was reminded of the blow he had received from that soldier who used to drink coconut water from his farm to keep himself healthy. A spark of anger ignited within him. 'Who are these people to touch my balls?' But, in reality, the six-and-a-half-feet-tall officer had not touched his testicles or penis – these officers are trained to search from a hair's distance away, without actually touching them. At the end of the search, they permitted Tharumalingam to carry on. Tharumalingam was livid and shaking in anger by then. He felt lightheaded and even thought of abandoning the trip. It was the singular thought of Asokamalar waiting eagerly for him in Chennai that compelled him to continue his journey that day.

He had to alight at the airport in Dubai and catch the flight to Chennai. He had not anticipated that he would be put through another humiliating security check again. 'Did they not examine everything over there? Just what is a passenger going to find in the middle of the sky to try to sneak past them?' he grumbled to himself as he stood in line.

Two Arabs examined him from head to toe. This time, too, Tharumalingam thought that they stroked his testicles when he was standing with his hands raised above his head and legs apart, trembling with anger.

It was only after he reached Chennai airport that Tharumalingam regained his composure. Still, a doubt lingered within him about them trying to touch his testicles here as well. Luckily, nothing of that sort happened. As he collected his baggage, walked through the doors of the airport and took the first step out of the building, he saw Asokamalar among the crowd, waving her arms with a shy smile on her face. But before he took his next step, a large hand grabbed his shoulder from behind and pulled him back into the airport. Tharumalingam stuck his head out, his gaze fixed on Asokamalar as he was pulled in. Asokamalar's face was frozen with fear.

They took Tharumalingam into a private room, stripped him down to his underwear and searched him thoroughly. Apparently, they had a special suspicion on him. The search was carried on coarsely, and this time the white gloved hands unmistakably touched his testicles and his penis. It was at that moment when those words burst out of Tharumalingam's mouth, loud and blistering:

'A Tamilian shall not do this to a fellow Tamilian!'

3

Days passed delightfully in Chennai. Asokamalar was brimming with exuberance and joy. Neither had the slightest interest in visiting any of the temples or shops on Ranganathan Street. In the mornings, the two of them walked together to the shop down the street to buy fish, crab or meat and cooked together. On Fridays alone, they ate vegetarian food. In the evenings, they sat on the terrace snacking on peanuts and such and chatting endlessly. Asokamalar relished with pride the few French words that popped up when Tharumalingam spoke. She would occasionally whine about that too. 'If you speak in French, how will I understand what you are saying?' The nights were spent making love to their hearts' desires. Asokamalar looked blossomed, Tharumalingam's youth reemerged energized. He was proud beyond words that Asokamalar enjoyed every bit of their intimacy. One morning, after drinking a cup of raw egg that Asokamalar handed him, Tharumalingam stood up and threw two air punches. One was for Uday and the other, for Fernando. Truly, they discovered all their happiness within those four walls.

One evening, the couple decided to go to the movies. They went to a movie theatre located in an enormous mall in Aminjikarai. It was only after he had bought the entry tickets and was standing in the queue at the entrance to the movie theatre that Tharumalingam noticed it: the cylindrical scanning machine that was placed right outside the movie theatre. On either side of it stood two stiff guards.

'Malar, come this way,' said Tharumalingam, grabbing his wife's arm and pulling her out of the queue. When Tharumalingam observed the guards, he saw that they were emptying a man's pocket, removing his cigarettes, lighter and other things, and putting them aside. When the next person in line stepped forward, one of the guards instructed him to spit out his chewing gum into a dustbin. He then frisked that man from head to toe.

'Malar, my dear, my stomach hurts,' he said, and the two returned home without watching the movie. The minute they entered home, Tharumalingam's stomach 'felt better'. After that, Tharumalingam did not step out of the house at all. If asked to, he said, 'The dust and dirt bother me, Malar.'

Two days before Tharumalingam had to depart for France, Asokamalar grabbed his hands, placed her teary face in them and declared that she had become pregnant. Tharumalingam's happiness knew no bounds! He put his hands together, raised them above his head in veneration and exclaimed 'Pillaiyaarappa!' with gratitude. He then said to Asokamalar, 'This is extraordinary ... everything is beautiful. Everything is right.'

The next day, Asokamalar had to leave for Colombo. Tharumalingan saw her off lovingly and left for France the day after.

The man who was so jubilant until he got to the Chennai airport lost some of that cheer as soon as he was inside the airport. But this time, it was more indignation than trepidation. In Chennai as well as in Dubai, he went through similar detailed searches again. Each time he got searched, he assumed they were teasing him by bringing their fingers very close to his testicles as if to grab them, and consequently suffered a fresh bout of anger and shame.

Back at the airport in France, he almost lost it. He could see why they would want to check him when departing from there. But why on earth would they want to frisk him upon alighting from a plane as well?

Tharumalingam decided to ignore the customs official who repeatedly called out 'Monsieur … Monsieur' after him. Instead, he sped up his pace walking away from the official, pushing his luggage trolley with all his luggage loaded in it. From the corner of his eye, he saw that the officer got busy checking some other passenger and was not following him.

Tharumalingam walked on adamantly, shaking his head and pushing his luggage trolley. Within the next two minutes he was confronted by two customs officers in civilian clothes. 'Ça va pas, non!' he shouted, so loud that the whole airport turned to look at him.

What happened after was that was a very, very thorough search. Their gloved hands crawled all over his body – every atom in his body was examined. They even made him lie down and took an X-ray of him. The search lasted for nearly four hours. All to find out why Tharumalingam had to run away when a customs officer called out for him. Surely, there was no reason to. As Tharumalingam got out of that office, one of the officers stepped forward to shake his hands affably, but Tharumalingam refused to mirror the sentiment. He glared at him instead. 'The next time you are here and are called for an examination, please comply. If you do, then we can avoid wasting so much time…' explained the official. But just as he was finishing his sentence, Tharumalingam's suitcase fell from his hands and skidded across the airport floor. Its mouth split wide open and all the contents, including the Tirunelveli Iruttu Kadai halwa, holy ash, sandalwood paste and Ayurveda oil, lay scattered on the floor. Tharumalingam squeezed his feet together, placed his hands on his hips, stuck his neck out, looked directly at the officer and asked him in Tamil, 'Why are you inviting me to come here again? Are you not satisfied with the humiliation you put me through this time around?'

4

Even though the weariness from the journey forced Tharumalingam to bed, the frustration from what happened at the airport did not let him sleep a wink. Moreover, he was worried about leaving his pregnant wife all by herself. But since he had to wake up by five to go to work, he finally managed to force himself to sleep.

The alarm rang an hour later. He showered, smeared the holy ash over his entire forehead and headed to the factory. After an hour-long train ride, he reached the factory. The labourer in him sprang up enthusiastically the minute he stepped into the factory premises after two months. The tall edifice of the factory, with its façade made entirely of glass, sparkled in the morning sunlight. As he approached the main entrance to the building, he saw a small crowd of workers standing there. Finding it to be very unusual for anyone to stand around at that time of the day and wondering if, possibly, there had been an accident, he quickened his stride. When he got to the entrance, he froze completely. His eyes stared at the entrance in disbelief; he grabbed his chest with one hand and covered his mouth with the other.

There, at the entrance, stood a circular scanning machine, the type that scanned people. Next to the machine was a young French man adorned in security uniform, shoes, cap and all, smiling grandly. Before Tharumalingam left on vacation, there was neither the scanner nor the guard. That door used to be wide open. This was a new arrangement.

Once the workers went through the scanner, the security officer examined them with his hands, one by one, before permitting them to go into the factory. Tharumalingam took off and ran around the building towards the rear exit, which the workers used to leave the building at the end of the day. But just like he had suspected, there was a circular scanner installed at that doorway also.

Tharumalingam slowly walked back to the factory's front entrance. He was already late by two minutes. He climbed the stairs, fatigue sweeping over him. He greeted the young security officer and showed him his identity card. The smiling young man greeted him in return and stood ready to search him. When Tharumalingam tried to circumvent the scanner to enter the factory, the officer stuck out his strong hands and stopped him from doing so. Tharumalingam gave him a glare and, with no option left, went through the scanner. The officer smoothened his bright white gloves and approached Tharumalingam with a smile to conduct the body search. Tharumalingam began to feel lightheaded. He tilted his head backwards, covered his testicles with his left hand and forcibly pushed away the young man's hands with his right hand. In a flash, all the alarms around the factory were activated. The factory's main door automatically closed shut. Guards came rushing towards the main door from all directions.

A mini panchayat gathered right there with Tharumalingam in the forefront. Tharumalingam stood strong in his grounds that no one had the right to place their hands on him. The manager tried to convince him that conducting a search was a common practice and that he too was searched before being allowed into the factory. He even performed a small demonstration, walking his heavy body through the scanner a couple of times with his arms up high. Out of breath but with arms still in the air, he stood before the officer to enact the procedure for Tharumalingam.

The workers' trade union representative also tried to assuage Tharumalingam: 'Look here, Tharumalingam ... there are security issues all around the world. For example, there's Al-Qaida...' and before he completed that sentence, Tharumalingam interjected, 'Do I look like Al-Qaida to you?' The spokesperson who had an encyclopaedic knowledge of world politics, replied calmly with a smile, 'Why my friend, aren't Sri Lankan Tamils quite the specialists in planting bombs too?'

Tharumalingam helplessly sank down right there on the entrance step. Then he rose, walked through the scanner, and stood in front of the young security officer with his legs apart and hands lifted high. The manager softly clapped his hands in appreciation, as if to encourage Tharumalingam. The officer very proudly patted down Tharumalingam's body. Tharumalingam felt that this officer too touched his testicles. He couldn't focus on his work all day. He didn't sleep well that night either. He lay on his bed the whole time stroking his testicles. Just at the crack of dawn, he had a flash of clarity in his mind. He sat up on his bed with his hands spread out sideways, flapped them up and down as though he were flying, and exclaimed, 'There is a way to solve any problem! This is good. A little lion cub is growing in Malar's womb ... All is well, everything is falling into place.'

That morning, Tharumalingam was the first person to arrive at the factory. He wore a pair of loose-fitting pants made of a very thin material. He walked crisply through the security scanner and stood in front of the young officer with his legs apart and hands lifted. The security officer adjusted his gloves and, very slowly, began to pat Tharumalingam's legs, starting at the bottom. Tharumalingam noticed that the security officer's fingers began to tremble when he looked up while making his way upwards. Tharumalingam had deliberately not worn an underwear that day. His stiff penis lengthened and, in a flash, fell into the hand of the officer. The officer withdrew both his hands instantly and permitted Tharumalingam to enter the factory floor without completing the search.

In the evening, after the shift was done and it was time to leave, the same officer was at the exit as well. Tharumalingam went up to him and stood with his hands lifted. He observed with a stifled smile of joy, the trembling in the officer's hands. When those hands reached his thighs, Tharumalingam suddenly thrust his hip forward. The young officer pulled his face back in reflex and, yet again, let Tharumalingam go.

When Tharumalingam arrived at the factory the next morning, the security officer turned his gaze away from him, avoiding him. Tharumalingam went over to him and stood in front of him, his pelvis pushed forward. The officer quietly murmured to him that he could go in.

From that night onwards, Tharumalingam ate only energy foods, like dates and almonds. Right before entering and exiting the factory, he chewed on Kola seeds, which were imported from the Republic of Congo and could induce a prolonged erection. Tharumalingam could evoke one of his secret fantasies and have one whenever he wanted to.

Apparently, there were a couple of women he would think about when he wanted to have an erection. Never was it Asokamalar at such a time, nor was it any of the women he saw on the streets, or actresses or relatives. It involved a few specific prime ministers or presidents of certain countries – admittedly a habit of his since childhood. He inadvertently mentioned this detail in the flow of his narration to this storyteller.

The security officer was subjected to an inquiry after his higher officials observed through security cameras that there was a certain employee whom he allowed to enter and exit the facility without physical examination. The poor young officer fidgeted and squirmed as he explained with great hesitation how he was unable to examine

Tharumalingam because he did not wear underwear and always had an erection.

When the manager asked Tharumalingam about this, his reply was: 'Not wearing underwear is a matter of personal choice. The factory management cannot interfere with that.' The workers' union sided with Tharumalingam in this respect. The manager could not push back either because, while there were rules requiring everyone on the work floor to wear uniforms, shoes and helmets, there was no stipulation on wearing underwear. Thereafter, the manager changed the security officer instead. In the place of the young French security officer, an old polyglot from Poland who was going into retirement the following year was instated.

The old man was resolute to frisk Tharumalingam even if he showed up without pants. However, the next day when Tharumalingam arrived at work, about thirty people were already ahead of him waiting to be searched. They were all well-built Arabs, the most affected and most disrespected during body searches in France. The inquiry conducted on Tharumalingam the previous day had induced a new uprising in them. Each one standing in that queue had done away with his underwear. Just how many penises could the poor man examine! The beaten Polish security officer effected a truce. With a hint of a smile hovering around the corner of his lips, Tharumalingam walked right into the facility past the defeated officer who remained seated with his hands to himself.

About half the labourers in that factory were Africans. When the security officers subjected them to security search but not Tharumalingam or the Arabs, they construed that as discrimination against their race. The next day onwards, they, too, decided collectively not to wear any underwear. The old Polish security officer cursed the gods in all the languages he knew and took a medical leave of absence from work. Anyone who took on the role of a security body-search officer in that factory panicked and vanished without trace, barely lasting a day. Finally, it was a lackadaisical old man, who could neither see nor hear clearly, who was assigned that post simply for the sake of filling it.

The factory management was stumped. This was a matter of honour for them. In that factory where three hundred people worked, only the ten of them, the management, wore underwear. And every morning, it was only the ten of them who were searched by the old security guard per the factory protocol. For the rest of the time, the guard sat in a corner with his hands folded.

When the news about the uprising of these workers slowly spread to other factories, the workers there too began to opt out of wearing underwear to work. The press printed this surge comparing it to the American women's bra-burning movement in the 1960s. Members of the nudist association sent their wishes and support to the factory workers of Paris. Through a statistic released by the Paris Airport authorities, it came to be known that about 32 per cent of men and 34 per cent of women who travelled through that airport did not wear underwear. In his speech at the parliament, the Minister of Home Affairs raised the question in frustration of whether 'we should protect our people from terrorism, or protect the rights of those who do not wear undergarments.' The catholic church released a statement that 'the action of the factory workers was savagery'. The anarchists' organization issued a rebuttal to that stating: 'When the soldiers apportioned Jesus Christ's clothes avidly amongst themselves, there was no undergarment in that pile.'

The association of owners held several brainstorming sessions. They were of the opinion that such unity among workers did not have any immediate significant negative impact on production – that is, in businesses other than ones involved in manufacturing underwear. However, this sort of unity may become the basis for workers to demand many more rights over the coming years. Therefore, they concluded that, until they identify a better and a subtler way to conduct a body search, for the time being, they would do away with the body-scanning machines that were installed in the factories, along with the security guards. A letter was issued by the factory owners' association that all body scanners will be removed from factories as of the following Monday.

The first person to arrive early that Monday morning was Tharumalingam. As anticipated, there wasn't a trace of the scanner at the entrance, nor a security guard. The doors to the factory were wide open. A few pigeons sat on the steps leading up to the front entrance. Tharumalingam cooed to the birds: 'Everything is bright … everything is right.'

As he climbed the steps to the factory, Tharumalingam's mobile phone rang. He pulled it out and answered cheerfully. On the other end was Asokamalar's devastated voice. Asokamalar had gone to a maternity doctor for a body scan. She was told there was nothing growing in her uterus. In the end, with a deep sigh filled with sheer despair, Asokamalar uttered the words *'endra rasa'*.

Tharumalingam climbed down the steps quietly. He kept walking and headed out of the factory premises. After that day, he was never seen around that factory ever again.

SACRIFICIAL STONE

Jeyamohan

TRANSLATED BY SUCHITRA RAMACHANDRAN

I HAD NOT PREVIOUSLY met the gentleman who was at my door. I lowered the newspaper and rose to my feet. 'Who is it?' I asked.

He brought his palms together. 'No, I just came to meet you…' he said. 'Auditor Ashtamoorthi?'

'Yes, that's me,' I said.

'My name is Paramasivam … I'm from Puliyarai, on the far side of Tenkasi…'

I greeted him. 'Please come in,' I said. I was not sure why he was here. His face didn't ring a bell. I had only worked in Kerala all my life. I knew nobody from Tenkasi.

He sat down. 'I came for a reason,' he said. A furtive note had come into his voice. 'Muthaalam Sankaran Pothi…'

'Yes, my father,' I said.

'I would like to meet him.'

'Why?' I asked. 'How do you know him?'

'I don't know him. I came on behalf of someone else. Someone whose life is intimately involved with your father's.'

'Look, do you know how old my father is now?'

He shook his head.

'I am sixty-three. My father is ninety-four. Bound to his bed for the last seven years. And it has been thirty years since he lost his memory. What do you want from him now?'

'I'll explain everything, sir. I'm a real estate broker. One of my clients wanted me to help sell his property in Puliyarai. His name is Shanmugalingam. He is an auditor in Madras. The land was purchased back in his father's time – a hundred and forty-seven acres of coconut, mango and jackfruit. Very fertile land, sir, no lack of water. There is even a small stream running through the estate. There's also a bungalow. It's old, but a great big house…'

'Oh.'

'But they had left their land in the trust of the watchman of the estate and moved to Madras. No one from the family went there any more. The watchman kept the profits from the land. That's why they decided to sell it.

'I looked for a buyer. The land would sell for ten or fifteen crores. A politician could perhaps afford that price. But it's hard to get them to pay up. So I made inquiries about whether there was someone in Kerala who might be interested.'

'Okay?' I said. I was still wondering why he was telling me all this.

'The person who came forward to buy the land was a Christian from Kerala. George Thomas Vadakked. He used to have a store in Dubai, but he lives here now. He took one look at the land and knew that there were no takers for it. He was adamant that he wouldn't pay a pie more than four crores. Shanmugalingam tried to explain. But these Kerala fellows know their way around. One price, he said; four crores. Take it or leave it. I was furious. A hundred and forty-seven acres for four crores was not a sale, it was practically charity. But Shanmugalingam said it's fine, four crores it is, let's finalize it.'

'Okay, but why are you telling me all this? I don't do any auditing these days.'

'Sir, please let me just finish what I'm saying. Otherwise you won't understand. All the negotiation was done, and the advance changed hands. A date was finalized for the registration. And then there was an accident. It was George Thomas's elder son. He was driving downhill from Idukki to Thodupuzha when his car plunged into a gorge. He died on the spot. It took four days to retrieve the body.

'George Thomas was broken. After three months, I went and asked him if we could proceed with the sale of the land. No, let's talk to an astrologer first, he said. I took him to meet the Allimangalam Namboothiri. You might have heard of him … in Mavelikkara? They are an ancient line of astrologers. I don't know him personally. They had made some inquiries on their own and told me that he was a fine astrologer, with rare intuition and foresight. They asked me to take them there.

'Sir, I can see it now. George Thomas, his wife and I, sitting in front of the astrologer. He takes up the horoscope, looks through it. Even before we could tell him about the recent loss in the family, he remarks, "Your son died recently. Yes?" He folds up the horoscope. "You have invited a great curse upon your head. *Arjitha dosham* – a referred curse. It's nothing you did. You caught it elsewhere, and it holds fast on to you now."

'It didn't make any sense to me. "How?" asked George Thomas. The astrologer looked at the horoscope again. "Did you buy a new house?" he asked. "No," said George Thomas. "Anything else? Gold? Property?" he asked. George Thomas hesitated. "I had paid an advance to buy a piece of land. But ever since then, I have been feeling somewhat restless in my mind," he said.

'"Have you been having any dreams?" asked the astrologer. "Yes," he said. "What kind of dreams?" "A really old man is at the bottom of an ancient well. He is crying. I am looking at him from above." "Anything else?" "No. Just this one dream." The Namboothiri looked at the wife and asked, "And you? Did you have any dreams?" "Someone at the door, rapping on it, crying. That was it. But I have had the dream more than ten times," said the lady.

'"Where is this land? Whose is it?" asked the Namboothiri. I explained everything in detail. "There is a great curse on the land. It is not going to be easy to escape it. Forget the advance. The rest of your family survived, take that as your gain from this. Don't invite more of the curse on your head." Saying so, the Namboothiri placed the horoscope down.

'When they bowed and made to leave, the lady was weeping, her hands clasped on her chest. "Why should my son die for this?" she asked. "Sin is like a contagious disease," the Namboothiri said. "That is its nature. A mouthful of food – sometimes that's all it takes to spread. That's why they say, avoid the sinner like the plague." "But why?" wailed the woman. "The astrologer can say just one thing, madam. These are the machinations of fate," he said, and made to go.

'When we came outside, George Thomas turned to me and said, "It's all right. I don't need my advance back." I tried to convince him. I told him there must be propitiations we could do to relieve the curse. He would not agree. I could do nothing more. I went to Madras and told Shanmugalingam what had happened. "What can we do now?" I bemoaned. "I'll return the advance," he said. "Why should I hold on to his money?"

'As we were talking, his wife rushed in. "I want to meet that Namboothiri. Our family has not been spared either! Take me to him," she said. She was hitting herself on the head. and collapsed to the ground as she was speaking.

'I took her to the Namboothiri. He took one glance at the horoscope and put it down immediately. "There's a great curse upon your line," he said, "and it won't stop until it has had its fill. Throw in what you will, its fire will not be quenched." The lady was weeping. She narrated all the happenings in her family. That was when I learned of it too.'

I got a sense of where this was going. But I kept my silence.

'The Azhagiyanambiyapillai family, sir, they are. When your father was embroiled in the case, Shanmugalingam's father, Azhagiyanambiyapillai, was the executive officer of the temple.'

'Mm,' I said.

'He made a lot of money at the time. Bought this land too with that wealth. The whole family came up in the world then.'

I nodded.

'Azhagiyanambiyapillai had three children. The first was Subramaniam. The second was a girl, Meenakshi. Shanmugalingam was the youngest. Subramaniam is dead. He was an engineer, fell to his death from a height. He had one son, who also died in an accident. The son's wife, she went to her parents' place with her only child. And the child is dead, too, it's been three years now. He had gone to bathe in the Chembarambakkam Lake, and drowned. Now it's just the lady. She lives near Rajapalayam someplace. The whole line has been wiped out.'

'Azhagiyanambiyapillai's daughter Meenakshi is also no more. Both her sons – gone. Both had a sudden heart attack. Four deaths in their family too. Three children, all slow in the head. The whole family has gone to seed – lying holed up somewhere in Tiruvannamalai.'

'Is that so?'

'Yes, sir. Shanmugalingam is an auditor. Two sons and a daughter. The daughter died four years ago in childbirth. The elder son had an accident last year. He's bedridden now … they get bad news every three months, he says. It has been so all their life. He has been on sleeping pills since he was twenty. He gripped my hand and wept like a child. "I should never have married. My line should have stopped with me. At least the rest of them would have been spared."'

'What should I do now?' I asked.

'Sir, they have spared nothing. No propitiation has been left undone. They've gone to all the temples. They have given crores in charity. They have done all they can to atone. Nothing more to do,' said Paramasivam. 'His father Azhagiyanambipillai died when he was seventy. He had a disease called fistula. Couldn't stop the shit flowing out of him. That was when he came out with the whole story. "I have been impaled for seventeen years," he wept. "God has impaled me…"'

I sat with my head bowed so as to control myself. I was clenching my teeth.

'It was he who did everything. Two of the watchmen were in on it. Their lives are also completely ruined now. When he was caught, he pointed to your father, who was innocent. He paid everyone, the lawyers and everyone else, through the teeth in order to escape. But he could not escape from God, see?'

'Okay, what about it now?' I asked.

'All this while, they thought that your father had died. They had made some inquiries. That was what they were told. How could we have expected that he would still be alive? It was the astrologer who said, "There is no point doing all these propitiations. The person who was destroyed by you placed a curse on you. That is still raging. Go there. Fall at his feet and ask for forgiveness. Unless he forgives you, there is no freedom for you." "But no one from that generation is alive now," Shanmugalingam had said. "Then their children," the astrologer said. "Go to them and ask for forgiveness. If they forgive you with all their heart, it would be like their ancestors forgiving you."

'We did not know then that your father was still alive. I asked around. I thought I could find some of his descendants. No one knew anything in Neelamanickapuram. I went to Parvathipuram Agraharam in Nagercoil. Nothing there either. I searched everywhere. Finally, I got this address and came here.'

'You could have asked for the address in the jail,' I said.

'Yes, sir, that's where I got it. But it was the Kochi address. I went there and inquired, and they pointed me to your old office address.

They told me that your pension is being sent to you here from the Thiruvananthapuram office. It's from there that I got this address.'

'But why is all this any of your concern?'

'They promised to reimburse my expenses, and pay me a commission too. This is my job, you see.'

'Okay, what do you need from me now?'

'I have told them that your father is alive and here. They wish to come here and seek his forgiveness.'

I pondered over it for a while. Then I got up. 'Please come,' I said. 'Come in, see my father for yourself.'

He came with me.

'This is just for their peace of mind,' Paramasivam said. 'They are not able to sleep in their beds at night. They have been dying of fear for two generations now. Let them come. Let them fall at his feet, as they wish. Do whatever ritual feels right to them. You see, this is not just a profession for me. These are human lives at stake, no? To smoulder like that for generations, to die smouldering ... that's torture.'

I took Paramasivam to the inner room. It was removed from the rest of the house. That smell – part Dettol, part urine – always made me want to throw up.

Appa – my father – was sitting up in his bed, gazing at the window. He looked very tired. It had been more than a month since I myself had seen him.

He was all alone even in my house. A male nurse named John stayed with him all day to help with his needs and went home in the evenings. It had been many days since I had encountered him as well. At nights, an old servant-woman stayed with him. Appa slept soundly through the night.

I realized that it had been many years since I had taken a good look at Appa's face. It was usually my nature to take one look at him and then lower my gaze. I had no idea why he made me so anxious. I avoided thinking about him if I could. It was like that from my younger days. That was how I was able to forget a man with whom I lived under the same roof for the past thirty years. It was by forgetting that I was still able to go on living.

Appa's face was different now, more sunken, longer. The skin on his face appeared as though it was burned and charred, his protruding cheekbones strained against it. The muscles on his face had all but melted away, making his big eagle-like nose even more prominent. Tufts of white hair sprouted out of his nostrils. Hardly any lips. The whites of his eyes were cloudy and streaked with red. The irises had whitened. I could never get rid of the feeling that his eyes were like two pus-filled open wounds on his face. I had to struggle to push the thought away of my head.

His body was badly shrunken. The muscles on his arms had all wasted away, the nerves taut as if he was in a state of permanent seizure. He was like a wax statue that had dissolved into a shapeless mass. Even the skin was waxy. His feet were puffy and shiny.

His hands wouldn't stop trembling. He could not grasp anything with his fingers. Even a glass of water – someone had to pour it into his mouth for him. Or he needed a flask with a straw to sip it. Appa held both his hands fast under his thighs. I could see that his wrists were convulsing. He heard our footsteps and turned around. I felt like Appa did not recognize me either. 'Who is this?' he asked.

'He has come to meet you,' I said. So he did recognize me after all.

'Dei, the sparrows are coming in now. Those tiny house sparrows, in here…' Appa pointed in a general direction. 'Who is this?'

'Appa, he has come to see you.'

'About the temple?'

'Appa, he wants to ask something about your case.'

Appa turned to me and smiled. 'The theft case of '76? The Neelamanickapuram theft case? And who is this?'

'Just an interested party,' I said. 'He just wants a few details.'

'Sit down. Let me tell you,' said Appa. 'It was a glorious case back in those times. There was a lot about it in the papers. It's all forgotten now, dead and buried. You know the Neelamanickapuram temple? A grand robbery there. The ritual priest was a man called Muthaalam Sankaran Pothi. A good man. Never one to get into any scrapes. A bit of a simpleton, to be honest.'

Paramasivam was startled. He looked at me. There's more, listen, I signalled with my eyes.

'Muthaalam Sankaran Pothi … now this man was known to everyone in town. He was also an astrologer. The family fell on hard times. Very hard times. I mean, they couldn't have more than a meal a day. Just boiled rice. Or cassava. Sometimes they could not afford even that. So this man, he would go to the old riverfront in the dead of the night and come back with peippoosanikkai pumpkins. Very poisonous. Sometimes there was enough poison in it to kill a man. They wouldn't feed it even to the cows. This man boiled that and gave it to the children. Kaattuchembu – wild taro – was even more poisonous. He would feed them that too. That's what happens when hunger climbs on top of you and dances on your head.

'In those days, most of the temples in Kanyakumari district were not part of the Department of Religious Endowments. The temples attached to the Travancore kingdom had their own administration. There were two kinds of temples: those attached to the government, and those that were unattached. It was not like the temples attached to the government were paying proper salaries back then. What to say of the unattached ones? If they pay you, they pay you. Otherwise, no money. Tell me, what was a poor priest to do? Maybe a rupee here, eight annas there, if there was a ritual to be performed in someone's home. But the general order of life was – hunger. Now, what was I saying?'

'About Sankaran Pothi,' I said.

'Yes, him ... Then that fellow came. Enticed him. There were a few panchaloha idols in the temple. Small ones, for the processions. Two hundred pounds of gold for the deity. Our man was starving. His father, bedridden. His father had been a great tantri back in the day, a great scholar of the Tantrasamuchayam text. He had been felicitated by the Maharaja himself. All gone. Times had changed. The Nayar and Vellalan who held the lands had managed to convince the rest that the Namboothiris and Pothis were scoundrels. No regard. No respect. No money. They were living like beggars. It's all the will of God, what do you say, eh?'

John entered. Appa looked at him for a few moments as if he was a stranger. Then he continued speaking to me.

'This Sankaran Pothi, he had four or five children. Three of them girls. One was old enough to be married. The second was a boy. In eleventh class. He also had a part-time job, as a ritual priest in a local Sastha temple. No earnings except what fell on his plate. Three more girls after that. Hunger stalked them, like a seven-birth-long curse. And somehow, he got his hands on the temple deity. First the jewels. He took them one at a time, sold them, and squirrelled away the earnings here and there. Then the idols. How he took them, where he sold them – the police knew everything. That's how they caught him. They spelt out everything in court. He got ten years in jail. I mean, it was god-sin, wasn't it? Doesn't spare you so easily now, does it?' A smile on Appa's face again. A sly smile, as if he knew something others did not. 'I was then the executive officer in eight temples, including Suseendram. It was I who discovered the theft, all of it. I mean, half the evidence in the case was mine. The court punished him ... Well, he had committed a crime, he should face the music, what do you say? The man had placed his paw on Perumal's property. Do you think the Lord would spare him? His eagle Garudan swoops down on scoundrels, snatches them away...'

'Yes,' I said. Paramasivam looked at me in sheer terror.

Appa nodded and laughed. 'Poor thing. Jail was hell for him. There was not a day when he was not beaten up. But what else could he expect? Look at what he did. He sold away the God he worshipped. No, they weren't going to spare him,' he said. 'Dei, bring me the water.'

John brought the water. Appa bent low and sipped on the water very slowly.

Very gently, Paramasivam turned to me. 'Sir.'

'Yes.'

'This Muthaalam Sankaran Pothi?'

'It's him,' I said. 'He thinks he is somebody else now.'

'Why do these sparrows keep coming in? I keep telling him to keep the windows shut … he doesn't listen…' Appa said.

'Shall we leave?' I asked.

'Yes,' said Paramasivam.

We returned to the living room. 'Well, you see?' I said.

'What is all this, sir?' Paramasivam was trembling.

'Jail life made him like this. He is no longer Sankaran Pothi, but someone else,' I said. 'He went to prison in '77. Came out only in '88. The sentence was for ten years. But he was in for eleven. More than twelve, if you include the time he was in jail during the trial. That's a life sentence. A double murder in the middle of the road in broad daylight, and you can still get out in five years on Nehru's birthday or Periyar's birthday. He did not even get parole. Stayed in for the whole term.'

'Sir, but why?' Paramasivam was in tears now.

'You need to know somebody for all this. In politics. In the government. Whom do we know? We're Brahmins. And Tulu Pothis at that. There may perhaps be four hundred of us in this town. In a democracy, number is everything, isn't it? How did the investigation take place? All of six months. It just flashed by, and the verdict was handed. No appeals. Straight to jail. The court had appointed an advocate to appeal Appa's case for free. All of twenty-six years … he knew nothing. Half the time he did not even turn up. That was it. The case was closed.

'And then there was the general pervasive hatred for Brahmins. Now the temple priest had been caught with his hands on the temple jewels. What jubilation! The papers were full of it. A politician who came to Nagercoil around that time spent an hour and a half on stage taking the piss out of this one incident. People need to see a good slaughter sometimes. And don't they always drag in a white goat for the sacrifice?

'I tell you, there are very very few families in this country who have not feasted on temple property directly or indirectly. They may feel a little guilty about it. So they all got together and placed my father on the slaughterstone. Justice, fairness – the society decides what is just and what is fair. Whatever the society decrees as justice, that is justice. That is all.

'I had just finished the eleventh class then. No job, nothing. The house we lived in belonged to the temple. When the police took him away, the townspeople practically drove us out of our home – the pitchforks were missing, that's all. Our grandfather couldn't get up from his bed. We placed him on a single-bullock cart and went to Puliyoorkurichi. Our Chithappa who lived there didn't want to have anything to do with us. Go away, don't spoil my family too, he said. We headed to Thiruvattaru. Periyappa, my father's older brother, met us halfway at Aatroor. He didn't even want us to enter the town, ruining his family by association.

'We had no choice but to turn back. On the way, I discovered that our grandfather's body had turned stone-cold. I told my mother. My mother told the cart driver. She wept, pleaded. He got up on his seat and slapped her right across the face. I was sixteen years old. I just stood there and watched. My eighteen-year-old sister was right next to me. Three younger sisters … what did we do then? I can't tell you that. Not with this tongue, which she who birthed me gave me.

Nothing else to do but think of that wretched woman, every day, every single day, and fall at her feet, over and over…

'The cart driver paid for the body to be burnt in a burning ground in the jungle near Unnamalaikadai. I did the rites. He then took us in his cart to Marthandam. Also gave us cash for the bus fare up to Thiruvananthapuram. We went there. Stayed in the front yard of a pilgrim house for eight days. Then we found jobs in a hotel. My mother became the hotelkeeper's keep. What else?

'For a year I waited and bussed in that hotel. Then, on the basis of my eleventh-class marks, I got the job in the post office. I studied hard. Became an auditor. Married my elder sister off when she was twenty-nine. And then my younger sisters. We did not have the means to visit my father in the meanwhile. To tell you the truth, I had forgotten him. It was difficult, but I managed to forget. I told myself that he was dead.

'They transferred him from Palayamkottai to Vellore. Ten years … and then a year more. There are a number of procedures to release a convict, you see … He came out like this. Now he is no longer Sankaran Pothi. He is someone else. Sankaran Pothi committed the theft, so he was sentenced to jail, he deserved everything – that's what he thinks now.

'After he came back, we took him to many doctors. They all say the same thing. His delusion is the only reason he is still alive. He thinks that Sankaran Pothi is a different person. He learned to hate the man. Then it justifies everything, doesn't it? The jail, the daily beatings, and all the other unspeakable horrors they inflicted upon Sankaran Pothi?

'Sankaran Pothi committed no theft. The thief was Azhagiyanambiyapillai. There is not a single person who is unaware of this. All the witnesses knew. Even the judge knew it. But if righteousness dies, then it means that there is no God. Appa had depended on God for his life since the day he was born. How could he let go of God? He could he stay in jail after forsaking God? He would have died in agony. So he simply let go of Sankaran Pothi. Sankaran Pothi was a thief. So he languished in jail. That must mean that a just God does exist, no? He holds on to that knowledge. That's how he lives on. For thirty-two years this man lives. But Sankaran Pothi is gone.'

'Sir, he said something else now.'

'What?' I asked.

'No, he said that he was the executive officer of eight temples, including Suseendram. He said that he had caught the thief in the act,' said Paramasivam.

'Yes,' I said. 'I did not notice then.' I felt a sudden alarm. 'So he thinks that he is Azhagiyanambiyapillai,' I said. And all these days, I had not noticed!

'Yes,' said Paramasivam.

I sighed. 'Look. This is how he is now. Now if we bring in Azhagiyanambiyapillai's son, what will Appa know? How will he forgive?'

'He doesn't need to forgive anyone,' said Paramasivam. 'I'll bring Shanmugalingam over. He just wants to fall at the feet of your father along with his family and seek forgiveness. For their sake. If a God exists somewhere, for the sake of that God.'

I hesitated. 'But my son or daughter – they don't know anything about their grandfather's jail term. Their children know nothing either. There will be trouble if Shanmugalingam's family comes here.'

'Then let's meet elsewhere,' said Paramasivam.

'I can't take him out anywhere,' I said. 'Okay. The family will go to Mattancherry next week for a wedding. Only my father and I will be home. I will call you then. You can ask them to come then.'

'Okay.'

'But no ritual, no propitiation, none of that. Whatever their astrologer or priest might say,' I said. 'They can come here if they like. They can meet him. But just half an hour. He won't understand anything. They can come and see him for their satisfaction.'

'Okay.' Paramasivam got up and took leave. 'Thank you for your help. I will talk to them and let you know.'

Only after he had left was I able to grasp entirely the state Appa was in. If he had transformed himself into Azhagiyanambiyapillai, was that just so that he could distance himself from Sankaran Pothi? Why should he transform into Azhagiyanambiyapillai? He knew very well that Azhagiyanambiyapillai was a thief.

That means he thinks that Azhagiyanambiyapillai won in the end. He was the victor. And Sankaran Pothi, the loser. So my father had taken a leap from being the loser and swathed himself around the winner. It was as Azhagiyanambiyapillai that he was celebrating Sankaran Pothi's suffering. Did he really think that the theft was a great victory?

All these thoughts made me very uncomfortable, and my discomfort only grew by the day. I felt like I had ingested something cheap and spoilt by mistake; I felt like throwing up. I had thought Appa was moving towards God. Instead, he had made himself a thief.

Normally, I didn't speak much to him. Now, I went to his room often and tried to get him to talk. 'Appa, did you meet Sankaran Pothi in jail?' I asked.

'Of course! Many times,' he said. 'He would take one look at me and start crying. I have sinned Pillai sir, I have erred, he would wail. All right, the wrong was done and the punishment has been doled out. All will be well now, I'd say. It is a very hard life in jail. And our man, he was fair-skinned, he had a weak frame. Always the sissy ... hehehehe.'

'Appa, it was Azhagiyanambiyapillai who committed the theft, wasn't it?' I said.

'Who?' he asked.

'You?'

Appa's eyes narrowed. His mouth tightened like the drawstrings of a purse. 'Which son of a bitch said that?'

'No, I heard someone say so.'

'Did he say that? That Sankaran Pothi?'

'No, someone else…'

'Who? It is he. He is going around saying that. Because he is the thief. Which thief would accept his thievery? He will claim that he is a good man. Then who is the bad man? The other one. The one he doesn't like. It was I who caught Sankaran Pothi in the act. He must hate me … so much … of course he'll say that. Scoundrel.'

I got up with a sigh. I was really anxious now. Should I let them come and meet Appa? What kind of an effect will such a meeting have on him? I went to meet my friend and Appa's doctor, Balakrishnan Nayar. I told him everything.

'It is a real puzzle. I can't understand it either,' said Balakrishnan Nayar. 'How will he talk to them? From whose perspective? How can he talk to them as Azhagiyanambiyapillai? Will he talk to Shanmugalingam as father to son? Or will he transform into Sankaran Pothi and forgive them? For Sankaran Pothi to reappear in this man … after all these years … does your father have the strength of mind today to withstand such an event?'

'Will something happen to him?' I asked.

'Well, he is going to be a hundred. The bodies of old people are very weak. Very little life in there. And the mind is but a projection of the body. If he gets too excited, he may not be able to bear it. He may die.'

'I think I will tell them not to come.'

'Perhaps that is for the best. However…' Balakrishnan hesitated. 'This could be a spiritual liberation for your father. His soul could make its way out of the dark prison where it has been incarcerated all these days and finally find some peace. It could be that he has lived all these days for this moment to arrive. We do not have the right to deny him that, do we?'

I was irritated. 'So what do you recommend?' I asked.

'As a psychiatrist I think it is better if he does not meet them. But as a human being, I think it is imperative that he does. I don't understand it myself.'

'I came here for your guidance,' I said.

'They should meet,' said Balakrishnan abruptly. 'That's what I feel. If all this was fated to happen, then let the meeting also take place. What will happen? He could die. So? He is going to be a hundred. If he can recover before his death, that's a good thing, isn't it?'

'Can we consult an astrologer?' I asked.

'Yes, I thought so too,' he said. 'Astrologers can speak decisively on certain matters. That is because they don't need to take responsibility for anything. They feel they are simply pointing towards fate. Only psychiatrists like me have to weigh every word with care, take responsibility…'

'I have visited Melamanakkadu Achuthan Namboothiri a couple of times. Why don't I pay him a visit now?'

'Does he know about your father?'

'No, I never told him.'

'If you have belief in astrologers, you may go.'

'Please come with me,' I said.

'Me!' Balakrishnan laughed.

'Please come,' I said. 'You can't be someone who does not believe in astrology. There is no such Malayali on earth.'

He laughed again. 'I will come,' he said.

That very day, we made an appointment and went to see Melamanakkadu Achuthan Namboothiri. His was an old house, he was also an old man. I felt like I had suddenly entered a world from a century ago. I had been there once before, to consult him about my son Raghavan's marriage. I had had the same feeling then.

I told Achuthan Namboothiri everything. He sat on the lotus seat in a padmasana, eyes lowered, the index finger of his right hand touching the ground, and listened. Then he lifted his eyes and looked at me. 'There is nothing the stars and signs can say about this. He has to meet them,' he said.

'But…'

'We cannot predict what will happen. Whatever happens, it is for the good. So what if he dies?' asked Achutan Namboothiri. 'Sankaran Pothi's self lies imprisoned in his depths. Set it free. Let it take its course.'

I felt much more clear-headed about everything on our way back. Balakrishnan laughed. 'This is why we need astrologers. We doctors give you the responsibility of making decisions. The astrologers make a decision for you and tell you what to do.'

'Please be with me when they come,' I said.

Balakrishnan hesitated. 'Will it be okay if I am present there?' he asked. 'What if they want a personal meeting?'

'We have the right to have you there. You are Appa's doctor,' I said.

'Yes, you could say that. I will come,' he said.

After that, my anxiety vanished. I became normal and went back to my usual routine. But I was anticipating their visit.

On the appointed day, my family left for the wedding. Dr Balakrishnan arrived in his car. We waited in the living room. John was with Appa.

'I have some tranquilizers with me. If he gets too agitated, we can put him to sleep. Don't worry,' he said.

'Let's see,' I said.

As I sat with my arms folded across my chest and my eyes closed, I remembered my mother. When I had found employment at the post office in Thiruvalla and rented a house, I had asked her to move in with me. She had said no. 'Take your sisters along. It wouldn't be the same if I came with you now.'

I could not comprehend why Amma would say so. I got very angry. 'Do you not want to live with honour at least now? Come with me,'

I insisted. At one point, I broke down. Then I got incensed. I swore at her. 'So you are now used to this life, aren't you?' I said.

She sat with her head lowered. I had gone off to Thiruvalla with my sisters. At first, I was bitterly revolted. In a week, though, my heart melted. I wanted to go and see her, fall at her feet and bring her home. But I got the news that she had died. Her corpse was found in the storeroom where she usually lay. She burned in a cremation ground in Thiruvananthapuram.

A car drew up on the street. Paramasivam got out and came into the house, his palms pressed in greeting. 'Sir, they are here. If you please, come, ask them to come in.'

I went out. Husband and wife were in the car. Shanmugalingam got out on my side. When he greeted me, I thought he would cry. He could not utter a word. His wife could not meet my eyes.

'Please come in,' I said.

They sat in the living room. Paramasivam looked at Balakrishnan. 'This is Dr Balakrishnan, my friend,' I said.

Shanmugalingam seemed relieved to see the doctor.

'There is no one else at home,' I said. 'If you would like some tea…'

'Thank you, we just had some,' said Shanmugalingam.

'Both of them felt a bit faint on the way,' said Paramasivam.

'Would you like to rest a little?' I asked.

'Sir, no,' Shanmugalingam cut in quickly. 'I am well now.'

'Paramasivam might have told you about my father…'

'Yes,' he said.

'He is a different person now…' I could not complete the thought.

'Yes,' said Shanmugalingam, 'Paramasivam told us. That in his mind, he is now Azhagiyanambiyapillai.' The strain told on his face, his mouth was crooked. 'Sami is a spotless man. He should not identify with that scoundrel even in his mind. At first, I was not sure if I should come at all. Then I thought, let the atonement for my family and descendants be. The first thing to do is to free your good father from all thought of that reprobate wretch. That is my duty. I have to do that. He will understand if I tell him.'

'You have to explain carefully,' said Balakrishnan. 'He is almost a hundred. He cannot endure any emotional drama.'

'We will try,' Shanmugalingam said. 'We just want to fall at sami's feet. That's why we came. And everything else is in God's hands…'

I rose. 'Please come,' I said.

He was trembling. He crossed his arms across his chest.

'Please come,' I said again.

'Let the doctor come as well.'

'He will.'

'Paramasivam, come.'

'Yes, sir.'

'Etti…'

'Coming,' said his wife.

He walked very very slowly, halting from time to time. He was breathless. 'Sami! Muruga! Senthilandava!' he muttered the names of the gods under his breath.

Appa was sitting on his bed, dressed in white. His hands were trembling. He had placed his palms tightly under his thighs. His arms continued to quaver. When he saw us, he broke into a smile. He looked at me. 'The sparrow keeps coming into the room. I tell him to close the window, he just won't,' he said.

'Appa, these people have come to meet you.'

'Come, please come,' he said pleasantly. 'What is it? Something about the temple? You can discuss everything with Ramu first. We cannot do anything these days without a receipt, you see.'

'Appa, they have come to talk to you about the case. The old theft case.'

Appa nodded, smiling. 'Yes, it was a grand affair in those days. There was a lot about it in the papers. All forgotten now. A great theft, at the Neelamanickapuram temple here…'

'Appa, this is Azhagiyanambiyapillai's son.'

'Who?' Appa's eyes narrowed.

Shanmugalingam fell in a heap at Appa's feet. He caught hold of his feet and placed them on his head. 'Sami, please forgive us. Sami, please forgive me, please forgive my family. Please wish us well. That great sinner Azhagiyanambiyapillai who stole the temple property and sent you to jail for it ... I am his son. Our family is entirely gone to ruin. Torn to shreds, nothing left ... Sami, please forgive us, wish us well ... my children should not suffer any more...'

His voice seemed to knead away at my heart. I turned away. I felt the tears on my cheeks, I wiped them away.

The lady simply sat on the floor. Then she collapsed to one side. Her face hit the ground. Her body quivered, as if she was having a seizure.

Appa's face remained unchanged. He took out one trembling hand from under his thigh and placed it on Shanmugalingam's head. 'All right, let it go. They are both little ones. They are all the same for me,' he said.

'Sami, bless us,' said Shanmugalingam, raising one hand as if he was begging. 'Please give us your blessing, sami.'

'Live prosperously with your children ... May you be blessed with everything good and great for the next eighteen generations. Go, be happy,' said Appa. 'Take good care of the women.'

Shanmugalingam broke into sobs and stretched himself out on the floor. Paramasivam had clasped his hands on his chest. He was weeping. 'Take them out,' I said gently. I signalled to John to put Appa to bed.

The doctor also became emotional. We both came out to the living room and sat down. Paramasivam took Shanmugalingam and his wife to the porch out in the front. They were still weeping. But the tenor was different now.

Paramasivam came to me. 'We will leave, sir. There is nothing more to say. Your father has given us a great blessing indeed. What else can be said?'

'Yes,' I said. I rose to my feet.

'I'll take your leave, doctor,' said Paramasivam, and went out.

We sat down again. I felt like all my energy had drained out of me. My limbs were weak. My eyelids drooped. I breathed heavily, feeling weaker by the minute.

Balakrishnan turned to me. His voice was hesitant. 'Just a small doubt,' he said.

'What is it?' I asked.

'Who spoke out of your father's mouth just now?'

I got up with a start, stared hard at the doctor's face. I slowly went to Appa's room and peeped inside. John had laid Appa to rest on the bed and spread a blanket out over his body. He had his hands on his chest, his mouth was slightly open, he was sleeping.

ACKNOWLEDGEMENTS

OUR GRATITUDE TO the writers, editors and publishers of the books and magazines where the Tamil stories were published. Every effort was made to trace the copyright holder for each story. For any that might have been inadvertently omitted, the publishers would be happy to make the necessary amendments in future editions.

'Harmonium': Ashokamitran, 'Harmonium', in *Nanbanin Thanthai* (Chennai: Natrinai Pathippagam, 2012).

'The King's Way': Kanmani Gunasekaran, 'Rajapattai', in *Athandar Koil Kuthirai* (Chennai: Tamizhini Pathippagam, 2000).

'The Saga of Butchery': Keeranur Jakirraja, 'Kasappin Ithikasam', *Kalam*, July 2015.

'The Breaking of a Story': Sundara Ramaswamy, 'Oru Storyin Katai', *Kalachuvadu*, August 2004.

'The Flight': Vannanilavan, 'Thappitthal', in *Mazhaippayanam* (Chennai: Sandhya Pathippagam, 2019).

'Cheenalatchumi's Queue': Latha, 'Cheenalatchumiyin Varisai', in *Nagarmanam*, the Tamil edition of the Commuting Reader series, ed. Kavitha K. and Kokilavani S. (Singapore: Marshall Cavendish International [Asia], 2017).

'The Rules of the Game': J.P. Sanakya, 'Attatthin Vithimuraikal', *Atcharam*, January–March 2002.

'The Known, the Unknown': Sa. Kandasamy, 'Arintathum Ariyatathum', in *Iravin Kural* (Chennai: Kavitha Pathippagam, 2002).

'Cycle': Charu Nivedita, 'Cycle', *Dinamalar Kathaimalar*, February 1994.

'Football and Her': Sureshkumara Indrajith, 'Kalpanthum Avalum', *Uyir Ezhuttu*, August 2013.

'Screening': Aravindan, 'Thiraikal', *Uyir Ezhuttu*, June 2023.

'The Horsewoman': Ambai, 'Kuthiraikkari', in *Sivappuk Kazhuttudan Oru Pachaip Paravai* (Nagercoil: Kalachuvadu Pathippagam, 2019).

Ambai's 'The Horsewoman', translated by G.J.V. Prasad, originally published in *A Red-Necked Green Bird* (Noida: Simon & Schuster, 2021). Used by permission.

'Catch a Chunky Goat': Appadurai Muttulingam, 'Kozhuttadu Pidippen', in *A. Muttulingam Kathaikal* (Chennai: Tamizhini Pathippagam, 2003).

'Soundaravalli's Moustache': S. Ramakrishnan, 'Soundaravalliyin Meesai', *Ananda Vikatan*, 26 December 2007.

'Black Beads and Television': Salma, *Karugamani TV, Balyam* (Nagercoil: Kalachuvadu Pathippagam, 2022). This translation originally published in *The Curse: Stories* by Salma, translated from the Tamil by N. Kalyan Raman (New Delhi: Speaking Tiger, 2020).

'The Goddess Was Watching': Nanjil Nadan, 'Ammai Partthiruntal', *Ananda Vikatan*, 25 October 2020.

'The Tool of His Trade': Devibharathi, 'Karuvi', in *Bali* (Erode: Kalam Pathippagam, 1993). This translation originally published in *Farewell, Mahatma: Stories* by Devibharathi, translated by N. Kalyan Raman (Noida: HarperCollins, 2014), reissued by Harper Perennial India as a special edition in January 2024.

'Mirage': Tamilnathy, 'Mayakkuthirai', *Amrutha*, May 2012.

'Heartbreak': Imayam, 'Manamurivu', *Uyirmmai*, September 2022.

'The Blouse': Perumal Murugan, 'Koditthuni,' *India Today*, 21 January–5 February 1997.

Perumal Murugan's 'The Blouse', translated by N. Kalyan Raman, originally published by Juggernaut Books, 2016. Used by permission.

'Uprising': Shobasakthi, 'Ezhucchi', in *Kandi Veeran* (Chennai: Karuppup Pirathikal, 2014).

'Sacrificial Stone': B. Jeyamohan, 'Palikkal', in *Ezhukathir* (Coimbatore: Vishnupuram Pathippagam, 2022).

ABOUT THE WRITERS

Ashokamitran, the pen name of Thyagarajan Jagadisan, is one of India's most distinguished writers to have emerged in the post-Independence era. In a prolific career that began in 1955, he wrote over 250 short stories, fourteen novellas and eight novels, with works like *Karaintha Nizhalkal* and *Manasarovar* receiving widespread critical acclaim, in addition to a steady output of columns, essays and book reviews. His works, which secured him a central place in contemporary Tamil literature, have been translated into many Indian and European languages. Five major novels as well as four collections of short fiction from his oeuvre are available in English translation. His years of rich and diverse contribution to Tamil literature brought him many honours, including the Sahitya Akademi Award (1996) for his short-story collection *Appavin Snekitar*. He passed away in 2017.

Kanmani Gunasekaran has authentically captured the lives of people from central Tamil Nadu, employing their everyday language and dialect in a realistic style in his works, for over twenty-five years. He has authored twenty-three books: ten poetry collections, five novels including *Anjalai* and *Vantharankudi*, five short-story collections, a lexicon focusing on the central Tamil Nadu region and two works of non-fiction. He received the Neithal Award in memory of Sundara Ramaswamy (2007), the Tamil Development Department Award (2007) and the Kalaignar Porkizhi Award (2019). Kanmani Gunasekaran lives in the village Manakkollai in Cuddalore district.

Keeranur Jakirraja was born in Keeranur, near Palani, into a Tamil Muslim family. He began his literary career with small magazines, and has authored ten novels, including his celebrated debut, *Meenkarat Teru*, which vividly articulates the cross-sections of everyday life and the issues faced by Tamil Muslims, particularly those living in poverty and under exploitation. In addition to his novels, he has published five short-story collections, six essay anthologies and two children's books. He has received several awards, including the Vikatan Award (2010 and 2020) and the Inkulab Award for Literary Voices from Marginalized Communities at the Hindu Lit for Life (2018), for his literary accomplishments.

Sundara Ramaswamy was a prominent figure in post-Independence Tamil literature, who authored three novels, seventy-four short stories, and over a hundred poems and articles respectively. He translated two Malayalam novels by renowned Indian writer, Thakazhi Sivasankara Pillai, and founded the magazine *Kalachuvadu* in 1988. His highly acclaimed debut novel, *Oru Puliyamarattin Katai*, has been translated into English, Hindi, Malayalam, Kannada and Hebrew. His second novel *J.J.: Sila Kurippukal* marks a pinnacle of Tamil modernism, breaking away from the conventional form of its time by exploring the literary milieu with self-awareness and a nonchalant, sarcastic tone, while deliberately maintaining a distance from emotive evocations. This novel, as well as the author's third, have been translated into English. Sundara Ramaswamy received the Iyal award for Lifetime Achievement (2001), given by the Tamil Literary Garden based in Canada, and the Katha Award (2003). He passed away in 2005.

Vannanilavan, the pen name of U. Ramachandran, is an acclaimed Tamil writer noted for his distinct style of prose. He has authored a poetry collection, over one hundred short stories and seven novels, including his celebrated debut novel *Kadalpuratthil* (*By the Sea*). He was honoured with the Lifetime Achievement Award (2019) by the Coimbatore District Small Industries Association and the Puthumaipithan Memorial Award (2021) by Vilakku Ilakkiya Amaippu, based in the USA. His works of fiction predominantly explore the everyday experiences of ordinary people, blending elegance and simplicity with nuanced storytelling. His works have been widely translated into languages such as English, Hindi, Malayalam and German.

Latha, the pen name of Kanagalatha, is a distinguished Tamil writer recognized for her contributions across poetry and short stories. She has published three poetry collections so far. Her short-story collections include *Nan Kolai Seyyum Penkal* (2007), which won the biennial Singapore Literature Prize in 2008, and *Cheenalatchumi* (2022). Latha's works have been translated into English, French and German, and featured in various multilingual anthologies. She holds the role of Associate Editor at the Singapore-based Tamil-language newspaper, *Tamil Murasu*, and is a founding director of Poetry Festival Singapore.

J.P. Sanakya is a notable fiction writer who also works as a screenwriter for Tamil films. Focusing on short stories, Sanakya has penned unique tales exploring the inner conflicts of human beings, often unfolding amid social norms and iniquities. He has published four short-story collections to date: *En Veettin Varaipadam* (2003), *Kanavup Puttagam* (2005), *Mutal Tanimai* (2013) and *Perumaikkuriya Kadikaram* (2023).

Sa. Kandasamy was born in Mayiladuthurai, Thanjavur district. A versatile author and creator, he excelled across diverse genres: as a fiction writer, essayist, critic and producer-director of documentaries. Known for his minimalist narrative style, he authored over 150 short stories and eleven novels, with his debut novel, *Sayavanam*, published in 1969. He was honoured with the Sahitya Akademi award (1998) for his novel *Visaranai Commission*. His contributions to the arts include the documentary, *Kaval Deivangal*, on terracotta idols, created with Doordarshan; it won the first prize at the Angino Film Festival in Nicosia, Cyprus, in 1989. His novels *Sayavanam*, *Suriya Vamsam* and *Visaranai Commission* have been translated into English. He passed away in 2020.

Charu Nivedita is the author of nearly a hundred works in Tamil, including essays, novels, poetry anthologies and short stories. Known for his postmodern and transgressive writing, he focuses on autofiction and metafiction. His novel *Zero Degree* was longlisted for the 2013 Jan Michalski Prize and featured in HarperCollins' *50 Writers, 50 Books: The Best Indian Fiction*. His latest novel, *Conversations with Aurangzeb*, was published by HarperCollins in 2023. Charu Nivedita lives in Chennai with his human and animal family.

Sureshkumara Indrajith, originally named N.R. Suresh Kumar, was born in Rameswaram and spent much of his life in Madurai, where he studied, worked and lived. He retired in 2011 as a senior administrative officer from the Madurai District Revenue Department. An accomplished writer, he has published eight collections of short stories, two anthologies of selected short stories, two collections of microfiction, one novella, and five novels, including *Kadalum Vannattuppoochikalum* and *Oru Padaki Oru Mayappiravi*. He received the Vishnupuram Award in 2020 and the Ma. Aranganathan Literary Award from the Munril Foundation in 2023.

Aravindan was born and raised in Chennai. As a writer, translator and journalist, he has authored over twenty-five works, including fiction, literary essays, film critiques and translations. In addition to his two novels, *Ponnagaram* and *Payanam*, he has written more than forty short stories. His fiction primarily explores the complexities of everyday life in the metropolis. Aravindan's Tamil translation of Douglas Knight's *Balasaraswati: Her Art and Life* received the award for Best Translated Work from the Tamil Literary Garden, based in Canada, in 2017.

Ambai, the pen name of Dr C.S. Lakshmi, has been an independent researcher in Women's Studies for the last more than forty years. She has a PhD from Jawaharlal Nehru University, New Delhi. She explores themes of love, relationships, quests and journeys in her works, and her short-story collections have been published in Tamil and also translated into English. Recognized for her significant contributions to modern Tamil literature, she has received numerous honours, such as the Tata Lifetime Achievement Award (2023), the Iyal Award for Lifetime Achievement (2008) from the Canada-based Tamil Literary Garden and the Sahitya Akademi Award (2021) for her short-story collection *Sivappuk Kazhuttudan Oru Pachaip Paravai*. She is currently the Director of SPARROW (Sound & Picture Archives for Research on Women).

Appadurai Muttulingam is an award-winning writer with numerous works in Tamil to his name. His novel, *Kadavul Todangiya Idam* (*Where God Began*), and three of his short-story collections have been translated into English. His stories have been part of anthologies like, *Many Roads Through Paradise* (2014) and *Uprooting the Pumpkin* (2016), and several magazines, including *Narrative Magazine* and *Words Without Borders*. He was also a finalist for the 2023 Armory Square Prize for South Asian Literature in Translation.

S. Ramakrishnan has been a prominent figure in Tamil literature for the last thirty years. A prolific writer, his extensive body of work includes twenty short-story collections, ten novels, such as *Urupasi* and *Nedunkuruti*, nine plays, seventy-five essay collections and fifteen children's books. His short stories and articles have been translated into English, Malayalam, Hindi, Bengali, Telugu, Kannada and French. He received the Iyal award for Lifetime Achievement (2011), given by the Tamil Literary Garden based in Canada, and the Sahitya Akademi award (2018) for his novel *Sanjaram*.

Salma, the pen name of Rajathi Samsudeen, is globally acclaimed for her contributions to contemporary Tamil literature. She has authored three volumes of poetry, three novels, two short-story collections and a travelogue. Her novel, *The Hour Past Midnight*, was shortlisted for the Man Asian Prize (2009) and the Crossword Book Prize (2010). Her other novel, *Women Dreaming*, was longlisted for the Dublin International Literary Award (2022). The recipient of numerous prestigious awards, Salma has represented Tamil literature at the Frankfurt, London and Beijing Book Fairs. She was also an honoured guest at the 2014 Writers of India Festival in Paris.

Nanjil Nadan, the pen name of G. Subramaniam, hails from Veeranarayana Mangalam in Kanyakumari district. He gained fame with his very first novel, *Talaikeezh Vigitangal* (1977). He has authored six novels, twelve volumes of short stories, six poetry collections, and twenty volumes of essays on social and literary topics. He has received the Kannadasan Award (2009), the Kalaimamani Award from the Tamil Nadu Iyal Isai Nataka Mandram (2009), and the Sahitya Akademi award (2010) for his short-story collection *Soodiya Poo Soodarka*, among many other accolades. He is also a renowned orator of the *Kamba Ramayanam*, the regional retelling of the *Ramayana*, and classical Tamil Literature.

Devibharathi grew up in a small village in western Tamil Nadu. He has worked as a political activist, government employee, journalist, managing editor of a literary magazine, and scriptwriter for TV programmes. Over a career spanning more than forty years, he has published two collections of short stories, two novellas, four novels, a play, two memoirs and three non-fiction anthologies. His first novel, *Nizhalin Tanimai*, and some of his works of short fiction have been translated into English. He was honoured with the Tannaram Award (2002) and was also the recipient of the Sahitya Akademi award (2023) for his novel *Neervazhi Padooum*.

Tamilnathy, the pen name of Kalaivani, was born in Trincomalee, Sri Lanka, and graduated from the University of Jaffna. She has eleven published works, encompassing poetry, short stories, novels and plays. She moved to Canada in 1992 due to the civil war in Sri Lanka. Her experiences of adapting to a new climate and feelings of alienation inspired her love for travel. She now divides her time between Canada, Sri Lanka and India.

Imayam, the pen name of V. Annamalai, made his literary debut with the novel *Koveru Kazhuthaigal* in 1994. One of the foremost contemporary writers in Tamil, he has since written eight novels, eight short-story collections and one novella. He received the Sahitya Akademi award (2020) for his novel *Sellata Panam*. He was the first Tamil writer to win the prestigious Kuvempu Rashtriya Puraskar National Award (2022). Other honours include the Agni Akshara Award (1994), the Tamil Nadu Progressive Writers' Association Award (1994), the Iyal Award for Lifetime Achievement (2018) and *The Hindu's* Jayakanthan Award for Contemporary Tamil Literature (2018). He has been recognized by the state governments of Kerala and Tamil Nadu and the Indian government for his literary contributions.

Perumal Murugan, one of the most acclaimed writers and scholars in Tamil, has authored twelve novels, six collections of short stories, five poetry collections and fifteen non-fiction books. His works, including *Seasons of the Palm*, *Current Show*, *One Part Woman* (winner of the ILF Samanvay Bhasha Samman) and *Pyre* (shortlisted for the International Booker Prize) have been translated into English. His novel *Poonachi* was shortlisted for several awards and was longlisted for the National Book Award for Translated Literature (2020), set up by *The New Yorker*. His novel, *Fire Bird*, translated by Janani Kannan, won the JCB Prize for Literature (2023). His books are available in several languages, including Malayalam, Kannada, French, German and Italian.

Shobasakthi, the pen name of Anthonythasan Jesuthasan, was born in 1967 in Sri Lanka and now lives in France. He is a well-known, critically acclaimed forerunner among the exiled generation of writers from Sri Lanka's bloody civil war. He writes fiction and political essays in Tamil. He is the author of *Gorilla* and *Traitor*, both translated into English by Anushiya Ramaswamy. He has acted in several plays and films, including *Dheepan* by Jacques Audiard.

Jeyamohan is a prolific Tamil writer who has authored over two hundred works, including novels, short fiction, travelogues, and books on literary criticism and Indian philosophy. His critically acclaimed novels include *Vishnupuram*, *Pinthodarum Nizhalin Kural*, *Kadu* and *Kottravai*, as well as a modern reimagining of the Mahabharata titled *Venmurasu*, a twenty-six-part novel series. He has received the Akilan Memorial Prize (1990), the Katha Award (1992), the Sanskriti Samman (1994) and the Iyal Award for Lifetime Achievement, given by the Tamil Literary Garden based in Canada. Jeyamohan is also well-known for his contributions to feature films as a screenwriter. He lives in Nagercoil.

ABOUT THE EDITOR

Perundevi is a poet, writer and translator, who has been contributing regularly to the Tamil literary milieu across various genres over the past two decades. She has to her credit ten collections of poetry, including her recent works, *Avan Kannatthil Hybrid Sevvarali Pookkirathu* (2023) and *Un Chinna Ulakatthai Tharumarakatthan Punarnthirukkiray* (2021), two collections of translated poetry, two volumes of micro-fiction, and three essay collections, one of which focuses on literary criticism of modern Tamil poetry. In addition, she has also edited an anthology of essays on Ashokamitran's works. In 2022, she was a visiting writer-in-residence with the Asia Creative Writing Programme (ACWP) in Singapore. An academic with a PhD in interdisciplinary human sciences, she is now a Professor of Religious Studies at Siena College in upstate New York.

ABOUT THE TRANSLATORS

N. Kalyan Raman is a translator of contemporary Tamil fiction and poetry into English. Over the past twenty-five years, he has published fifteen works of Tamil fiction in translation, by important writers such as Ashokamitran, Poomani, Devibharathi, Perumal Murugan, Vaasanthi and Salma. His translations of contemporary Tamil poets have been published widely in journals and anthologies in India and abroad. In 2022, he was awarded Sahitya Akademi's Translation Prize (English) for his translation of Perumal Murugan's *Poonachi*. He lives and works in Chennai.

Yashasvi Arunkumar began translating as an undergraduate at Ashoka University, where she was mentored by translator Arunava Sinha. After earning an MPhil in English Studies from the University of Cambridge, she now works as an English teacher in a secondary school in England. She often finds herself pondering about bilingualism, the rationale behind school curriculums for language and literature, and more recently about the startling similarities between Korean and Tamil.

Suchitra Ramachandran is a writer and translator. *The Abyss*, her debut book-length translation of Jeyamohan's Tamil novel, was published in 2023 to critical acclaim. She won the 2017 Asymptote Close Approximations Fiction Prize for 'Periyamma's Words', a short story by the same author. Suchitra lives in Bengaluru.

G.J.V. Prasad, a former Professor of English at Jawaharlal Nehru University, is a writer, critic and translator. He has translated two notable works from Tamil to English: Ambai's *A Red-Necked Green Bird* (2021) and Imayam's *A Woman Burnt* (2023), the latter earning the KLF Award for Translation.

Nandini Krishnan is a writer and translator based in Madras. Her books include *Hitched: The Modern Indian Woman and Arranged Marriage* and *Invisible Men: Inside India's Transmasculine Networks*. Her first novel is forthcoming from Westland. She is also the award-winning translator of *Estuary* and *Four Strokes of Luck* by Perumal Murugan, and *Ponniyin Selvan* by Kalki Krishnamurthy. Her translation of Sajjad Haider Yaldram's 'Save Me from My Friends' was shortlisted for the 2022 Jawad Memorial Prize for Urdu-English Translation. Her translation of Charu Nivedita's novel, *Conversations with Aurangzeb*, won the Crossword Book Awards 2024 in the Popular Choice Award for Translations category. Nandini lives in Madras.

Janani Kannan is an interior architect, marathon runner and a Carnatic musician. Originally from Chennai, she rediscovered her love for everything Tamil as a young adult and enjoys translating Tamil novels and short stories into English. Her translation of Perumal Murugan's novel *Fire Bird* was awarded the 2023 JCB Prize for Literature. Her self-professed anthropological interests also include collecting and chronicling anecdotes, recipes and architectural nuggets from Tamil culture. She lives in the United States.

HarperCollins *Publishers* India

At HarperCollins India, we believe in telling the best stories and finding the widest readership for our books in every format possible. We started publishing in 1992; a great deal has changed since then, but what has remained constant is the passion with which our authors write their books, the love with which readers receive them, and the sheer joy and excitement that we as publishers feel in being a part of the publishing process.

Over the years, we've had the pleasure of publishing some of the finest writing from the subcontinent and around the world, including several award-winning titles and some of the biggest bestsellers in India's publishing history. But nothing has meant more to us than the fact that millions of people have read the books we published, and that somewhere, a book of ours might have made a difference.

As we look to the future, we go back to that one word—a word which has been a driving force for us all these years.

Read.